Left in the Ashes

Anna Britton lives on the Isle of Wight with her husband and their chronically clumsy Labrador. An avid reader, she began writing around ten years ago and hasn't stopped since. Anna works as a freelance editor and loves helping out other authors. When not filling her head with stories, Anna enjoys baking (and eating) cakes and exploring rivers in her kayak.

Also by Anna Britton

Detectives Martin & Stern

Shot in the Dark
Close to the Edge
Left in the Ashes

LEFT IN THE ASHES

ANNA BRITTON

CANELO CRIME

First published in the United Kingdom in 2025 by

Canelo Crime, an imprint of
Canelo Digital Publishing Limited,
20 Vauxhall Bridge Road,
London SW1V 2SA
United Kingdom

A Penguin Random House Company
The authorised representative in the EEA is Dorling Kindersley Verlag GmbH. Arnulfstr. 124,
80636 Munich, Germany

Copyright © Anna Britton 2025

The moral right of Anna Britton to be identified as the creator of this work has been asserted in accordance with the Copyright, Designs and Patents Act, 1988.
All rights reserved. No part of this publication may be reproduced or transmitted in any form or by any means, electronic or mechanical, including photocopy, recording, or any information storage and retrieval system, without permission in writing from the publisher.
No part of this book may be used or reproduced in any manner for the purpose of training artificial intelligence technologies or systems. In accordance with Article 4(3) of the DSM Directive 2019/790, Canelo expressly reserves this work from the text and data mining exception.

A CIP catalogue record for this book is available from the British Library.

Print ISBN 978 1 80436 528 1
Ebook ISBN 978 1 80436 529 8

This book is a work of fiction. Names, characters, businesses, organizations, places and events are either the product of the author's imagination or are used fictitiously. Any resemblance to actual persons, living or dead, events or locales is entirely coincidental.

Cover design by Dan Mogford

Cover images © Shutterstock

Printed and bound in Great Britain by Clays Ltd, Elcograf S.p.A.

Look for more great books at
www.canelo.co | www.dk.com

For those who dance with fear every day

Crash.

Her eyes snap open. Sleep falls away as her throat spasms. The room isn't big, but she can't see the far wall. The window and ceiling are lost in swirling smoke. Grey and ashen. She cringes at the crackling roar as she fumbles her scarf over her mouth and nose, heaves in stuffy air.

Move.

She rolls off her sleeping mat and onto the concrete floor. On hands and knees, she squints around the room. Tears prickle. She blinks them away. They're not helpful. Boxes loom beside her makeshift bed, the top of each stack lost in thick fog. She crawls alongside them. Sweat stings under her arms, trickles down her neck.

Crack.

Her head smacks into the doorframe. Panting shallowly behind her scarf, she scans the main room. Flashes of red on the far side break through the clogging grey. More boxes create columns of darkness. Her eyes sting: smoke and hopelessness combining. She can't remember where the front door is.

Fuck.

Smoke and flames consume the main room. She turns around. Knees aching, she crawls towards the window. Her shoulder thumps into a pile of boxes. They lean and she shoves back, heart hammering. They crash out of sight. Lungs burning, she shuffles forward. Her head thuds into the wall.

Reach.

Her skull throbbing, she spreads a hand across the uneven plaster above her. It's cool against her feverish skin. She weaves back and forth until her fingers catch on jutting wood. Stretching her other arm, she pulls herself up to the windowsill. The smoke is thicker when standing. The scarf across her lower face does nothing to block out the acrid stink.

Breathe.

She takes a pained breath, eyes watering, and leans close to the window. The latch is painted shut. She braces her arms where the panes join and pushes. It doesn't budge. Moaning, she scrabbles at the gloss. Her nails catch on stray flecks. She huffs out a breath, coughs when she takes another. She presses her cheek to the window pane. Streaming eyes don't allow her to see outside, but the trees are right there. Fresh air is so near.

Push.

She shoves the window, then slumps to the floor. She cannot breathe. Cannot see. The roaring and crackling in the main room grows louder. She lowers her face to the rough floor. Even there, the air is poison. She closes her eyes for the length of a single heaving sob, then hauls herself to her knees. She must keep trying. Her back thumps into a box. It shifts. The third blow to her head defeats her. She chokes as more boxes fall, pinning her legs. Cardboard presses on her shoulders, forces her face to the floor. She opens her eyes to darkness, but the smoke finds her.

Day 1

Monday, 4 August

Call connected at 8:22.

'999, how can I direct your call?'

'I, ah. I think I need the police. Not an ambulance.'

'That's fine. Please wait while I connect you.'

PLEASE HOLD. PLEASE HOLD. PLEASE HOLD.

'Hello, you're through to the Southampton Central Police control room. What's your emergency?'

'I checked on my boat before work and found a barrel caught up in the rope.'

'Where is your boat moored?'

'In Hythe. At the shipyard.'

'Okay. What do you need police assistance with?'

'I. Well. The barrel isn't empty.'

'What's inside it?'

[Coughing.]

'Take your time.'

'Sorry. I was sick. When I saw it.'

'What did you see?'

'A body. There's a poor kid in there.'

[Rapid typing.]

'A unit is on its way. They'll be with you in under ten minutes. Is the barrel secure?'

'Yes. I left it on my boat.'

'Please make sure no one else goes near it.'
'Oh, I will. No one should see that, not unless they have to.'

Gabe

Cloying smoke snuck into my car's ventilation system as we neared the Dunlow Estate. It wasn't the same smell as bonfires or burning charcoal. The stink of melted plastic combined with overheated metal. Stinging chemical undertones deepened as I drove through the New Forest.

My feelings at an investigation once again causing Juliet and me to bump up against the Dunlows would have been a weighted mixed bag anyway, but the prospect of heady smoke clinging to my clothes for the rest of the day made my stomach churn with dread. If we were lucky the estate owner, Timothy Dunlow, would be absent. Another fire had destroyed half the manor ten months ago, so he and his sons couldn't be living on the grounds.

I turned onto a single-track lane. The low stone wall around the estate was an ineffective barrier against the white clouds wending through the trees. The smell intensified as I drove towards the front gates.

Hunched in the passenger seat, Juliet wrinkled her nose as she tapped at her phone. My partner's blonde hair was tied into a low ponytail, her pink blouse paired with flowing grey trousers. Hopefully she'd be able to throw them in the washing machine, rather than waiting for dry cleaning. I'd never checked the labels in my dark green chinos and blue shirt, but they would be doused in detergent as soon as I got home.

The Dunlow Estate gates stood open, an Incident and Response car parked across them. I pulled up behind. Red vans sat inside the grounds, their polished wording proclaiming that various branches of Fire Control and Investigation were present.

Taking a last breath of vaguely unsullied air, I opened my car door. Juliet tucked her phone in her pocket and unclipped her seatbelt. The wet warmth outside swept over us, competing with the thick stink of burning. This was our eighth straight day without rain but this close to the coast, the air hung heavy with humidity.

Alice hurried over as we rounded the car at the gates, her light brown forehead shining with sweat. 'This was most likely a torch job but the water squirters aren't letting us near the building.'

Juliet's jaw tightened. She strode into the estate. I nudged Alice with my elbow as I passed. 'Name calling is juvenile.'

'I guess I'll sign you both into the scene log then?' she said.

I shot her a smile over my shoulder as I followed Juliet. Although Alice had worked several cases with us in the last few months, I couldn't be certain Juliet retained her name. To her, Alice was part of the sea of uniformed officers who worked at Southampton station. Juliet didn't care about Alice's dream to become a detective or respond to her dwindling questions about her weekends. Juliet barely noticed anyone in uniform unless they did something wrong. Even then, it was only for long enough to shove them out of her way.

Juliet didn't recognise Alice as an asset. Juliet and I had been shot in the spring by a woman twisted up by years of hate. Her father was dismissed from the force following allegations, triggered by Juliet, that he had been abusing his position. Alice helped me apprehend the shooter and pursue a number of other cases that alone I wouldn't have had the physical strength for while recovering.

Despite not spending more than a weekend away from the station before, Juliet was off work for a surprisingly long time after we were shot. Once she returned, her slight favouring of her right side betrayed that she'd suffered an injury and Alice was relegated back to her regular patrols. I couldn't decide if I preferred Alice's over-investment in my life to Juliet's cool disinterest, but I certainly got more work done with my fellow detective sitting across from me in our shared office.

Juliet marched towards a cluster of firefighters standing beside a smoking wreck of a building, her steps sure. Her preference for impractical heels was a thing of the past. Since she'd moved in with Keith and their daughters instead of living in a flat in the city during the week, the sharp edges of her appearance had softened. Sensible shoes brought her inches closer to my height and although her clothes were always flawlessly matched, her trimmed nails were bare. The purpling bags under her eyes lingered, despite the shorter hours she'd worked since moving permanently to Eastleigh.

Three months after we were both shot, and I still wasn't sure if these changes were a good sign. The confidence built between myself and Juliet after the joint attack had been severed at the earliest moment. Any mention of her family and she clammed up, her lips a thin line and her eyes blank.

I didn't know the details of her homelife before the shooting, but Juliet had been living separately to her family long before I moved down to Southampton a year and a half ago. She seemed neither more or less happy that her free time was now filled with her daughters and husband rather than spent alone in a studio flat, but I couldn't quell a hunch that Juliet's life hadn't changed for the better.

'Morning.' She stopped outside the ring of broad-shouldered men, forcing a couple to twist to look at her. 'I'm Detective Inspector Juliet Stern and this is Detective Sergeant Gabe Martin. We're heading up the investigation into the cause of this fire, so need immediate access to the site.'

The firefighters blinked at her. They shuffled out of the way as one man at the far side of the group stepped forward. My stomach flipped when he smiled, revealing the gap between his front teeth. His rich brown skin shone in the dappled sunlight and his eyes lingered on me. I resisted the urge to check my choppy pixie cut wasn't curling around my ears in the damp heat.

'I've met you before?' He was either unaware of Juliet's reputation or spectacularly brave. If I didn't know the smoke surrounding us was caused by the blackened hulk to our left, I'd have wondered whether it plumed from Juliet's ears.

'You have. At the other fire on this estate.' I extended my hand, suppressing the shiver of pleasant friction as his calloused palm brushed mine. 'I seem to remember you barred access to the property then too.'

'A necessary evil.' He held out his hand to Juliet. His smile dimmed when her arms remained firmly crossed over her chest. 'I'm the Forensic Fire Officer. Matt Lam.'

I remembered his name. His card was tucked in the bottom drawer of my desk. No one had accompanied me here when I first met him, one half of the Dunlow Manor reduced to a crumpled ruin. Even if Juliet had, she wouldn't have been able to confirm whether Matt had been flirting when he passed over his details.

It was irrelevant, anyway. I was happy with my boyfriend, Ollie. It might be flattering to be smiled at by a handsome stranger but my days of meaningless physical encounters were over. Exchanged for dimpled smiles and familiar lips on mine after I walked through our front door each evening.

'There's no way we can inspect the building?' I checked before Juliet butted in and put Matt's back up. He didn't strike me as someone who would be easily pissed off, but Juliet was adept at pushing even the calmest person past their limit.

Matt shook his head, his black hair falling in sweaty tendrils over his forehead. 'No chance. The site is structurally unsound. We'll need to make it safe before anyone pokes around, and we can't do that until twenty-four hours since the last flames were extinguished.'

That would be sometime tomorrow morning, if the smoke billowing from the wreck of the estate outbuilding was any indication. Beams of charred wood jutted towards the surrounding trees. Their summer green leaves had been withered by extreme heat.

Juliet and I had last seen this cottage after Karl Biss absconded. The previous estate groundskeeper was now languishing in prison, found guilty of all the charges brought against him. I'd initially interpreted his flight as the desperate move of a frightened man, but it eventually compounded his guilt.

This fire and the last were not the sole crimes haunting these ancestral grounds. Karl shot Melanie Pirt, a young woman in a secret relationship with the youngest Dunlow son, Leo, between these close-packed trees to exact revenge. Karl believed himself shunned by his family, while the Dunlows hadn't been aware of his relation to them. Karl was the illegitimate oldest son of Timothy Dunlow and he'd refused to remain hidden in the shadows. He'd ended an innocent teenager's life in a sick bid to gain his father's attention. I didn't feel undue sadness that his previous home had been destroyed.

I pulled my notepad from my trouser pocket. 'What can you tell us about the fire?'

'You're likely looking at an arson investigation,' Matt said, again displaying either obliviousness or bullheadedness as Juliet rolled her eyes. 'The fire started at around four a.m. and quickly spread through the property. It wouldn't have done so at such a rate without an accelerant. Probably petrol.' He looked at the charred branches stretching over the cottage. 'During a drought like this, it's lucky the blaze didn't spread into the forest.'

I scribbled notes, too aware of Matt's dark eyes on my hands. 'The last fire on the estate was deemed arson as well, but they can't be linked. The perpetrator is in prison.' Before Karl was arrested, he managed to lash out in a myriad of ways against his relatives.

Matt shrugged, his tight navy T-shirt shifting over honed muscle. 'Could be a coincidence.'

'We don't like those,' Juliet snapped.

I made a note to dig out Matt's report on the manor fire. Karl Biss couldn't have started this blaze, but he'd maintained he wasn't involved in the other. After witnessing his propensity to lie at every opportunity, especially if it would harm the Dunlows, I hadn't been inclined to believe him.

If the fires were connected in any way, that could mean Karl was innocent of one of the charges brought against him and someone else was targeting the Dunlows. The list of possible suspects would be long. The number of people with good reason to adamantly dislike Timothy Dunlow would have grown over the course of his consultancy career as he assisted in the demise of one small company after another.

'Have you been able to ascertain anything else?' I asked.

'The spread of the fire was aided by the amount of flammable material in the building.'

I squinted at the crumbling brickwork. 'Last time we visited, there was barely anything inside.' It had been a sad place. A single mattress on the concrete floor, dusty sofas and undecorated walls.

'Things had changed.' Matt scratched his stomach through his top. 'The two rooms are packed with boxes. Some have fabric inside, which provided ample fuel for the fire.'

We needed to ask Timothy Dunlow if he'd been using the cottage for storage. What a pleasure it would be to talk to him again. No doubt he would invent new and exciting ways to convey exactly how far beneath him he believed Juliet and me to be.

'Have you been in touch with the estate owner?' I asked.

'Not yet.'

'Leave that to us.' Juliet turned to stare at the remains of the cottage.

'Fine.' One corner of Matt's mouth twitched upwards. 'If I remember rightly, the bloke who owns this place is a bit of an ogre.'

'That's one way to describe him.' My lips tugged into a half-smile. If one person deserved to be made fun of behind their back, it was Timothy Dunlow. He was rude at best, habitually obstructive at worst. So much so that we'd believed him capable of Melanie Pirt's murder.

'Do you have anything useful to tell us?' Juliet swung around. 'Or do we have to wait for helpful input for our investigation?'

Matt's shoulders stiffened: the first sign that Juliet's attitude bothered him. He'd outlasted many others.

'You're in for a wait, I'm afraid.' Matt held out his hand. I fumbled my notepad before taking it. 'I'll send over my report as soon as I can.' One rough squeeze and he stomped over to where his team lingered beside the cottage.

Juliet glared after him before falling into step beside me. We walked to the estate gates, where Alice was hovering.

'Rushing over here was a total waste of time,' Juliet muttered.

'We couldn't not come,' I said gently.

Fires had been extinguished on several monied estates in the last couple of weeks. All deemed purposeful. This was the first that had claimed a whole building, even if it was only a two-room cottage. The other detective inspector at Southampton station had overseen the previous investigations but couldn't take charge of the latest; Paul and his partner, Nicole, had been called away to a dock. Even the beginnings of cases didn't stay secret at the station but that was all our assistant, Maddy, could tell us before we left.

'All done?' Alice pouted. I'd learn the reason why she was put out later. We hadn't had a traditional start to our friendship but once she'd wormed her way into my affections, it was impossible to oust her.

Juliet hurried over to my car. I pressed the key. Despite her rudeness, which I wanted to believe was unintentional, I wouldn't begrudge her escaping the stench of smoke.

'Let us know anything important,' I urged Alice. A few warm smiles from Matt hadn't convinced me that he'd complete his investigation until he'd adhered to the letter of the law concerning fire safety inspections.

'Will do.' Alice's eyes fixed on the men grouped over my shoulder.

I didn't look back as I walked to my car. Attractive or not, Matt Lam was a roadblock in this case. I wouldn't be mulish about it like Juliet, but his strictness wasn't endearing. This string of estate fires didn't pose a serious threat to anything but property, but that didn't mean they weren't dangerous. We needed to catch the arsonist before they caused significant damage or someone got hurt.

Detective Sergeant Nicole Stewart: Witness statement recorded with permission of the interviewee on the 4th August at 9:27 a.m. at Hythe Sailing Yard. This interview is being conducted by Detective Inspector Paul Willis and myself, Detective Sergeant Nicole Stewart. The interviewee is Bruno Bowdler. This interview is concerning a barrel containing the body of a child found by Mr Bowdler this morning at Hythe Sailing Yard.

Detective Inspector Paul Willis: Thank you for talking with us, Mr Bowdler. I know it's been a difficult morning.

Bruno Bowdler: Can't say I won't be glad to see the back of this place today. Not sure it's ever going to be the same.

DI Paul Willis: That's understandable. We won't keep you for long. Can you please tell us, in as much detail as possible, about your arrival here?

Bruno Bowdler: I was meant to work at the fishing shop down the way this morning and arrived early to check on my boat. I drove in. Got here about eight. Parked up behind the shop and walked through to the yard.

DS Nicole Stewart: Did you notice anyone unusual around the boat yard?

Bruno Bowdler: Only saw three people. Regulars around here. Nick, Ed, and Stan. They use the shop for bait and whatnot, so their details will be in the accounts book.

DS Nicole Stewart: What made you decide to check on your boat today?

Bruno Bowdler: I look in on her most days, especially if I'm at work.

DS Nicole Stewart: Did you notice anything strange on the walk from your car to the boat?

Bruno Bowdler: Nothing at all. I know this yard like the back of my hand. I'd have clocked it if anything was amiss. There was nothing out of the ordinary until I saw the barrel knotted in the excess rope by my boat.

DI Paul Willis: What can you tell us about the barrel?

Bruno Bowdler: Someone had waterproofed it. It was tarred along the seams. Almost floated off after I untangled it, but I managed to grab onto the top and haul it aboard.

DI Paul Willis: Why did you keep hold of it? Why not let it float away?

Bruno Bowdler: It's probably not what you want to hear, but there's more of a sense of finders-keepers at sea than there is on land. The barrel was caught up in my rope, so anything inside was rightfully mine.

[Silence.]

DS Nicole Stewart: Mr Bowdler, are you alright to continue?

Bruno Bowdler: Yes. I'm fine. Thank you, lass. I just wish I'd never laid eyes on that damn thing.

DS Nicole Stewart: It must have been terrible.

DI Paul Willis: We're not going to ask you to recount what you found when you opened the barrel. The forensic team is going over it now and we'll get all we need from them. But I did want to ask if you noticed anything as you were opening it or once it was open that would give any indication as to who had handled the barrel before you?

Bruno Bowdler: No. There was nothing. And once I saw what was inside, it was all I could do to get away.

DI Paul Willis: You've not seen a barrel like this before or seen anyone at the yard with one?

Bruno Bowdler: I've seen barrels like it before. It's not anything special, as far as I could tell. Not an antique or anything. Just a bog-standard barrel. But it's the kind of thing I'd notice someone lugging around.

DI Paul Willis: Okay. Thank you for your time, Mr Bowdler.

Bruno Bowdler: Is it him again?

DS Nicole Stewart: Sorry, who?

Bruno Bowdler: The Barrel Man.

DI Paul Willis: We cannot comment on an ongoing investigation.

Bruno Bowdler: I get it. I hope you catch him this time. The sick bastard.

Call connected at 9:43.

'Most people would take it as a sign that the person they're calling is busy when they don't pick up the first five times.'

'I'm not like most people. I'm much better.'

'What do you want, Jessica?'

'Well, dearest brother of mine, I thought you might want to know our father has had a stroke.'

'What?'

'Dad's in hospital. Mum's there with him. She insisted I call you, even though I said we'd be lucky if you picked up the phone since you're probably arsing around in your underwear. Too important to talk to the likes of us.'

'Can you stop being awful for one moment and tell me what's going on?'

'I've already told you. Dad's had a stroke.'

'But what do you mean, a stroke? How bad is it?'

'How would I know? I'm not a doctor.'

'Should I come home?'

'I don't know, little brother. Can you take a break from your glamourous life to help your family when they're in need?'

'Please tell Mum I'll be there as soon as I can. And I'm not your little brother.'

'The minutes count, Oliver.'

Angela. Sent 9:51

> Please bring Gabe straight to my office as soon as you get back to the station.

Juliet. Sent 9:51.

> Will do.

Juliet. Sent 9:54.

> Have I had another complaint? If it involves Gabe, it's wrong.

Angela. Sent 9:55.

> I'll explain to you both what's going on once you're here. Just bring Gabe to me. Don't go to your office or talk to anyone else.

Gabe

'We need to go to the eighth floor,' Juliet said.

I looked at her, my hand hovering before the lift's buttons. She'd been in a staring contest with her phone since we exited my car. If she wouldn't have shuddered away like I had a contagious disease, I would have held her elbow to guide her across the car park and through the station entrance. Juliet offered as little explanation for her aversion to touch as she did for almost every aspect of her person, but I tried to respect it if possible. Even when I was scared she would faceplant on uneven concrete.

'Why?'

Juliet stabbed one finger at her phone then slotted it into her trouser pocket. 'Angela asked us to come to her office.'

Anxiety spiked through me. I tried to ignore it. I was not a naughty school child and Angela was not a stern headmistress. Southampton station's superintendent was hands on, which meant this summons could be for praise or censure. And if one of us was going to be told off, Juliet was the more likely candidate.

I pressed the button for the eighth floor. As the lift rose, Juliet tapped one sensible shoe while I checked my hair in the mirrored walls. The short brown strands flicked upwards. I couldn't flatten them properly without water but I patted at the worst offenders. My skin was a warmer shade of off-white than it was over the winter, visits to beaches with Ollie during quiet weekends bringing a faint hint of tan. I straightened the collar of my shirt, my fingers brushing my overwarm neck.

Over the top of my head, Juliet's eyes flicked to the lift doors as we passed the seventh floor.

'Do you know why Angela wants to see us?'

Juliet raised her shoulders. 'We'll find out soon enough.'

When we reached the eighth floor, I followed her from the lift and down a corridor lined with offices. The Major Investigation Team one storey below was open-plan. There were only two offices: one for Paul and another for myself and Juliet. Those who worked on the eighth floor were far too important to endure hot-desking in clusters. We walked past closed doors, the white paint bright and unscuffed.

Angela's door at the end of the corridor stood open. Our superintendent sat at a desk cluttered with piles of paperwork. Her long black braids were bound in a loose bun on top of her head and her starched uniform was perfect as always. I wouldn't suspect she was suffering with the heat like the rest of us if it wasn't for the fan whirring in one corner and the faint shine of perspiration on her brown skin.

She gestured to the chairs opposite her desk as she stood and rounded it, reaching behind us to push her door shut. 'Thank you for heading straight here.'

Angela leant against the side of her desk, arms folded above her plump stomach. She wasn't the kind of boss who played power games but it was hard to not feel small as she loomed over us. Her lips pressed together, lines pulling across her forehead.

All signs pointed towards a bollocking.

'Have I done something again?'

I glanced at Juliet. Although that was the more probable scenario, she didn't look nervous. She sat straight backed as usual, hands resting on her lap.

'No.' Angela breathed deep. 'But I thought you should be here.'

Dread flickered through my stomach. If Juliet hadn't stepped out of line, then Angela had summoned us here for another reason. Judging by the immovable frown on her face, it couldn't be anything good.

'What's going on, ma'am?' I asked, unwilling to wait any longer.

Angela dropped into a crouch beside my chair. Her pressed trousers strained across her thick thighs as she reached out and clasped my hands. I hoped she didn't notice how clammy they were.

'Max Powrie has been found.' She swallowed. 'His body was discovered earlier this morning.'

Seven-year-old Max had been abducted almost three weeks ago from a church picnic. Neither of his fathers nor anyone else saw anything to indicate who took him. He was last seen running for the swings with a couple of friends. Minutes later, he was gone.

Following his disappearance, a concerted effort had been launched to find him. Everyone at the station joined a sweep across the city, conducting door-to-door interviews and searching parks. Max's face made regular appearances in local Facebook groups alongside increasingly desperate appeals from his family for information.

From the moment Max vanished, no clue or sign of what had happened to him was found. The investigation was still a priority, but without direction. Paul had been leading the residual searches but, without any evidence to work with, Max had been assumed irretrievably lost.

Angela knew the initial stages of the investigation had taken a toll on me. I suspected many of my co-workers had delved into my file and read about my sad childhood but, as my superintendent, Angela had a duty of care. It was kind of her to call me to her office so that I didn't have to cope with the emotional fallout of a child's death in front of a floor full of colleagues.

'I'm sorry to hear that, ma'am.' My voice held steady. Later, I would allow myself to think of Max's parents and all that had been taken from them, to remember my long dead brother. But not yet. I had a job to do. Finding Max's killer would fall under Paul's remit while Juliet and I investigated the latest fire.

'How did he die?' Juliet asked.

Angela's hand atop mine flinched. Maybe she regretted asking Juliet to sit in on this. If Angela had expected tact or support from my partner, then she had seriously misunderstood Juliet's character.

Angela's fingers tightened. 'That's why I called you here.'

Chill fear spread through my veins. Alarm bells pealed in my mind, demanding I push my superintendent away and run.

I exhaled and met her eye. 'What happened to Max?'

'He was killed by strangulation and his body placed in a barrel.'

I floated away. No longer a detective sat in my boss's office, I was a young girl. Desperate and starving. Across a warehouse, an empty barrel waited.

I came back to myself with a full-body shudder. Angela's thumb moved across my knuckles. I lowered my head and squeezed my eyes shut against the tears gathering.

'The investigation to find Max's killer will be conducted from this station, but I've instructed Paul and Nicole to use the Major Incident room on the sixth floor,' Angela said, slow and soothing. 'We want to make this time as stress free as possible for you, Gabe.'

I nodded, but was unable to vocalise my gratitude. It had been difficult walking past Max's smiling portrait on the seventh floor at the start of the search. It would have been impossible to pass by once it was joined by many others, now that he'd joined the ranks of the bad man's victims. I wouldn't have been able to function with my brother's smiling face stuck on the wall outside my office.

'Paul will need to take a statement from you,' Angela went on. 'He'll keep it brief.'

Any time the bad man struck again, I was hauled in to share patchy memories I wished I could erase. It didn't matter that nothing I said would ever be of any help. The investigations had to be thorough. I couldn't be left in peace.

I opened my eyes and raised my head. 'I understand. That's fine.'

I hadn't worked at the station one of these investigations was conducted from before. Paul would question me carefully and his whole team had been moved to another floor, but I wouldn't be able to escape it. I might not have to look at the victims but I'd know the bad man was being hunted nearby.

Fruitlessly. Just like every other time.

'Our arson case will keep us busy,' Juliet said.

Despite the stench clinging to our clothes, I'd forgotten the fire. Everything apart from the bad man had been swiped away.

Angela squeezed my hands, then stood. She walked around the desk to take her seat. Her touch removed, my skin numbed. My brain was sluggish, working through smoke as thick as the clouds that wound through the trees on the Dunlow Estate. I felt just as lost as I would be in that ancient forest.

'Keeping occupied is a good idea.' Angela rested her forearms on her desk. 'But I want you to take care of yourself, Gabe. It's completely understandable that you might need a break from work. This is a difficult time. If you want anything to change, don't hesitate to ask.'

'I'll be okay, ma'am.' On legs as insubstantial as brittle twigs, I stood. 'We need to get on.'

'I'm here if you need to talk,' Angela said as I opened her door. The corner caught on my boot. I lifted a hand to acknowledge her without getting tangled in more conversation.

In a dazed blink, Juliet and I arrived at the lift. She tapped the button for the seventh floor. The swooping sensation as it lowered mirrored the dip of my heart.

Terror, pungent and heavy, dragged at me.

'You go on.' I jabbed the button for the ground floor after Juliet walked out of the lift. 'I need to grab something from my car.'

Her eyes narrowed but the doors slid shut before she could speak. My throat constricted when the lift descended. Time stopped as the display above the door flicked to six, my heartbeat impossibly loud.

The relief when it switched to five was temporary. Despite the heat of the day, goosepimples rose on my arms. I gripped the lift's rail and leant into the wall. The bullet wound on my shoulder pulsed, the injury flaring as my muscles tensed.

On the ground floor, I stumbled out of the lift and pushed through the shining glass doors at the front of the station. The road was quiet. The press would gather once the news broke. Serial killers were intriguing to people whose lives hadn't been torn apart by one.

Keeping my face averted from everyone I passed, I walked to my car. My head clipped the roof as I climbed in. I had a brief thought that I shouldn't drive in this state before I pushed my keys into the ignition. I gripped the steering wheel hard and blinked away tears.

The bad man had struck again. He'd taken my brother, had taken countless others, and now he'd taken Max.

My colleagues would attempt to find him. To do that, they would delve into my past without restraint, dissecting my memories. They would look at me and see nothing more than a poor victim.

I couldn't stay here. I needed to get away.

I lowered the handbrake and drove.

Retrieved from police archives.

Detective Inspector Mohammad Allon: Witness statement recorded on the 8th February at 10:20 a.m. with the permission of Gabriella Martin's mother, as Gabriella is an eight-year-old minor. This interview is being conducted by myself, Detective Inspector Mohammad Allon. Our Family Liaison Support Officer, Bethany Wilde, is also in attendance, as is Gabriella's mother, Romilly Martin. Now I've got all of that out of the way, can you tell me who this is?

Gabriella Martin: Mr Duck.

DI Mohammad Allon: He looks like a friendly fellow.

Gabriella Martin: He broke his wing. I'm taking care of him.

DI Mohammad Allon: I'm sure you'll do a good job of that, especially because you've broken your wing too.

Gabriella Martin: I've got a broken arm.

DI Mohammad Allon: You're quite right. Silly me. Gabriella, how did you break your arm?

[Shuffling.]

Gabriella Martin: The bad man hurt me.

DI Mohammad Allon: I'm really sorry he did that. What does the bad man look like?

[Shuffling.]

Romilly Martin: It's alright, darling. You can tell us.

Gabriella Martin: Big and scary.

DI Mohammad Allon: Can you remember what colour his hair was?

Family Liaison Support Officer Bethany Wilde: For the benefit of the tape, Gabriella is shaking her head.

DI Mohammad Allon: How about his skin? Was it more like yours or mine?

Gabriella Martin: Mine.

DI Mohammad Allon: That's great, Gabriella. Thank you. You're doing a great job. Now, can you remember anything else about the bad man?

[Shuffling.]

Gabriella Martin: He wore a hat.

DI Mohammad Allon: What kind of hat?

FLSO Bethany Wilde: For the benefit of the tape, Gabriella is shaking her head.

Romilly Martin: Can you remember what colour it was?

Gabriella Martin: Black.

DI Mohammad Allon: What else did the bad man wear?

[Shuffling.]

DI Mohammad Allon: It's alright if you don't remember. Did the bad man talk to you?

FLSO Bethany Wilde: For the benefit of the tape, Gabriella is nodding.

DI Mohammad Allon: What did he say?

Gabriella Martin: We had to come with him. He said Daddy told him to take us home because we'd been naughty.

DI Mohammad Allon: What else did he say?

FLSO Bethany Wilde: For the benefit of the tape, Gabriella is shaking her head.

DI Mohammad Allon: Did the bad man mention your daddy after that?

Gabriella Martin: No.

DI Mohammad Allon: Okay. Can you remember anything about the bad man's car?

FLSO Bethany Wilde: For the benefit of the tape, Gabriella is shaking her head.

DI Mohammad Allon: That's alright. Where did the bad man take—

Gabriella Martin: Mr Duck wants to go home.

Romilly Martin: We'll take Mr Duck home soon, sweetheart.

Gabriella Martin: No. He needs to go now.

DI Mohammad Allon: That's okay. We can stop. But can you do one thing for me, Gabriella? I'm going to try to catch the bad man and all the information I have will help me to do that. So if you remember anything else about him, I need you to tell your mummy and she will make sure to pass it on. Okay?

[Shuffling.]

Gabriella Martin: Are you going to find Barney?

DI Mohammad: I'm going to try my hardest.

You have one new voicemail. Voicemail left today at 10:49 a.m.

'Hello, Mr Dunlow. This is Detective Inspector Juliet Stern. I'm calling about a fire on the Dunlow Estate this morning in one of the outbuildings. The site is unsafe, so please do not attempt to visit. Currently, we do not believe the fire was accidental. When you get this message, please call me to discuss your whereabouts over the last twenty-four hours. Please also consider if anyone would have a strong reason to set fire to one of your buildings.'

From: Paul Willis **paul.willis@mit.gov.uk**
To: Madison Campbell
madison.campbell@mitadmin.gov.uk
CC: Nicole Stewart **nicole.stewart@mit.gov.uk**
Date: **4 August, 11:15**
Subject: **Operation Mercury – contact details**

Maddy,

Can you please collect up-to-date addresses and contact details for the following men? They are regular customers at Hythe Fishing Supplies, so likely live in the surrounding area.

- Nick Aubrey
- Ed Simpson
- Stanley Cooper

She probably won't appreciate me meddling, but I imagine Gabe will need extra support over the next few days.

Thanks,

Paul

Jordan. Sent 11:37.

Do you need me to cover for you at the chippy again later?

Tyler. Sent 11:39.

Shit yeah. Do you mind? And tomorrow as well?

Jordan. Sent 11:39.

It's fine. I need the money.

Tyler. Sent 11:39.

If you ever want extra, you know who to call.

Jordan. Sent 11:41.

I can't do that shit. I have to look after Mum.

Paloma Robins @WiseGirlHiker. Sent 11:49.

> Hi, lovely. I hope your hike is going well! Really looking forward to joining you tomorrow! Drop me a pin of your location when you stop tonight and I'll see you in the morning xxx

Call connected at 12:43.

'Hello?'

'Hello. Is that Terence Dunlow?'

'Yes. Who's this?'

'It's Detective Inspector Juliet Stern. I don't know if you're already aware, but there was a fire on your family estate this morning. The groundskeeper's cottage was badly damaged.'

'Oh. Right.'

'I've called your father but had no reply. Do you know where he is?'

'I've not spoken to him in weeks. Not since Leo moved in here.'

'I see. Can you tell me your whereabouts from yesterday evening to this morning?'

'I've been at home with my boyfriend, Benedict Hogan. Leo was on the night shift. He arrived here late this morning and went straight to bed.'

'What were you doing at home last night and this morning?'

'Benny and I watched TV and went to bed. At about eleven? This morning we got up at eight and had breakfast together. We both work from home, so we started at nine.'

'Okay. Is Mr Hogan there?'

'Hello. Teddy's got you on speaker.'

'Mr Hogan, I'm sure you heard Terence's account of your whereabouts yesterday evening and this morning?'

'Yes. Everything he said is true.'

'At no point was Terence out of your sight for a significant period?'

'No. We've been together the whole time. He couldn't have left for long enough to start a fire or anything. Neither could I.'

'Do you have any idea where Mr Dunlow is?'

'I couldn't have. That man and I have never had a single conversation.'

'Thank you, Mr Hogan. Terence, do you know of anyone who would want to burn down the cottage on your family's land?'

'That's a question for my father. I've not been over there since the last fire.'

'Fine. Thank you for your time.'

Alice. Sent 13:03.

> It's not enough that Gabe locked down Ollie before anyone else got a look in. She's also got hot firebugs panting at her heels.

Maddy. Sent 13:05.

> What are you on about?

Alice. Sent 13:05.

> A ridiculously gorgeous fireman asked about Gabe after she swanned off

Maddy. Sent 13:08.

> You need to get a life.

Alice. Sent 13:08.

> I need to get a boyfriend.

Maddy. Sent 13:08.

Are you at the station?

Alice. Sent 13:09.

Yeah. Just got back. My hair stinks.

Maddy. Sent 13:09.

Have you seen Gabe?

Alice. Sent 13:09.

No. And she's not answering my messages. Rude.

Maddy. Sent 13:10.

Something's wrong. Juliet asked if I knew where Gabe was, which is Juliet-speak for 'I can't find Gabe and I'm worried about her.'

Alice. Sent 13:10.

They're usually attached at the hip. I'll have a quick look around. See if I can find her.

Maddy. Sent 13:11.

Thank you x

Alice. Sent 13:46.

Shit. I've just found out what's going on. Do you think that's why Gabe's disappeared?

Maddy. Sent 13:47.

Maybe. God. This is going to be such a shitshow.

Call connected at 14:20.

'Hello, how can I help you?'

'Good afternoon, is that Mrs Martin?'

'It is, but please call me Romilly.'

'Hello, Romilly. I'm Detective Inspector Paul Willis. I work with Gabe at Southampton station.'

'Gosh. Is she okay?'

'Yes, she's fine. Although she's had a bit of a shock this morning. I'm sorry to say that the body of Max Powrie has been found.'

'Oh no. The poor lamb.'

'I'm very sorry to have to tell you this, but Max's body was found in a barrel.'

[Clattering.]

'Romilly? Are you okay?'

'Yes. Yes. I'm sorry. I dropped the phone.'

'We can't say for certain at this point in time that Max was killed by the same person as Barnabas, but the similarities between their deaths are there.'

'Every time I pray he won't do it again. No one deserves this.'

'I'm sorry, Romilly. I know this must be difficult, but can I please speak to your husband?'

'Oh. Yes. I forgot you'd want to do that. He's in his workshop. Let me just—'

[Shuffling and indistinct voices.]

'Hello? This is Ellis Martin.'

'Hello, Mr Martin. Has your wife explained why I've called?'

'She said the bastard has killed another child.'

'Yes. Now, I know this is a hard time but can you please tell me your whereabouts on the day Max went missing. The sixteenth of July.'

'Let me check Romilly's calendar. The sixteenth. Let's see. I was at my allotment in the morning. Came home for lunch with Romilly. Was in my workshop in the afternoon. We had dinner together and watched TV in the evening.'

'Can anyone confirm your whereabouts in the morning?'

'Some of the lads down at the allotment saw me. I'll get them to give you a call.'

'Thank you, Mr Martin. I know this is a tough time for you and me asking questions like this only makes it worse.'

'It's alright, son. Ever since Gabriella and Barnabas went missing, I've been answering detectives' questions. You've got to be thorough.'

'Thank you for your understanding.'

'How's Gabriella taking it?'

'I imagine she was shocked, but I've not seen her today.'

'Right. I'll let you get on.'

'Thank you for your patience.'

You have one new voicemail. Voicemail left today at 2:31 p.m.

'Hello. This is a message for Nicolas June. My name is Detective Inspector Juliet Stern. I need to speak to you about the fire you reported on the Dunlow Estate early this morning. Please call me back on this number as soon as you can.'

From: James Knowles **james.knowles@police.gov.uk**
To: Juliet Stern **juliet.stern@mit.gov.uk**
CC: Gabriella Martin **gabriella.martin@mit.gov.uk**
Date: **4 August, 14:53**
Subject: **Leonard Dunlow's whereabouts**

Juliet and Gabe,

Sorry I've not gotten back to you sooner.

Leo was with me for the entirety of our shift last night. We did paperwork before setting off on a planned patrol across the city. We dealt with a domestic disturbance and aided a young woman who was concerned about a group of men following her home. Before leaving this morning, we returned to the station to complete more paperwork. I dropped Leo off at his brother's house at about 8 a.m. – he's been living there for the past few weeks.

I hope Leo's okay. He's a good lad.

James

You have one new voicemail. Voicemail left today at 3:46 p.m.

'Hello, darling. It's Mum. We've had a call from Paul, who works with you. Gabriella, I'm so sorry you're dealing with this again. It's horrible whenever it happens but especially as it's so nearby this time. Your dad and I love you and we wish we could take this away. I don't know if time off is an option, but you can always come home for a while. Let us know what you want to do. Please look after yourself.'

News Archives – Daily Echo

FIRES BLAZING ACROSS COUNTRY ESTATES

Several fires have been doused in the last couple of weeks across estates in Southampton and the New Forest. Moore Estate outside Eastleigh suffered structural damage to its stables, Whitelaw Manor in the north of the New Forest has had to condemn a disused outbuilding, and Duckworth Estate near Hythe has lost the use of its garage.

Forensic Fire Officer Matt Lam explained that none of the fires were accidental. He said, 'There is clear evidence of purposeful ignition of each of these fires. All had accelerants to aid the spread of the flames.' He has asked anyone with information about who may be setting the fires to come forward. 'There has been no loss of life yet, but fire is unpredictable and fast. These fires have been started in places where people are unlikely to be but that doesn't mean terrible accidents can't occur.' Please call the number at the end of this report if you have any information that might be relevant.

We spoke with the estate owners, who were confused about why they had been targeted. Prior to and following the fires, no communication came from any parties who might have had reason to single out these families. Lord Whitelaw said, 'We're all upstanding citizens who conscientiously involve ourselves in our local communities. These fires are nonsensical and completely irresponsible. The perpetrators should feel ashamed of themselves.'

Chase Nolan @ChaseTheDream. Sent 16:22.

Have you heard from Zara today?

Paloma Robins @WiseGirlHiker. Sent 16:22.

Not yet. Should I have?

Paloma Robins @WiseGirlHiker. Sent 16:24.

You're such an arsehole. You know I can see you've read my message, right?

Paloma Robins @WiseGirlHiker. Sent 16:25.

I'm going to assume you're just being a twat, rather than anything actually being wrong.

Keith. Sent 16:50.

> Juliet, leave in the next ten minutes to be home in time for dinner. I'm making macaroni cheese with the girls. They're excited to see you x

You have four new voicemails. Voicemail left today at 5:01 p.m.

'Gabe. It's Juliet. I'm heading home. I've made a start on investigating the fire. As much as I could without anyone useful being allowed to examine the scene. I'm not sure where you've gone but I'll see you tomorrow morning.'

Gabe

A warm breeze whispered across the grass. I shivered and leant into the cool headstone.

It stood straight and proud. Immovable. I wondered if Barnabas would have been as strong and dependable if he'd been allowed to reach adulthood. Mum had passed her short stature on to me. Perhaps my brother would have been broad and muscled like Dad.

The sun had been high in the sky when I arrived. The drive to North London did nothing to calm the shrill alarms clashing in my brain. Abstractly, I'd known leaving the station mid-morning to visit my brother's grave wasn't normal but my foot hadn't moved from the accelerator.

Coming here was necessary. As I'd sat on the parched grass and traced my finger over the grooves of my brother's name, my mind had stilled.

The bad man had struck again, but he didn't have Barnabas anymore. My little brother was right here.

After an hour or so, I'd considered returning to Southampton. I could have crammed a day's work into what was left of the afternoon. But I shrivelled into myself at the thought of standing. I crowded close to the grey stone and closed my eyes. My phone buzzed in my pocket, making me flinch. It had recently gone still.

Now the sun hovered above the roofs of the terraced houses butting up to the edge of the graveyard. This far from the sea, the air held a baked dryness. No salty brine but the combined smells of thousands of people packed together. The aroma of home. Sweet rot around overflowing bins and enticing fried onions from takeaways and sun-softened tarmac.

'Hello, petal.'

I snapped my head around, but relaxed as Dad eased onto the grass. He rubbed my back, the ingrained callouses on his palm rough through the thin fabric of my shirt. His T-shirt was smeared with grease, his shorts adorned with ripped pockets. He must have been in the workshop today. Varnish and sawdust combined into a scent that never failed to make me feel safe.

This was the most contact we'd had since I'd moved to Southampton. Recently, Dad had relented from his campaign of total silence but the smile curving his thick grey moustache hadn't been aimed in my direction for over a year. Mum responded to my absence with fretful phone calls and care packages, whereas Dad fought without words to bring me home.

'Hi,' I croaked. I leant into his side when he curled his arm around my shoulders. 'How did you know I would be here?'

'Paul from your station called to ask my whereabouts when Max was taken,' Dad stated. 'He hadn't seen you, so I wondered if you'd come to visit Barney.'

I cringed at my brother's perfectly maintained headstone. I wasn't the only person subjected to another round of questioning each time the bad man resurfaced. Paul had to follow every lead if he was going to run an airtight investigation while under more scrutiny from the press and our higher-ups than ever before. That didn't make me want to shove him away from my family any less.

Mum, Dad, and I just wanted to be left alone, but that was impossible. We were inextricably linked to the periodic hunts for the bad man. We always would be, until he finally stopped.

'I'm sorry.' This wasn't the first time I'd apologised for the interest in my dad. The bad man had used him to lure my brother and me into his car. I didn't know if he'd planned for my dad to become a smokescreen he could hide behind while he carried on, unknown and undetected.

Dad's hand tightened around my shoulder, pulling me close. 'Gabriella, it's not your fault.'

This became my parents' mantra after I was found alone and starving outside a disused warehouse on a vast industrial estate. It wasn't my fault Barnabas and I had been taken, wasn't my fault my brother defended me against the bad man, wasn't my fault Barnabas had disappeared by the time I'd regained consciousness. I wasn't to blame when his broken body was found, stuffed in a barrel floating on a lake a couple of miles from home.

My parents believed me completely innocent in the abduction and murder of my younger brother. They told me this again and again.

It had yet to sink in.

I'd chosen to go with the bad man. I could have said no, could have grabbed Barnabas's hand and run to safety. I'd left our hideaway in the warehouse to search for food, exposing us both. I'd let the pain of my broken arm overwhelm me, choosing unconsciousness instead of fighting beside my brother. The bad man had seemed unconquerably big and strong but if we'd both fought, we would have stood a chance at stopping him. Barnabas and I could have escaped from the warehouse. We could have returned home together.

Despite the pressing heat of the evening and Dad's warmth at my side, I shivered. 'I just needed to come here,' I murmured, eyes on the daisies Mum must have arranged in the vase at the base of the headstone within the last couple of days. 'It's difficult when it happens again. It'll be worse since it's being investigated at my station.'

Dad's grip intensified, awakening a flare of pain in my shoulder. The bullet wound was fully healed but extreme pressure or stress had the power to jolt echoes of seemingly relentless hurt.

'You're not part of the search.'

'No.' I shifted and Dad's arm loosened. 'I was involved in the initial effort to find Max but won't be included from now on. They'll want the usual interview, then I'll be left alone.'

I didn't know if it would be more or less excruciating to have Paul, my friend, witness me stumbling through my useless memories rather than an impartial stranger. At least nothing I said would be new. He must have read my previous accounts of my time with the bad man, would have gone over them a second time after Max was found.

I could often tell when one of my co-workers used an idle minute to dip into my file. The week after Alice discovered my history had been filled with soft smiles and careful words. Showing her photos of mine and Ollie's weekend on the Isle of Wight, my boyfriend's tattooed torso on full display, had returned her to her normal self.

'Come home for a while,' Dad urged. 'Mum left you a message about it.'

I pulled my phone out of my pocket. I tapped at it, rather than look at Dad. It didn't respond, the screen stubbornly blank.

'Must not have charged it last night,' I muttered.

'Gabriella?' Dad's arm dropped from around me. 'I hope you're not going to try and work at the same station where they're looking for Barnabas's killer.'

I stared at my brother's name. My parents' response every time something affected me negatively was to swoop in and whisk me away. I'd endured it for years after my brother died but had finally broken free when the detective sergeant position came up at Southampton a year and a half ago.

Moving had broken my relationship with my dad, and it just kept fracturing. I wished I could tug his arm back to my shoulders and hold it there until he realised offering some comfort was better than withholding it all unless he could shelter me from everything. I breathed deep and looked at him.

'The investigation will be conducted on another floor. My co-workers will do everything they can to minimise the impact on me.'

Dad's cheeks flushed red and his forehead creased with the lines that had appeared when Barnabas and I had been taken, then never left. He stood and patted the top of Barnabas's headstone. Without another word, he walked towards the entrance of the graveyard.

Leaning against the polished stone, I drew my legs up to my chest and rested my head on my knees. Mum was baffled by my decision to leave home and work down in Southampton; she wanted to hold me close but she understood that wasn't what I wanted. Needed.

Dad couldn't accept that. He thought it best for me to live at home and find a quiet job, and he wouldn't deviate.

Barnabas had been stubborn too. His urge to protect me, even if it cost him his life, probably came from our dad.

I clenched my eyes shut and pressed into my brother's headstone. I'd stay here a while longer; recover from Dad's removed comfort, then head back to Southampton. Back to Ollie. And Artie. I could rest with my boyfriend and my dog until I had to face the world again tomorrow.

I'd give Paul an account of my time with the bad man, pass over my vague recollections, then focus on the arson investigation. Juliet wouldn't be thinking of any other case. This once, I would emulate her and develop a cold disinterest in victims outside my workload.

Call connected at 19:10.

'999, what's your emergency?'

'I need to report a missing person. My girlfriend.'

'Alright. I'll connect you to Southampton station.'

PLEASE HOLD. PLEASE HOLD.

'Hello, this is Southampton station. Camilla speaking. How can I help you?'

'I need to report a missing person.'

'Okay. What I'll do is take some details then a member of our team will give you a call back. What's the name of the missing person?'

'Zara Everett.'

'Thank you. And what's your name and relationship to Zara?'

'I'm Chase Nolan. She's my girlfriend. We live together.'

'How old is Zara?'

'Twenty-three.'

'And when did Zara go missing?'

'I'm not sure. I don't know if you've heard of her? She's pretty big on Instagram and TikTok.'

'I haven't. Sorry.'

'She's a travel blogger. Hiking, mostly. She's been all over the country, gone to Europe a few times. Her big thing is that solo hiking is beautiful and women shouldn't be afraid to go out on their own.'

'She's gone hiking alone?'

'Yeah, but we have a system. She always texts me last thing at night, then first thing in the morning. Only, she didn't text me yesterday evening or today. I've tried calling but her phone goes straight to voicemail. I drove over to where she planned to make camp last night in River Hamble Country Park, east of the city. There's no sign of her.'

'Is there anywhere else she might have gone or anyone else she could be staying with?'

'No. Zara was careful to stay where she said she would be. Just in case anything happened. And I've asked around our friends. No one has seen or heard from her.'

'Her parents?'

'Zara doesn't have any. She was put into care when she was seven and hasn't seen them since. She lived with foster carers until she was eighteen, but she isn't in contact with them either.'

'Okay, Chase. Thank you for all of this. I'm going to pass it on and someone will be in touch soon.'

'Thank you. I'm worried about her.'

You have one new voicemail. Voicemail left today at 8.12 p.m.

'Hey, mate. It's Tyler. Got some stuff I picked up last night on that job I chatted to you about at the pub. It's good shit, should be easy enough to move on. Let me know if you want in. I've got another guy who's keen.'

Hey Gabe,

I've tried calling and texting, but nothing's getting through. Did you forget to charge your phone again?

I'm sorry I couldn't wait until you got home from work but Dad's had a stroke and I need to get over to Cornwall to be with him. I spoke to Mum a little while ago and she said he's stable, but I want to go anyway.

I'm taking Artie with me. I wasn't sure how long you'd be working today and I didn't want you to have to worry about him if a new case has come in and you'll be out of the house lots.

I'll call later. Love you.

Ollie xxxxx

Gabe

I stared at Ollie's note, as if by sheer desperation I could change what it said. He couldn't be speeding miles away from me. He'd popped to the shop, would be back in five minutes, his voice ringing through the house as he delighted in whatever bargain he'd found this time.

The promise of falling into his arms had sustained me during the drive home. I'd grown no better at expressing my feelings for him in the months we'd been dating but after today's shitshow, the only person I wanted to be around was him. I needed Ollie's soft touch, his kind words, whatever cheesy concoction he'd made for dinner.

It took reaching for my phone, sitting uselessly in my pocket, for the correct response to register. On finding Ollie's note, my first thought should have been a fervent wish that nothing too bad had happened to his dad. Followed by concern for Ollie, who had cried when his mum fell in the kitchen last month and bruised her knee.

Self-recrimination swamped me as I traced the line of kisses at the bottom of the page. Ollie always thought of others first, always thought of me before himself, yet all I wanted was for him to appear and comfort me. I should have been worried about what my boyfriend was going through, not purely focused on my own struggles.

The house was too silent. The two-up two-down Ollie and I had recently started renting together was fresh after a between-tenants scrub. We were making it our home. Ollie and I with photos and soft blankets, Artie with black and brown fur that nestled in every tight corner. Unsure of an Alsatian owned by a police officer, our new neighbours had been wary of him until they got close. Then he covered them in drool and demanded they throw his ball.

I'd depended on Ollie and Artie's rambunctious welcome. I wasn't prepared for oppressive quiet. Cars occasionally swept past but inside no heavy footsteps or panting breaths broke through my swirling thoughts.

I wanted to be a good girlfriend and detective, to care for others and do my job well. That felt an insurmountable task with the bad man lurking. Each time he struck, I told myself it had to be the last time. He couldn't keep getting lucky and slipping away without a trace. Technology was advancing. CCTV cameras multiplied every day. The number of spaces where it was possible to commit secret, horrendous acts undetected was diminishing. He had to stop, had to know he would be found if he didn't. Even if he wasn't sensible enough to recognise the odds were stacked against him, he had to get too old for it someday.

But then he did it again. Another child snatched away. Another family irreparably broken. Another life snuffed out for no good reason.

Raised voices clattered through the open living-room window. I flinched, sending Ollie's note to the floor. Indistinct words sliced through the air, high and slurred.

People near my home, and I had no idea who they were.

Anyone could be outside. Watching and waiting. Biding their time until my guard dropped.

The kitchen-diner had a U-shaped counter. I rushed into the recess and plunged to the floor. Tucking myself into a ball, I pushed my back into the corner of the cupboards.

The shouters moved on. Quiet descended.

I pressed my forehead into my knees. My ears strained with the effort of listening, searching for any indication of danger. My blood throbbed, twisting the growl of passing cars into swooshing roars.

The bad man was strong enough to crash through my front door. He would find me and he would grab me and he would take me away.

My left arm ached. Phantom pain, one doctor called it. There was no physical reason it would continue to hurt. The bone had so wholly fused back together that it was difficult to tell on an X-ray where the break had been.

I knew. I grasped my arm where the bone had snapped, pressing my thumb into my skin.

A car door slammed. Or a monster smashed against my front door. A gun shot.

'He can't get me now.' I cowered deeper into myself. 'He can't get me. He can't get me.'

I'd whispered the same thing in the hospital after I'd been found. Small and shivering and broken.

Tears soaked through my trousers, wetting my knees. The words formed a poor defence against the horrors looming in my mind. My memories of the bad man might be confused and vague, but he was always with me. He waited in my nightmares and pressed into my waking fears. I saw snatches of him in each unknown man's face, searched for him at every sudden noise, spent sleepless nights guarding myself from his next attack.

'He can't get me,' I whispered. 'He can't. He can't.'

I willed it to be true, to feel true, but the past pressed in. The bad man might not be here right now, but he had taken me and my brother years ago. I'd returned home. Barnabas had been forever stolen.

Nothing could ever undo that.

Nothing could stop the bad man.

Recording started: 21:45.

Police Constable James Knowles: Hello, everyone. Thank you for coming in at such short notice. We know this is later than we'd usually gather you, so thank you for taking time out of your evenings. Detective Inspector Paul Willis will now make a statement, after which there will be a short time for your questions.

Detective Inspector Paul Willis: Following a phone call from a distressed member of the public just after eight a.m. this morning, officers were dispatched to Hythe Sailing Yard. A barrel had become tangled in rope beside a boat and, upon opening the barrel, the member of the public discovered the body of seven-year-old Max Powrie. His parents have been informed and are being supported by their family and a member of our Family Liaison team. We are gathering forensic evidence from the barrel and Max's body, and searching for any sign of Max's killer in CCTV footage surrounding Hythe Sailing Yard. We would ask members of the public to report sightings of anyone acting strangely around the sailing yard late last night or this morning.

PC James Knowles: Any questions?

[Indistinguishable voices.]

DI Paul Willis: One at a time, please.

Hally Jenks: Hally Jenks, *Guardian*. Since Max's body was found in a barrel, does that mean the Barrel Man has claimed another victim?

DI Paul Willis: At this time, we are looking into a number of different lines of enquiry. There are similarities between

Max's death and the murders of other children but we cannot be blind to the evidence presented to us in this instance. However, I will say the similarities are stark and the possibility that this was the work of the serial killer commonly known as the Barrel Man is not an avenue we're ignoring.

Anna Yen: Anna Yen, *Independent*. The Barrel Man has been active for thirty-five years: what makes you think you will be more successful than the other attempts to catch him?

DI Paul Willis: As I just said, we are not yet convinced this was the work of a serial killer. We are working through a wealth of evidence and will make informed decisions based on that. Unlike some other professions, detective work takes a lot of determination and effort. If anyone can bring Max's killer to justice, it will be myself and my team.

Anna Yen: But is there anything significantly different this time? Is there a reason you think you'll be able to catch a killer who has eluded other detectives for years?

DI Paul Willis: I cannot reveal details of an ongoing case. Does anyone have any sensible questions, or shall we draw this to a close?

Robert Browning: Robert Browning here, *Daily Mail*. At what point will you concede this is a hunt for a serial killer, and will it be helpful that his only surviving victim is a fellow detective at Southampton station?

DI Paul Willis: If the investigation progresses towards searching for the serial killer known as the Barrel Man, then I will ask Detective Sergeant Gabriella Martin for a short statement and a description of her brother's killer. We will attempt to make both the investigation as a whole and our questioning cause as little distress to her and her loved ones as possible. I know it's not in your nature, but I'd ask you to leave her in peace. I'm done here.

PC James Knowles: If you'd please follow Detective Sergeant Nicole Stewart through the door at the back of the room and sign out before you leave the building.

Ollie. Sent 22:28.

I've tried to call but my signal here is useless. If you really want to chat, I can try using the home phone. It's ancient though, actually attached to the wall, and I'd rather not risk waking up Mum. Are you okay? x

Gabe. Sent 22:30.

That's fine. Just got home. How are you? And your dad?

Ollie. Sent 22:31.

Dad's fine, thank god. It was a mild stroke and apparently it's a good sign that he didn't lose any speech or movement. He's cross Mum even made him go to hospital, and even more cross that the doctors are insisting he stays until they've sorted out his blood pressure x

Gabe. Sent 22:34.

I'm glad he's okay.

Ollie. Sent 22:34.

I'm going to go to sleep now. I'm covering for Dad at the farm and that means getting up ridiculously early x

Gabe. Sent 22:35.

That's okay. I'm tired too. I'm going to head to bed.

Ollie. Sent 22:35.

Okay. We'll catch up properly tomorrow. Sleep well xxx

Gabe. Sent 22.37.

You too x

Day 2

Tuesday, 5 August

THE BARREL MAN STRIKES AGAIN – TWO YEARS AFTER OLGA BERT'S BODY WAS DISCOVERED IN THE RIVER TWEED…

Scroll.

MAX POWRIE'S BODY FOUND – HIS DISTRAUGHT FATHERS SHARE THEIR RESPECT FOR THE POLICE AND ASK FOR PRIVACY…

Scroll.

DETECTIVES REFUSE TO COMMENT ON SERIAL KILLER THREAT – DO THEY SUSPECT CATCHING THE INFAMOUS BARREL MAN IS BEYOND THEM?…

Scroll.

Ollie. Sent 8:32.

> Morning – hope you slept well. The poster of McFly in my bedroom gave me sweet dreams. I chatted to Mum over breakfast and she asked if I can stay for a few days to help on the farm, at least until Dad's out of hospital. He's disgusted they want to keep him in for up to a week. Talk to you later xx

Gabe. Sent 8:35.

> That's fine. See you when you get home.

Call connected at 9:04.

'Hi, Juliet. You didn't need to call. I'm getting in my car now. I'm sorry about—'

'Don't come to the station. Reroute your ridiculous satnav to the Dunlow Estate.'

'Is Matt allowing us into the cottage?'

'He has to. He's found a body.'

'Shit.'

'Indeed. Race you there.'

Retrieved from police archives.

Detective Inspector Mohammad Allon: Witness statement recorded with the permission of the interviewee on the 8th February at 1:16 p.m. The interviewee is Romilly Martin. This interview is being conducted by myself, Detective Inspector Mohammad Allon, and our Family Liaison Support Officer, Bethany Wilde, is also in attendance. Romilly, you are under no obligation to continue with this interview and please let us know if you need a break at any time.

Romilly Martin: I can't stay for too long. I need to get back home to Gabriella.

DI Mohammad Allon: That's understandable. Thank you for coming back into the station. How is she doing?

[Sniffing.]

DI Mohammad Allon: I apologise. That was a thoughtless question.

Romilly Martin: No, no. Please don't be sorry. It's just been the most awful time.

Family Liaison Support Officer Bethany Wilde: It must be incredibly difficult to have Gabriella home but Barnabas still missing.

Romilly Martin: It's horrendous. That's why I'll answer all your questions. Anything to bring my boy home.

DI Mohammad Allon: Thank you, Romilly. I know it's only been a few hours since I spoke to her, but has Gabriella shared any more details with you about the man who took her and Barnabas?

Romilly Martin: She's barely spoken. The most she says—

[Sniffing.]

FLSO Bethany Wilde: Take your time.

Romilly Martin: It's just. Oh gosh. She keeps asking me and Ellis when Barnabas will come home. Neither of us knows what to say.

DI Mohammad Allon: I can't imagine how difficult it is for her to understand what's happened.

Romilly Martin: I hope she never does.

DI Mohammad Allon: I'd like to talk about something Gabriella mentioned about your husband. She said their abductor told her and Barnabas that Ellis was cross with them and that's why they had to go with him.

Romilly Martin: It boils my blood that such a monster used Ellis like that.

DI Mohammad Allon: Your husband has an alibi for the time when your children were taken but, I wonder, is there a reason the threat of Ellis being unhappy with Gabriella and Barnabas would have been so effective?

[Short pause.]

Romilly Martin: I'm not sure what you mean.

DI Mohammad Allon: I wonder why the man didn't use the threat of you being cross?

Romilly Martin: You'll have to ask him once you catch him.

DI Mohammad Allon: Romilly, please understand: I'm not trying to make a villain out of anyone. To perform a successful investigation I must delve into every avenue, no matter how unpleasant. Your daughter said that the man who took her and Barnabas mentioned Ellis. That's not something I can ignore. I need to establish if there has been prior contact with their abductor, if there is any kind of link between him and Ellis.

[Short pause.]

Romilly Martin: I understand that. But I think he just said whatever he thought would be most effective to get them to go with him.

DI Mohammad Allon: Is there a reason your children would have been more scared of Ellis being cross, rather than yourself?

Romilly Martin: Only because it would be so unusual. I'm the one who tells them off when they leave their toys in a mess or won't eat their dinner. Ellis is much more of a softie.

DI Mohammad Allon: There's no reason for Gabriella and Barnabas to fear your husband?

Romilly Martin: Are all your questions going to be like this? Because if so, I'd rather leave now. Ellis is a wonderful father and husband. He was broken when our children were taken, blames himself completely. He's barely eaten, hasn't slept. He sits at Gabriella's bedside each night so he's there when she wakes from nightmares. He is the gentlest and kindest man I know, and you need to remove him from your thinking right now. You're wasting your time on my husband, when you need to find my son.

Gabe

The smell of smoke was muted as I parked up outside the Dunlow Estate behind Juliet's Toyota Yaris. She'd not driven before she moved out to Eastleigh, preferring the position of passenger. Even now, she abandoned her car for most of the day at the station whenever possible. Juliet didn't welcome even the shallowest of personal enquires, but I wondered if she didn't like driving for some reason. Or perhaps it was simply avoidance of a menial task that wasted her precious time.

She wouldn't be scared of driving. Juliet wasn't scared of anything. Not like me.

I took a deep breath. It did nothing to calm my fractious thoughts or stumbling heart. After another of the bad man's victims was found, there always followed a period of time when the world felt distant yet bruisingly close. I just had to get through it. Gradually, I'd return to normal.

Ollie's absence wasn't helping. I tried to concentrate on concern for his dad but I missed the comfort my boyfriend would have offered. I wanted him here, wanted him close, needed the distraction of his body to free me from my spiralling thoughts. I'd used meaningless sex with strangers for years when my brain wouldn't quiet, but Ollie and I had agreed to exclusivity early on. I'd had no reason to regret it before.

I grabbed my notepad and climbed out of my car. The lingering stink of burning intensified as I walked over to the uniformed officer managing the scene log. I didn't recognise them. Usually, I'd ask for their name. Today, I gave my own and offered a faint smile before walking into the estate. I needed all my energy for this case, couldn't waste any on pleasantries.

Another day of relentless sun had been predicted. It was a relief to step under the shelter of charred trees as I neared the cottage, half the building engulfed by a white tent. Juliet stood beside Matt Lam just outside the crumpled front wall, both of them tall and strong. I felt particularly stunted when I stood on Juliet's other side.

'Morning.' I coughed and flipped open my notepad, willing my thoughts away from a night of horrible dreams and listening intently for strange sounds. 'Have I missed much?'

'Nothing.' Juliet didn't look away from the shadows moving inside the white tent. 'And nothing would have been missed at all if those trained to detect crimes had been allowed into the cottage in a timely manner.'

A muscle in Matt's jaw twitched. 'As I've already explained to your colleague, there was no reason to expect a body in the building.'

Apparently Juliet had been deploying her own brand of unhelpfulness before I arrived. My nerves might be frayed but I was always more diplomatic than her, could see beyond the petty annoyance of a delayed investigation to how helpful Matt would be as the case progressed.

'We all thought the building had been abandoned,' I conceded, ignoring the sharp flick of Juliet's eyes. 'Mr Dunlow had previously housed groundskeepers in this cottage. With the main house vacated, it was reasonable to assume no one would be living here either.'

Matt's face relaxed as he twisted to look at me, his habitual T-shirt and patched fluorescent trousers largely devoid of ash this morning. 'I don't think it was someone employed here.'

I readied my pencil over my notepad. 'What makes you say that?'

'The building was being used for storage.' Matt gestured at the cottage, its innards bared to the world by blackened walls and collapsed sections of thatched roof. Charred boxes teetered in uneven stacks across the section of living room uncovered by the tent. 'Unless the groundskeeper had way more stuff than would actually fit in their home, I reckon the boxes and the body are unrelated. We also discovered a big backpack. They could have been homeless.'

Juliet sniffed. 'I haven't been able to make contact with Timothy Dunlow. When he surfaces, we can ask if he'd employed a new groundskeeper or was using the cottage for storage.'

She would have tried to talk to Dunlow yesterday during my unexplained absence. Juliet didn't seem bothered by the reminder that I'd absconded after exiting Angela's office. She had shown no curiosity around where I'd been when I should have been helping to establish the basic facts of this case.

'There are a lot of outbuildings on this estate closer to the main house,' I offered, unwilling to be flaky and useless. 'It doesn't make sense that Dunlow would have used this cottage for storage when he could have moved a couple of his cars and had ample and easily accessible space in the garage.'

Matt shrugged. 'The estate is fairly remote. Could be that Mr Dunlow wasn't aware someone else was using one of his buildings, either to stash stuff or live in.'

I looked over at the entrance. A camera that had once topped the fence post beside the front gate was absent. It must have been removed after the family vacated the grounds. It had relayed a live feed, but would have deterred all but the boldest of trespassers. It seemed Melanie Pirt's murder hadn't converted Dunlow from his entrenched views around CCTV and privacy.

'When did you find the body?' I prompted.

'Just before I called Detective Stern,' Matt said. Presumably, Juliet hadn't given him permission to use her first name. Either a petty one up of someone who'd stood in her way or she hadn't noticed. More likely the latter. 'Twenty-four hours had passed since the fire was doused and I'd deemed the area stable enough for an initial assessment.'

The cottage was no longer smoking but looked far from safe to me. The inches of height and breadth Matt had on me, along with his years of experience searching through ruined buildings, likely made examining a one-storey house a pleasant break from more daunting explorations.

'First, I worked to ascertain the cause of the fire.' Matt's deep voice slipped into a practised monotone. 'A glass bottle filled with petrol and rags had been set alight and thrown through the front door.'

'Is that the same process as the other recent estate fires?' Juliet asked.

'Very much so,' Matt said. 'It's either the same group or person, or an accurate copycat.'

I frowned. I couldn't recall the details of the other fires. I was unwilling to ask Juliet about them in front of Matt and reveal my ineptitude, but it was likely we were dealing with a newly active serial arsonist.

'Do you think they knew there was someone in the building?' I asked, determined to provide what little help I could.

Matt shook his head. 'The previous fires caused no loss of life. This could be an escalation, but they had been targeting uninhabited buildings. Once you join your forensic team you'll see that, even if the arsonist entered the building prior to setting it alight, they could have missed the person inside. The individual was surrounded by boxes.'

'Is that why you didn't spot them earlier?' Juliet asked, her tone cool and clear. I didn't think she was purposefully needling Matt, but his jaw tightened.

'They were buried underneath boxes. When I moved a couple to check for potentially volatile substances, I found them.'

His narrowed eyes fixed on Juliet, who calmly regarded the rippling white tent. I didn't know how often firefighters discovered bodies. As a Forensic Officer, it had to be more common. Matt's brown skin was beaded with sweat, but no more than anyone else's would be as the sun rose on another sweltering day. He'd not stumbled over his words or shied away from discussing what he'd found.

Yet another person able to compartmentalise the more unpleasant aspects of their job. Perhaps only I continued to struggle when faced with dead bodies, even years after working with my first. Examining the latest couldn't be delayed for much longer.

I flicked to a new page in my notepad. 'What can you tell us about the body?'

Juliet didn't roll her eyes, but disdain oozed from her crossed arms and tapping trainer. One of the many things we disagreed about was asking those who arrived at the scene of a crime before us for their impressions. One day, someone would share an important detail and she'd have to concede that people outside her trusted few could bring something of merit to investigations.

'Nothing really.' Matt winced, betraying that he wasn't entirely comfortable with unexpectedly finding a corpse. 'I moved the box, realised what was underneath, then called in your forensic team.'

Juliet waited for him to finish, then strode towards the cottage. Her progress was impeded by the necessity of donning a paper jumpsuit. That didn't make for a triumphant exit from the conversation. Not that she'd care.

'Thank you for talking that through,' I said, while Juliet pulled covers onto her trainers. An indistinguishable member of the forensic team passed her a pair of gloves and protective glasses, their face obscured by a thick mask.

Matt's toothy smile had been wholly absent in Juliet's presence. 'Not a problem. I'm going to do what I can for my report around you, then I'll have to wait for the rest.'

I nodded, even less equipped than normal to discern if explaining his movements was some flirtatious code. I suspected not, as my appearance today was very much thrown together. My eyes were sunken due to lack of sleep and, although I'd showered, I couldn't recall whether I'd checked my hair before hurriedly leaving home.

While I pulled on a jumpsuit, my skin passively protesting the addition of another layer, Juliet walked into the cottage. The front door had fallen to one side, the wooden frame where it once stood sagging. Juliet ducked underneath and used stepping plates to pick her way across the main room. The squares of thick plastic had been placed by the forensic team to provide a safe route through the site that wouldn't compromise any material they needed to collect. Her jumpsuit crinkled as she edged around boxes.

My own protective gear reluctantly pulled into place, I followed Juliet's path. I breathed the already stuffy air behind my mask, reminded of Covid lockdowns when fabric had pressed across my nose and mouth for long hours each day.

Juliet paused outside the white tent. She held up the flap, a silent invitation for me to enter first. I didn't have to ask who was working inside. If Juliet was reluctant to march in, it had to be David Rees. The head of the forensic team had become minimally more bearable recently but his unwavering attention towards Juliet was off-putting, even as a bystander.

I grimaced as I took an awkward step closer across plates positioned by someone with much longer legs than me. The enclosed space promised more swampy warmth than had been generated outside on an already humid morning.

I'd braced myself with one last breath of relatively cool air behind my mask when pounding footfalls approached from the estate entrance. A uniformed officer ran through the gates. They ignored Matt's shout and rushed over.

Leo Dunlow panted on the other side of the crumbling pile of bricks that had previously formed the front wall of the cottage. His auburn hair was cropped close to his olive-toned scalp, his thick glasses slipping down his straight nose.

He couldn't have good feelings towards this place, the home of the man who'd killed the girl he loved.

'Is it Dad?' he asked breathlessly.

James Knowles puffed up behind him, his cheeks flushed. 'Leo, I told you not to run off.'

'What's going on?' David Rees poked his head out of the tent. His pale blue eyes lingered on Juliet for longer than was comfortable, before sweeping over to the two uniformed officers outside the ruined cottage.

Leo and James made an odd pair. Leo was beginning his time on the force as James neared the end. The younger man was tall and lean while James was stocky. Their similarities were less obvious. Gentleness, kindness, a hardworking attitude. Leo had been a Police Constable for a matter of weeks and had already gained a reputation as someone to depend on.

'What do you want?' David snapped.

Uneven blush rose across Leo's neck and cheeks. 'I heard a body was found.' He turned his wide brown eyes on me. 'Is it Dad?'

I looked to David. Only he could say with certainty that the body wasn't Timothy Dunlow. He seemed inclined to tell Leo and James to get lost, until Juliet coughed. David's eyes softened behind his protective glasses.

'Unless your father is a woman in her twenties or thirties, then I'm going to say no,' he pronounced, before ducking back into the tent.

Leo sagged, his magnified eyes swimming. I left James to console him. Confronting the body had been delayed for long enough.

I walked into the tent then reared back, nearly stepping on the toes of Juliet's covered trainers.

Jagged thoughts of the bad man and Paul's investigation had distracted me too much. If I'd been more present, I would have been forewarned of the smell inside the tent.

A body had been found following a fire. That body had been blasted by the intense heat that ripped through the cottage. It had then been left in late-August warmth for over twenty-four hours.

The tent was packed with the fetid stench of cooked meat gone bad. Juliet gasped when she walked around me onto an adjacent stepping plate, her gloved hand rising to her already covered nose. Our masks did little to block out the stink, designed to filter potentially harmful gases released by the fire's extreme heat rather than odours.

David crouched beside a pile of collapsed boxes. I squared my shoulders and breathed shallowly through my mouth as I followed Juliet across the room.

'What can you tell us?' she asked.

David stood. His bent legs had concealed the head and shoulders of a young woman. Her face was partially turned towards the concrete floor. The rest of her body was buried under misshapen cardboard. Considering the state of the cottage, she was remarkably untouched. Boxes that had buried her had also protected her from direct contact with flames. The angle of her head, half-pushed into the floor, made it hard to distinguish her features beyond the strange wax-like quality imparted by death. One eye, half-visible under strands of dark brown hair matted with sweat, was closed. Her beige skin was mottled by bruises. Faded blue straps hooked over her shoulders, the fabric of her vest streaked with grey ash.

'Not a lot,' David said. 'We're removing the boxes, but they're unstable. We have to work slowly to minimise disturbance to the body.'

'Have you found any ID?' I gripped my notepad. Behind my mask, my upper lip was damp. I breathed shallowly through my mouth.

'None.' David pointed a gloved finger at one of his colleagues, who was writing on a series of wide plastic evidence bags. 'We found what we believe to be her rucksack beside a mat she was most likely using as a bed, but there's nothing to identify her.' He pointed to another white-suited person photographing a charred yoga mat. 'Our theory is that she woke after the fire was well established and became trapped under boxes while attempting to escape.'

A shiver trickled down my spine despite the oppressive heat inside the tent. To awaken to smoke and burning, then to have any chance of flight taken away. Buried, left in the ashes of a building that had offered refuge before it was set ablaze. I swallowed and looked anywhere but at the young woman on the floor.

'You'll be able to use DNA and dental records to identify her?' Juliet checked.

It was more difficult than usual to discern if she was completely unaffected with a mask covering half of her face. I hoped I was rendered similarly unreadable. The death of this young woman tugged at me more than it should, the temptation to weep over this unknown person's death strong.

The bad man weakened me.

'Should be able to,' David said. 'The other case has to take precedence, but I'll get the tests done as soon as I can.'

Despite knowing the bad man was being hunted by my colleagues, such casual mention of the investigation sent a strange frisson through my bones.

Juliet had no visible reaction. David was denied the pleasure of more unadulterated staring when she spun and stalked out of the tent.

'Good work,' I muttered. David frowned at me, before dipping into a crouch beside the body.

I pulled down my hood and shook out my hair once I exited the tent. Gulping great breaths of earthy air, I retraced my path along the stepping plates.

Matt shot a grimace my way as I stripped off the rest of my protective gear and passed it to an unknown member of David's team.

I raised a weak hand in Matt's direction before following Juliet towards the estate entrance. I couldn't face talking to him right now, but I needed to get a grip. My personal problems couldn't affect my work. Angela had already hinted at time off. I couldn't display any weakness that would turn that into a command.

Our cars waited outside the estate gates. James and Leo must have left. I wondered if Terence would be so concerned when he heard a body had been found, whether he would be grieved by the thought of his father mouldering under a pile of boxes.

From: Nicole Stewart **nicole.stewart@mit.gov.uk**
To: James Knowles **james.knowles@police.gov.uk**
CC: Paul Willis **paul.willis@mit.gov.uk**
Date: **5 August, 9:52**
Subject: <u>**Operation Mercury – CCTV footage**</u>

James,

Please can you retrieve and check footage from around Hythe Sailing Yard in the forty-eight hours before Max's body was found? It's likely the barrel was put into the river nearby, so look for anywhere it would have been easy to get the barrel close to the water and place it in without being seen by members of the public.

Thanks,

Nicole

Paloma Robins @WiseGirlHiker
Shirley, Southampton

Unlike some people *pointed eyeroll in a certain direction IYKYK* I've spent the last few days enjoying short hikes with friends. Each night, I stayed with mates or in highly rated hostels. I made my phone trackable to two trusted fellow hikers and checked in at several points during the day.

This might sound overcautious but I refuse to close my eyes and pretend the world is a lovely place. In case you didn't know it – the world is fucked! Sorry not sorry to burst your bubble.

I hike to find peace but as a woman I know all too easily how that peace can be torn away. I'm never going to stop enjoying the natural world via my own two feet, but I am going to do so in a safe and responsible way that takes into account the realities of the fucked-up world we live in.

Be safe out there, my fellow girlie hikers xxxx

From: David Rees **david.rees@forensics.gov.uk**
To: Paul Willis **paul.willis@mit.gov.uk**
CC: Nicole Stewart **nicole.stewart@mit.gov.uk**
Date: **5 August, 10:16**
Subject: **Operation Mercury – forensic results**

Willis,

Attached are the full forensic results from MAX POWRIE's body and the BARREL he was discovered in. A number of these findings will not be news to you, as you were present when the body was extracted and examined, but there are a few details I wanted to highlight.

The pathologist has determined with a reasonable degree of certainty that MAX POWRIE had been asphyxiated prior to being placed in the BARREL. His hyoid bone is broken and the pattern of bruising around his neck supports a case for strangulation. The BARREL was tarred prior to being placed into the water but was not airtight. Had MAX POWRIE been alive when placed in the BARREL, there is a good chance he would have remained so until the BARREL was found.

The marine biologist and forensic metallurgist I consulted with agree that the BARREL was in the water for a minimum of six hours and a maximum of twelve, due to the lack of algae growth and corrosion. As the tides around Hythe Sailing Yard were not strong during this time frame, this would suggest the BARREL was placed into the water in the approximate area it was found.

On close examination of MAX POWRIE's hair, we were able to isolate several loose strands that differed in colour and texture. DNA has been extracted and is a match to DNA discovered in the WAREHOUSE where GABRIELLA MARTIN was found. The DNA shows no familial links to MAX POWRIE or GABRIELLA MARTIN.

There was also a partial fingerprint embedded in the tar at the bottom of the BARREL. This is a match for two fingerprints found on the BARREL containing OLGA BERT's body two years ago and the partial fingerprint found on the BARREL containing PRINCE BAILEY's body seven years ago.

Rees

Gabe

Juliet was slouching in her driver's seat when I pulled into the station car park. She hadn't suggested a race back but she would have been the undisputed winner. I'd taken slower side roads, aware my reactions were lacking in a way they shouldn't be when behind the wheel. Her head jerked up as I climbed out of my car. Her hair was in a perfect ponytail, unruffled by the protective gear she'd donned at the estate.

I sniffed at my shirt as I slammed my door shut, sure the pungent stink inside the tent lingered. Thick and meaty.

I wondered if it smelt similar to the inside of a barrel, whether the same stench had belched forth when Barnabas was found.

I'd only seen the barrel before it was put to use. Large, but decidedly placed in the background. The bad man overshadowed it. I'd learnt its significance over time. No one wanted to tell an eight-year-old the details of her brother's demise. I'd picked up a rough idea during repeated rounds of questioning, from screaming headlines and gossip on the playground whenever he struck again. My parents tried to protect me, but they couldn't keep the truth hidden forever.

I'd read the case file as soon as I joined the force. Barnabas was dead before he was placed in the barrel. Strangled. At most, he'd been in there for seventy-two hours. It was February when he was found. Frigid and wet.

He would have smelt nothing like the unknown woman in the cottage, but there would have been something. Even the most cared for corpse wasn't odourless.

'Gabe?' Juliet said as we walked towards the station entrance. Her tone suggested it wasn't the first time she'd said my name. I wasn't often on the receiving end of her impatience. Left exposed by the reappearance of the bad man, her casual ire stung.

I struggled to recall anything she'd said. 'Sorry?'

A line formed between her thin eyebrows but her voice softened. 'It's fine. Don't worry about it.'

Shit. I presented such a pathetic front that even Juliet was taking it easy on me.

I rolled my shoulders as we rounded the corner from the car park. This couldn't continue. Before I could insist Juliet treat me with her normal casual disregard, she stopped walking.

'Fuck.'

It took me two seconds too long to realise what she was staring at near the glass fronted entrance to the station. The normally quiet pavement swarmed with people.

Like a hound catching a scent, the milling reporters turned our way. Camera lenses flashed, obscuring faces. I stood rooted to the spot as the crowd stormed closer.

'Gabriella, how does it feel to have your brother's killer strike so nearby?'

'Martin. Look here.'

'Would you be willing to give a message to the families of his other victims?'

'Detective Martin, did Barnabas's death influence your decision to join the force?'

Fear clogged my throat. Journalists jostled for the best position in the tight ring around me. Juliet had been pushed out of reach, her blonde hair just visible beyond the braying riot.

'Hey. Over here.'

'Gabe, do you think the Barrel Man striking so close to home is a sign?'

'Don't say that name.' I wanted to shout. It came out as barely a whisper.

On seeing my mouth move, the crowd pressed in. Tears sprang to my eyes as I span, searching for an escape route. There was none. Only a howling mass of demands and unfamiliar faces. Juliet had disappeared, lost behind the seething group.

My knees weakened. I wanted to hide my face, scream into my hands. Generally shorter than other adults, I felt tiny surrounded by screaming strangers.

I was a little girl again. Terrified and alone.

Firm fingers grasped my upper arm. 'Get the fuck away from her, you bloody vultures.'

Paul had fought his way to my side. Instinctively, I huddled close to him. His gait uneven, he marched through the pack. One arm curled around my shoulders, he used the other to roughly push people out of our way. His chest heaving, he shoved the station door open and pulled me inside.

The door slammed shut, closed by Juliet. The shouting was abruptly muffled but the words echoed around my head, their barbs embedding.

Paul stepped back. I wished he hadn't. Juliet handed over his stick, her eyes on the journalists pressing into the other side of the glass.

'We should move out of sight.'

She strode towards the bank of lifts. Paul and I followed at a slower pace, his limp less pronounced now he could distribute some of his weight to his stick. He'd been injured years ago in a badly handled hostage situation. His sons had reluctantly conceded, after close examination of both when Paul invited Ollie and I over for dinner a couple of weeks ago, that the long scar stretching down their dad's leg was far more impressive than the puckered wound on my shoulder.

'You alright, Gabe?' Paul's black-and-grey hair was more mussed than usual, the bags resting under his eyes as heavy as mine. Lines crossed his forehead, the freckles that had appeared during his recent holiday to Malta faded after too many hours spent inside the station.

I nodded, willing myself to leave behind what had happened outside. It was a shock to be suddenly accosted, but it shouldn't make my whole body tingle with suppressed shudders. My skin crawled even though none of the journalists had touched me. I wanted to be small, to curl up in the nearest corner and close my eyes.

'I needed to come get you anyway.' Paul squeezed my shoulder and my desire to become unnoticeable intensified. It was inevitable that he would need to take my statement about the bad man, but I'd hoped against reason to avoid it.

'Can't it wait?' Juliet snapped. The lift opened and she glowered at Paul as we all stepped inside. 'We've just gotten back from the scene of a homicide. The forensic results are already going to be delayed because of your investigation. Gabe and I at least need a minute to focus on our own case before she helps with yours.'

Intentional or not, it was kind of her to label what I would offer Paul as helpful and, under her waspishness, to provide a quiet moment for me to slink off. Usually, after facing a dead body for the first time, I hurried to the most private toilet in the station to heave. I'd suspected Juliet knew about my involuntary ritual, but it wasn't something we spoke about. I didn't let it affect my work so she happily ignored it.

I bit my lip and moved focus from my over-sensitive skin to my guts. By this point, saliva would normally be gathering in sickly waves over my tongue as my stomach clenched.

My insides sat still and hollow. Seeing a dead body, even one so unpleasantly altered by summer heat, paled when faced with everything else clamping down around me.

'I'd rather get this over and done with,' I said as we rose to the sixth floor. 'I'll go with Paul now.'

Juliet regarded me when the lift stopped, her expression unreadable as Paul and I walked out into the wide corridor. 'Don't take too long.'

'I won't,' I said as the lift doors slid shut.

I couldn't. I didn't have much to say. Never did, no matter how much detectives poked and coaxed.

The quicker this was over, the quicker I could find my way back to some semblance of normal life. My past would ebb away as the days passed and nothing was found to bring the bad man to justice.

From: Juliet Stern **juliet.stern@mit.gov.uk**
To: Madison Campbell
madison.campbell@mitadmin.gov.uk
CC: Gabriella Martin **gabriella.martin@mit.gov.uk**
Date: **5 August, 10:32**
Subject: **Operation Pyrite – list of missing persons**

Alice,

Please collate a list of missing persons matching the following criteria:

- Female
- Aged in their twenties or thirties
- White skinned – either IC1 or IC2
- Dark brown hair – around shoulder length

Start the search with those who have been reported missing from Hampshire in the last two weeks.

Juliet

A joint arson and homicide investigation has been launched following an incident on the Dunlow Estate in the New Forest.

The Fire Service was called at approximately 4 a.m. on Monday 4 August to a report of a fire on the Dunlow Estate. A cottage at the entrance to the estate was ablaze. The fire is believed to be non-accidental.

Fire engines from the New Forest and Southampton attended the scene of the fire. Forensic Fire Officer Matt Lam said, 'Our crews worked hard to bring the blaze under control as the cottage was alight on our arrival. The fire was quickly extinguished and did not spread to the surrounding woodland. Regrettably, the body of a young woman has been found on the premises. The fire service is working closely with the police to establish her identity and the cause of death.'

The young woman is as yet unidentified. Dental records and DNA will be consulted to provide a formal identification.

No other details have been released but police are anxious to speak to anyone who may have been in the area around the time of the fire.

The police and fire service remain at the scene.

Detective Inspector Juliet Stern, who is leading this investigation, said, 'If anyone has any information about the woman found in the wreckage, then please come forward. Similarly, if anyone knows anything about who set the fire, we would welcome this information.'

No arrests have been made; enquiries continue.

Gabe

'We'll make this as quick and painless as we can,' Paul said as he ushered me along the corridor.

At the end, the door to the Major Incident room was firmly shut. Overlapping voices burbled from the briefing room on our right. Paul steered me into the meeting room opposite. Windows stretched across one wall, giving an unimpeded view of the sunlit city. Gulls rested on chimneys, their patience with the endless baking days exhausted.

A table occupied the middle of the room. A young man with spikey white-blond hair fiddled with a laptop at one end. I'd met Gunter several times since the investigation to find the person who shot Juliet and me. I'd admit he was a talented sketch artist, adept at wheedling details out of witnesses and compiling approximations of guilty parties that had a high success rate for bringing in helpful information, but no amount of innate or trained talent would help him create anything useful from my memories of the bad man.

Paul sat down heavily in the padded chair beside Gunter. I slid into the one on the other side of the table. A steaming mug of coffee, the pale brown colour I preferred, waited before me.

Paul had done what he could to make this conversation comfortable. I wouldn't tell him that none of his efforts made the slightest difference. Question me in a formal interview room or in a relatively cosy meeting space; my answers would be the same.

Hopelessly vague. Unhelpful. Draining.

'Hi, Gabe.' Gunter looked up from his laptop. He pushed black framed glasses up his nose, his slender fingers shaking.

'Hey.' I aimed for a reassuring smile. Even without a mirror, I could tell I'd botched it. It wasn't Gunter's fault today's sketch would be a resounding failure, but it was beyond me to offer comfort.

I curled my chilled hands around the coffee mug. The temperature outside was soaring into the mid-thirties but my fingers remained cold and inflexible. I took a sip, the hot liquid bitterly tasteless. It had been at least a day since I'd had a proper drink, longer since I'd eaten. My stomach, which usually protested the hours between meals, was empty and silent.

'We thought we would combine the interview and sketch.' Paul shifted in his chair, a slight wince the only sign that rescuing me had exacerbated his old injury. 'We'll be done soon and you can get back to working with my bestie.'

The tenor of Paul's teasing of Juliet had changed in the last few months. His previous regimen of name calling and bitching had been abandoned once he'd discovered she'd been targeted by a serial abuser of women who'd held a position of power at the station until she toppled him. Immediately after, Paul had become quiet and polite. Over time, he seemed to notice Juliet tensed every time he enquired about her day or asked about her weekend. He'd not quite reverted to overt aggravation, but had settled on a middle ground of gentle needling Juliet happily ignored.

I benefited the most; no longer refereeing between a partner I admired and the colleague-turned-friend who'd informally mentored me until we both moved down here from North London. Paul and I had expected to work together after I took the promotion here but I'd been paired with Juliet instead. I'd had to adjust from the expectation of banter and warmth to Juliet's caustic approach, but I didn't regret the move.

'That's fine.' I lowered the mug to the table, glad of a prop to hold onto if not for its contents. 'I want to say sorry now for not being of much use. You'll have seen my other interviews. I haven't remembered anything since.'

Paul's mouth pinched. Despite working with individuals who made a career out of poking through the dirty secrets of strangers, it was an unacknowledged rule that we kept anything we found out about one another's pasts to ourselves. A rule I'd been particularly glad of, since my childhood was a minefield best avoided. I might know when someone read my file, but at least they didn't try to talk to me about it.

Until now, when the bad man killed another child and forced me to relive the worst moments of my life.

'Let's get on with it.' Paul pulled a dented Dictaphone from his shirt pocket and recited the relevant information for a witness statement. Placing it on the table between us, he sat back. 'Gabe, in your own time, can you please tell me about the day you and Barnabas were taken?'

I swallowed, the hint of coffee sour on my tongue. 'I was eight. Barnabas had just turned six. Our parents had taken us to a car boot sale. Dad took us to a park across the road while Mum looked around.'

'You're doing good, Gabe,' Paul murmured.

'Dad needed the loo. There was one at the end of the playground. He made us promise to stay on the swings until he got back.'

It was a cold day. The swing's freezing chains bit through my knitted mittens. Barnabas started whining as soon as Dad walked out of earshot. He didn't want to play on the swings. He wanted to hide under the slide. The wind wouldn't be able to get us under there.

'We didn't.' I pressed my boots into the thin carpet, willing myself to stay completely in the room. 'We moved to under the slide. Cuddled beneath the stairs. A—'

Paul waited a beat. 'Take your time.'

Time wouldn't make this easier. I needed to get it done.

'A man found us. He said Dad was cross, that we had to come with him.'

Why did we go? Why did we believe him?

These two questions had wound through my life ever since I was old enough to understand that the bad man had tricked us. He'd lied, had used our dad to bend us to his will.

'What did the man look like?' Gunter asked gently.

My eyes snapped to him. I hoped Paul had warned him to not expect much.

'White. Tall. Broad.' I rattled off the details. 'He wore jeans and a blue jumper. And a black hat. His hair was grey.'

Gunter tapped at his keyboard. As his mouth opened for a follow-up question, I blurted out, 'That's all I remember. I'm sorry.'

Barnabas and I were with the bad man for six days. We'd hidden for most of that, but had spent enough time in his presence that I should have been able to remember more.

My eight-year-old self had chosen protection over precision.

'That's okay, Gabe.' The expression on Paul's face was familiar. I recognised it from when my parents protected me from the terrible things of the world by shutting it all out. Kind, but it didn't help. No one could take away the horrors that had already happened.

'We walked to the man's car. It was white. Big.' Again, details eluded me. I couldn't tell if the car had seemed large to an eight-year-old or had been objectively so. 'The man told us Mum and Dad had left, that they'd asked him to take us home. Dad didn't want us to mess around and be late. We got in.'

Barnabas and I had been taught about stranger danger. We'd been warned that odd men with sweets could attempt to lure us away from our safe homes.

The bad man hadn't seemed strange. I remembered that. To a child, he slotted easily into the category of adults who knew things. He talked about our parents, knew they would be cross if we didn't come home. I didn't think to ask for our mum and dad's names or why they would have left without us. The bad man wasn't pushy. His calm assurance that getting into his car was the right thing to do was compelling.

'He drove for a while.' I clutched the mug, the coffee cooling. 'He stopped at a warehouse and took us inside.'

That was the first moment we'd known something wasn't right. The building was dark and cold, the bad man's grip on our arms too tight.

'Barnabas asked where our parents were. The man threw us on the ground.' My voice quietened. 'He left and locked the doors. We were alone most of the time. For days, he came and went. Anytime the door opened, we hid.'

We had no way to mark the passing of time in the warehouse. We cried after the bad man left, tight in each other's arms. Then we tried to open the door. All the windows were high and covered in grime. Impossible to get to. We walked amongst the piles of boxes, searching for a way out.

'He didn't feed us. Or give us water.' Facts, offered as excuses. 'We drank from puddles under broken windows, but we were starving.'

Paul had been on the force for a decade longer than me. He could listen to stories of the worst that human beings did and remain impassive. Maybe, if I didn't know him so well, I'd believe he was sympathetic but ultimately unaffected by my history. Lines tightened around his eyes. The muscles of his forearms bunched. At his side, Gunter stared at his computer rather than chancing a look at me.

Best to end this quickly. The worst was to come, the parts that made me burn with shame and haunted my nightmares.

'I decided to search for food so I left our hiding place.' I gripped the mug. 'We must not have heard the doors open. The bad man was there.'

I cringed at my slip of the tongue. I refused to use the name the press and public had adopted for my brother's killer, usually referred to him out loud as *the man*. I didn't like people to know what I called him in my head. It sounded childish. *Bad* was far too mild to encompass all that he'd done.

'He caught me. Broke my arm.' My shirt was rolled up to my elbows. No mark showed where my bone had sheared. 'He dragged me across the floor. Over to the barrel. Then Barnabas appeared. He distracted him.'

The bad man usually took one child. I'd probably never know why he abducted us both. How he had chosen who he would kill. Who he would leave alive.

'I passed out. When I came to, they were both gone.' So was the barrel. 'The warehouse doors were open.'

I'd been left where the bad man dropped me, discarded like unwanted rubbish.

Paul pressed the button on the side of the Dictaphone. His movements slow but firm, he reached across the table and pulled the mug from my unrelenting hold. He cupped my hands in his. His broad palms were warm.

I flinched when the door clicked shut behind Gunter. I hadn't noticed him move, too caught in a moment I tried my hardest to forget.

I was glad he'd left. Paul was my friend. I could break apart in front of him.

'All done, Gabe.' Paul's grey eyes shone. 'You're all done.'

Call connected at 10:59.

'Mate, I've been—'

'Look, Ty. I can't chat long. I ain't taking that shit you sent me pics of.'

'What? Why?'

'Keep a better eye on the news, lad. I'm not touching that stuff, not 'til the heat's died down.'

'Fuck. I didn't think you'd be so chickenshit that a little attention would scare you off.'

'Guess I am. And I guess you'll have to get one of your other guys to take it. Isn't that what you said before? Other people are keen? Fucking offload your mess onto them, then.'

'Maybe I will.'

'Do whatever the fuck you want. Don't call me again unless you've got something I can work with.'

From: Nicole Stewart **nicole.stewart@mit.gov.uk**
To: James Knowles **james.knowles@police.gov.uk**
CC: Paul Willis **paul.willis@mit.gov.uk**, Leonard Dunlow **leonard.dunlow@police.gov.uk**
Date: **5 August, 11:12**
Subject: **Operation Mercury – barrel purchases**

James,

I'm not sure if you'll have time around combing through the CCTV footage to take a look at barrel purchases, which is why I've CC'd Leo into this email. If you're not able to do this yourself, can you please oversee his search?

We're not sure how likely it is that the barrel was bought in the local area but it's worth checking. It's made from oak. Trace amounts of good quality soil were found inside.

Ask for purchase reports from local fishing supply shops, antique shops, homeware stores, and garden centres. If you're able to get customer details, please retrieve these alongside any CCTV footage.

In the first instance, limit the search to the week immediately before Max went missing to the day his body was found.

Thanks,

Nicole

Call connected at 11:25.

'Hi. Um, this is Gabe. Detective Gabe Martin. Detective Sergeant.'

'Hello, it's Matt.'

'Who?'

'Matt Lam. The Forensic Fire Officer.'

'Oh, Matt. I'm sorry. My head's all over the place.'

'It's fine. I'm still at the estate and wanted to let you know the owner is here.'

'Timothy Dunlow?'

'The very same. He's insistent he be allowed into the cottage. I've managed to deter him for now, but he shouted about contacting his solicitor before he stormed off to his car. He's been on the phone in there for the last few minutes.'

'Right. Juliet told him not to come over to the estate, but he's not great at listening to the police. God. Sorry. I shouldn't have said that. It was unprofessional.'

'But fair. I'm not sure he has much time to listen to anyone.'

'Yeah. Anyway, me and Juliet will come over now. If you can keep Mr Dunlow out of the cottage until we get there, that would be great.'

'I'll try my best.'

Gabe

My arm tangled in the seatbelt as I got out of the car. I extracted myself, avoiding Juliet's gaze. After we'd walked out to the station car park via the side entrance to avoid the lingering journalists, she'd given me a long look when I'd told her I didn't have my car keys. I wasn't capable of bare faced lies so hadn't said I'd forgotten them. The worst was over, I'd given my statement, but my brain was a fuzzy mess. I couldn't keep driving when compromised, even if Juliet was pissed to lose out on time to fiddle with her phone.

She shot me another assessing frown as we walked towards the gates of the Dunlow Estate. At least Juliet wasn't like Maddy or Alice. She wouldn't ask how I was doing, not unless my mental state affected my work. I was determined it wouldn't. I might not be able to hold it together at home, especially if Ollie stayed away for much longer, but I would maintain a solid front at work.

'About damn time.' Timothy Dunlow marched over to us. His pale skin was unchanged from when we'd last had the displeasure of seeing him, his thick white hair and blue eyes compounding his air of colourlessness. He wore a pristine grey suit, apparently unaffected by the day's pressing heat.

He'd parked his black BMW in front of the burned cottage. Though the forensic van was absent, a white tent remained. The body and most obvious materials would have been removed, but that didn't mean it was safe or wise for Dunlow to rifle through the charred contents of the wrecked building. The fire had done significant damage but information could still be gleaned between the fallen beams and burned boxes.

Dunlow's hands rounded into tight fists at his sides. 'That man is refusing me access to my own property.'

Matt waved, then turned back to examining the fallen front door of the cottage. Apparently, he was happy to hand the irate landowner over to us.

'Rightly so.' Juliet stood a head taller than Dunlow, a fact that wouldn't have passed unnoticed by the short bully. She looked down her nose at him. 'I assume you received and promptly ignored my voicemail, which asked you to contact me rather than coming here?'

'This is my property,' Dunlow growled, his face blooming with uneven patches of puce. 'I can come here whenever I damn well please.'

'Not when there's been a fatal fire,' Juliet countered.

I pulled my notepad from my pocket. Not for the first time around Dunlow, I was glad of Juliet's unflappable presence. I felt like an animal forced from its protective shell. Vulnerable. Unable to fight off unwanted aggressors.

'Mr Dunlow?' I reluctantly drew his attention my way. I couldn't claim to do my job unimpeded if I didn't say a single word. 'We apologise for the inconvenience, but until the fire service and forensic teams have finished working in the cottage we cannot allow you to enter.'

Dunlow's nostrils flared. His eyes darted to the white tent. 'You said the fire was fatal. Who died?'

Not quite the panic Leo had displayed, but another death on his estate at least caused Dunlow some discomfort.

'We don't know yet,' I said. 'No identification has been found, but it was a White woman in her twenties or early thirties. She had brown hair and was wearing a blue vest. Have you given anyone matching that description access to the estate?'

Dunlow shook his head before I finished the question. 'No one but myself and my sons have keys for the gates and the various properties. Building work is due to commence on the manor next month but the project manager hadn't requested a visit in over a week.'

'You've not invited anyone else onto the estate?' Juliet checked.

'No,' Dunlow said flatly.

'And you've not changed your stance on CCTV cameras around the grounds?'

I was relieved Juliet asked. My current fragility could lead me to cower under the full weight of Dunlow's glare. His thick white eyebrows lowered, the lines criss-crossing his forehead deepening.

'I have not.'

'How helpful,' Juliet said.

'Where were you on the night of the third and morning of the fourth of August?' I asked, before Dunlow could snap back. His fists hadn't unclenched. Even though Matt Lam wasn't paying close attention to us, his presence comforted me. It wasn't likely Dunlow would lash out but the proximity of a witness lessened the possibility.

'I've been visiting clients around the country.' Dunlow's voice adopted the same bored tone as when we'd requested details of his movements around the time Melanie Pirt was shot and killed on his land. I hadn't missed it.

'We'll need confirmation of that.' I noted to follow up on his alibi. Despite the probability Dunlow had set fire to his own cottage being low, he wasn't above lying to the police. His acting skills had been honed over a lifetime of convincing small companies that the mergers and acquisitions his larger clients suggested were in their best interests.

'Why didn't you return home immediately after you got my voicemail?' Juliet asked.

'Your message was devoid of pertinent details.' Dunlow's glower fixed on Juliet. He'd evidently decided she was most at fault. Since his anger wouldn't affect her, I didn't feel too ashamed she would take the brunt of it. 'I had no idea of the location or scale of the fire, nor the damage it had caused, until my son rang this morning. He informed me that a major fire had ravaged the groundskeeper's cottage.'

It must have been Leo who'd called. Terence was estranged from his father, wouldn't contact him unless the situation was truly dire. He likely wouldn't consider the death of someone on the estate reason enough to break their stalemate.

'At the time of my message, we were not aware of the body.' Juliet rightly or wrongly assumed part of the damage Dunlow referred to was the loss of life. 'Is there a reason you rushed home if someone unknown to you had died?'

A moment of sparking tension I refused to turn away from, even though I wanted to, and Dunlow's anger faltered. His fingers jerked open. He turned towards the cottage and his face fell into less familiar lines of sadness.

'As work was to begin on the manor soon, the project manager asked that all valuables be moved to prevent further damage. I stored everything in here, as the site team would be using the room above the garage for breaks.' Dunlow raised a shaking hand to push strands of white hair from his forehead. 'I didn't want them poking around in any of this.'

Dunlow always made it difficult to fully sympathise with him. He hadn't rushed home on finding out someone had died in the cottage, was more concerned his possessions may have been ruined.

'What was in the boxes?' I asked.

He blinked, and it went through me like an electric jolt when I realised he was struggling to contain tears. We'd seen Dunlow under pressure, had seen him reduced and shocked. Nothing had come close to breaking past the outer battlements of his well-maintained façade.

'These were my wife's things.'

During the investigation into Melanie Pirt's murder, Dunlow had recited from memory the exact number of months, weeks, and days since his wife's death. I wouldn't force him to perform such a sad party trick again.

'I'm sorry,' I said reflexively.

Juliet shuffled. I didn't attempt to read into the movement. If offering shallow condolences when the bulk of Dunlow's dead wife's things had been destroyed wasn't what Juliet would do, then we had another point to differ on. Add it to the pile.

'We aren't being difficult,' I continued. 'Once our teams have everything they need and the cottage is declared safe, you'll be able to go through the boxes to see what can be salvaged.'

'Actually, that would be helpful,' Juliet added. 'We can't assume homicide and arson were the only crimes committed here. If you placed valuables in the cottage, it may have also been burgled. The cottage could have been set alight to cover their tracks.'

I stared at the side of Juliet's head. She might not have thought it appropriate to express meagre sentiments for Dunlow's loss, but I would never so tactlessly prod at an open wound. Suggesting his late wife's things may have been stolen as well as ruined in the fire seemed needlessly cruel.

I looked away to the white tent undulating in the faint breeze between the trees. Juliet might be brutal but she was doing her job. Our job. We had to relentlessly pursue every lead that might help us find whoever set the fire and killed a young woman, either purposefully or accidentally. I couldn't let my softness get in the way.

'If you could let us know whether any items are missing, rather than damaged by the fire, then we would appreciate that,' I added, attempting to lessen the blow of Juliet's blunt request.

'Of course.' Dunlow straightened his shoulders, his voice steely once more. 'Is there anything else?'

'Just one more question.' I tapped my pencil on the side of my notepad. 'Is there anyone who had good reason to lash out at you in this way?'

Dunlow sniffed. 'I may have had disagreements with people in the course of my life, but none of them would resort to such destruction to make their displeasure known.'

I struggled to keep a frown off my face. Dunlow seemed to have erased his illegitimate son from his memory. Karl Biss had been violent and erratic in his quest to make his father notice him, to get revenge when Dunlow refused to. All of Karl's attempts had ultimately failed.

'We're done here.' Dunlow's words were half-question, half-statement. A clear dismissal, but not an unwelcome one.

If his alibi was robust, then he wasn't a suspect. After he'd revealed what was in the boxes, I didn't think it remotely likely he would have set the cottage alight. He was wholly motivated by family. If he'd thought there was a chance his late wife's belongings would come to harm here, he never would have left them so unprotected.

His arrogance reached wide. Fires has been started on other local estates in the last two weeks but Dunlow couldn't conceive of the same happening on his. He was not a man who learnt his lesson, no matter how brutally it was applied.

'We'll be in touch with any further questions.' Juliet turned towards the estate gates.

I raised a hand in Matt's direction as I fell into step beside her. I didn't need to speak to him. I couldn't stop my past from intruding, but I could limit my present distractions. Juliet and I had work to do before the body was identified. I needed to shed my memories and throw myself into the investigation. Focusing on the case would keep me from falling deeper into remembrances I wished could be forever left behind.

'Good afternoon. You're listening to The Darker Side on Radio Four with Narinder Ghoshal-Allen, the show where we explore more difficult aspects of human nature and their origins. Joining me for today's show is world renowned expert in present-day serial killers, Dr Travis Gaffney. Dr Gaffney, welcome.'

'Thank you for having me.'

'Dr Gaffney, what drew you towards this field of study?'

'It was woefully undeveloped, at least to my eye. The police and various agencies are, at specific times, actively involved in tracking the movements and motives of current serial killers, but these investigations are highly charged and constrained by the understandable limitations of working for government funded organisations. What I have attempted for several individuals is to collate the work of these various groups into a more coherent whole.'

'One of the serial killers you've studied is colloquially known as the Barrel Man.'

'Indeed, and let me first say how awful it is that he has taken another young life. My deepest condolences go to the family and friends of Max Powrie. I cannot imagine the sadness they're suffering.'

'It's unfathomable. Is it difficult for you, at times like this, to continue working in this field?'

'It's always an emotional blow but, much like the police and other emergency services, a divide has to be created between what I as a father feel whenever a serial killer like the Barrel Man strikes again and what I as a scholar can ascertain from this latest incident.'

'Have you been able to glean any important information from Max Powrie's death?'

'Details of investigations are, very understandably, usually not shared with me until the initial phase has passed. I make my research freely available so, if my insights are helpful, they can be applied without the rigmarole of bringing a civilian into a criminal investigation. However, the details around Max's death that have been shared mean I can, with a reasonable degree of academic certainty, claim he was murdered by the serial killer known as the Barrel Man.'

'Max would be his seventeenth victim?'

'Known victim. However, that is a reasonable assumption. The Barrel Man has a particular set of signifiers. It's unlikely one of his victims would go unnoticed or their killer be misidentified.'

'Can you talk me through these signifiers?'

'Most obviously, there's the barrel. The presentation of bodies is often incredibly significant for habitual killers so it's probable that each of the Barrel Man's victims have been positively identified as such.'

'I believe it was in the noughties that the moniker was first used?'

'You're quite right. The Sun newspaper used it in a headline proclaiming the death of Jamal King. It quickly became a shorthand afterwards.'

'Alongside the barrels, what else makes it clear that it's the Barrel Man at work?'

'The placement of the barrels is consistent. They are left in rivers and bodies of water across

England and are found mere hours after being left. His victims are often kept alive for a number of days or weeks before they are killed and evidence suggests they are strangled shortly before being placed in the barrel. The victim profile is incredibly similar as well. All children between the ages of five and ten. A mixture of ethnicities, but all able to speak basic English and all with loving families. They were all taken from outdoor events, not their homes.'

'With so much to link these killings, it has to be location that sets them apart?'

'The downfall of most serial killers is geography. They work within a small area, so victims are selected from a limited pool. These murderers are easier for police to detect because the number of possible suspects is dramatically reduced.'

'That's certainly not the case with the Barrel Man.'

'No. As one of the most prolific serial killers of our time, his evasion of the authorities is only possible because he works over such a broad area. His movements are seemingly random, although they likely have deeper meaning to him. His first known victim, Lisa Blunt, was taken from Durham. He then struck two years later in Cheshire, a year later in Essex, and three years after that in Dorset. Even when at his most active in the late noughties, within nine months he took children from Derbyshire, Suffolk, and Herefordshire. His geographical reach is such that until his victims are found, there's no way to ascertain that it's this particular serial killer at work.'

'Have the police ever come close to catching him?'

'Unfortunately, no. His movements are impossible to predict and too little is known about him to begin to make a profile. It's impossible to narrow down the kind of man he might be and where he may be found when not actively engaged in abduction and killing. No images of him have ever been captured and the fingerprints and DNA that have been extracted have no match on the police system.'

'Surely Gabriella Martin being found several days after she and her brother, Barnabas, were abducted from a car boot sale in North London has been helpful for creating a stronger understanding of who the Barrel Man is?'

'Her witness statements confirmed the Barrel Man is, in fact, a man but little else she has been willing and able to share has been particularly insightful. We have to remember Gabriella was eight years old when she was abducted. The human brain has incredibly powerful mechanisms in place to ensure we are not overly haunted by the trauma of our pasts.'

'Gabriella is one of a very small number of people who have escaped from the clutches of a serial killer. Have you ever had the opportunity to speak with her?'

'That would certainly be an incredibly interesting interview, but sadly I have not. Understandably, her parents were protective of her following her safe return. Until Gabriella turned eighteen, they blocked all attempts by myself and other interested parties to question their daughter. Since then, Gabriella has made it clear she is not interested in speaking about her experiences. She is interviewed as part of the police investigations, but that is the extent of her willingness to participate in any dialogue about what she witnessed.'

'It's interesting that she's now a police officer at Southampton station, where Max's murder is being investigated.'

'She's a detective sergeant. I'm sure every attempt will be made to distance her from the investigation.'

'Do you believe her career choice was influenced by her horrific early brush with a killer?'

'Most likely. We are all changed and moulded by the experiences of our youth, especially those as significant as Gabriella's. To have been so helpless against a dangerous criminal must have created within her a powerful urge to help those in similar situations.'

'This has been such an illuminating discussion so far. Next, we'll unpack the motives of serial killers and talk about those who remain undetected alongside the Barrel Man. You're listening to Radio Four. Now, a summary of today's news with Gianna Lilley.'

Zara Everett @SoloHikingGirl
Woolston, Southampton

Hi there everyone. Not Zara this time – it's Chase!

As you all know, my amazing girlfriend is off on one of her solo hiking adventures this week. She doesn't publicly share where she's headed beforehand, but now she's done with the first stretch I can tell you she hiked across to the River Hamble, then up towards the country park and off into the greenery to the east of Southampton city. She'll have so many beautiful pictures to share once she's safely back home, but here are some we snapped during a recent weekend spent on our SUP boards!

While she's hiking, I know she would love to hear about your adventures. And, more importantly, have any of you spotted Zara on your rambles? Please DM me if you have.

Look after yourselves, Chase xxx

Gabe

Shame blossomed anew as I stood before the evidence wall with Juliet, hands cupped around a mug of coffee. She'd insisted on making drinks before we discussed her findings from yesterday and had forced a packet of Hobnobs into my hand as we left the kitchenette.

The main open-plan area of the seventh floor was eerily quiet. Most of our co-workers had been relocated to the floor below. I squirmed at the amount of effort being extended to accommodate me, but couldn't pretend I wasn't grateful. Walking past empty desks and Paul's abandoned office was strange, but constantly passing a wall of victims would have been unendurable.

'I've put up the recent estate fires, along with a couple across the city that match in ways other than location.' Juliet pointed at a map dominating one side of the corkboard affixed to one wall of our cramped office. 'Three fires have been started on similar ancestral estates in the last two weeks. Unless Matt's report from this one is drastically different, we can be reasonably certain they were all set by the same individual or group.'

A skitter of nerves broke through my numb malaise. I needed to pay attention and find this arsonist. I couldn't let my distracted state be the reason someone else got hurt.

'Any leads on who started the fires?' I asked, determined to get up to speed before we headed back out of the station to attend the young woman's autopsy.

'No, but not for lack of trying.' Juliet sipped her steaming black coffee like she needed to fortify herself for her next words.

'Paul did a thorough job. The surrounding areas were canvassed for witnesses but none came forward. CCTV footage is minimal and reveals nothing. The arsonist knew they wouldn't be spotted, even in the city. All the buildings are remote and surrounded by far too many chances to disappear.'

'Does there seem to be any reason why these places were targeted?'

Another sip. 'None. Alongside the usual enquiries, Paul did a major search across social media for anyone speaking out against the families or boasting about playing with fire. It returned nothing.'

Blue twine connected pictures of a half-burned three-storey car park and a blackened disused bowling alley to the map. The fires in the city and on the estates were randomly spread across Southampton and the New Forest. This wasn't someone with a grudge against a neighbour or lashing out on their own turf. The arsonist followed a pattern I currently found impossible to discern.

I wrinkled my nose. 'So apart from the fact the fires were started in the same way and on similar estates, or at least in places it was easy to escape from, there's no link between them or clue who might have set them?'

I needed to check whether my sluggish mind wasn't making the right links or if Juliet, unaffected as always, was stumped as well.

'Nope.' Juliet took another sip. 'The Dunlow cottage fire doesn't illuminate anything further. There's no links between the landowners or ties to the other properties.'

'We've got nothing,' I summarised.

'Except for an unidentified body.' Juliet nodded at a piece of paper she'd pinned up, a large question mark printed in the centre. We must not have the crime scene photos yet. Juliet would have displayed them on the corkboard with no consideration for whether I wanted to work watched over by a corpse.

'She could be the key to figuring out who's been setting the fires,' I said.

It was horrible that she'd died but once we knew her identity, we would at least have a place to start our search. Although there had been no other fatalities, we couldn't rule out a link to the arsonist.

'Any joy with this lot?' I angled my cooling coffee towards the right side of the corkboard. During my interview with Paul, Juliet had pinned up columns of missing persons' posters. All women in their twenties or thirties with brown hair and pale skin.

'None.' Juliet's grey eyes darted between the smiling photos. 'Most reports have so little information that it's impossible to say what might have happened to the women, or too much time has passed and they could be anywhere by now. Without inviting each woman's next of kin to view the remains, we won't have any leads until the DNA and dental records provide a match.'

It was a rare show of humanity that Juliet wasn't already on the phone to friends and family members, inviting them to the morgue. Her single-minded pursuit of criminals usually led her to leap over lines I'd never cross.

Maybe there were simply too many candidates. Three lines of posters ran down the whole height of the corkboard, overlapping to show just the photo and name of each woman.

I glanced at the clock over our door, a pile of discarded paperwork wedging it open. 'We should head off soon if we don't want to be late for the autopsy.'

Juliet grabbed her car keys from her desk and I suppressed the urge to explain myself. She didn't require my fumbling apologies.

I set my coffee on the desk next to the unopened packet of Hobnobs just as Maddy tapped on the door and leant into our office. She'd ditched her habitual cardigan; her burnt-orange blouse paired with a flowing brown skirt patterned with tiny roses. I avoided her curious gaze, staring instead at the parting of her wavy hair. I didn't want her to ask how I was. I had no clue how to answer.

'Sorry to disturb, but I've just had a call from the front desk. They've got Benedict Hogan down there. He said he needs to speak to someone about the fire on the Dunlow Estate.'

Juliet straightened, an idle wolf awakening at the scent of prey. 'Tell him we'll be there in a minute.'

'They've put him in meeting room three.' Maddy's skirt whispered as she departed.

'What do you think he has to say?' I grabbed my notepad and walked with Juliet across the quiet floor towards the lifts. 'Is it worth missing the autopsy for?'

I had to mention it, despite the leap in my heart at the thought of not attending. In-depth explorations of bodies weren't my favourite activity to witness on the best of days, and today was far from good.

'Ideally, we'll do both,' Juliet said, unaware or uncaring of how her words activated a cage in my chest.

She jabbed at the lift's call button. It was still strange to see her nails without colour coordinated polish. I shook my head. I couldn't let questions around Juliet's living situation derail me. I cared about her and hoped she was happy, but I didn't have the bandwidth to search for an arsonist and the smallest sign Juliet was being mistreated.

'I called Benedict and Terence yesterday,' Juliet said as the lift doors opened and we walked inside, unaware of the inner turmoil her nails had caused. 'They're one another's alibis.'

My empty stomach swooped as the lift lowered, but the doors remained firmly closed as we passed the sixth floor. 'You think they lied?'

'Wouldn't be the first time.'

Juliet wasn't referring to couples who covered for one another. During the investigation to find Melanie Pirt's killer, Terence had been supremely unhelpful. He'd dodged outright lying by hiding behind the falsehoods he'd already told his father about his whereabouts at the time of the murder. After it was revealed he'd spent the weekend with Benedict, he'd refused to divulge the nature of their relationship until forced.

Sympathy twinged, dull under the layers of fog I was fighting through. Terence had been reluctant to share the truth because he was certain his father's wrath on discovering his sexuality would be harsh and swift. It didn't seem Dunlow had disproved his son's theory that he would be disowned if he publicly declared he had a boyfriend.

'Surely Terence wouldn't have set alight a building full of his mum's things?' I mused.

Barnabas's clothing and toys remained in the bedroom we'd once shared. I'd slept in my parents' bed for a month after returning home from the warehouse, then climbed into the loft to sleep under the gently sloping eaves. The thought of someone taking anything of my brother's, of wantonly destroying the items he'd touched and loved, made me want to smash my fist into the smudged metal of the lift walls.

'Maybe Terence didn't know the boxes were there,' Juliet suggested as the doors slid open on the ground floor. 'He and his father aren't on speaking terms.'

Movement caught my eye through the glass frontage as I followed her across the station's reception. Too late, I averted my gaze from the journalists clustered outside. They wouldn't storm the station, but their presence was a pressing shadow. Hopefully they didn't recognise me as I scurried from the lifts to the corridor of informal meeting rooms opposite.

'Mr Hogan. I'm Detective Inspector Juliet Stern.' Her greeting as we walked into the third meeting room snapped me from irrelevant thoughts about the photos that might have been taken during the earlier onslaught. Juliet held out her hand, shaking Benedict's for a brief second before her arm snapped to her side and she sat on one of the boxy sofas.

'Nice to meet you. And a pleasure to see you again, Detective Martin.' Benedict's smile was warm and his palm smooth. His deep brown eyes darted over my face. 'Please, call me Benedict.'

The first time we met, I'd been distracted by the changes to Benedict's boyfriend. Terence had been diminished by the months that had passed since he'd moved out of the family manor. Benedict had seemed bright beside him. Even without his unkempt partner in attendance, Benedict shone. His black hair flowed artfully from his unlined forehead. He was as pale as me, but I suspected his skin tone was due to sunny days spent lounging under carefully angled fabrics to protect his delicate complexion.

The slight pinch to his eyes hinted he wasn't drawing favourable conclusions about me. I'd last seen Benedict when recovering from a bullet wound. I didn't want to think too hard about how much the bad man striking again had affected me that I could possibly look more pitiful now.

'What can we help you with?' I sat beside Juliet and flipped open my notepad. The autopsy loomed, but I wouldn't be sad to end this interview with a stupidly good-looking man soon.

Benedict adjusted his navy suit jacket as he settled on the opposite sofa. His trousers rode up to reveal green socks with an unfamiliar monogram embroidered on each ankle.

'I appreciate you taking the time to speak with me.' His posh voice wasn't as annoying as Terence's. Perhaps because he wasn't actively trying to piss us off.

'That's alright,' I said, after a pause that indicated Benedict's unwillingness to launch straight into whatever he'd come here for. Juliet crossed her legs, her fingers whitening around the edge of the sofa's scratchy fabric.

'You'll likely think this a tad ridiculous,' Benedict went on. His lips parted on a self-deprecating smile that revealed unnaturally even teeth.

'We're in the middle of an incredibly time sensitive investigation,' Juliet cut in before he offered any more useless small talk. 'Is there something important you need to share with us? Otherwise we'll get on.'

She uncrossed her legs, as though she was about to leap up and leave the room, but paused when Benedict spread his hands.

'I need to talk to you about the fire at Teddy's old home. On the estate,' he said, eyebrows rising. 'I'm sorry I didn't say this before. You caught me unawares on the phone yesterday.'

'What do you want to share now you've had time to gather yourself?' I nudged.

Benedict's eyes flicked between Juliet and me. 'What I say here stays between us?'

I could sense Juliet readying herself to actually leave if Benedict didn't get to the point soon.

'That depends on the nature of what you divulge,' I said. 'If it's important to the investigation, we'll have to pursue the leads it reveals. We can keep your name confidential.'

Any ties binding Juliet to this interview frayed to breaking point as Benedict bit his plump lower lip. I wasn't quite as impatient, but I did wonder why he'd gone to the trouble of coming here just to dither over whether to tell us his secret.

'This most likely won't be of any use, but I didn't want it to come to light later and you be perplexed as to why I hadn't said a word.'

'What is it?' Juliet asked, each syllable sharply distinct.

Benedict's shoulders slumped. 'I was caught starting a fire on a similar estate when I was fifteen.'

Juliet and I froze. I'd expected Benedict to share flawed aspects of his and Terence's shared alibi, not something that incriminated the polished man sitting before us.

Juliet leant forward, her attention finally captivated. 'Can you tell us about that?'

Benedict looked anywhere but at us. If I didn't know better, I'd think something far more interesting than a poster about drug awareness sat on the wall behind my head.

'I got mixed up in a bad crowd after I was forced to leave private school. My father lost a great deal of money in a short amount of time and suddenly my tuition fees were insurmountable. I had to attend the local state school.'

I'd briefly looked into Benedict's family and financial situation when he'd been named as Terence's alibi during the investigation into Melanie Pirt's murder. Whatever monetary hardships his family had faced were temporary. Benedict and Terence often spent weekends at his family's cottage in Cornwall, one of several holiday homes they owned across Europe. He had no mortgage on his house in Southampton and his family might not live on an estate like the Dunlows', but no other Hogan offspring would have to suffer a state school education with all its corrupting influences.

'I don't know how comprehensive the files are around crimes committed when one is under the age of eighteen, especially if no charges were brought forward,' Benedict mused.

It was a common misconception of the general public that police records were wiped clean when a person legally reached adulthood. We felt it better to remember youthful misdemeanours, rather than work in frustrated ignorance.

I frowned as I made a note to check Benedict's file again. An entry of this nature would have grabbed my attention when we were investigating the first fire on the Dunlow Estate. Benedict had sat firmly on the periphery of the investigation to find Melanie Pirt's killer but would have been dragged into the limelight once the manor was set ablaze if he'd had a known history of arson.

Benedict eased a folded piece of paper from his jacket pocket and passed it to me. His name was written at the top, a series of first names in the same neat cursive underneath. 'This is the group I started the fires with. I'm sorry, but I can't remember their surnames. They led me to believe they were my friends. Once I was caught, I learnt they'd used me for my knowledge of the estates around the county.'

'Why did you go along with it?' I leant into Benedict's narrative that he was an innocent youth preyed on by state-school plebs.

'My old friends ditched me when my parents lost their money.' Benedict picked at imaginary lint on his trouser leg. 'I was lonely, desperate to be liked and included. Once I realised those boys were interested in the estates, I couldn't tell them enough. I was angry at my old friends, cross enough that I wanted to teach them a lesson. When my new supposed friends suggested torching their outhouses, I foolishly thought it was the perfect way to show those who'd ghosted me that their place at the top of the pile was as precarious as mine had been. We threw bottles of petrol and burning rags through open windows. It sounds insane now. but that's what we did.'

The details of Benedict's childhood arsons were startlingly similar to the recent fires that had culminated in the death of a young woman. Perhaps there was a historic link to a group who wanted to teach arrogant poshos a lesson.

'Your interviews will be on the system.' Juliet's voice was far more animated than it had been before Benedict told us of his past. 'But can you explain in more detail how the fires were started?'

Benedict shifted his weight. 'That's the rub. I'm not sure what records there will be.'

I glanced at the list of names he'd given me. 'What do you mean? Arrest records for those under the age of eighteen are kept. You would have been questioned when you were brought in.'

'I was arrested. Technically.' Benedict grimaced. 'Dad might not have had money to splash around at the time, but he knew the superintendent here. They read law at university together. They had a chat and I walked away with a slap on the wrist after I promised to never play with fire again.'

Juliet barely seemed to breathe beside me. I'd only need one guess at which former superintendent would have let a young arsonist walk free because one of his chums had asked him to. During the investigation into our shooting, I'd met Juliet's old boss. Douglas Frey's departure from the force was precipitated by accusations of sexual misconduct. In his youth, he'd abused his position in many ways. He would never answer for it. The man I'd met three months ago was powerless, his physical and mental strength stripped by illness. Incapable of shooting us and incapable of shouldering the due punishment for his crimes.

At least Benedict's arrest being expunged meant I'd not overlooked a connection between him and arson in the past. That was paltry comfort given the details lost. Benedict's statement after being caught should have been recorded and preserved.

'I've never done anything like that again,' Benedict said into heavy silence.

His hunched back and downturned face screamed discomfort. Another way he differed from his boyfriend. Terence wielded his posh-boy privilege with impunity while Benedict was fully aware he'd gotten away with a crime in his youth due to the moneyed connections of his family.

'We're going to need your whereabouts during several recent fires,' I said. Benedict's remorse seemed sincere and it would certainly be a strange move to confess to his youthful arson if he'd had anything to do with the more recent fires, but we couldn't take his word that he wasn't involved, especially given the similarities.

Benedict swallowed. 'I understand. If you give me the dates, I'll check my diary when I get home. But I promise I've not started another fire since.'

Unmoved by his earnest assurances, Juliet rattled off the dates of the estate fires. I jotted them down and handed the page from my notepad to Benedict, my handwriting lacking the casual elegance of his.

'We'll need a DNA sample as well,' Juliet stated as Benedict tucked the list into his jacket pocket. 'An officer at the front desk will take one from you before you leave.'

Benedict nodded, his manicured hands spreading across his thighs. 'Of course. Is there anything else?'

'What are your feelings towards Timothy Dunlow?' I asked. Benedict might have come here of his own accord and might have an alibi, but he also had the means and knowledge to have started the fire. As our sole suspect until the victim was identified, a motive would make his voluntary confession seem much less innocent.

Benedict's jaw twitched. For the first time, I thought the calm expression on his face was a mask. 'I don't know the man.'

'Terence must have spoken about him?' Juliet prodded.

'Barely.' Benedict linked his fingers together atop one knee. 'We have far better things to talk about.'

Translation: Terence had shared about his father and Benedict had less than friendly feelings towards the man who'd rejected his boyfriend. I wasn't sure if that was enough to have reawakened Benedict's dormant pyro tendencies.

'Do you know anything about the recent fires?' Juliet asked.

'No,' Benedict said. 'I've not heard from the boys I started fires with since we left school. I only thought I should bring it up because I didn't want to be accused of involvement if my past was revealed and I'd not mentioned it.'

'What did you think you might be accused of?' I willed everything clouding my mind to clear away and focused wholly on Benedict, watchful for the smallest indication of guilt.

His dark brows drew together, his face softening as we moved away from discussing his boyfriend's father. 'Arson?'

'Not manslaughter?' Juliet asked. 'Or murder?'

Benedict's eyes widened, his mouth slack. 'What?'

'Leo hasn't told you a body was found in the cottage?' I checked.

'Oh, God. No. Leo doesn't talk about work at home.' Benedict shook his head. 'Who is it?'

'A young woman.' Juliet pursed her lips. 'We're awaiting identification. Any idea who she might be?'

Benedict rubbed a hand over his eyes. 'No idea, but how awful. That poor woman.'

Juliet and I exchanged a look while Benedict sniffed down at the straight crease of his trousers. His sadness seemed genuine, which made his relationship with Terence even more baffling.

That someone caring and honest, perhaps foolishly so, would fall for someone wholly selfish was a mystery.

'Once she's been identified, we'll get in touch to check there's no connection between the two of you.' I looked up at the clock. No chance we'd get to the autopsy on time, but that didn't mean we had to linger here.

'Of course.' Benedict nodded jerkily. 'I know it will be infinitely worse for her loved ones, but this is going to crush Terence and Leo. They grew up on that estate. Despite their father, it was their home. For it to be the site of a shooting and now this.' He pressed his lips together. 'All their happy memories there will be ruined.'

Benedict was right; the greatest sympathy had to be reserved for whoever the young woman had left behind. Soon, Juliet and I would create a drastic line between their lives before and after tragedy struck.

Yet I could too clearly understand Benedict's sadness for the Dunlow brothers. When horrifying acts smashed into our lives, it was hard to stop them from marring everything.

Retrieved from police archives.

Detective Inspector Mohammad Allon: Interview commencing on the 8th February at 3:24 p.m. at Southampton station. The interview is being conducted by myself, Detective Inspector Mohammad Allon, and Detective Sergeant Craig Fellows. Our Family Liaison Support Officer, Bethany Wilde, is also in attendance. The interviewee is Ellis Martin. Mr Martin, you are not currently under arrest but you are under caution. You do not have to say anything but it may harm your defence if you do not mention when questioned something which you may later rely on in court. Anything you do say may be given in evidence. Mr Martin has been given the opportunity to invite a legal representative to this interview but declined. If at any point he changes his mind, then a solicitor will be sought for him. This interview is concerning the abduction of Gabriella and Barnabas Martin on the 2nd February.

Family Liaison Support Officer Bethany Wilde: Ellis, this interview is voluntary and can be stopped at any time. The detectives are gathering information to aid the safe return of Barnabas.

Ellis Martin: I understand. I'll do anything you like if you bring my son home.

DI Mohammad Allon: Thank you for your cooperation, Mr Martin. We asked you to come in because following an interview with Gabriella this morning, we have reason to believe the man who took your children may be someone you know.

Ellis Martin: Who? Who the hell is it?

Detective Sergeant Craig Fellows: Mr Martin, please calm down.

Ellis Martin: Don't ask me to calm down when you're saying someone I know could have Barnabas. You tell me who it is. I'll get my boy back right now.

DI Mohammad Allon: Unfortunately, we've still not been able to identify who has Barnabas.

Ellis Martin: Why do you think they know me?

DI Mohammad Allon: Gabriella said that the man who took her and Barnabas used the threat of you being cross to lure them away.

[Sniffing.]

FLSO Bethany Wilde: Take all the time you need.

Ellis Martin: Sorry. It's just the thought he used me to get to them. It's sickening.

DI Mohammad Allon: I understand this is difficult.

Ellis Martin: Go on, then. What else did Gabriella say?

DI Mohammad Allon: How do you know she had anything else to share?

Ellis Martin: I assume the man said something else to her to make you think I know him.

DS Craig Fellows: Why would you assume he said anything else?

Ellis Martin: Because he must have done? Anyone can go up to a kid and tell them their dad is cross so they need to come with them. He must have said something else for you to think he knows me in some way.

DI Mohammad Allon: It doesn't mean he doesn't know you.

Ellis Martin: Bloody hell.

DS Craig Fellows: There's no need to get angry, Mr Martin.

Ellis Martin: Yes, there is. You're meant to be out there, looking for my son, and instead you're in here asking me pointless questions about something any fool could tell you is no real link whatsoever.

DI Mohammad Allon: This is a complex case. The smallest detail could lead to bringing your son home safely.

Ellis Martin: That's what I want more than anything in the world, and that's why I'm not leaving right now. You ask me whatever questions you need to if it will satisfy your curiosity and get you back to looking for whoever actually took my kids. I've been through worse: when they first went missing and you decided I was to blame because I'd left them. Do you not think I blame myself, that I'm always going to be forever hating myself for looking away for one second?

REPORT ON THE FIRE AT THE DUNLOW ESTATE

At 4:30 a.m. on Monday 4 August the Hampshire and Isle of Wight Fire and Rescue Service responded to and extinguished a major structural fire in a cottage at the entrance to the Dunlow Estate in the New Forest. Local police units were also in attendance.

The senior fire officer was informed by the senior police officer present that arson was considered a possibility. A request was made for a full Forensic Fire Service examination.

We evaluated the scene from exterior to interior, then from the least damaged to most damaged areas. We worked first to establish the area of origin, then worked to determine with a reasonable degree of professional certainty the cause of the fire. This examination was conducted twenty-four hours after extinguishing the fire and once the building had been deemed structurally sound.

The cottage is a single-storey building, built circa 1850. The walls are a mix of stone, bricks and mortar, which were in disrepair prior to the fire. The roof was wooden beams covered with straw thatch. This provided ample combustible material and poor insulation to smother the blaze.

The heaviest fire activity was observed in the main room of the cottage, which was the most damaged area. Boxes of papers and clothes stored in the cottage provided ample combustible material to accelerate the fire. Burn marks on the walls indicate the fire took hold swiftly and reached high temperatures.

The fire spread to the wooden beams and thatched roof, much of which subsequently collapsed. The fire was largely contained to the main room. It was during a search of the lesser-damaged backroom that a body of a young woman was found under several boxes. The investigation of the body has been passed over to the police forensic team. Preliminary examinations suggest she died due to smoke inhalation.

Fragments of a glass bottle were found near the front door, along with fragments of cloth. Initial testing suggests the bottle contained petrol. It is highly likely that this was the cause of the fire.

Due to the speed and nature of the fire, significant damage was caused, which will result in a need for demolition of the building to avoid further risk of harm. It was noted that one of the reasons for the speed and ferocity of the fire was the availability of combustible materials stored inside the cottage. The loss of life could have been avoided if there was a clear path to the front door: the only exit.

The fire was determined to be purposeful in nature. Police can expect full cooperation from the Fire Service as they investigate further.

REPORT COMPILED BY: Forensic Fire Brigade Officer Matt Lam.

You have one new voicemail. Voicemail left today at 3:46 p.m.

'Hello. This is a message for Nicolas June. My name is Detective Inspector Juliet Stern. Please call me back as soon as you get this message. It is of the utmost importance that I speak to you about the fire you called in on the fourth of August on the Dunlow Estate.'

From: Madison Campbell
madison.campbell@mitadmin.gov.uk
To: Paul Willis **paul.willis@mit.gov.uk**
CC: Nicole Stewart **nicole.stewart@mit.gov.uk**
Date: **5 August, 16:23**
Subject: **Operation Mercury – contact details updated**

Hi Paul and Nicole,

The contact details for the three men who visited Hythe Boat Yard on the morning of 4th August are now updated. Sorry it took a while – none of them have mobiles and it was difficult to track them down.

I don't know if this is helpful, but my parents have always been interested in the origins of names. I cannot believe someone would be this blatant, but coopers used to be barrel makers. I thought it was strange that one of the men you need to speak to has such a coincidental surname.

Maddy

Gabe

Juliet slammed her mobile onto her desk. I flinched, then tried to wipe all vestiges of the spike of terror her unexpected movement had induced from my face.

Juliet couldn't have paid less attention to my struggle to appear normal. She stabbed at her keyboard, her jaw clenched. My partner was the one person at the station I could depend on to leave me to deal with what was happening a floor below in my own way with zero prying.

It wasn't that Juliet didn't care. Maybe. More that she trusted me to be an adult and ask for help if I needed it.

Nothing would help. The worst had already happened many years ago. I lived through the bashing echoes.

Across our desks, Juliet stood and snatched her jacket from the back of her chair. 'I have to go home,' she said in the same way others would announce a painful dental appointment.

The time at the bottom of my screen was later than it should have been. I'd written a two-line email to Matt thanking him for his report at least half an hour ago. Instead of pressing send, I'd gazed vacantly at the blinking cursor and twitched at every sound from the unusually quiet main part of our floor.

'I've got a few more things to get through.' At my current rate, a handful of emails would take well into the night. Maybe if I hung around for long enough, the reports from the autopsy we'd missed because of Benedict's rambling confession would come through. Lingering at the station wouldn't be a hardship. All that awaited me at home were empty rooms.

I'd lied. One thing might help me wade through the aftermath of the bad man striking again. One person. If I could sink into the arms of my boyfriend, everything else might become slightly more tolerable.

I'd tried not to think about Ollie's warm smiles and gentle touch today. They would have been a balm against these battering times, but he wasn't here. Wishing he was made everything worse. I was a novice girlfriend but I knew calling Ollie away from his seriously unwell father was a no-go. He might need to explain a lot of things about committed relationships since I was such a newbie, but I could figure that out on my own.

Juliet shrugged on her jacket and dropped her phone into the pocket. 'See you tomorrow.'

'Have a good evening.'

I turned back to the email, intending to read it once more before sending. I needed to check I hadn't written something odd in my addled state.

I twisted in my chair when Juliet's footsteps paused at the doorway. She was frowning at the unopened packet of Hobnobs on my desk.

'I won't get crumbs everywhere.' Not if I didn't eat them. I cranked a smile across my face. 'Or I'll at least contain them to my desk if I go full savage.'

Juliet looked to the panelled ceiling, the heel of one trainer digging into the greying carpet. Her eyes hardened when they snapped to me.

'Don't stay for too long,' she commanded.

I raised my eyebrows, but she turned and marched away.

Before Juliet lived with her family during the week, I'd had to pry her away from her desk each evening. Despite her departure a mere handful of minutes after five now that she returned home to her husband and daughters every day, her order was the height of hypocrisy. I might not be sure if her unpainted nails and sensible footwear were signals of discontent or shifted priorities, but I knew she'd stay at the station for longer if she could.

Five minutes passed before I caught myself staring through the doorway at the empty desks beyond. I swung back to my computer. At least the bulk of my colleagues being relocated meant no one would notice when I zoned out. Maddy had said her goodbyes at five and, now Juliet had left too, I was the only person on the seventh floor.

The click of my mouse when I finally pressed send on the email to Matt was loud in the unnatural quiet. On the floor below, it was unlikely my colleagues would head home before the sun dipped beneath the horizon.

Neither would I. I had hours of skiving yesterday to make up for. If I wanted to pull my weight with this case, to find the arsonist who'd intentionally or accidentally killed a young woman, I couldn't let Juliet carry the investigation on her own.

I pulled up Benedict's records. There was no listing for youthful arson. My notes from his unprompted confession today had been added to his status as Terence's alibi on several occasions.

Benedict was twenty-seven. Six years younger than me. Working backwards in a way that would have been less laborious if my brain didn't feel packed tight with cotton wool, I figured out when he was fifteen.

Several arsons were reported that year. I narrowed the search to blazes that had gone unsolved, then trawled through the list for those on monied estates. There were four. All affected outbuildings. All started with petrol and rags. All non-fatal. Benedict hadn't given an exact date for his erased arrest, but it seemed his cronies had abandoned their crusade against the landed rich once their inside man was caught.

I printed the details and added them to the map on the corkboard, gold stars nabbed from the overflowing stationery supplies on Maddy's desk marking their status as historic fires. The delineation was pointless. Even without the fires jumbled together, no clear link appeared except for the targeting of wealthier families across Southampton and the New Forest. None of the estates were close or owned by friends. Their occupants worked in different industries or lounged in centuries-old wealth.

The sole connection between the recent fires was the probability that they were being set by the same person. They were all started with bottles of petrol in places devoid of CCTV coverage over a short period of time. The older fires also matched these criteria so, despite Benedict's innocent act, he remained a suspect.

I couldn't let the fact that Benedict seemed less of a twat than his boyfriend confuse me. He'd set fires in the past. He could be doing it again.

After staring at the blue twine stretching between the map and properties for far too long, I slumped into my desk chair. Benedict's neat list of names sat next to my notepad. Straightening, I googled the state school he'd been forced to attend during his family's brief financial downfall. It was still open. It had a new building and had achieved Outstanding in its last Ofsted inspection.

'What a dump,' I muttered as I tracked down the admin team's contact details.

The email to request the surnames of previous students didn't take as long to send as the one to Matt Lam. Hopefully we would be able to match individuals to Benedict's list. The chances any of them had restarted their mission after so many years of dormancy was unlikely, but it was a lead to follow. Until David gleaned useful forensic information from the young woman's body or the cottage, Juliet and I would be spending far too much time twiddling our thumbs.

I couldn't be idle. Though my brain wandered off on tangents when I tried to focus, it would be a hundred times worse if the pretence of useful activity was removed. I shied away from memories of last night. My broken sleep and nightmares had combined, the dark corners of my bedroom full of unknown threats.

Shaking my head to clear the pressing fog, I searched for Matt's report about the first fire on the Dunlow Estate. The cause of the blaze had initially been difficult to determine. Dunlow had been adamant it didn't have anything to do with his fireplace but had been caused by the cigarette butts strewn around the manor. Matt's report was decisive though; the fire originated inside. A jury had concluded that Karl must have snuck in and caused the blaze, despite his not-guilty plea.

Jordan Haines, the litterer of cigarette butts, was exonerated. I squinted at my computer screen. Since Melanie Pirt's murder, Jordan hadn't been linked to any other investigations. His connection to the Dunlow family had been severed when his girlfriend's killer was sentenced. He had no reason to lash out at them now. The Dunlow Estate was probably somewhere he strove to avoid.

'Gabe?'

'Fuck.' I lurched to the side and my knee slammed into the desk.

'Shit. Sorry.' Alice rushed over from the door, holding a dripping mug. 'I didn't mean to scare you.'

'It's fine.' I winced and rubbed my leg. I hadn't heard her walking across the floor, too absorbed in staring at Benedict's precise handwriting.

Alice used a crumpled tissue from her trouser pocket to mop the sides of the mug, then offered the drink to me. 'Coffee. Just how you like it.'

Rings of differing shades of brown marked the spot where my mug usually sat on my desk. Maddy must have cleared away my undrunk coffee from earlier while Juliet and I were downstairs with Benedict. I needed to remind her that her duties did not extend to cleaning up after us, no matter now incapacitated she might deem either of us to be.

'Thanks.' The sides of the mug were tacky but warm against my chilled hands.

Alice leant one hip on my desk, the square holster of her taser jutting. 'Do you want to talk about anything?'

One long blink, then I set down the pity drink. Paul's team relocating minimised the amount of sympathy I had to endure from my colleagues. I was more than happy to be left alone until the investigation was inevitably declared a failure and everything returned to normal.

'No. Thank you.' I carefully kept my voice even, betraying nothing of the mass of sadness and anger and grief roiling under my skin.

Alice's almost-black eyes flicked over me. I wondered if this was how Juliet felt when asked simple personal questions. I'd search her face for clues, keen to discover what she was thinking and feeling. Perhaps she wanted to be left alone as desperately as I did.

The difference between us: my problems were in the past, whereas I was fairly certain something wasn't right with Juliet's life now. I'd had to make peace with her silence. She knew I cared. She would reach out if she needed to.

'Well then.' Alice switched from gentle concern to an aggrieved pout. 'I have a bone to pick with you.'

The relief washing through me was palpable. 'What have I done now?'

'Stolen another beautiful man from my clutches.' Alice glared at me. 'Did you even notice the water squirter on the Dunlow Estate yesterday was giving off more heat than the building that had literally been on fire hours before, or are you so loved-up with Ollie that no other man gets a look in?'

I bent to rummage in my bottom drawer. 'You're talking about Matt Lam?'

'Have you chatted to any other ridiculously gorgeous fire-fighters lately?'

I pushed aside a stack of post-it notes. 'Aha.' I grabbed the card and showed it to Alice. 'Matt gave this to me after the first fire on the Dunlow Estate.'

Alice's nostrils flared. She pointed at me as she walked backwards out of the office. 'We need to get you a sign. *This woman is taken. Stop giving her attention.*'

'Lovely to see you,' I called as she disappeared.

'Drink your coffee,' she shouted.

Steam curled from the murky brown liquid. I wondered who had told Alice I liked my coffee milky with sugar. The back of my neck burned. At the moment, it was reasonable that my colleagues would talk about me when I was absent. That didn't make it any less uncomfortable.

Matt's card perched next to the mug on my desk. Instead of relegating it back to my bottom drawer, I tucked it into my notepad. Instant access to a fire expert could prove essential during this investigation.

Banishing thoughts of Matt's work-roughened hands, I reawakened my computer. An email from Benedict Hogan waited in my inbox.

He had alibis for each of the recent fires. He'd been with Terence, Leo, or various Hogan family members with increasingly pretentious names.

My coffee had gone cold by the time I emailed Benedict to thank him for his prompt response. I turned to look at the missing persons' posters on the wall.

The young woman killed in the fire could be up there. Juliet had started looking into each of them, but maybe a deeper dive was needed to discover her identity.

Her DNA and dental records would come through soon, but I didn't need to wait for them. Every minute that passed before we knew her name was another her killer could use to cover their tracks. Maybe even target their next victim.

Telling myself I was relentlessly pursuing the truth sounded better than simply not wanting to go home.

Call connected at 17:47.

'Hey, Ol.'

'Gabe, I can't tell you how much I'm missing you right now.'

'Yeah?'

'I don't know how my sister isn't driving Mum and Dad insane. She's literally the worst person on the planet.'

'What's Jessica done this time?'

'Everything she can to be unhelpful. She was here when I arrived but had to leave because of a super important work thing. An especially dickish move after she moaned about how long it took me to get here. Then she sent Mum an article about how Alsatians shouldn't be allowed to roam free with other animals, so now Mum is all worried anytime I walk Artie around the farm. And she told Dad I didn't want to come see him, which is not true.'

'She's really going for it.'

'It's the stress. It makes normal people cry and snap at each other. It turns Jessica into a spiteful monster intent on using our parents against me. I wish you were here. You'd be on my side.'

'I can't come. There's a big case.'

'Yeah? Are you looking after yourself? Sorry I can't be there to help out.'

'I'm fine. You don't need to worry about me.'

'It's probably best you're distracted with an investigation. I'm going to be here for a few more days at least.'

'Yeah?'

'Dad won't be out of hospital until they're sure his blood pressure is sorted and I need to help Mum while he's recovering. All my time today has been spent at the hospital or tramping around the farm.'

'That makes sense.'

'Are you sure you're okay? You don't sound right. I'm sorry I've not called before but my signal is shit here apart from in very select places that change every day.'

'I'm fine.'

'What's the case you're working on? Is it upsetting?'

'It's arson. Someone died, but it's not a bad case. Look, Ollie, I need to go. I'm still at the station and I want to finish up here and go home before it gets dark.'

'Okay. Let's talk again tomorrow, yeah?'

'Sure. I hope your dad is okay. Bye.'

'Bye, Gabe. Love you.'

BREAKING NEWS – THE BARREL MAN ARRESTED?

Independent Online – Anna Yen

Reports have come in from Marchwood in Southampton that a gentleman has been arrested in conjunction with the investigation into the death of seven-year-old Max Powrie. It is believed Max was abducted and killed by the notorious serial killer known as the Barrel Man.

The gentleman was arrested by a large team of officers in the early evening. Detective Inspector Paul Willis has asked that the man not be named at this time. He said, 'A gentleman has been taken into police custody and is helping with our enquiries into the death of Max Powrie. A search warrant was executed at his address and several items have been taken away for further examination. I understand that there is considerable interest in this case but I'm unable to share anything more at this time.'

Neighbours were eager to talk to the press. One woman who would prefer to remain anonymous said, 'He's always been a strange one. Should have put it together when the poor lad was killed. If there was anyone who had easy access to a barrel, it was him.'

What several neighbours have revealed is that the man who was arrested has a large collection of barrels in his garden. We don't know yet if this was what turned police attention towards him.

This story will be updated as we gather more information.

Mum. Sent 18:52.

> Hello – how are you today? xxxx

Gabe. Sent 18:58.

> I'm fine. Busy x

Mum. Sent 18:58.

> Remember you can always come home xxx

Gabe. Sent 19:03.

> Thanks, but I'm fine here x

Mum. Sent 19:03.

> Love you, darling. Call any time you need to. Do you want to chat now? xxxxx

Gabe. Sent 19:08.

Can't now. I'm still at work. Maybe tomorrow x

Mum. Sent 19:08.

Okay. Take care of yourself xxx

Call connected at 21:10.

'999, which service do you require?'

'An ambulance. Please. Now.'

'Okay. I'll transfer you.'

PLEASE HOLD. PLEASE HOLD. PLEASE HOLD. PLEASE HOLD. PLEASE HOLD.

'Hello, what's your emergency?'

'My mum's hurt. She's unconscious.'

'Is she breathing?'

'Yeah. Her heart's beating too. I checked. But she's not waking up.'

'Is she in a comfortable position?'

'I think so. I haven't moved her. I'm scared I'll do more damage.'

'That's okay. Can you please tell me what's happened?'

'I don't know. I came home from work and found her like this.'

'What did you find her like?'

'She's at the bottom of the stairs.'

'Do you think she fell?'

'Maybe.'

'Can you see if she's hit her head?'

'I don't know. I don't want to move her.'

'That's okay. Can I take your name?'

'It's Jordan Haines. Is someone coming?'

'Yes. I've got your address from your phone. An ambulance is on its way. They'll be with you in seventeen minutes.'

Day 3

Wednesday, 6 August

HIS REIGN OF TERROR OVER – POLICE MAKE CRUCIAL ARREST IN THE HUNT FOR THE BARREL MAN…

Scroll.

HIS LOST VICTIM – EXHAUSTED GABRIELLA MARTIN SEEN ENTERING SOUTHAMPTON STATION YESTERDAY…

Scroll.

WHY WASN'T HE CAUGHT SOONER? – POLICE IGNORED REPORTS FROM NEIGHBOURS ABOUT HIS STRANGE BARREL COLLECTION…

Scroll.

From: David Rees **david.rees@forensics.gov.uk**
To: Juliet Stern **juliet.stern@mit.gov.uk**
CC: Gabriella Martin **gabriella.martin@mit.gov.uk**
Date: **6 August, 8:01**
Subject: **Operation Pyrite – victim identified**

Stern and Martin,

Attached is the transcript and documents from the autopsy of the Dunlow Estate arson victim. She has been positively identified using dental moulds and DNA as ZARA EVERETT. She suffered fatal smoke inhalation and several blows to the head. The pathologist has suggested these could have been as a result of the boxes found on top of her body and perhaps attempts to flee the building.

Rees

Retrieved from police archives.

Detective Sergeant Craig Fellows: Informal interview conducted at 6:39 p.m. on the 8th February at Cat Hill allotments. This interview is being conducted by myself, Detective Sergeant Craig Fellows. The interviewee is Fergus Symon, a friend of Ellis Martin. This interview is voluntary and can be terminated at any time. This interview is concerning the abduction of Gabriella and Barnabas Martin.

Fergus Symon: Bloody awful business. I'm not just Ellis's friend, I'm a friend of the whole family. Saw those kids down here every Saturday with their dad. Lovely nippers.

DS Craig Fellows: Thank you, Mr Symon. I realise this is a distressing time, but have you noticed changes in Ellis's behaviour recently?

Fergus Symon: Of course I bloody have. The poor man has been in pieces since his kids were taken. Can't say he's been much better since Gabe came home. El and Milly love those kids like nothing else. It's torn them apart that some beast would take them.

DS Craig Fellows: Have you seen Ellis much since the children were abducted?

Fergus Symon: I've popped into their house every day. Not much to do here at the allotments but I've told El not to worry about his plot. I'll take care of it for him.

DS Craig Fellows: Has Ellis said anything to you, either before or after his children went missing, that gave you cause for concern?

Fergus Symon: Now, lad. What are you getting at? El is a brilliant dad. He didn't have anything to do with his kiddies going missing. He doesn't have it in him to hurt a hair on their heads. Let me tell you; I found him down here crying a couple of months ago. He was turning over the soil and sliced clean through a frog with his spade. Now, the kind of man who cries for a frog isn't about to hurt his own flesh and blood, is he?

Gabe

Before admitting my brain had become a pool of slush, my final task to prove my usefulness last night had been sorting the missing women pinned to the wall into three categories. Those most likely to be the arson victim, those who could be, and those who were highly improbable. I'd been unable to identify her without the forensic results, but this reordering made the hours I'd spent in the office feel worthwhile.

Zara's Everett's poster sat in the middle section. She'd been bumped up from highly unlikely because she'd gone missing the day before the fire. I hadn't progressed her into most likely because her boyfriend had announced on Instagram that she'd headed off on a solo hike on the opposite side of the city.

Though I'd spent the bulk of my time delving into the records and social media of the four most likely women, I'd been so reluctant to return to an empty house that I'd briefly nosed into the lives of the middle pack too. Zara was well known in the online hiking community, if her follower count on Instagram was anything to go by. She regularly hiked alone across the country and encouraged others to do the same. Her mantra was that the world was to be enjoyed by all and that a few bad eggs shouldn't stop anyone from doing what brought their souls joy.

Her message wouldn't have quite the same carefree tone once news of her death spread. Zara hadn't necessarily been killed because she was a woman hiking alone, but she might have been more protected if she'd been with a group.

Now she'd been identified, the similarities between her smiling picture on the missing person's poster and the ashen head and shoulders on the floor of the Dunlow cottage fell into place. Glossy brown curls had become tangled and almost black with sweat. Tanned skin held a hint of the sun's warmth in death.

Taking down the other missing persons' posters felt callous, but keeping them helped no one. I couldn't spearhead a search to find them. It didn't matter that the women seemed to glare at me as I pulled each poster from the wall; my focus had to be on finding Zara's killer.

I looked around the seventh floor after I dropped off the papers in the recycling bin beside Maddy's desk. No one else had arrived yet. A combination of the early hour and a major investigation being housed elsewhere conspired to make me the last person here the night before and the first in this morning.

I didn't think I'd ever have reason to resent Juliet developing a healthy work–life balance. It meant more dinners and lazy weekends with Ollie, less continual worry about my partner's home life when she avoided her family at all costs.

With our arson victim identified, every minute I waited for Juliet to appear felt doubly long.

Retreating to our office, I printed the information I'd gathered about Zara. A task completed with much more efficiency than it would have been the evening before. I wouldn't describe last night's doze on my sofa as restful, but some of the swirling fog had dissipated. My mind still lagged but a sharpness had returned.

The shock had started to clear. The bad man resurfacing knocked me off course, but a couple of days had passed. I could reaffix my eyes on the present. In another few days, the investigation to find him would wind down. Everything could begin to return to normal.

Until next time.

I flinched when the lift doors opened across the floor. I'd gotten stuck in a daze, derailed by one errant thought. They would lessen too. As time passed, the bad man would be consigned to memory. To nightmares.

'You've been busy.' Juliet strode into our office. Her eyes snapped to the remaining missing person's poster. 'The victim's been identified.'

She threw her jacket over her chair, the navy fabric of her matching straight-legged trousers swishing as she walked to the corkboard. I didn't need to check my grey chinos and dark green shirt for biscuit crumbs as I stood. The packet of Hobnobs Juliet thrust on me yesterday sat unopened on the edge of my desk.

'She's Zara Everett.' I moved to Juliet's side. 'Reported missing by her boyfriend – Charles Nolan, who goes by Chase – on Monday evening. He thought she was heading off on a solo hike on the other side of Southampton.' I pointed at the map. I'd traced the route Chase said his girlfriend went on, plus the most likely one she'd taken to the Dunlow Estate.

'She lied to him. Or he's lying about her plans.' Juliet bent to read Zara's five most recent Instagram posts from another printout. The latest was from her boyfriend, asking her followers if they'd spotted Zara. Since he'd told them to look in completely the wrong direction, it wasn't a surprise they'd failed. 'What's all this?'

'Zara was very active on social media,' I explained. 'She hiked all over the country, often on her own, and encouraged others to do the same.'

Juliet straightened. 'I can't imagine they'll follow her advice now.'

'Probably not.' Having witnessed too much of the darker side of humanity, I couldn't be disappointed people would be discouraged from wandering remote places alone. Although, I wouldn't choose for a young woman to die in a burning building to keep others safe.

'What do we know about her?' Juliet asked.

'She was twenty-three years old. A care leaver. Her last foster placement ended when she turned eighteen. There's no evidence she's been in touch with them since.' Zara documented her life faithfully on Instagram. There was no hint of any parental figures. 'She runs a SUP shop with her boyfriend, down near the seafront.'

'What's SUP?' Juliet's pale brows drew together.

I fought to keep a grin off my face. 'Stand-up paddleboards.' I continued when her expression didn't clear: 'They're a cross between surfboards and kayaks.'

Ollie and I tried them when we spent a weekend on the Isle of Wight in July. He'd fallen off a lot. Even when laughing at him, I'd managed to stay on my feet until he dragged me into the startlingly cold sea. He said I found balancing easier because my centre of gravity was that much lower than his.

'Chase, the boyfriend, lives in a flat above the shop. Zara lived there too,' I went on. 'If we head over, we'll likely catch him in one or the other.'

'Perfect.' Juliet reached for her jacket, before turning to me. 'Shall I drive?'

I gathered up my notepad and keys. 'No need. I'm fine.'

Not strictly true, but close enough. I rolled my shoulders as we walked across the abandoned floor towards the lifts. A few more weird days of using the side entrance to avoid journalists and ignoring the news on my phone, and everything would settle.

I would return to my normal life. Driving was a move towards that.

Step by step, I'd leave the bad man behind once again.

Call connected at 9:05.

'Hi?'

'Hello. This is Detective Inspector Juliet Stern. I'm—'

'Oh God. What's happened this time?'

'I'm sorry?'

'Johnny said he was staying with a friend last night. I assume that was bullshit? Do I need to call his social worker?'

'I'm not calling about Johnny. I need to speak to you about Zara Everett.'

'Zara? Oh, Zara. How is she?'

'Can I confirm you are Holly Simmonds, Zara's last foster carer?'

'Yes, that's me. Is Zara okay?'

'When did you last hear from Zara?'

'God. Years ago. She's such a lovely girl. We told her she had a home here as long as she needed one, but she wasn't interested.'

'Do you know why?'

'Our house is always busy with kids coming and going. I don't think she liked that. Plus, she felt like she had a better option. She'd started up with that boy. Can't remember his name now but it was something stupid. And she had a friend who kept her out late. Sometimes they'd disappear for days and Zara would seem shocked when I was cross. Like I was the stupid one for worrying.'

'Can you remember the name of this friend?'

'It was such a long time ago. She was posh. Black. Can't remember much more than that. Anyway, why do you want to know about this? Is Zara okay?'

'Zara died of smoke inhalation on the fourth of August on the Dunlow Estate in the New Forest.'

'God, no. How awful.'

'Do you know why Zara would have been on the Dunlow Estate?'

'What? No. Sorry. Is it alright if I go? This is such a shock.'

'One more question. Did Zara ever lie to you about where she went?'

'No. She didn't bother to tell us most of the time, but she didn't lie if she did. Sorry, I really do have to go. I need to get my head on straight before I deal with Johnny whenever he comes home.'

'That's fine. I'll be in touch if we have any other questions.'

From: James Knowles **james.knowles@police.gov.uk**
To: Paul Willis **paul.willis@mit.gov.uk**
CC: Nicole Stewart **nicole.stewart@mit.gov.uk**, Leonard Dunlow **leonard.dunlow@police.gov.uk**
Date: **6 August, 9:16**
Subject: **Operation Mercury – CCTV of barrel purchases**

Paul and Nicole,

Leo and I have been searching CCTV footage from shops around Southampton that sell barrels. A full list is attached to this email, but I wanted to highlight that Stanley Cooper was filmed buying a barrel from Sharp and Link garden centre in Allington on the 23rd July.

I've attached the full clip, along with several stills. His face isn't clear at any point due to dust and cobwebs covering the camera, but he paid with his credit card so we were able to confirm that it's him.

One other man bought a barrel from the garden centre on the same day. He paid in cash and looks quite different to Mr Cooper, so it's unlikely that it was him a second time.

Leo has been a great help looking through the CCTV footage. The lad has a keen eye.

I hope this is useful,

James

Keith. Sent 9:27.

> Have fun at your pottery class later. The girls will miss you for dinner but I've told them you're making something special we can all use. I can't wait to see your latest creation x

Gabe

'Hold on a minute.' Juliet stopped outside a sun-drenched charity shop. 'I need to get something.'

She ducked inside, the bell above the door jingling. I eyed the wares in the window. Battered puzzles and floral dresses wouldn't tempt Juliet. Racks of clothes filled the shop. Beyond them, a blonde ponytail dipped as Juliet grabbed an item from a shelf.

We'd left my car a minute away in a car park tucked around the back of the shops. The businesses neighbouring Chase and Zara's SUP shop faced right out onto the River Itchen. Juliet and I had walked past tourist traps full of tacky T-shirts nestled beside boutique clothes shops. None of them had distracted Juliet from our visit to the arson victim's boyfriend.

I looked out at the water, the sun glinting off lapping waves. Breathing deep, I closed my eyes as the warmth of the day washed over me. The heat wasn't so bullish this close to the sea. A cool breeze and occasional bursts of salty spray across the sea wall kept the temperature manageable.

The bad man robbed me of moments like this. In the first days after he resurfaced, I was too stuck inside my own mind to appreciate the present. My vision tunnelled to identifying safety and threat, my brain unable to comprehend that the danger had passed years ago.

'Done.' Juliet stepped out of the charity shop holding a misshapen pot. Garish green and orange paint wound around the uneven sides. She didn't offer an explanation for her sudden need for strange pottery, instead turned on her heel and walked along the baking concrete to *The SUP Shack*.

The shopfront was dominated by a wide window. Three paddleboards stood upright behind the glass, blocking the interior. A sign on the door was turned to a cheerful shark who declared the shop open. A blackboard outside decorated in looping chalk proclaimed a one-day sale on flip-flops.

A wind chime clanged as we walked inside. The walls were decorated with more paddleboards. Paddles and wetsuits stood in rows in the middle of the floor, making the already small room cramped. No customers milled but rustling sounds drifted through an open door at the back.

'Be with you in a minute,' someone called.

Juliet and I walked over to a wooden counter while the rummaging continued. An old-fashioned till sat at one end and the wall behind was filled with tote bags extolling the virtues of spending time on the water. Twisted metal hung from the ceiling, lightbulbs attached at odd angles. They gave the shop an uneven feel. Shadows loomed across the packed walls, the bright plastic boards a jarring contrast.

'Hi.' A man emerged from the back room. His blond hair was twisted into thick dreadlocks, which he'd knotted at the top of his head. Sparce facial hair covered his tanned chin and upper lip. His green board shorts hissed with each step towards us and a multicoloured vest hung from his narrow shoulders. 'How can I help you?'

'Are you Chase Nolan?' I checked as I pulled out my notepad. He looked familiar, although the pictures on Zara's Instagram had to have been heavily curated and edited. Chase looked taller and broader in the seemingly impromptu shots of him hauling SUP boards out to sea or laughing with Zara around a campfire.

'That's me.' His chapped lips curved into a gentle smile, hands loose at his sides.

'I'm Detective Inspector Juliet Stern and this is Detective Sergeant Gabe Martin. We have unfortunate news about Zara.'

Juliet gestured at the stool behind the till. 'You might want to sit down.'

'Zara?' Chase rounded the counter with a loping gait. 'What do you mean?'

'I'm sorry, but Zara was found dead in the New Forest yesterday morning,' I said. Juliet and I hadn't discussed who would share this but, of the two of us, I was far gentler with victims' friends and family. I'd winced at Juliet's side of the conversation with Zara's past foster carer on the drive over.

Chase slumped onto the stool, his face slackening. 'Zara's dead?'

'She is.' My hand tightened around my notepad. 'We're sorry for your loss.'

'This can't be true.' Chase raised his hands to rub at his face. 'It's a nightmare.'

His words pulsed through me. I knew too well the pain of horrifying dreams brought to life. I bit the inside of my cheek. Now was not the time to think about any of that.

'We know this is difficult, but can you please tell us about your relationship with Zara?' I raised my notepad like a shield.

Chase pressed his palms over his eyes. 'Yeah. She's my girlfriend. Was, I guess.' His jaw jutted between his forearms. 'We've been together for about five years. Started renting this shop and the flat above three years ago.'

'When did you last see Zara?' Juliet asked while I scribbled notes.

'On Sunday,' Chase said nasally. He sniffed, then lowered his hands. The redness around his eyes could have been due to sadness or pressure. 'You said Zara was found in the New Forest?'

'Yes.'

Chase jumped off the stool as Juliet finished the word and rushed to the backroom. Juliet and I had time to exchange a look that told me nothing of what she thought of Zara's boyfriend before he returned holding a large piece of cardboard. He placed it on the counter.

I recognised this from Zara's Instagram as well. After each hike, she shared a collage. Inspirational quotes, photographs, and drawings merged with her intricate handwriting, snippets from her diary, route maps, and pressed flowers.

Chase nudged the half-finished board towards us. 'It must not have been Zara you found. She hasn't gone anywhere near the New Forest.'

A map sat in the centre of the incomplete collage, a circular route out to the east of the city and through the surrounding countryside marked with a dotted line. The places Zara planned to stay each night were highlighted by a pink heart. She must have started each board before her hikes then added all the finer details once home.

'Her plans must have changed.' Juliet's eyes roved over the board. 'Positive identification was achieved via DNA and dental records.'

'Can they be wrong?' Chase's fingers dug into the top of the board.

'That's incredibly unlikely.' I softened my voice. 'You reported Zara missing on Monday. Was that because she wasn't where you expected her to be?'

The desperate energy powering Chase slipped away. 'God. You're right.' He let go of the board and slouched onto the stool, his hands pressing over his eyes again. 'Zara didn't call or text when she stopped that first night and I couldn't get hold of her. I didn't worry too much because signal can be spotty away from the city but when she didn't make contact the next day, I went out to find her. There was no sign of her along the route or where she'd planned to stay the night.'

'Why would Zara have lied to you about where she planned to hike?'

I'd worked with Juliet for long enough that I wasn't shocked anymore when she ploughed through an interview like a wrecking ball. Her difficult questions allowed me to maintain rapport. People didn't fall for overt good cop bad cop routines, but they did respond differently to detectives who were gentle or all hard angles.

Chase's hands dropped to his lap. He glared at Juliet with bloodshot eyes. 'I don't know. That wasn't the kind of relationship me and Zara had. We told each other everything. If she went off in a random direction, it would have been because something happened rather than some pre-planned conspiracy against me or whatever you're thinking.'

'Zara was found without her phone,' I said. 'Could she have gotten lost?'

'She didn't have her phone?' Chase blinked down at the board, then shook his head. 'Even without it, she wouldn't have gone so far off track. She would have come home if she'd lost it. Some people think Zara's stupid for going on long hikes on her own but she's not. She cares about being safe. Cared. Without her phone, she couldn't reach out to me. Let me know she was okay.' Chase folded in on himself, once again burying his face in his hands. 'God. I should have known something was wrong as soon as Zara didn't call that first night. I should have gone out and found her.'

I wished Chase wouldn't keep covering his face. It made it difficult to tell if the red tint to his skin was due to distress. His eyes were watering when he straightened, his fingers digging into his hair.

'You said you had to use her DNA to tell it was her?' he asked. 'Didn't she have her purse with her?'

'Nothing we could use to identify Zara was on her person or in the bag we found with her,' I said.

Chase leant against the wall, cushioned by a tote featuring a seagull holding a chip in its beak. 'I don't know what happened to make Zara change course, but something must have gone wrong before she died. She wouldn't have continued without her phone and purse. If she didn't have them, she would have been helpless.'

A young woman, lost and alone, who believed she'd found shelter for the night, only to be awakened by smoke and flame.

'Where were you on the night of the third and morning of the fourth?' I asked, avoiding revealing the circumstances of Zara's death. Assumptions could be telling. 'And can anyone confirm your whereabouts?'

'I was here.' Chase's mouth formed an unhappy line. 'I guess our neighbours might have noticed I'd stayed in.'

Chase had no alibi but he didn't seem overly concerned. Perhaps because his mind hadn't turned to the possibility of foul play yet, though two detectives appearing in his shop surely hinted at such. I didn't know if his lack of curiosity around Zara's death should be blamed on shock or prior knowledge.

'Is there anyone who would want to hurt Zara?' Juliet pointed at the collage with one finger, the rest curled around the strange pot. 'Anyone who didn't agree with her solo hiking?'

Chase's face scrunched. 'No one wanted to hurt Zara, not even the people who thought she was an idiot. Everyone who met her loved her.'

'Is there anyone in particular who disagreed with her?' Juliet persisted.

'Loads of people did.' Chase scrubbed at his patchy beard. 'The loudest was Paloma Robins. She's always talking shit about how hiking alone as a woman is an unnecessary risk. Even calls herself wise in her Insta handle, like anyone who doesn't do things her way is stupid.'

I wrote down the name. 'Do you have contact details for Paloma?'

'It'll be in Zara's address book. Upstairs.'

I hadn't pegged Zara as the kind of person who would own a physical address book. With so much of her life lived online, I'd assumed she would keep her friend's details on her phone. Ollie would approve of her writing addresses down on paper. When we moved in together, he'd proudly shown me his flower-covered address book.

Chase slid off the stool and walked to the backroom. He turned at the door, rubbing his elbow. 'I guess you want to take a look at our flat?'

'That would be helpful,' I said.

Usually, we had to request a search through victims' belongings. I didn't know what it said about Chase that he assumed we'd want to. His understanding of this part of an investigation was at odds with his lack of interest in the circumstances around his girlfriend's death. He could simply have watched enough police dramas that he knew the routine. The knowledge that his girlfriend was dead at all could be too loud. Curiosity would follow later.

We followed Chase into the backroom. Stacked cardboard boxes reached to the ceiling alongside deflated boards folded into multicoloured piles. A narrow staircase led straight up into a studio flat. A double bed occupied one side of the room, next to a packed clothes horse and a ratty sofa. A kitchen stretched across the far wall, while the others were decorated with Zara's hiking collages. Her artful handwriting danced across them all.

Chase searched the drawers of a bedside table topped with a vase of wilting flowers while Juliet and I pulled on plastic gloves. She placed her newly purchased pot on the kitchen counter.

'Here.' Chase flicked past the mid-point of an address book decorated with multicoloured stars. He ripped out a page. 'I won't need this. You can have it.'

I took the paper and slotted it into one of the handful of evidence bags I'd stuffed into my chino pockets alongside my car keys, phone, and notepad. Spikey handwriting directed us to an address across the city.

Gentle chimes sounded from the shop. Chase swung towards the stairs.

'Have a look around,' he said over his shoulder as he descended. 'I won't be long.'

Juliet walked to the bedside table Chase had ransacked. I moved to the matching cabinet on the other side of the bed.

'What do you think of him?' Juliet murmured, flicking through craft supplies.

'Not sure.' I rifled through the top drawer. Nothing more exciting than a pack of condoms and a tube of out-of-date lube alongside paracetamol and a pair of crumpled boxers. 'He doesn't seem too upset.' I waved at the stairs. Muffled voices rose from the shop. 'He's serving a customer, rather than crying.'

Juliet abandoned the chest of drawers and opened a narrow wardrobe. 'Could be shock.'

'Maybe.' I lowered to my knees to check under the bed. More hiking boards. Perhaps ones not pretty enough to deserve a space on the walls. 'But Chase reported Zara missing. He must have thought about the possibility that something could have happened to her.'

Juliet stretched to examine the top of the wardrobe. 'Some people are determined to think the best until they encounter the worst.'

I hummed in agreement, then worked through the debris scattered on and beneath a round coffee table. I wondered where Juliet would put me on that scale. I liked to believe the best of people. I hoped not to a foolish degree.

I ran my hands around the fixed cushions of the sofa. I couldn't judge anyone for how they responded to bad news. Shock, no matter how lessened it should be, made people act in strange ways.

Juliet ducked into the bathroom while I checked the kitchen. We met minutes later at the foot of the bed. Her hands were empty, mine occupied by Paloma's address.

'Do you think he's lying about where Zara was headed?' Juliet pulled off her gloves and retrieved her pot. 'Or did her plans change after she left?'

'Chase showed us the board.' I tugged off my gloves and placed them with Juliet's in a second evidence bag. 'Zara used them a lot on her social media. I don't see why she would have wasted time starting one for a hike she didn't intend to go on. Her plans must have changed at the last minute.'

'That must have been after she was parted from her phone, unless what Chase told us about their relationship was wrong,' Juliet mused. 'According to him, Zara would have told him she was headed in a different direction if she could, or she had some reason to keep the change from him.'

I nodded, then followed her down the stairs. In the shop, Chase talked to a lanky man about different wetsuit options. I tried not to judge him too harshly for not telling the customer to go away while he dealt with the news of his girlfriend's death. Perhaps a small business owner couldn't afford to close, not for anything.

'Give me a second, mate.' Chase met us next to the counter. 'You done? I need to help this guy.'

I searched Chase's face. Nothing indicated the news we'd so recently given him. Maybe he would crumple when alone, once the initial disbelief and confusion had worn off.

'Can we take this?' Juliet picked up the incomplete board.

Chase's eyes widened. The skin around them had returned to a neutral tan. A moment of indecision passed before he jerked his head down once. 'Yeah. Take whatever you need.'

'A forensic sample would be helpful.' I pulled the kit from my cluttered pocket. Ollie had laughed when I explained I chose trousers based on pocket size. 'Then we can eliminate your DNA from the samples gathered from Zara's body and bag.'

Chase's eyes flicked to the customer, who was doing a passable impression of someone not avidly listening, before he twisted off the tab. He dug the swab around his cheeks before dropping it into the tube. His hand was steady as he passed it to me.

'We'll be in touch with any more questions,' I said, as Juliet turned to the door.

I looked back before following her out of the shop. I couldn't get a good read on Chase. He might be closed off, but I suspected the fault was with me. The bad man emerging always threw me off.

My detective instincts would have to come back online before our arsonist struck again. Chase may not be guilty, but I needed to be able to recognise who was. I couldn't keep floundering in the dark.

Detective Sergeant Nicole Stewart: Interview commencing at 10:40 a.m. on Wednesday the 6th August. This interview is being conducted by Detective Inspector Paul Willis and myself, Detective Sergeant Nicole Stewart, at Southampton station. The interviewee is Stanley Cooper, who is under arrest. Mr Cooper has been given the opportunity to consult with a solicitor prior to this interview, but has declined. Should he change his mind, arrangements will be made to provide him with legal counsel. This is the second interview concerning Mr Cooper's involvement in the abduction and murder of Max Powrie and the abduction and murder of several other children, the details of which can be found in the attached notes.

Detective Inspector Paul Willis: Now you've had a night to cool down, I hope you'll be more cooperative with our investigation.

Stanley Cooper: You think a night in this shithole has made me want to talk to you more than I did yesterday? Mate, you've got a screw loose if you think I'm going to say anything but what I already have.

DS Nicole Stewart: I hope you'll change your mind, Mr Cooper. If, as you say, you're innocent, then it's in your best interest to answer our questions as fully as possible.

Stanley Cooper: That's exactly what you want me to do, isn't it? Shout my mouth off and I might say something you can twist up to make it fit that I'm a murderer of little kiddies. That would be perfect for you, right? You'd get to be heroes and a bastard is thrown in prison. At least, it would be perfect until the actual killer came out of the woodwork and offed another kid. Then you'd have a whole lot of hard questions headed your way.

DI Paul Willis: We are already well aware of your ability to declare your own innocence. What we would prefer to clarify in this interview is the reasoning behind items found on your property, and we'd like to talk to you about your whereabouts on certain key dates.

Stanley Cooper: It's the barrels, isn't it? They're the damn problem.

DS Nicole Stewart: For the benefit of the recording, I'm showing Mr Cooper photographs NS003 and NS007. These were taken during a search of Mr Cooper's home and garden.

DI Paul Willis: Can you understand why we would be interested in speaking to a man whose name originates from barrel making, whose garden is full of barrels when we are searching for a killer whose trademark is a barrel, and who, on the morning it was left, was near where the barrel containing Max Powrie's body was found?

Stanley Cooper: Of course I can bloody understand, but it doesn't mean I've done anything wrong.

DI Paul Willis: Can you explain why there is a collection of barrels on your property?

Stanley Cooper: You're not going to stop asking, are you?

DS Nicole Stewart: The more information you give us, the better idea we will have of whether or not you were in any way involved in Max and the other children's deaths. If you are innocent, we no more want to be spending time interviewing you than you want to be here.

Stanley Cooper: That's not true. You didn't spend the night in a cell for no good reason.

DI Paul Willis: That could have been avoided if you'd been forthright with us yesterday. The quickest way for you to get out of here is to prove, one way or another, that you're completely uninvolved.

[Heavy breathing.]

Stanley Cooper: Fine. I'll answer your questions and, if you decide to keep me any longer, then we'll all know sooner or later that you're damn fools.

DS Nicole Stewart: Thank you for your cooperation, Mr Cooper. Can you please explain the barrels in your garden?

Stanley Cooper: You said about my surname. Dad was a barrel maker and his before him and on and on. I broke from tradition because they're all made in factories these days. My old man nearly bankrupted us because he refused to move with the times. He wanted to disinherit me, but he died before he sorted his will. Mum left everything to me when she passed a year later. That's where the barrels came from.

DI Paul Willis: All the barrels came from your father?

Stanley Cooper: I said when he kicked me out that I'd never have anything to do with those damn things. But then Mum died and I went round to their house. It seemed wrong to get rid of them all. Dad made barrels his whole life. It wasn't his fault no one gave a toss anymore if something was quality, made to last. In the end, I carted them back to my place. You've seen: they take up most of the garden. Dad didn't intend them for this, but they're great for growing veg. Don't have to bend my bad knee.

DS Nicole Stewart: You mentioned your knee yesterday. When was it injured?

Stanley Cooper: It's an old rugby injury. When I was fifteen, a lad from a visiting school tackled me badly. Didn't think much of it at the time, apart from being annoyed I couldn't play the rest of the game. It was only as I got older that it's caused me gip.

DI Paul Willis: Apart from causing you pain, does your knee limit your movement at all?

Stanley Cooper: I guess you're asking because you need to check if I'm physically capable of stuffing a poor lad into a barrel? Let me tell you, no weakness in my body would stop me from doing that. There has to be something gone seriously wrong in the head for someone to think that's a fine thing to do. No matter how little my knee would hold me back, my conscience would always hold me back a hundred times more.

DI Paul Willis: The barrels were all from your father?

Stanley Cooper: That's right.

DS Nicole Stewart: For the benefit of the recording, I'm showing Mr Cooper CCTV still JK014. It shows Mr Cooper purchasing a barrel on the 23rd July from Sharp and Link garden centre in Allington.

Stanley Cooper: This is what has you so bloody convinced I had something to do with that poor lad's death, then?

DI Paul Willis: This, along with your lack of alibi for the time of Max's abduction and the suspected time of his murder, is causing us to believe you were involved in his death. Your inability to provide your whereabouts for the dates of the other children's abductions and deaths is also highly suspicious.

Stanley Cooper: Who the hell knows what they were up to every day years ago? That doesn't make me guilty, just a normal man who doesn't constantly keep tabs on his comings and goings.

DS Nicole Stewart: Why did you buy a new barrel, Mr Cooper?

Stanley Cooper: Because I wanted to, alright? One of Dad's broke and I needed to replace it.

DI Paul Willis: I thought you said your father's barrels were made to last?

Stanley Cooper: You're a damn wise arse. They were good barrels that Dad made but that doesn't bloody mean they last forever. And haven't you found the new barrel in my garden?

DI Paul Willis: There did seem to be a newer barrel there. However, there's no barcode or other identifying details, so we can't know for certain it's the same barrel you bought on the 23rd July, one week after Max went missing. We've sent it off for forensic testing to see if it can be matched to the barrel you bought at Sharp and Link.

Stanley Cooper: Me buying that barrel on that day is just bad timing. Nothing else.

DS Nicole Stewart: We would like to talk to you in more detail about the dates other children went missing. If you can remember anything about your whereabouts or anyone you would have had contact with at these times, that would be helpful to our investigation.

Stanley Cooper: You want to know something helpful for your investigation? I didn't bloody do it. None of it. If you want to find the sicko who's killing these kids, stop wasting your time with me and get back to any other clues you've got.

DI Paul Willis: Since you're our strongest suspect at the moment, I think we'll continue to talk to you for a while longer.

Tyler. Sent 10:57.

> Mate, I popped into the chippy to get my slip and they said you've called in sick. You alright?

Jordan. Sent 10:57.

> Yeah, I'm fine. It's mum. I can't leave her for the next couple of days.

Tyler. Sent 10:57.

> She okay?

Jordan. Sent 10:58.

> She will be.

Tyler. Sent 10:58.

> Was it him again?

Jordan. Sent 10:58.

She says it wasn't.

Tyler. Sent 10:58.

Do you need me to sort it?

Jordan. Sent 11:05.

Na, Ty. Keep your distance. I've got a plan. Just need to see it through.

Zara Everett @SoloHikingGirl
Woolston, Southampton

It's Chase again. I'm so sorry to have to share this, but Zara died during one of her solo hikes. I'm completely heartbroken. One half of my soul is gone. Zara would have wanted you all to know how much she loved her life. She lived it to the fullest right to the last moment. I can't say anything else about her death but please take care of yourselves out there. I'll share here again once I've sorted the funeral. Maybe we could do a group hike along one of Zara's favourite routes? I can't think of a more beautiful way to remember her. The most wonderful woman I've ever known and will ever know. Please look after yourselves if you're a solo hiker. Zara loved it so much, but the risk wasn't worth it in the end.

Gabe

I knocked on the brushed metal door of flat seventeen a second time. Paloma Robins had buzzed us into the building, but Juliet and I had been left waiting in the corridor for over a minute. No sounds from within hinted at whether Paloma was readying herself to invite us inside or had changed her mind about chatting in the time it took for us to rise to the ninth floor in the sleek lift.

The door swung open. 'It's fucking true then? Zara's dead?'

The woman standing in the doorway was about my height, but much fitter. Her arm muscles bulged as she leant on the heavy door, her smooth brown skin showcased by a pink crop top and matching shorts. She glared at Juliet and me, her dark eyes bloodshot and her blonde hair in a messy bun on top of her head.

'Unfortunately, Zara Everett died on the fourth of August,' I said. 'Can I ask how you know about her death?'

Paloma pressed away from the door and waved us inside. 'Her fucking tool of a boyfriend posted about it.'

We hadn't told Chase not to share the news of his girlfriend's death but I'd expected more than an hour to pass before he disclosed it on social media. I should have known better. So much of Zara and Chase's relationship had been played out online. Why wouldn't her death and his grieving be as well?

Paloma's flat met the expectations set up by the building's glass and metal exterior, which stood out amongst roads of neat semis. Polished concrete floors stretched across the open-plan living room towards huge windows. A stark white sofa sat in the centre, a grey kitchen tucked in one corner.

'You're Paloma Robins?' I checked as we followed her to the L-shaped sofa.

'Yes.' She flopped onto one side. 'Who are you again?'

We'd given our names before she buzzed us into the building. The intercom was crystal clear. Apparently, detectives' details weren't worth retaining.

I caught myself. That was ungenerous. I'd barely interacted with Paloma so shouldn't assume she was as privileged as her home and perfect outfit – which matched the scrunchy containing her bleached hair – suggested. Her voice might be refined, but her language wasn't what I'd expect from someone of her apparent class.

Half the people we interviewed probably forgot our names immediately. Paloma was forthright enough to actually ask again, rather than hoping it wouldn't be an issue.

'I'm Detective Sergeant Gabe Martin,' I said, as Juliet and I sat down on the other side of the sofa. It was surprisingly comfortable, despite looking more like a piece of art than useable furniture. 'This is Detective Inspector Juliet Stern.'

'Right.' Paloma tugged a tissue from a white box on top of a glass coffee table and blew her nose. The noise was unexpectedly trumpet-like, bouncing across the monochromatic room. 'I guess you're here because of how Zara died? That dick was all cryptic in his post, but the police wouldn't be involved if she'd fallen over a log or something.'

'That's true.' A rare light shone in Juliet's eyes, one that occasionally warmed me after I'd done a particularly good job with one of our cases. She wasn't the type to have friends, but she evidently clicked with the young woman slumped on the sofa.

'Zara died of smoke inhalation,' I cut in. Misplaced admiration might cause Juliet to believe Paloma could cope with her signature bluntness, but Paloma's hand shook as she dabbed at her eyes. 'She was caught in a building set on fire. We're fairly certain the blaze was arson, but we're not yet sure if the perpetrator knew Zara was inside.'

'Fuck,' Paloma breathed. Her eyes swam with tears. 'How absolutely horrifying.'

Juliet's features dimmed as she sat back on the sofa. Paloma had seemed promising, but apparently her emotional reaction to her fellow Instagrammer's death placed her firmly in the average human category.

'What was your relationship to Zara?' I asked. Given Chase's description of their animosity, I hadn't expected such sadness from Paloma.

She sniffed. 'She was my best friend.'

Juliet tipped her head to one side. 'That's not what Chase told us.'

'That arsehole.' Paloma's grief was banished. She pointed a finger topped with a long pink nail at the notepad on my knee. 'One thing you need to get straight about that man-child is every word he's said to you is a lie, or at least some shady version of the truth that suits whatever he's decided is fact.'

'Why would Chase say you and Zara weren't friends?' I asked, my pencil hovering.

Paloma laughed harshly. 'Because he doesn't understand friendship? Because he can't see how two people could disagree and get along? Because he's unable to conceive of Zara having a support system beyond his clingy stick arms? Take your pick.' Her eyes narrowed. 'Or I guess it could be because the boyfriend often gets a lot of heat when a woman dies in suspicious circumstances. Chase would have been delighted to turn you away from him and on to me.' She stuck her tongue into the side of her cheek. 'Twat.'

A hint of a smile played around Juliet's lips as she sat forward. 'What did you think of Chase and Zara's relationship? Did you get any sense they didn't get along?'

'Oh, they got along just fine.' Paloma rolled her eyes. 'Because Zara falls over herself backwards to please him. Fell over.' Her shoulders drooped. 'Since those two got together, she twisted and squeezed herself to be everything he wanted. The only thing she wouldn't give up was hiking.'

'Chase didn't like Zara's hiking?' I checked. Her Instagram page painted Chase as her biggest supporter.

Paloma tucked her hands under her toned thighs. 'He was a total arsehole about it. He even tried getting me onside since he knows I don't support people, especially women, hiking alone. But I never agreed with him when Zara was around. I would never take her independence from her. That's what he wanted: her small and under his thumb.'

I wondered which picture of Zara and Chase's relationship was true. We'd found no evidence of a coercive dynamic in the couple's flat but if Chase was as insidious as many master manipulators were, he would have made sure his moves against Zara couldn't be tracked.

'Chase was surprised Zara's body was found in the New Forest,' Juliet said, the hint of a smile gone. 'Did she often change her plans at the last moment?'

'What?' Paloma's lip curled. 'Zar had been planning to hike that way for weeks.'

'Chase gave us one of Zara's collages.' If Paloma was familiar with Zara's Instagram, then she'd know what I was referring to. 'It shows she planned to head east of the city.'

Paloma jumped up and grabbed her phone from an angular desk in front of one of the floor-to-ceiling windows. 'I don't know whether he showed you Zara's plan for another hike or what, but she was one hundred per cent heading over to the New Forest this time.'

She came back to the sofa and held out her phone for inspection, displaying messages between her and Zara. Similar to the map in the centre of the board Chase had shown us, a route across the New Forest was marked out with a dotted line in a photo sent from Zara five days ago. The chatter beneath, full of emojis, detailed her excitement over wild horses and pigs. She thought it might be cute to be woken by them one morning.

Juliet pulled her card out of her pocket. 'Can you send us a copy of those messages?'

Paloma nodded, then placed the card and her phone on the coffee table. 'It's weird that Chase lied about where Zar was going, right?'

'It's something we'll ask him about.' I tapped my pencil on my notepad. 'We'd appreciate it if you left that to us and didn't make any of this information public.'

Normally, people allowed us to conduct our investigations unimpeded. Chase had proven with his Instagram post that explicit instructions were needed with this case.

'Can you tell us your whereabouts on the night of the third and morning of the fourth of August?' Juliet asked.

Paloma's neat black eyebrows grew together. I didn't allow mine to do the same. The question shouldn't have shocked me, which was further proof I wasn't back to normal yet. I could be getting innocent vibes from Paloma because she had nothing to do with Zara's death or because I couldn't cope with another guilty person in the world.

It was reasonable to need to rule her out as a suspect, despite her seemingly genuine response to Zara's death. She'd already admitted she'd known where Zara was when she died. Perhaps their friendship had been an act Chase had seen through.

'I was here.' Paloma bit hard at her lower lip. 'I live alone, so no one can tell you if that's true or not.'

She was more concerned than Chase about a lack of alibi at the time of her friend's death. That was a point in her favour.

'When did you last see Zara?' I asked, determined to bring something of worth to this conversation if I couldn't seem to figure out any of our suspects.

'The morning of the third.' Paloma's chest rose and fell with a heavy breath. 'I helped her with last-minute prep for the hike, packing her bag and stuff.'

I pulled a DNA sample kit from my pocket, since eliminating Paloma was a necessity now too. 'Do you mind—'

'It's fine.' Paloma snatched the tube from my hand. She unscrewed the top and rubbed the cotton swab around her mouth. She grimaced, then passed it back to me. 'I know the drill.'

Guilt twisted my insides. A dynamic that couldn't be taken out of the equation was that Paloma was a Black woman being implicated for homicide by a White man. Chase hadn't hesitated to bring up Paloma's name. Being party to that didn't sit right with me, but we had to take what Chase said seriously. Just as we would follow up on what Paloma had told us.

Paloma seeming genuinely sad about Zara's death didn't make me feel any less culpable. I wanted to comfort her, tell her that taking the DNA sample was a formality, but such reassurances would be premature. At this stage of an investigation, we knew too little to rule anyone out. Paloma was fit, knew where Zara would be, and might have had reason to dislike her if their disagreements went deeper than she'd suggested. The lack of an alibi didn't help either.

'Is there anyone you can think of who would have wanted to hurt Zara?'

I'd meant the question as a lifeline, a chance for Paloma to exonerate herself by implicating others, but she blinked to contain a fresh onslaught of tears.

'You never met her so you can't know this, but Zara was the kindest and loveliest person. Only she would be patient enough to put up with that arsehole. Literally no one would want to hurt her. She was an angel.'

Salted droplets cascaded down Paloma's face. If what she'd said was true, then Zara was an unintended victim of the fire. The arsonist might not have meant to kill anyone but a young woman had still met her end in that dank cottage, her head battered and lungs blackened.

Detective Sergeant Nicole Stewart: Witness statement recorded with the permission of the interviewee commencing at 12:18 p.m. on the 6th August at Sharp and Link garden centre in Allington. This interview is being conducted by Detective Inspector Paul Willis and myself, Detective Sergeant Nicole Stewart. The interviewee is Lily French. She has asked that her manager, Bella Watts, accompany her for this interview. Lily, if you feel uncomfortable or wish to stop this interview for any reason, please say.

Detective Inspector Paul Willis: Thank you for taking the time to talk to us.

Lily French: It's fine.

DS Nicole Stewart: We've looked through CCTV captured here and you served two gentlemen on the 23rd July who bought barrels. Can you remember them?

Lily French: I remember the first one better.

DI Paul Willis: Why's that?

Lily French: We don't sell many barrels. It was weird to sell them to two guys who looked so similar in such a short space of time.

DS Nicole Stewart: The two men looked alike; in what way?

Lily French: They were both old. White. Had grey hair.

DS Nicole Stewart: For the benefit of the recording, I'm showing Lily stills taken from CCTV footage. JK014 and JK103. These are the two gentlemen who purchased barrels on the 23rd July.

Bella Watts: I'm sorry the pictures are so terrible. I've told the area manager about it but he's not interested. He says the cameras are there as a deterrent, but if that's the case then they're worse than useless. People assume because they don't look like they work that they're not real. We've had a few shoplifters walk out brazen as anything. The ceilings here are so high, we can't even clean the cameras ourselves.

DI Paul Willis: It's not a problem. Lily, can you remember anything else about these two men?

DS Nicole Stewart: For the benefit of the recording, Lily is shaking her head.

DI Paul Willis: I want you to really think about this; is there any chance that it was the same man who bought both barrels?

Lily French: No, it wasn't.

DI Paul Willis: What makes you so certain?

Lily French: They looked alike but they were different. The first guy had trouble with his card and I remember he said something about needing the barrel to replace one that had broken. He made a right song and dance about getting it out to his car. I wasn't sure he would be able to get it in the boot, but he managed in the end. The second guy wasn't interested in chatting. He paid in cash and took his barrel out to his van with no fuss.

DS Nicole Stewart: The first man struggled with the barrel?

Lily French: Yeah. He rolled it outside instead of picking it up and he was huffing around for ages getting it in his boot. I couldn't go out to help because I was the only one on the tills and we're not allowed to leave them.

DI Paul Willis: He mentioned he was replacing another barrel?

Lily French: He said something about his dad being a barrel maker. I didn't know that was a thing.

DI Paul Willis: It is. Not so much anymore. You said the second man you served didn't talk much, but can you remember anything else about him?

Lily French: Not really. He was just a normal guy. I probably wouldn't remember him if the other man hadn't bought a barrel on the same day and made such a fuss.

DI Paul Willis: Those are all our questions. Is there anything else you want to tell us?

Lily French: Just that I hope you catch him. The Barrel Man. He shouldn't be allowed to carry on hurting kids.

From: Matthew Lam
matthew.lam@hampshirefireandrescue.gov.uk
To: Gabriella Martin **gabriella.martin@mit.gov.uk**, Juliet Stern **juliet.stern@mit.gov.uk**
Date: **6 August, 12:40**
Subject: **Mr Dunlow's search of the cottage**

Gabe and Juliet,

Mr Dunlow conducted an aided search of the fire-damaged cottage on the Dunlow Estate earlier today. Overseeing his search was necessary as, although the fire had been fully extinguished, there is significant structural damage to the property and civilians entering unchaperoned is not advised at this time.

Mr Dunlow had compiled an inventory of the contents of the boxes stored in the cottage prior to the fire. He agreed that several items would have been lost to the blaze, but there are a number that would have left evidence had they been burned or melted.

There is a full list of the missing items attached to this email. They are all valuable pieces of jewellery. As these belonged to his late wife, Mr Dunlow is understandably anxious to be reunited with them. They hold significant sentimental value for him and his sons.

I have assured Mr Dunlow that, in addition to an investigation into who started the fire and killed the young woman, due time and attention will be given to finding whoever took the jewellery and returning it to him.

I hope you're having a good day, Matt

Paloma Robins @WiseGirlHiker. Sent 13:00.

Hey motherfucker. I don't know why you're going around telling detectives that me and Zar were enemies or some pre-school shit but you need to stop running your mouth. I know you don't get this because you're incapable of removing your head from your arse and engaging in empathy, but black girls don't always get the fairest treatment from the police. You could have caused me a major problem by telling them that Zar and I had beef. No thanks to you, everything's fine because the detectives aren't total arseholes. Keep out of my business and I'll keep out of yours, but come at me again and I'll make sure the police know exactly what kind of shithead they're dealing with.

Paul. Sent 13:17.

> Hey Juliet. Can you please bring Gabe to the smaller briefing room on the sixth floor when you get back to the station?

Juliet. Sent 13:19.

> Why?

Paul. Sent 13:19.

> I need her to look at a photo of a suspect.

Juliet. Sent 13:22.

> Is that necessary?

Paul. Sent 13:22.

> I wouldn't ask otherwise.

Juliet. Sent 13:26.

> Fine. We're on our way back now. Don't keep her for too long.

Gabe

'Do you think it's significant that Chase didn't ask how Zara died?' I climbed out of my car. My mind kept snagging on his lack of curiosity. I had no idea if that was because it was significant or just odd.

We hadn't used the drive back to the station to compare thoughts on our two recent interviews. Juliet was busy on her phone and I might be feeling more present, but the more of my focus reserved for driving, the better.

'Maybe he was in shock and didn't think to ask.' Juliet manoeuvred the collage from the back seat. 'Or maybe Paloma's right and he's incredibly controlling. Perhaps he was more concerned that Zara lied to him about where she'd gone.' She nudged the door closed with her hip and we headed towards the side entrance of the station.

'It was annoying that he kept covering his face. Made it hard to get a read on him.'

'All the usual motives for a partner committing murder apply.' Juliet gestured idly with the hand holding the charity shop pot. Another thing I kept turning over. I wouldn't get an answer if I asked about it. 'Chase's lack of an alibi for the time of Zara's death means he's certainly a suspect.'

I tapped my ID on the sensor at the side door and held it open. Almost everyone acted strangely when told someone significant to them had died. I couldn't assume Chase's lack of curiosity or overt emotion was a sign of guilt, but I was glad he was being considered seriously by Juliet. I'd have to make sure to do more of the grunt work on this case. She would be shouldering the bulk of actual detecting.

'What did you think of Paloma?' Juliet swept inside.

'I'm inclined to believe her about the nature of her friendship with Zara. She has the messages to back it up.' I pulled the door closed behind me and followed Juliet along the winding corridors to the bank of lifts. 'No alibi again, but I'm not sure what her motive would have been.'

'Jealousy?' Juliet stepped into reception and pressed the call button for the lifts. 'She was particularly vehement about her dislike of Chase. Perhaps too much. She could have been playing nice with Zara but waiting for a chance to take her out of the picture.'

'Maybe, but I'm not sure Paloma would pine over something she couldn't have.' The lift doors opened and we stepped inside. My shoulders loosened as the glass front of the station and the waiting journalists moved out of sight. 'We mustn't forget Benedict as well.'

'It would be strange for him to throw his own name into the mix if he had anything to do with the fire.' Juliet jabbed a button. 'But then maybe—'

'No.' I rushed to her side as the lift doors slid shut. 'You pressed the wrong one.'

Juliet stepped back, eyes flicking across the line of buttons. The sixth glowed gold.

'Paul asked me to bring you to him when we got back.'

I wanted to demand she tell me how long she'd known about this and why Paul hadn't summoned me directly, but all my energy went into remaining upright. Weight dragged at me, threatening to buckle my knees. I'd just begun shucking off the bad man. I should have known that with him being investigated so close by, that had been too easy.

I braced one hand on the rail around the lift and concentrated on breathing.

'Gabe?' Juliet's voice was soft. Unfamiliar. 'You can leave it for now.'

I shook my head, swallowing against the thick lump in my throat. 'No. I need to get it done.'

Whatever it was, I couldn't leave Paul and his team hanging. It didn't matter if I took time to attempt to centre myself; that was impossible. I couldn't clear my mind when it was crowded with the terrible possibilities of what might be revealed once I stepped onto the sixth floor. All waiting would do was make me look even weaker in everyone's eyes.

I'd been called back to investigations before. Most often, detectives believed a second round of questioning would shake loose hidden memories. They didn't realise parts of my past were encased in steel vaults, no hint of light or air getting through.

Paul wouldn't do that to me. He knew I'd given everything I could.

Which meant he needed me for another reason. When I was eighteen, a detective had used a second interview to focus ruthlessly on my relationship with my dad. He had no alibi for the time of mine and Barnabas's abduction other than the claim of a weak bladder refusing to be ignored. He couldn't have taken us anywhere because he had raised the alarm about our absence minutes after we disappeared, but some detectives were convinced he must have a connection to the bad man.

After that interview, I'd walked out of the station and driven home. I'd closed my front door, then fallen apart when Mum asked if everything was okay.

I was good at compartmentalising, at holding myself together until it was safe to break down. Gripping the lift's rail, I forced in deep breaths.

I had been moving on, clawing my way to normality. It wasn't fair that I had to sink back into the mire.

Not a helpful thought. Fairness didn't play into any of this.

I heaved another breath through my nose. If I'd learnt anything when I woke on that warehouse floor, it was that life didn't deal the same set of cards to every person. Some people got knocked down again and again. I'd gotten very adept at picking myself up.

By the time the lift doors opened on the sixth floor, I was ready to face whatever Paul might throw at me. I'd answer his questions and, afterwards, I'd find a place to be alone. Then I would let the howling inside take over.

At the end of the corridor, the door to the Major Investigations room snapped shut. I walked out of the lift, nails creeping over my skin at the thought of people keeping watch for me.

'They're in the small briefing room,' Juliet said.

I flinched, too on edge to not react. I hadn't expected her to exit the lift with me.

'You don't need to come,' I offered.

Juliet wouldn't want to stand beside me while I jumped through whatever hoops Paul had devised. Spending time with her fellow detective inspector was one of her least favourite activities, especially when he held up progress on our investigations.

I cringed inwardly. Paul hadn't been the main roadblock with the arson investigation.

'It's fine.' Juliet's face was impassive, giving no sign of whether she was annoyed by this detour before we continued the search for the arsonist.

I turned away as we walked into the smaller briefing room. The space in my mind reserved for puzzling out the subtle emotions and whims of my partner was choked out. The noise of too many other thoughts built to fever pitch.

I needed to get out of here as quickly as possible. Juliet's presence would facilitate that. She wouldn't allow Paul to keep me for a second longer than was necessary.

Too many people looked over when I entered the room. I'd made peace with Juliet witnessing this, but the pealing bells in my head grew louder as my eyes jumped around the group. All people I trusted, but I didn't want them observing my fight against the pressure building inside my skull.

Maddy and Alice stood off to one side of the table in the centre of the room. Alice gripped Maddy's hand, both their mouths set in narrow lines. Maddy's dress was plain blue, her cardigan dark green. Disconcertingly sombre, especially paired with Alice's bulky black uniform.

Paul sat at the table, his greying hair in greater disarray than ever before. The bags under his eyes bulged as he shot me a tight smile. His shirt was creased, his chin peppered with more than a day's worth of stubble.

Nicole hovered at his shoulder. I tried not to frown at her. She was a consummate professional and clearly felt no rivalry towards me as the other detective sergeant at the station, but that might have been because she was winning. Nicole was always smartly dressed and calm, her brown skin clear of blemishes and her lips always ready to curve into an easy smile. She was valued by her partner and leagues ahead of me in her personal life. While I held myself together with stinging fingertips, Nicole was a fully assembled whole.

'Gabe.' Paul's face settled into grim lines. 'Take a seat.'

I walked to the chair opposite him, acting too much like a lost child as I glanced at Juliet. She leant against the doorframe, her hands empty. She must have left the collage and her mystery pottery in the corridor. Of all the people gathered here, she was the least likely to offer comfort. That wasn't what I was hoping for. Juliet's disregard for the rules and investigations other than her own made her the perfect candidate to yank me out of here.

I'd thought I wanted this over and done with. Now I was here, all I wanted was to escape.

Juliet didn't say a word as I took a seat. Paul's Dictaphone sat in the middle of the table. A pile of papers waited at his elbow; a plain page set on top blocked the others from view.

I eyed them as Nicole rattled off the information for the recording. Everything connected to the investigation to find the bad man would be in the closed-off room down the hall. Anything brought in here was relevant to whatever Paul needed from me. The reason for this interview hid on those sheets of paper.

I wanted to grab them. Find out what was on them. I wanted to rip them to shreds. Never be involved in hunting the bad man again.

'Thank you for talking to me a second time,' Paul said when Nicole straightened, tucking a black braid behind her ear. 'I know this isn't where you want to be, but I wouldn't have asked if it wasn't important.'

'It's fine.' I'd learnt over the years that if I said that enough times, people believed it.

Paul frowned, clearly unconvinced, but he let it slide. He needed my help so regard for my wellbeing had to be shoved away. I didn't blame him, despite how easy it would have been to redirect my fraught emotions towards him. We were detectives. To find criminals, we often had to push innocent witnesses further than was comfortable.

'I invited Maddy and Alice here to support you,' Paul explained.

They shifted to stand behind me. Maddy gripped my shoulder, her long nails rasping on my shirt. A show of solidarity, but one that made me feel trapped. Flanked by prison guards.

'If you need to stop for any reason, let me know,' Paul went on. 'This line of enquiry is important to the investigation, but you must take all the time and space you need.'

This build-up was excruciating. Under the table, I balled my hands into fists so tight it would be a miracle if my nails didn't cut into the skin of my palms. Every second in this room inched closer to being intolerable.

Paul sighed. 'If you need anything else—'

'Bloody hell,' Juliet snapped through Paul's agonising litany of care. 'Can you hurry up so that Gabe and I can get back to work?'

Her motives might be faulty, but Juliet was my solitary point of light in the room. No one else would force Paul to stop being painfully considerate.

His nostrils flared, but he didn't argue. 'Gabe, I'm going to show you some stills from CCTV footage. All you need to do is tell me if you've seen this man before.'

My heart clenched as Paul listed the picture codes. No investigation had gotten this far before. I'd not had to brace myself for potentially seeing the man who'd stepped into my childhood and torn it apart.

I squeezed my hands, sending cramps up my arms. 'I'm ready.'

Paul slid the plain piece of paper off the top of the stack, then pushed the first picture to the middle of the table.

Heart thundering, I examined the top-down image of an older man. Grey hair spun in untidy tufts around his head. He wore a green jumper and jeans.

Paul placed more pictures next to the first. Despite the poor quality, small details crystalised. Wide shoulders. A slight gut. Work roughened hands.

None of it familiar.

My brain had been an elastic band, pulled ready to snap. As my eyes darted between the stills and no spark of recognition lit, the tension eased. I straightened my fingers, hands shaking as I pressed them flat on my thighs.

'I don't think it's him.' I examined the photos one last time. 'I'm not totally sure I would recognise the man who took me and Barnabas, but this man isn't familiar.'

One picture waited off to the side. I glanced over to check if this new angle—

A steel door crashed open inside my mind.

A man walked over to Barney and me. His greying hair was tucked under a black hat. Thick stubble grew across his chin and neck, spanning his upper lip under a prominent nose. The smell of smoke and oil drifted off him. He told us Dad was mad, that we needed to come with him if we wanted to make our parents happy. His strides were long as he led us across the field. Barney's hand slipped into mine.

No.

He didn't talk during the drive. We would have been excited, on any other day, to sit at the front of such a big car. We were silent, huddled into one another. I watched the man as he drove. His bulbous nose was red. He looked over, caught me staring. He didn't smile. His brown eyes flicked between Barney and me. I cowered closer to my brother's side.

No. No.

He didn't drive to our house. He parked beside another big car. He got out, walked around the front, yanked open our door. He grabbed us each by the arm. His grip was too firm. I didn't scream but tears streamed down my face as he dragged us. He threw Barney and me on the floor of a huge warehouse. Light streamed in through the wide doorway behind him, leaching his shirt and jeans of colour, making his craggy face featureless. He was dark dark dark.

No.

He muttered about complications, his voice rough. We ran and hid after he left. For a long time, we didn't see him again. We heard him though, over our rumbling tummies. He sang to himself, to us. Strange songs. I'd not heard them before. They wormed their way into my mind, haunted me during brief snatches of sleep between towering stacks of boxes. When he left, his scent remained. Smoke and car oil and stale sweat.

No no no.

Barney called him the bad man first. He must be bad, to have lied and taken us. To not let us go home. We wanted that more than anything. We thought we might starve if we didn't find food. I told Barney to stay hidden and I crawled out from our hiding place. The bad man found me. Broke my arm. His lips curled as he pulled me across the rough concrete. His teeth flashed, white and even. Then my brother roared, and the warehouse and the bad man and the waiting barrel were gone.

NONONONONONO.

'No. No. No.'

My lips caught on my wet palms. Screwing my mouth shut, I pressed my forehead into the scratchy carpet.

I'd been gone, but now I was back in the briefing room. My knees and elbows pressed into the unrelenting floor. My head burrowed into my hands.

'Give her space.' A familiar voice. I couldn't connect it to a person.

My body felt impossibly heavy. Images that had been locked away for too long flooded me. Drowned me. My stomach rolled, my throat constricting as I rasped in each breath.

A hand rubbed up and down my back, rucking my shirt against my sweaty skin. 'You're okay, Gabe. We've got you.'

I wanted to believe them. I wanted to trust there would be someone to catch me. But I'd awakened in the warehouse alone. No one helped me stand or explained what had happened. I'd stood for a long time on my own, waiting for Barnabas to come back.

He didn't. I was alone. Left and abandoned.

I breathed into my salty skin. I couldn't remember, but I must have fallen to the floor after I saw the picture. I'd made a total fool of myself already, so emerging from the temporary cave I'd formed with my arms before I was ready to face everyone was pointless.

I scraped the shattered parts of myself together. New details of my time with the bad man had been unleashed, but the result was no different than when he'd been a murky blur. He was part of my past, not my present. He took other children, was no longer interested in me.

He never had been. Or his interest only extended until the moment he'd determined whether my brother or I would become his victim. I'd been so insignificant to him that he hadn't even worried that I'd seen his face.

His confidence wasn't misplaced. I hadn't remembered his sharp details until forced to confront them.

The hand on my back helped me place myself firmly in my skin. I wasn't a terrified little girl anymore. I was older. Stronger. The bad man couldn't hurt me. I wouldn't let him.

I turned my head to wipe the worst of my tears on the sleeve of my shirt. The hands on my back spread across my shoulder blades as I slowly levered myself up to kneel. I rested my weight on my boots, each muscle protesting as though pressed on with a brick.

Alice and Maddy sat either side of me, their presence a blanket I wanted to pull close. With them there, I could curl up small and hide.

That wasn't an option. I raised what I hoped wasn't too pathetic a smile. They didn't leave my sides, Alice's arm firm around my middle as I regained my footing.

'Gabe.' Paul stood on the other side of the desk, his face stricken. 'I'm so sorry. We didn't realise—'

'It's fine.' I shook my head, but stopped when the room swayed. Alice and Maddy guided me to the chair. I melted onto it, my muscles whining.

Nicole stood next to Paul, her eyes contorted with pity. Yet another way I was weaker than her. I looked away.

Juliet stood in the doorway. The photos from the table were clutched against her chest. She must have snatched them up during my embarrassing episode.

Relief sank through my heavy limbs. I wouldn't have to look at the bad man again, not if Juliet had a say in it.

'I'm sorry about that.' I turned back to Paul.

He thumped into the seat opposite and rubbed a hand over his face. 'You have nothing to apologise for.'

I licked my lips, tasting salt. 'Who was that?'

'Another man who bought a barrel from Sharp and Link garden centre in Allington.' Paul's gaze flicked to his Dictaphone. The light on top shone red. 'Can you please clarify your reaction?'

'It's him.' I closed my eyes, but the bad man's face was waiting. I snapped them open and stared at Paul. 'It's the man who took us.'

From: Juliet Stern **juliet.stern@mit.gov.uk**
To: Angela Dobson
angela.dobson@superintendent.gov.uk
Date: **6 August, 14:01**
Subject: **Gabe**

Angela,

On returning to the station this afternoon, Paul asked if Gabe would take a look at several CCTV stills. Gabe reacted particularly strongly to one of these images. Paul suggested she take the rest of the day off. I agreed this was a good idea. She won't be of use to our investigation until she's calmed down.

I understand Gabe identifying the man who abducted her is an important development in Paul's case, but from now on I would prefer that interruptions to mine and Gabe's investigation be kept to a minimum.

Juliet

Gabe. Sent 14:33.

> Hey. This is Gabe Martin – one of the detectives on the arson case. Are you free tonight?

Matt. Sent 14:36.

> Hi Gabe. I wondered if you were ever going to make use of my card. I've got an hour or so left on my shift, but then I could hang out.

Gabe. Sent 14:36.

> Do you want to come to mine when you're done?

Matt. Sent 14:38.

> I'd love to. Let me know your address and I'll be there right after I finish.

From: Paul Willis **paul.willis@mit.gov.uk**
To: James Knowles **james.knowles@police.gov.uk**
CC: Nicole Stewart **nicole.stewart@mit.gov.uk**, Madison Campbell **madison.campbell@mitadmin.gov.uk**, Leonard Dunlow **leonard.dunlow@police.gov.uk**
Date: **6 August, 15:04**
Subject: **Operation Mercury – summary of action points**

James,

Gunter is currently creating a sketch using the CCTV footage you isolated. Once he's done, Maddy will send over the appeal for info poster. I want you and Leo to head up a team canvassing the city. We need these posters up in every public space possible.

Make sure to visit hotels and campsites. There's a chance he used one of them, since his movements around the country suggest he doesn't select victims from his local area.

Thanks,

Paul

Call connected at 15:43.

'Hello, this is Detective Inspector Juliet Stern.'

'Hello, Detective. This is Gladys June, Nicolas's wife.'

'I've called several times to speak to your husband with no joy.'

'I know. I'm sorry. It's such a busy time of year at the farm.'

'That's fine. Is Mr June available to answer a few questions now?'

'He's not in, I'm afraid. It's hard to predict when he'll be about when there's so much to be done. But he told me to tell you he doesn't know anything about how the fire started.'

'I see. We really do need to speak to your husband, Mrs June.'

'I told him that. Right. Can you come over on Friday first thing? I'll make sure he's here.'

'We can't speak sooner?'

'I'm sorry. He's got a market tomorrow and around that he's got all the crops to tend to and the animals.'

'Right. We'll see you on Friday then.'

Gabe

I perched on the edge of the sofa, gripping my phone. Matt had texted ten minutes ago to say he was leaving the fire station. I'd checked his route. He should get here soon.

Alice and Maddy had shepherded me home after Paul and Juliet agreed it was for the best if I finished work early. My shock at them coming to an accord without name calling or snarling was dampened by the combined weight of the horrible memories running riot in my mind and the crushing shame of how I'd reacted to seeing the photo of the bad man. I'd managed to give an updated description of him before I left the station, cringing each time I stumbled over simple words.

On delivering me home, Alice and Maddy had bundled me into a shower and laid out a soft jumper and pyjama bottoms on my bed. They made coffee and a sandwich and only left when I pretended I was going to take a nap.

I'd needed them gone before Matt arrived. I'd sat on my bed, my wet hair dripping onto my shoulders, and pulled his card from my notepad. I'd focused on the logistics of him coming over, rather than the hollow guilt added to the emotions churning through my guts.

Ollie wasn't here, he couldn't be here, but I needed someone. I needed the thoughts to stop, for my mind to still for one minute. I couldn't think properly with all the noise inside my skull. If I could quiet it, then I could begin to put the past back in its place.

My boyfriend wasn't here for a good reason. That hadn't changed because I desperately wanted him. I couldn't ask Ollie to come home just so that I could forget myself in his touch.

Shame had plucked at me as I made plans with Matt but I needed this. Before Ollie, sex with willing strangers had always worked to push away the darkness. I couldn't think too hard with someone else's hands on my skin, my heart thumping in pleasure and my breath short.

I almost hadn't gotten rid of my friends. On the doorstep, Alice had asked what time Ollie would be home. Too addled by fear and aching tiredness, I'd not thought before telling her and Maddy he was in Cornwall.

I'd blinked at the shock on their faces. It had taken all my remaining energy to assure them I was fine alone and that Ollie looking after his dad was far more important than rushing home to my side.

I'd been desperate for Maddy and Alice to leave, but as their footsteps faded I'd swung into the clutches of terror.

My phone dug into my palms as I waited. I hated this, hated what I was about to do, but I didn't have any other options. I couldn't call Ollie home and I couldn't think of another way to claw out of the howling abyss seeing the bad man's picture had hurled me into.

I jumped at a firm knock on my front door, dropping my phone. I left it on the floor, steadying my hands on my thighs as I stood.

Matt smiled when I opened the door, the gap between his top front teeth winking. His black hair was damp, his brown skin flushed like he'd rushed straight here after a shower. A clean black T-shirt strained across his muscled chest and navy tracksuit bottoms showcased his thick thighs.

He was what I needed right now. A distraction. I suppressed the urge to shut the door in his face, instead held it open wide.

'Hey.' I breathed in the warm scent of his shower gel as he walked inside. 'You're up for this, right? Sex? With me?'

I had no brain space for finesse or embarrassment. I needed one thing from Matt, and I needed to know right away whether he was able to provide.

His eyes widened before he laughed. 'Yeah. I'm up for it.'

'Great.'

I shut the door and stepped closer to him. His smile dropped, his gaze lowering to my mouth as I lifted onto my tiptoes, narrowing the distance between us. Neither of us was wearing more than one layer. His muscled chest pressed into me as I arched against him, a burgeoning hardness hot on my hip.

Clanging bells clashed in my head, but I ignored them. They'd quiet soon. I needed to do this, to lose myself in another person. Then I'd be able to find peace from all the noise.

It didn't matter that Matt's hands were too rough as they spread across my back, that he smelt wrong and his hair was too thick. That his lips were too wide and his teeth too present.

Matt wasn't who I really wanted, but he was here. Ollie wasn't. I had to make do with what I had. Anything to make the vicious cyclones in my mind stop.

Matt traced his fingers down my spine. I shuddered and hoped he would misinterpret that as an overload of sensation. Not disgust. His palms were too broad, too different. I burrowed my face into the side of his neck, cringing at the unfamiliar scent of bodywash and hint of smoke.

He lifted the hem of my jumper and his fingertips brushed my skin.

The sound that escaped my mouth wasn't a gasp or anything that could easily be conflated with pleasure. I whimpered, and Matt stilled. His hands retreated to the small of my back, my jumper firmly in place. He leant back and his dark eyes cleared of desire.

'Do you want this?' he asked.

It should have been easy to lie. I'd lied to many people today. Would it hurt to hide the truth from one more?

I opened my mouth, allowing another whimper to sneak out. I wanted to forget in the only way I knew how when my demons got too demanding, but I couldn't. Matt was handsome and willing and right here, but he wasn't Ollie. He wasn't the man I loved.

I didn't want to hurt Ollie just so that I could stop hurting.

The whimper was followed by a galloping legion of sobs. Our embrace shifted from being remotely sexual, Matt's strong hands rubbing my back. His breath was soft in my hair as he shushed me.

I permitted myself one long moment of sadness tinged with glimmering relief before pulling back.

'I'm sorry.' I wiped my sleeve over my face. 'This isn't what you came here for.'

Matt shrugged, as though sex being abruptly swapped for comfort genuinely didn't bother him. 'It's okay. I'm not keen on fucking someone who's clearly not into it.' His brow furrowed. 'Do you want to talk about anything?'

'Not really.' Not with him.

Matt chuffed out a laugh. 'Thank fuck. I'm no good at emotional stuff.'

I half smiled and stepped to the side. 'You can go, if you like.'

I didn't want him to disappear, to leave me with my crowding memories, but I couldn't expect a virtual stranger who I'd invited over for sex to retain interest in my presence once the possibility of mutual orgasms had been removed.

Matt looked at the door, then at me. His eyes narrowed. 'When did you last eat?'

The sandwich Alice and Maddy had made sat untouched on the kitchen side, a cold mug of black coffee beside it. The milk had gone bad. I'd eaten a dry handful of cornflakes this morning. I didn't think Matt would be impressed by that.

He took my silence as answer enough and nudged past me into the living room. With the confidence of someone accustomed to quickly orienting himself in unfamiliar buildings, he beelined for the kitchen.

'I'm always starving after a shift,' Matt said over his shoulder as I followed slowly. I wasn't sure if he was serious or would depart once he realised sex was definitely off the table. 'I don't know how to cook much but I'm epic at toasted cheese sandwiches.'

He grabbed cheddar from the fridge and pulled half a loaf of bread from the cupboard. I watched from the doorway, resting against the angular wood. Matt may not have been able to chase away the darkness, but it was at least kept at bay while he clattered around my kitchen.

He wouldn't stay forever, would likely be gone in under an hour, but I sank into the security of another person's presence. Someone who didn't want to talk about my problems and wouldn't ask any question more complicated than where I kept my frying pan.

Police Constable Alice To: Witness statement recorded with the permission of the interviewees. Interview commencing at 5:20 p.m. on the 6th August at Southampton General. This interview is being conducted by myself, Police Constable Alice To. The interviewees are Jordan Haines and Jennifer Haines. Jordan, you requested a police officer come to the hospital to discuss your mum's injuries.

Jordan Haines: Yeah. I wanted the detective.

PC Alice To: I know you asked for Detective Inspector Juliet Stern. Unfortunately, she's working on a high priority case at the moment so couldn't come out. She's asked me to talk to you and your mum, and I'll make sure to pass anything important on to her as soon as I return to the station. Why don't you start by telling me why you wanted to talk to the police?

Jordan Haines: My dad hurt my mum again. He can't get away with it this time.

PC Alice To: Can you talk through what happened?

Jordan Haines: I came home from work late last night and found Mum at the bottom of the stairs. She was unconscious. I had to call an ambulance. The doctors said she has a broken arm and two fractured ribs, plus concussion.

PC Alice To: Where was your dad when you arrived home?

Jordan Haines: Who the hell knows? He pushed Mum down the stairs, then buggered off. He should be done for murder. He didn't give a shit if she was dead or not.

PC Alice To: To clarify; you didn't witness your dad hurting your mum?

Jordan Haines: No, I didn't. But that doesn't mean it didn't happen. I've seen him slap her around enough that I can one hundred per cent say this was him.

PC Alice To: Okay. Mrs Haines, could you please tell me how you were injured?

[Long pause.]

Jordan Haines: Come on, Mum. You have to say something.

PC Alice To: Jordan, give your mum a minute. Mrs Haines, I understand that if your husband has been violent towards you then it can feel impossible to break free of the situation. If that is the case, I can make sure you go straight from the hospital to a women's refuge. You won't need to see your husband again.

Jennifer Haines: I've read about those places. Jordan wouldn't be able to come with me.

PC Alice To: Unfortunately, Jordan is too old to enter a women's refuge with you.

Jordan Haines: That doesn't matter, Mum. Just tell the truth and I'll deal with stuff at home.

[Sniffing.]

Jennifer Haines: My husband had nothing to do with this.

Jordan Haines: No, Mum.

Jennifer Haines: I just fell.

Jordan Haines: That isn't true. Surely, you can tell it isn't true.

PC Alice To: Jordan, if your mum says she fell, there's nothing I can do. You didn't witness the event so, even though you're sure your father was involved, we cannot arrest him for what you believe he has done. However, Mrs Haines, I would like to state I am concerned for your safety. I suspect what Jordan's said is correct and that your husband did hurt you and has done so on a number of other occasions. If you continue living with your husband, there is a high likelihood this abuse will continue and escalate into more serious injury or loss of life. Please know that if you ever want to talk to me, I will listen. Here's my card and a leaflet for the local women's refuge.

Jordan Haines: Everything you're saying. Fuck. You know it's true and you're not going to do anything?

PC Alice To: I'm sorry, Jordan.

Jordan Haines: If you're not going to help us, then fuck off. We don't need you here.

PC Alice To: I'll go. Mrs Haines, if you ever want to talk or tell me anything, please don't hesitate to call or come into the station.

Jennifer Haines: Thank you. I'm sorry I can't. I'm sorry.

Gabe

Matt hugged me again at the front door. He'd eaten three toasted cheese sandwiches to my one while telling stories of various mishaps that had happened at the fire station. His company was easy and light, his good humour settling over me like a soft blanket.

'Look after yourself.' He stepped back and I did the same, despite my desire to huddle into his warmth.

I shut the door behind him, and all the comfort he'd imparted swept away. The dull click of the lock was overloud, unchallenged by Artie's tapping paws or Ollie's humming.

Closing my eyes, I held onto the door handle. Chasing after Matt and pleading with him to stay the night was not an option. He'd been kind enough not to walk out as soon as the possibility of sex was taken away, had stayed way beyond what could be expected. I couldn't demand more of his time because I needed someone here to keep away the memories roaring for my attention.

'Find your phone,' I muttered. Calling Ollie wouldn't pull too much of his focus from caring for his parents. Maybe talking to him would banish the clawing darkness more effectively than Matt's casual kindness had done.

I walked to the living room, and it was like wading through thick sludge. Each step took far more effort than it should. I had to think about the mechanics of lifting my feet. Even then, my heels dragged across the hardwood floors.

The sun was low. Golden light shone from the kitchen and through the living room windows. The sofas and coffee table were lost in gloom.

I gripped the doorframe, short nails digging into the gloss. I'd dropped my phone when Matt arrived. I thought it had landed in front of the sofa but only a couple of Artie's well-loved toys cast long shadows there.

I needed to search under the coffee table and sofa – lower to my knees and reach under.

Those movements felt impossible.

I blinked against a sudden rush of tears. I needed my phone, but the ability to search for it had been robbed from me.

I shuffled backwards. Away from the light shining through the wide window. It would be too easy for someone to look in. To see me.

I gravitated towards an alcove under the stairs. Most of the sloping space was taken up with a cupboard where we stored the hoover and various products Ollie was determined would stop Artie's hair embedding in every soft furnishing. Under the tallest part of the stairs, our landlord had set a hanging rail into the remaining boxy space. Ollie had gushed over it on the day we moved in, a fan of houses with quirky surprises.

I'd not had any thoughts about it beyond wondering why the rail had been put in so high. I could just about reach it, had to yank my coat off its hanger.

I hadn't considered it as a potential hiding place, but I pushed the thick fabric of Ollie's coats to one side and crouched. I twisted into the space, my back hitting the far wall. My knees tucked into my chest as Ollie's coats swished into place, concealing me.

There had been a similar space in my parents' home. Before the bad man took me and Barnabas, I'd barely noticed it. After I returned home without my brother, I crept into it every chance I got. The tiny recess between our downstairs toilet and the pantry cradled me.

Mum said Dad made it into a cupboard with thick and immovable shelves because we needed more storage. She needn't have lied. Each time she found me hiding, her face was pulled down with sadness. She'd asked why I curled up in there.

I couldn't explain how that tiny space felt safer than our entire house. In there, I became small and unnoticed. I could close my eyes and dip my head. Not be for a while.

I did the same now. The plaster at my back was cool, Ollie's coats brushing my shoulders like a blanket. In this hidden place, I didn't have to run from the memories. Or fight them. I didn't have to think about anything at all.

Blurring white noise took over my mind and I forgot the world. Forgot myself.

You have one new voicemail. Voicemail left today at 7:05 p.m.

'Hey, Charlie. It's Neil. Just got off the phone with Mum. I'm sorry about what's happened to Zara, but you have to know being so upset about it really isn't on. You and her weren't even married or anything, and you can't pretend she was who you'd be with forever. Mum's already worried about you so don't call her again crying and shit. I can't come down for another visit until Christmas and I don't want Mum on the phone every day telling me what a wreck you are. Buck up and get on with it, or leave Mum alone.'

Recording started: 20:01.

Police Constable James Knowles: Thank you all for coming into the station at such short notice. Detective Inspector Paul Willis will now give a short update on the investigation into the murder of Max Powrie and the historic murders of several other children.

Detective Inspector Paul Willis: Thank you, James. Yesterday evening, a sixty-seven-year-old man was arrested in connection with this case. The gentleman has strong links to barrel making and due to the manner of Max and the other children's deaths, we considered whether he could have been involved. However, further evidence has since emerged that has given us strong reason to eliminate this gentleman from our investigation. Detective Sergeant Gabriella Martin participated in an exercise today to identify whether the man we'd arrested had abducted her and her brother. She did not recognise him, but she was familiar with another gentleman who bought a barrel from Sharp and Link garden centre in Allington. Using images captured by CCTV, we have been able to glean a strong understanding of what this man looks like. Police Constables James Knowles and Leo Dunlow will hand out a poster on your exit that they have already begun distributing around the city. We believe the man who killed Max and several other children is around 6'2, White, in his fifties or sixties, and is medium build. He was last seen wearing jeans and a green checked shirt. I've called you all here today to ask for your and the public's help in apprehending this gentleman. We urgently need to hear from anyone who has seen a man matching this description, particularly if he has ever been seen in the company of young children or barrels. A firm understanding of the appearance of the man who killed Max Powrie and Barnabas Martin, among others, has never been achieved before. We are hopeful that, with the cooperation of the public and press, we will be able to bring this man to justice.

Detective Sergeant Nicole Stewart: Any questions?

Anna Yen: Anna Yen, *Independent*. How do you know the gentleman arrested yesterday hasn't been working in conjunction with Max's killer?

DI Paul Willis: We believe that would be unlikely, but we're not ruling out any possibility at this stage. However, our primary focus is on identifying and apprehending the gentleman in the posters you'll be given when you leave.

Hally Jenks: Hally Jenks, the *Guardian*. You said Gabriella Martin identified this man. How could she do this when previously she's been unable to describe him? How can you be sure she's identified Max and her brother's killer correctly?

DI Paul Willis: I have enough faith in my fellow detective that I know she wouldn't send us off on a manhunt unless she was pretty bloody certain.

DS Nicole Stewart: As we all know, memories can be unreliable. Especially those around traumatic events. However, Gabriella may have been unable to give a detailed description of the man who abducted her as a child before, but we can say with a reasonable degree of certainty that she has identified him correctly now.

Robert Browning: Robert Browning for the *Daily Mail*. Reading between the lines, it sounds like you've stumbled across identifying the Barrel Man by lucky chance. Are you hoping for another stroke of luck to help you find him or is any actual policework going to be involved?

DI Paul Willis: Luck or hard work; I don't give a damn. No matter how we catch Max Powrie and Barnabas Martin's killer, I'll be happy once he's behind bars. We're done here.

DS Nicole Stewart: Please take a poster as you leave, and make sure to sign out before you exit the building.

Call connected at 20:23.

'Hello?'

'Hey, Ollie. It's Alice. Gabe's friend.'

'I know who you are, you numpty. To what do I owe this pleasure?'

'Gabe said your dad's ill?'

'Yeah. He had a stroke, but he's recovering really well. He's still in hospital until they get his blood pressure sorted but they're not going to be able to keep him there for much longer.'

'I'm happy to hear that, because you need to come home.'

'What?'

'Gabe is going to hate that I've said anything to you, but she needs you here.'

'What's happened?'

'Have you been reading the news?'

'No. I've not had time between visiting Dad and trying to keep the farm running with Mum. Why? Should I have been?'

'Do you know anything about the Barrel Man? He struck again a few days ago.'

'Oh, that's horrible. I don't know much about him. It's a bit grim for me.'

'Do you know who he is?'

'No, why should— Oh, fuck. Is he the guy who hurt Gabe and her brother?'

'Yup.'

'Shit.'

'You need to come home, Ollie. Gabe's putting a brave face on it, but she's falling apart.'

'Why didn't she say anything to me?'

'I imagine because she doesn't want to make you feel like you have to come home while your dad is poorly.'

'She still should have said.'

'I agree. Anyway, are you coming home? Otherwise, I'm going to have to look after Gabe whether she likes it or not.'

'Yes, of course I'll come back. Mum's already asleep but I'll chat to her in the morning. I'll sort things here, go see Dad, then head off.'

'Good.'

'Thank you for calling me, Alice.'

'Could you please tell Gabe it was the right thing to do before she gets cross at me for overstepping?'

'I'll try.'

I'm not sure how much longer I can continue volunteering at The Refuge. The team there are wonderful but I feel like I'm being dragged down by the problems shared in the group meetings.

Today, a young man told us his father had grievously injured his mother. He wasn't home at the time but he knew what had happened. In these situations, there's rarely any doubt. He tried to get his mother to talk to the police but she wouldn't. He shared how angry and helpless that made him feel.

When he cried, I felt it inside me. I know I'm meant to sympathise with my clients, but this is too much. I can't keep listening to these people, knowing the most likely scenario is that their loved ones or they themselves will continue in a violent cycle indefinitely.

It was good to see the young man talking to the tall woman. My fears that she would stop coming months ago were unfounded. She's been quiet during sessions but it's nice that she and this young man comfort one another on hard days.

Feelings to acknowledge: tiredness, overwhelm
Feelings to celebrate: not sure this time
Actions to practise healthy detachment: Talk to my supervisor about whether it's time to take a break from The Refuge. Acknowledge that this group is not about me and my ability to help, and stepping away doesn't mean I've let anyone down

Tonight I need to remember that pushing myself too far doesn't help anyone. All counsellors have different issues that trigger them and perhaps domestic abuse is one of mine. I need to make time for a long bath and cook myself a huge bowl of pasta.

Day 4

Thursday, 7 August

CAN YOU FIND THE BARREL MAN? – POLICE REQUEST HELP IN THEIR SEARCH FOR THE NOTORIOUS SERIAL KILLER…

Scroll.

COULD SHE BE HIS DOWNFALL? – TWENTY-FIVE YEARS AGO, THE BARREL MAN LEFT GABRIELLA MARTIN ALIVE AND NOW SHE'S LEADING THE HUNT…

Scroll.

POLICE INCOMPETENCE COULD RESULT IN MORE DEATHS – CHILDREN AT RISK WHILE DETECTIVES DEPEND ON LUCK TO FIND A KILLER…

Scroll.

From: David Rees **david.rees@forensics.gov.uk**
To: Juliet Stern **juliet.stern@mit.gov.uk**
CC: Gabriella Martin **gabriella.martin@mit.gov.uk**
Date: **7 August, 8:05**
Subject: **Operation Pyrite – forensic results from the cottage**

Stern and Martin,

My team has completed a forensic sweep of the COTTAGE on the Dunlow Estate. A full report is attached to this email, but I wanted to highlight a few points that may prove helpful.

A DNA sample taken from CHARLES NOLAN was a match for a large quantity of materials left on the body of ZARA EVERETT and her BACKPACK. There were also a smaller number of matches for PALOMA ROBINS. These are in such high quantities that it is likely they both came into direct contact with ZARA EVERETT and her BACKPACK shortly before her death.

A third match is for TYLER JENKINS. This is in much smaller quantities but these materials are spread across Zara's face, the BACKPACK, and the entirety of the cottage, particularly boxes where TIMOTHY DUNLOW indicated that valuable items are missing. TYLER JENKINS also left behind a fingerprint on the COTTAGE DOOR HANDLE.

We were not able to obtain forensic material or fingerprints from the items used to start the fire. They were too badly burned.

Rees

FORM 22A – FORMAL REQUEST FOR WARRANT: PERMISSION TO SEARCH A PRIVATE RESIDENCE

REQUESTING OFFICERS: Detective Inspector Juliet Stern and Detective Sergeant Gabriella Martin

CASE NUMBER: 17293074

CASE DESCRIPTION: Arson of a cottage on the Dunlow Estate in the New Forest and homicide of Zara Everett on 4 August

REQUESTED SEARCH AREA: Residence of Tyler Jenkins

REASON FOR WARRANT REQUEST: Following a forensic sweep of the burned cottage on the Dunlow Estate and the body and backpack of Zara Everett, significant amounts of materials provided a DNA match for Tyler Jenkins. The owner of the estate has confirmed that several highly valuable items are missing from the cottage. Tyler's fingerprints can also be found on the front door handle of the cottage. This leads us to believe he may have been involved in the fire and may have stolen items from the cottage beforehand. We are still working to establish whether Tyler knew Zara, and a search of his residence may provide us with crucial evidence. We would like to interview Tyler and search his home simultaneously. He has been questioned in conjunction with other investigations around stolen goods and is a known flight risk. We would like to minimise the chance he will abscond or hide important evidence.

Call connected at 9:04.

'Hello?'

'Gabe?'

'Juliet?'

'Why didn't you answer your mobile?'

'Oh. I can't find it. What's happened? I'm almost ready to head into work.'

'Don't come to the station. Stay at home and I'll collect you.'

'I can make my own way in.'

'Don't. It's a fucking circus out the front today.'

'Shit.'

'There have been developments in the case. I'll fill you in when I get you, but we need to chat to Chase again about why Zara would lie to him. We can go straight there from yours.'

'Fine. Okay. Thanks.'

'See you in twenty minutes.'

Gabe

My shoulders dropped after Juliet slammed her car door shut and marched off to sort a parking ticket. I hadn't asked how she knew my address. She hadn't attended the housewarming party Ollie and I threw after we moved in but I assumed she'd done as much snooping around in my file as I'd done in hers.

Mine would have been added to yesterday. I wondered if the transcript from my interview was in there yet, or Paul's notes. I didn't want to know how he'd described my episode after I saw the photo of the bad man.

I rolled my neck as I climbed out of the car. A hot shower this morning had knocked the ragged edges off a night spent curled in the alcove under the stairs, but my back protested.

During moments of lucidity, I'd decided to leave. Logically, I knew the tiny space was no safer than the rest of my home. But the thought of moving, stretching my legs and standing, kept me huddled in the darkness. The memories left me alone while I remained small. They wouldn't be so benevolent if I came out of hiding.

I'd woken slumped to one side, the hems of Ollie's coats forming an impromptu pillow. Morning light streamed over the wooden floor of the hallway. With a new day dawning, crawling out of the alcove hadn't felt insurmountable.

When the landline rang – which I would have gone without but Ollie insisted was the mark of a true adult – I realised what a dream-like state I'd been moving about in. I'd showered and dressed but until I heard Juliet's voice, I'd had no thought for how I'd get in to work or for how late I was already. My partner's commanding attitude saved me from navigating buses while barely grasping at reality. My car had been left at the station yesterday after my abrupt exit.

I longed for the quiet of the alcove but I couldn't miss work. My reaction to the bad man's picture yesterday had been beyond ridiculous. I needed to prove to my colleagues I wasn't a damaged little girl.

Juliet slotted a ticket on her dust-free dashboard, then we walked down an alley between two shops and onto the promenade. This time, Juliet was undistracted by the charity shop. Her head remained dipped as she frowned at her phone.

In the car, Juliet had updated me on the forensic findings from the cottage and Zara's body. We had a new suspect. Tyler Jenkins was a vaguely familiar name – a young man who had been at the periphery of several investigations. That he might have escalated from petty thievery to arson and homicide was unsettling.

After explaining she'd requested a search warrant for Tyler's home that she hoped would be ready for us to leap into action with once we'd finished questioning Chase, Juliet had lapsed into silence. She had no questions about how I'd spent the previous evening or whether the sore bags under my eyes were the result of a disturbed night's sleep. I revelled in her habitual disinterest, her trust that the weakness I'd expressed yesterday was done with. I needed to focus fully on our work and avoid invasive care until the protective shell I held around myself was no longer gossamer thin.

Today, looping words on the sign outside the SUP shop declared customers could claim a free tote bag when they spent fifty pounds or more. Wind chimes jangled above the door as we walked inside. Juliet slid her phone into the pocket of her lilac trousers. Her blouse was a crisp white, her hair tied into a low ponytail.

I'd given no thought to my clothes after showering. I glanced down. A green shirt tucked into brown chinos. Not too bad. I would fade into the background beside Juliet.

'Welcome,' Chase shouted from the backroom. His cheery smile dropped when he emerged and saw us.

'We talked to Paloma Robins,' Juliet launched straight in. We hadn't decided who would take the lead but perhaps my general air of absence made the decision. 'She knew Zara was heading to the New Forest.'

Chase frowned. His blond dreadlocks were twisted into a knot at the back of his neck and he'd paired a grey tank top with navy shorts. An attempt at mourning clothes. 'She's the only one who did, then.' His eyes widened. There was no sagging skin underneath from sleepless nights spent worrying about or mourning his girlfriend. 'Do you think Paloma killed Zara?'

His leap of logic jolted me from floating in a fuzzy malaise. 'Why would you say that?'

Chase's blue eyes darted between the two of us. 'No one else knew where Zara was going. She didn't even tell me, her boyfriend. If Paloma was the only person who knew where Zara was, then she was the only one who knew where to set the fire that killed her.'

Despite his lack of curiosity yesterday, Chase must have used the time between our visits to discover exactly how his girlfriend had died. It wouldn't have been too difficult to put together the press release about a body found in a burned cottage in the New Forest and Zara's death on the same morning.

'There have been a number of non-fatal arson cases on similar estates,' Juliet said. 'The one at the Dunlow cottage fits the pattern and our hypothesis is that Zara could have been killed accidentally. The arsonist may not have known she was in the building.'

Chase's shoulders rounded. I couldn't decipher his expression in the uneven shadows cast by the fiddly light fixture. He could have been disappointed his theory had immediately fallen through or that his girlfriend had been killed accidentally, with no reason she was targeted other than being in the wrong place at the wrong time. Either way, he didn't make a great show of emotion. Any hint of distress he'd displayed yesterday was gone.

'Paloma showed us a number of messages that prove Zara's intention to hike through the New Forest,' Juliet went on. 'Zara had no plans to follow the route detailed on the board we took from you yesterday.'

Chase shrugged. 'I don't know what to tell you. Zara made that board. I don't know why she would have gone to all that effort just to randomly change her mind.' He scrubbed at the uneven wisps of hair on his chin. 'I don't know why she wouldn't have told me.'

Frustration burned in my chest. I couldn't tell if Chase was strangely enigmatic or if my crumbling brain was at fault. He seemed most concerned that he'd not known where Zara had gone, rather than that she had met her end in a smoke-smothered cottage.

'Paloma mentioned your relationship with Zara wasn't always a happy one,' I said, determined to prove I was more than a walking prop of a detective.

Chase laughed, the sound devoid of humour. 'Of course she did.'

Juliet was still beside me. I waited a beat. 'What does that mean?'

'Paloma has always been jealous of me and Zara.' Chase's thin lips curled with distaste. 'She couldn't get over not being chosen.'

'Did you and Paloma have a relationship in the past?' Juliet asked.

Chase huffed. 'God, no. Can you imagine getting close to her? I bet her underwear is barbed.' His bravado diminished at the realisation he was playing to the wrong crowd. 'I met Zara and Paloma at the same time. Both of them liked me, but I picked Zara.'

I wondered what Paloma would have to say about Chase's version of events. She didn't strike me as the type to wallow over a missed opportunity for long, nor the kind of person who would lash out in thunderous jealousy. She had been blunt when we'd questioned her, not one for hiding her feelings for long enough for them to fester into something toxic.

She had to be considered as a suspect though. Her DNA was all over Zara's backpack. We had no way of knowing if it had appeared there as innocently as she claimed when she helped Zara pack or had been spread around before she torched the cottage. Chase might be hard to read but Paloma's abrasive bluster could be a smokescreen.

'You claim Zara and Paloma were rivals,' I said. 'Why would Zara have told Paloma about her change of plans if they didn't like one another?'

'I didn't say Zara disliked Paloma. Zara loved everyone.' Chase looked away, hiding any sign that he was affected by his girlfriend's death. 'Paloma's whole "women need to be careful of terrible men" thing must have finally gotten to Zara.'

'What do you mean?' Juliet asked.

Chase leant on the wooden counter. Someone passing his shop wouldn't suspect he was being questioned about the death of his girlfriend. His hands hung loose, his face calm and open.

'I don't know if you've taken a look at Paloma's Instagram, but it has a different vibe to Zara's. Paloma's all about group hikes and taking a thousand precautions against things that won't ever happen. She was always going on at Zara to be more careful, to not go out alone.'

According to Paloma, she wasn't the main person attempting to change Zara's approach to hiking. She said Chase had been chipping away at Zara's personality, that hiking was the sole thing she could claim as her own.

Maybe that was why Zara hadn't told Chase her changed plans. If he meddled in every other aspect of her life, he would have done the same with her solo trips.

'How did you feel about Zara's approach to hiking?' I asked.

Chase's eyes didn't move from the overflowing basket of flip-flops between me and Juliet. 'It was her thing. She checked in with me along each route, but she did the rest on her own.'

I wondered how Ollie would react if I decided to hike around the country alone. He'd be supportive, perhaps reassured of my safety because of my job. He knew I could handle myself in difficult situations and that I'd do what I could to avoid them.

Ollie would certainly have a contrasting reaction to Chase's if I was killed. I'd gotten a taste of his grief when I was shot earlier in the year.

The thought of my boyfriend made my ribs tighten. I'd let him down last night, even if I hadn't had sex with Matt. I needed to tell him about it. I couldn't imagine how he would react.

'We'll be in touch if we have any more questions.' Juliet turned towards the door.

Chase didn't reply. He watched us leave his packed shop.

'What do you think?' Juliet asked, once we'd walked past several window displays.

'I don't get him.' Pleased that Juliet thought I had anything of worth to contribute, I willed myself to focus on the case and not on the tiredness pinching at my weary muscles. 'He's not displaying much sadness over Zara's death, at least not in front of us. I can't figure out whether he or Paloma have a clearer understanding of his and Zara's relationship. And I don't understand why Zara would have told him she was heading on a different hike.'

Juliet pursed her lips. 'If Chase didn't know where Zara was headed, then he couldn't have set the fire that killed her.'

'And him being coercive is a good reason for her to have hidden the truth. Even if he doesn't want to admit that he's like that.' Paloma might be providing Chase with an alibi, which would delight her. I pivoted with Juliet towards the alley to the car park. 'What do you think of Chase's theory that Paloma started the fire?'

'Probably nonsense.' Juliet pulled her car keys from her pocket. With anyone else, I would have wondered if preference for Paloma over Chase was clouding their judgement. 'We can talk to her again, but if the warrant's ready then Tyler's up next. It could turn out that everything between Zara, Chase, and Paloma is a mess that has nothing to do with the fire.'

One of the difficulties of detective work was sorting pertinent details from the random currents of people's lives. Zara and Chase's relationship might not have been perfect and she might have lied to him about where she was hiking, but that didn't mean he wanted to hurt her. Paloma might be jealous, but that didn't have to lead her to killing her friend. Chase's lack of emotion could be reluctance to break down in front of strangers rather than an indication of guilt.

If Tyler did set the fire, then the discord between the three of them was noisy drama. Too easy to get distracted by and ultimately useless in our hunt for Zara's killer.

Call connected at 10:23.

'Yes?'

'Hello, is that Ellis Martin?'

'Who's asking?'

'It's Detective Inspector Paul Willis.'

'Hello, lad. Sorry for being a bit brisk. Sometimes journalists get hold of our number and try it on.'

'I understand. Do you have time to answer a couple of quick questions?'

'Sure.'

'I wonder if you've seen the sketch circulated by the press of the man we believe killed Max Powrie and your son?'

'I have. Can't say it didn't give me a shock.'

'I apologise. This investigation has moved along rapidly. I should have warned you.'

'No harm done. The times around each killing are full of moments like that. Little jolts.'

'Thank you for your understanding. I wonder if the man looks familiar?'

'No. Not at all.'

'You'll have already been told, but Gabe shared in her first interview that the gentleman who took her and Barnabas said he was acting on your instruction. Are you sure you don't know, even in a passing fashion, the man in the sketch?'

'No. I don't.'

'I'm sorry to press.'

'No. I'm sorry for getting cross. It's just, I thought all these questions would be done with now you've got proof I had nothing to do with it. That man doesn't look anything like me, or anyone I know.'

'I'll make sure to leave you alone for the rest of the investigation unless it's of the utmost importance.'

'Don't hesitate to call, lad. If there was anything I could do to help, I would do it. I wish I did recognise him, so I could give you an idea of who to search for.'

You have one new voicemail. Voicemail left today at 10:52 a.m.

'Hey, Gabe. I hope you're okay. All my calls are going straight to voicemail and I can see you're not reading my texts. Hopefully you're just busy with work. I'm setting off now so I'll be home whenever you finish today. Don't be mad at Alice for telling me what's going on; Dad is fine and I want to be around for you in the bad times as well as the good. Anyway, I'll see you soon.'

Gabe

Juliet and I walked up the short path to Tyler Jenkin's terraced house. Where his neighbours had sad collections of bins and discarded furniture cluttering the small spaces between their front doors and the pitted pavement, Tyler's front garden overflowed with rose bushes. Their sherbet lemon scent hung heavy in the muggy air.

Juliet pressed the doorbell beside a newly painted red front door. Tyler's house was as narrow as the others on the street but he or someone he lived with had obviously lavished far more care and money on its upkeep than most of their neighbours. Juliet had parked behind a souped-up Ford Focus. I suspected that belonged to Tyler as well.

The lock clicked and the door opened to reveal a middle-aged woman. Like the house, she was well taken care of. Her flowery knee-length dress showed off calves the same orange as her slim arms. Her bleached hair flowed over her shoulders, parted neatly above a face so made up I wouldn't have been surprised if she'd stepped off a TV set. The only discordant note was the stink of cigarettes that rushed out of the open door.

'Can I help you?' Her voice didn't match her appearance, the damage caused by a lifetime of smoking difficult to conceal.

'I'm Detective Inspector Juliet Stern and this is Detective Sergeant Gabe Martin,' Juliet said. 'We have some questions for Tyler Jenkins.'

The women flinched at a crash in the house. I moved to Juliet's side. The white walls of the hallway and the staircase stretching up didn't hint at what was going on further inside.

'My cat,' the woman said.

Juliet pulled the warrant out of her pocket as I stepped forward. For a moment, I thought the woman might block me, but she moved out of the way.

I ran down the hall and into an airy kitchen. A stool laid on its side next to a high counter.

The back door swung wide. I rushed through it, then across a garden of artificial grass to the gate. It was ajar. I yanked it open and hurried into an alley running along the ends of the adjacent gardens, the space narrowed by the high fences either side.

Empty.

My heart thumping with unspent adrenaline, I jogged to one end then the other. No sign of whoever had done a runner.

'Tyler's not home,' the woman said when I walked back into the kitchen. She and Juliet stood beside the toppled stool. 'I haven't seen him today.'

Neither of us challenged the obvious lie.

'This is Tyler's mum,' Juliet informed me. She passed her the warrant. 'We need to make a search of the property. Are you willing to cooperate? Otherwise we can ask uniformed officers to assist.'

The woman's pink lips pressed together. She scanned the warrant. 'It's fine.'

She trailed behind us as we walked back to the hallway. A huge vase of lilies sat on a side table beneath a wide mirror. Their heady scent competed with the ingrained stink of cigarettes.

'Can I please have your name?' I pulled my notepad and a pair of plastic gloves from my pocket.

'Nat Jenkins. Natalie.' Her eyes skittered between my pencil and the evidence bags Juliet held. 'I can leave you to start down here while I get on with some paperwork upstairs.'

'We'd rather go straight to Tyler's bedroom.' Juliet turned to the stairs, which were carpeted a plush blue. If Natalie was happy for us to look around the ground floor unsupervised, anything of interest would be upstairs.

'When are you expecting your son home?' I followed Juliet, my thighs protesting. A night scrunched on the floor was a much less enjoyable way of pushing my muscles to the limit than a weekend spent with Ollie. My aches used to result from hours in bed but more recently long dog walks followed by lazy pub lunches caused twinges on Monday mornings.

'I'm not sure,' Natalie said from close behind me.

I fought the urge to look over my shoulder, the skin on the back of my neck prickling at the unwelcome proximity. 'Do you know where Tyler was on the night of the third and morning of the fourth August?'

'I'm not his keeper,' Natalie muttered.

'Which room is Tyler's?' Juliet asked when we reached the top of the stairs.

Natalie's gaze twitched to a closed door on the left. She pointed to the right. 'That one.'

'Wonderful. I'll start in there.' Juliet pushed open the righthand door to reveal a bright room decorated in yellows. She jerked her head to the left. 'Gabe, why don't you search in there?'

'That's an airing cupboard,' Natalie said.

I opened the door. A rumpled blue duvet covered a double bed. Dark green walls were broken up by posters of flashy cars.

'I thought you meant the other door,' Natalie mumbled behind me.

I controlled my expression before turning. 'Some people find it difficult to watch a search of their home. Please don't feel like you need to stay.'

The tendons in Natalie's neck stood out. 'I'll be fine.'

Observed from the doorway, I started with the large wardrobe. Tracksuits hung in neat rows inside, spanning a spectrum of greys, blues, and blacks. The shelf at the top hosted thick hoodies, while a neat line of spotless white trainers was tucked at the bottom. My questing fingers only met fabric as I stretched my arm behind the smoke-tinged outfits.

'Nothing in there,' Juliet announced as she entered the room. Following some cue from Natalie that I'd missed while shoulder deep in Tyler's hoodies, she beelined for a desk in the far corner.

After rummaging in Tyler's bin, I placed a used condom in an evidence bag. It wasn't likely Tyler had sex with Zara but his fingerprints were found on her face and in the burned cottage. That could be a sign of a relationship between the two of them. Paloma thought Zara was happy with Chase despite his flaws, but Zara had hidden where she was going from her boyfriend. She was adept at keeping secrets from those closest to her.

Natalie folded her arms as I pulled back Tyler's duvet and felt beneath his pillows. Under the bed, dusty storage boxes held old school books with lewd drawings on the covers and more tracksuit sets. I slid them back into place and joined Juliet at the desk. She flicked through a notebook, most of the pages blank.

On top of the desk, a framed corkboard rested against the wall. A glittering card in the middle wished Tyler a happy eighteenth. Someone with artistic flair had tied string from each side of the wooden frame and used tiny pegs to surround the card with photos of Tyler and a multitude of family and friends. Natalie featured in several pictures, her face bright orange. A young man with piercings across his eyebrow stood at the centre of them all. I'd not had a chance to look at Tyler's picture before we headed here. His face rang a distant bell. Blue hair curled over his tanned forehead.

I pointed at a young man who laughed as he pulled Tyler into a headlock. 'Do you recognise him?'

Juliet set the notebook on the desk and peered at the picture. 'Maybe.'

'That's Jordan Haines.' I hadn't seen him since Karl Biss's trial but this was either a photo of him or his long-lost twin. I turned to where Natalie stood in the doorway. 'Are Tyler and Jordan friends?'

Her expression soured. 'They used to be. Don't see Jordan so much since the boys left school, even though they work at the chippy together sometimes.'

Their friendship might have deteriorated once the convenience of seeing each other every day was removed, but Jordan could be worth talking to. If Tyler didn't return during our search then his old friend might be more talkative about his whereabouts than his mother. Jordan hadn't been obstructive during the investigation to find Melanie Pirt's murderer. He'd hurt his girlfriend before she'd died and his actions were reprehensible, but a cursory look at his home situation gave an explanation. We'd visited Jordan's house twice. His father clearly ruled over his mother with a combination of violence and fear. I didn't relish the thought of going to their home again.

Juliet shuffled through the desk's drawers while I unpegged the picture from the board. She had likely forgotten Jordan and might not think him worth talking to, but I was willing to question him to gain even a small insight into this case. He'd been a suspect for the fire at Dunlow Manor last year, had lurked outside while Karl Biss started the blaze within. Jordan had nothing to do with that fire but Tyler might have asked him about it. Even the smallest of links could be the key to finding our current arsonist.

'Huh.' I stumbled when I moved to where Juliet had left a pile of empty evidence bags at the foot of Tyler's bed. I set the picture down beside them and crouched to look at the grey carpet in front of the desk.

Juliet pushed her trainer back and forth, the synthetic fibres bunching under the pressure. 'Does Tyler have a desk chair?'

I stood up. I hadn't noticed something was missing. Now Juliet had pointed it out, it was obvious.

'He used to.' The rasp of Natalie's voice grew more pronounced. 'He doesn't use the desk so much now he's not at school no more.'

I examined the desk. The corkboard and notepad were the only things on the smooth surface, compared to Tyler's bedside table, which was littered with aftershave bottles, beer bottle caps, and crumpled tissues.

The desk looked staged, while the carpet underneath was loose and worn.

'Help me shift this?' Juliet edged her fingers between the desk and the wall.

Natalie rushed into the room as I gripped the other end. 'Don't do that.'

Juliet straightened and pulled the warrant out of her pocket. 'As part of our search, we're allowed to move furniture. If you find this distressing, please wait downstairs until we're done.'

I braced for an explosion. The blood flooding Natalie's face turned her the shade of an overripe tomato. She glared at Juliet, then stomped out of the room. Her heavy footfalls could be heard all the way down the stairs.

Juliet raised her eyebrows as she slotted the warrant back into her pocket. 'Ready?'

The desk was light. We moved it to press against the bed and the carpet shifted with it, revealing paint-stained floorboards. Juliet squeezed into the new space and lifted one of the wooden planks with ease.

I leant over the desk, holding evidence bags ready as Juliet plucked items from a plastic box tucked into the revealed recess. Gold and silver jewellery I'd bet Timothy Dunlow would recognise had been tucked beside a phone protected by a floral case and a purse patterned with pink leaves. Juliet opened it and flashed the cards at me, Zara's driving licence battered but clear.

I wrote details on the bags, the marker moving awkwardly atop the uneven shapes. Juliet could be right about the drama between Chase, Zara, and Paloma. Finding Zara's belongings in Tyler's room might be a sign that neither of the people closest to her had anything to do with her death.

'Nothing else down there.' Juliet edged around the desk, then we shoved it back into place. 'I don't see Tyler coming home soon, do you?'

I shook my head as I pulled off my gloves. 'Natalie isn't going to say anything useful if she can help it. We should talk to Jordan. He lives nearby and he might not be so loyal. If we're lucky, Tyler might even be hiding there.'

Juliet's lips pinched before she nodded. I wasn't sure how to interpret that, my focus on the case and my partner hanging by a tenuous thread. I didn't have the energy to pick apart her reactions. She might think talking to Jordan was a waste of time, but at least it was something.

We needed to locate Tyler. Regardless of whether he had anything to do with the fire, he may have been the last person to see Zara Everett alive.

'I understand you're anxious. I'll make sure to pass this on to my colleagues and they'll follow up with you as soon as they can.'

'Absolute madness. I saw that sicko doing his weekly shop.'

'Are there any other details you would like to share?'

'No. You've got it all. The Barrel Man was in Chichester yesterday. Send the cavalry.'

'Thank you for calling this in. A member of the team will be in touch soon. Goodbye.'

'Bye.'

BEEP.
Call incoming. Caller number one of fifteen.
Call connected at 11:43.

'Hello, this is the police information centre at Southampton station. Do you know the case number your call is in reference to?'

'Sorry, love, no. I saw his picture in the paper and rang straight away.'

'That's alright. Can you give me a brief description of the case?'

'It's the Barrel Man one.'

'Okay. I can find that for you. Now, I need to warn you that we have had an unusually high number of calls from the public regarding this case so it may take slightly longer than normal for a member of the Major Investigations team to get back to you.'

'They're going to want to get a wiggle on. I've been living next to the bloke for the past two weeks.'

'I see. First, can I please take your name?'

'Meridith Coates.'

'Thank you. Your address?'

'I live on the caravan park in Hythe. Oak Hill Holiday Park. I'm in caravan 12. The Barrel Man was in 13 until a few days ago.'

'Do you know exactly when the gentleman you're referring to moved out?'

'Not sure. Might have been the same day that poor lad was found. Here one minute, gone the next without a peep.'

'When did the gentleman move in?'

'Couple of weeks ago. Sharon, that's the woman who owns the park, would know the date.'

'Did you interact with the gentleman?'

'The occasional hello and what have you. Nothing proper.'

'Did you ever get his name?'

'Didn't talk long enough for that.'

'What makes you believe he's the man the detectives are interested in?'

'He was the right spit of the picture in the paper.'

'Did you see him acting strangely?'

'I don't watch my neighbours day and night. Not like some around here. I saw him if he was coming or going at the same time as me. That's all.'

'Okay. Thank you for all of this. Like I said, the team is dealing with a large number of calls from the public. While they will get in touch as soon as they can, please don't be concerned if it takes a couple of days.'

'A couple of days? Didn't you hear what I said? The Barrel Man has been living next door to me.'

'Unfortunately, you're the fourth person I've spoken to who believes he's living nearby.'

'Well, I don't know what they're on about. He's been here the whole time.'

'Thank you for calling this in. My colleagues will be in touch soon. Goodbye.'

'Right. Bye.'

BEEP.
Call incoming. Caller number one of seventeen.
Call connected at 11:47.

'Hello, you're through to the police information centre at Southampton station. Do you know the case number your call is in reference to?'

'It's that barrel one. I saw him. Just now. Down at Lymington car ferry.'

'Please make sure you're at a safe distance, then tell me in as much detail as possible what you saw.'

Gabe

Jordan Haines lived a handful of streets from Tyler, but his home couldn't have given a more different impression. Sun-parched weeds stretched to my knees either side of the uneven front path. Yellowing net curtains hung in the downstairs windows, the glass greyed by countless lashings of salt-tinged rain.

We'd stopped at a chip shop between Jordan and Tyler's homes. We couldn't be sure it was the one both young men worked at but we'd attempted to make contact with the owners regardless. No one answered the door or the phone and we couldn't see much through the smudged windows.

I pressed Jordan's doorbell. A moment later, thumping footfalls preceded the off-white front door swinging open. Jordan's hair was longer than when I'd last seen him at Karl Biss's trial, the greasy blond strands tied into a bun on top of his head. He'd paired battered jeans with a T-shirt proclaiming him an employee of *The Cod Father*. We'd got the right shop, then. A faint whiff of batter joined the peppery stink of his neighbours' bins in the warm air.

His narrow face settled into a hard frown. 'What are you doing here? Mum told the other one she didn't want to press charges.' I'd forgotten how unusually high Jordan's voice was. It didn't fit with his tough man persona. Although he seemed less tough now than he'd attempted to be during the hunt for Melanie Pirt's killer. More worn down.

'Press changes for what?' I asked.

Beside me, Juliet tucked her hands into her trouser pockets and examined the peeling posters for local musicals in next-door's window. She might be doubly annoyed an interview she deemed unnecessary was taking a detour but she was at least professional enough to endure it in silence.

Jordan eyed her warily. 'You're not here about what happened to Mum?'

'What happened to your mum?' I nudged.

'I wasn't here. She says she fell down the stairs.' His jaw jutted and his eyes snapped to me. 'But we all know what really happened, don't we?'

From the first time we'd stepped inside Jordan's home, it was clear something was drastically wrong with their family dynamic. Jordan's father lashed out at his wife, apparently while his son was absent so that there would be no witness. Without his mother's testimony, we were powerless to act.

'Is your mum okay?' I asked.

Jordan blinked rapidly. 'She's healing. Actually, I need to sort her out before I head to work. What do you want?'

He leant against the door frame. We weren't being invited inside. I wasn't disappointed. A front step wasn't the perfect place to gather information but, even when Jordan's father was absent, the atmosphere of their home was oppressive.

I pulled my notepad from my pocket. 'Can you tell us your relationship to Tyler Jenkins?'

Jordan's eyebrows jumped up his forehead. 'We're mates. Work at the chippy together sometimes, but we've known each other since school. Tyler's always been good to me, came with me to Mel's funeral and helped me get the chippy job.'

That explained my flicker of recognition at the photos in Tyler's room. He must have been one of the crowd of youths surrounding Jordan at his girlfriend's memorial.

'Is Tyler in trouble?' Jordan's knuckles whitened at his sides.

'Why would you assume he's in trouble?' Juliet spoke for the first time.

Jordan licked his lips. 'Why else would you be here?'

'Do you know about anything that might land Tyler in trouble with the police?' I tapped my pencil on top of my pad.

'Not much.' Jordan's chest rose with a sigh. 'That's the truth, I promise. Tyler has tried to chat to me a few times about ways to make quick money. He knows I'm saving up. I want to get Mum out of here.' He frowned. 'Tyler was trying to be helpful, but I couldn't get mixed up in any illegal shit. I wouldn't be able to help Mum at all if I was in prison.'

'Do you know how Tyler makes his quick money?' Juliet pressed.

Jordan shook his head, his bun flopping. 'He's a good mate. When I told him I wasn't interested, he didn't push.'

Tyler's respect for Jordan's wishes was admirable, but it would have been more helpful for our investigation if he'd been determined to drag his friend down.

'We've not been able to locate Tyler,' I said. 'Can you think of anywhere he would go other than his home and the chip shop?'

'Not really. Tyler's a good mate but we don't hang out much outside work. I've got other odd jobs and he's off doing whatever.' Jordan scratched the back of his head. 'Maybe a month ago we got drunk at some random pub. Can't remember the name.'

'Has Tyler ever mentioned Zara Everett?' I asked. Since Jordan didn't know much about Tyler's illegal activities this was a long shot, but it was better to ask and be disappointed than leave a thread untugged.

Jordan's eyes widened. 'The woman who died on the Dunlow Estate?'

'How do you know about that?' Juliet straightened, more focused on Jordan than at any other point of the discussion.

'It's in the news.' Jordan's brows lowered as he and Juliet stared at one another. 'Once you get past everything to do with that barrel psycho, it's there.'

I dropped my notepad.

Face burning, I bent to pick it up. My heart thumping, I struggled to think of a question to move the interview on before

Jordan realised or remembered there was a link between me and the bad man.

'You didn't hear about Zara's death before it was reported on the news?' Juliet likely didn't know she was swooping to my rescue. Her obliviousness didn't make me less grateful.

'No.' Jordan shuffled, his bare toes dragging on the fibres of a welcome mat. 'I keep an eye on things over there. Don't know why. It's not like it will bring Mel back.'

Jordan wasn't the first person to take repeatedly illogical actions due to grief. My mum followed stories of missing children obsessively, even though it deepened the gaping wound in her chest.

'Tyler never mentioned Zara?' I clarified, sufficiently recovered to re-enter the conversation. My hand was clammy around my pencil.

'No.' Jordan smirked. 'Tyler's often got a girl on the go, but he's never—'

He was cut short by the creak of floorboards. He whipped around, inadvertently pushing the door wider.

Jordan's mum stood at the top of the stairs. Loose pyjamas swamped her slender frame. One bandaged arm pressed tight to her ribcage. The light was dim inside the house but the dark bruising across her forehead and cheek was unmissable.

'Jordan?' Her soft voice carried in the sudden quiet. 'You alright, love?'

'I'm fine, Mum.' Jordan's words were gentle in a way they never were when directed towards me and Juliet. 'Go back to bed. I'll bring up some tea in a minute.'

His mum shuffled out of sight. Jordan's face was pulled into tight lines when he turned back to us. His eyes met Juliet's, then darted to the ground.

'One more question before we go,' I said. 'Was Tyler interested in the first fire on the Dunlow Estate?'

'The one that fucked up the manor?' Jordan shook his head, shifting his weight. 'We talked about it when it first happened. Nothing since then though.'

'We'll let you get on.' I raised a smile, sure Jordan would appreciate being left to tend to his mum and Juliet would be pleased to end an interview that had done nothing to progress our case. 'If you hear from Tyler, please let us know.'

'Sure.' Jordan stepped back.

'I hope your mother feels better soon,' Juliet said.

Jordan didn't reply before closing the door.

Juliet didn't speak again as we walked to her car. There was no way to broach the subject of Jordan's living situation without it being far too obvious I was fishing for information about her own. Juliet had once likened herself to the young man, but her shields would come slamming down if I asked if things with her husband were difficult. I had to hope that whatever had previously caused Juliet to avoid home was in the past. She'd never come into work visibly injured and she certainly spent much more time with her family since she'd moved out to Eastleigh. Surely extra time with her daughters was a good thing.

'Can you email Maddy?' Juliet asked as we climbed into her car. 'We need a poster sorted for Tyler.'

'Yeah. Sure.' I should have thought of that myself. I could blame the fact I was usually the driver while Juliet tapped at her phone, but that was a lie I couldn't even tell myself.

Tyler was suspect number one and I needed to focus on that. Juliet probably wasn't ruminating on how Jordan's home life reflected hers and neither should I. If I wanted to prove I was fit to work, I couldn't let anything distract me from finding Zara's killer.

POLICE APPEAL – HAVE YOU SEEN THIS MAN?

Police are looking for the man in the attached images. They wish to speak to him regarding several incidents of arson and theft reported across Southampton and the New Forest. Police also wish to speak to him about the recent death of a young woman.

The man is White, 18 years old, slim build and average height, dyed blue hair, last seen wearing a light grey tracksuit, with several eyebrow piercings.

If you know this man's whereabouts or recognise the images attached/description, please call the number below and quote the case number.

Police ask that members of the public do not approach this man.

Call connected at 13:12.

'Hello, this is Detective In—'

'You need to come over here.'

'Who is this?'

'Stanley Cooper. The bloke you wrongly arrested.'

'Right. What can I do for you, Mr Cooper?'

'You can come to my house and clear the louts from my garden.'

'There's someone in your garden now?'

'Yes. A whole gang of them. They're bloody wrecking the place.'

'Okay. I'll send a unit over.'

'These yobos have decided to take the law into their own hands. They don't accept I had nothing to do with that kiddie dying.'

'Did they say that to you?'

'They've been shouting all kinds of things. Calling me a paedo. A kid killer.'

'I'm sorry about that, Mr Cooper. I'll make sure someone is assigned to monitor your home until the conclusion of this case.'

'That's not going to do much good, is it? They'll just wait until you've given up trying to find the actual guy who did it, then go back to harassing me.'

'We're following strong leads, Mr Cooper. We're closer than ever before to finding Max's killer.'

'I hope you're not full of hot air.'

From: Canada Lewis
canada.lewis@groveacademy.sch.uk
To: Gabriella Martin **gabriella.martin@mit.gov.uk**
CC: Juliet Stern **juliet.stern@mit.gov.uk**
Date: **7 August, 13:27**
Subject: **Alumni surnames**

Detective Martin,

Sorry for the delay in replying – I don't check my emails much over the summer holidays!

Looking at the time when Benedict Hogan was a student here, there are several options for who may have been his friends from the list you sent over, as they were quite popular names in those cohorts. Not a problem I can sympathise with!

James:
- Lester (same year as Benedict)
- Chime (two years below)
- Yeller (two years below)
- Stone (three years below)

Thomas:
- Chrome (same year as Benedict)
- Wright (one year below)
- Umbridge (one year below)
- Hater (three years below)

Neil:
- Nolan (same year as Benedict)
- Osbourne (two years below)

Brian:
- O'Hart (same year as Benedict)
- Allan (same year as Benedict)
- Inker (two years below)

I hope this is helpful! I'll make sure to check my emails over the next few days, so just let me know if there's anything else you need.

Have a lovely rest of your day,

Canada

Gabe

Back at the station, Juliet and I dove deep into Zara's Instagram to see if we could unearth a connection between her and Tyler. We'd found nothing, but examining her posts confirmed Chase's story about Zara's unexpected change of plans. She often playfully moaned about how long the hiking collages took to make, claiming she loved the hours spent playing with her calligraphy pens and sparkly glue gun. If she hadn't planned to head east of the city, it seemed strange she would begin the laborious process of creating a board for that hike.

Juliet printed off the messages between Zara and Paloma, which suggested Zara had kept her change of heart from her boyfriend. Perhaps she'd been keeping her options open, had only decided where to go after she set off.

'I know Tyler is our main suspect, and for good reason.' I stepped back from pinning a picture of Zara's incomplete collage to the wall. 'But why wouldn't Zara tell Chase where she was actually headed unless there was a problem between them?'

Juliet scrunched her nose at her computer. The skin of her forehead had been permanently wrinkled since we'd started working through Zara's Instagram. Juliet wasn't a luddite, but she couldn't comprehend the impulse to splash so much of life on the Internet for all to see. Even I'd wearied of Zara's longer posts. She seemed determined to detail every thought she had whilst walking alone. Maybe it didn't feel so lonely when constantly drafting missives to her thousands of followers.

'There might have been a problem between them, but the important thing is that Chase claims he had no idea where Zara was and we have no evidence to the contrary,' Juliet said as I sat down heavily at my desk. 'Him being a shitty boyfriend she hid things from is currently providing him with a perfect alibi for her death.'

I nodded and wiggled my mouse. The potential relationship issues between Chase and Zara were a dead-end I needed to stop straying down. My preoccupation wasn't a sign there was something more to Chase and Zara's issues but that my mind struggled to prioritise information worth clinging to over that which needed discarding. A night spent huddled on the floor was taking its toll. My brain strained, my eyelids rough with each blink.

On auto-pilot, I checked my emails. Benedict's state school had replied. I scrolled through the list of surnames, dreading making contact with each person.

'Oh.' I sat up, then clicked on the database and typed frantically.

'What is it?' Juliet's eyes remained on her computer screen.

'One of the surnames Benedict's old school sent back.' I waited for the page to load. 'It's the same as Chase's.'

Juliet looked up. 'Coincidence?'

'Nope.' Information flooded my screen. 'Chase Nolan has a brother called Neil who may have started fires with Benedict Hogan as a teen.'

I rubbed my forehead, struggling to sort through the possible implications. Was it a clear indication Chase could be guilty, or did it further implicate Benedict?

Juliet clicked her mouse and our printer whirred to life. She jumped up and brought the paper over to me. 'What are the odds Benedict started fires with Chase's brother, then just happened to bump into a future arson victim years later?'

Juliet had printed one of Zara's Instagram posts from two years ago. A group of sweaty faced men and women wearing matching bright orange T-shirts grinned at the top of a hill. Zara's familiar smile stood out near the middle. Benedict had slung a sun-burned arm around her shoulder. Chase posed at the edge of the group, his dreadlocks in an elaborate braid.

'We need to talk to Benedict again.' I wasn't sure why he would have told us about his previous brush with fire if he had anything to do with Zara's death, but his connection to both her and Chase's brother couldn't be ignored.

'Chase first.' Juliet tapped her finger on a clear space on my desk. For once, it wasn't littered with biscuit crumbs. 'Let's bring him in and ask about his brother, see if we can make contact with Neil as well. Then we'll have something concrete to throw at Benedict.'

My desk phone rang. I nodded absently, eyes on the familiar number scrolling across the pixilated screen. Heart sinking, I grabbed the receiver.

Call connected at 14:04.

'Mum? Is everything alright?'

'Yes, darling. I wanted to check you're okay. I couldn't get through on your mobile so thought I'd try your work number.'

'Oh, yeah. I lost it last night.'

'Did something happen?'

'No. I just misplaced it.'

'How are you?'

'I'm fine.'

'I read in the news that you saw a picture of the bad man. I'm sure it was helpful to the investigation, but that must have been hard.'

'It was fine. How are you? And Dad?'

'Oh, I'm alright. Everyone at church has been really kind. A couple of people brought over meals.'

'That's nice.'

'Dad is a bit down today.'

'Why?'

'He got another call from your friend Paul. Nothing unpleasant, but he wanted to check Dad didn't know the man in the picture. Dad always thought that if the bad man was ever discovered, it would mean he was finally free from suspicion. It's made him sad that it's not panned out like that.'

'I guess he doesn't want to talk to me about it?'

'He's out at the allotment at the moment, love. I'll see if he wants to call when he gets home.'

'Don't worry about it, Mum. We both know you'd be wasting your breath. You can tell him from me that I'll have a word with Paul. Tell him to back off.'

'Dad won't want you to do that. Gabriella, you know better than us that your friend is just doing his job. He can't leave Dad alone to spare our feelings.'

'Maybe. Look, I've got to go.'

'Send me a text when you find your mobile.'

'I will.'

'Love you, darling.'

'Love you too. Tell Dad I love him.'

'Of course.'

You have one new voicemail. Voicemail left today at 2:10 p.m.

'Hello, this is Detective Inspector Juliet Stern. I need to speak with Neil Nolan as soon as possible concerning the death of Zara Everett on the Dunlow Estate in the New Forest. Please give me a call back on this number any time before five, or call Southampton station and leave a message. Thank you.'

Call connected at 14:17.

'Hi. Who is it?'

'Hello, this is Detective Inspector Juliet Stern. Is this Paloma Robins?'

'Yeah. What do you want?'

'I wanted to clarify a couple of points with you. Is now a good time?'

'It's fine. Whatever.'

'You knew Zara was headed into the New Forest instead of hiking out eastwards from Southampton. Did she give you any indication why she would have kept this information from her boyfriend?'

'I told you before; Chase knew exactly where Zara was headed. I don't know why he's lying to you, other than because he's shady as fuck, but he is.'

'Why didn't Zara tell her Instagram followers where she was going?'

'Because the bulk of people are lovely, but there are serious whack jobs out there too. Zara didn't need some rando turning up while she was hiking alone. She may not have taken all the precautions I do, but she at least didn't invite the crazy in with open arms.'

'Would Zara have kept the truth about where she was hiking from Chase because she didn't want him to follow her?'

'She literally talked to him about everything. I might see him for what he really is, but my girl was blind to the truth. She wouldn't have hidden it from him because she thought he was perfect in every way.'

'Chase said he believes you might have claimed his and Zara's relationship wasn't perfect because you were jealous. He thinks you felt upset because he picked Zara over you.'

'That. Fucker.'

'It's not true?'

'Of course it's not fucking true. I don't know when Chase decided every woman in the world must want him, but I didn't get the fucking memo. Self-obsessed prick.'

'I see. One more question. Zara shared a post two years ago of a charity group hike. A man called Benedict Hogan is in one of the pictures. Do you know him?'

'Hold on. I'm having a look. I remember I couldn't go on that hike. I'd sprained my ankle the weekend before. Which one is he?'

'The dark-haired gentleman standing next to Zara.'

'He doesn't look familiar. But then, he's got that airbrushed look loads of guys who say they love hiking have, even if they only ever break out their boots when there's a photo op.'

'Did Zara speak to you about Benedict Hogan?'

'Na. Zar didn't chat about any guy but Chase. She was loyal. Shame she put her trust in someone who didn't deserve it.'

Gabe

As we walked along the short corridor to the informal meeting rooms, I pushed away lingering sparks of outrage. My phone call with Mum had been brief, but anger had burned through me as she spoke. Dad endured too much already every time the bad man resurfaced. Paul should have known better than to poke him when he was down. Maybe Mum was right and Paul was just doing his job, but I'd need a day or two before I could chat to him without an urge to kick and shove rising up.

We'd elected not to meet Chase in a formal interview room. He wasn't under arrest and we thought ousting him from his natural habitat might be enough to discomfit him. We wanted him on the back foot, where he was much more likely to slip up and reveal anything he was hiding.

His skin was pasty under meeting room two's glaring fluorescent lights, the roots of his dreadlocks brown with accumulated sweat.

'Mr Nolan.' Juliet and I sat down opposite him on a boxy sofa. She placed a Dictaphone on a scuffed table and rattled off the information for an informal interview. 'Thank you for coming in to speak to us.'

'Call me Chase.' He cringed as I opened my notepad, but didn't express unhappiness over anything but his name. His legs were thrown wide, his back slumped. He didn't seem overly bothered by the recording or change of scenery. 'I was happy to come in, but I don't know what else you want from me. I've told you everything I know.'

I wasn't sure that was true. Something about Chase sent alarm bells ringing. I didn't know if that was because of the chance he'd been involved in his girlfriend's death or his potential capacity to wear down those he claimed to love.

There was a third option; alarms already blared so loudly in my brain that it was difficult to distinguish between innocence and guilt. I was on high alert for incoming threats. Chase wouldn't stop feeling like one until we found Zara's killer.

Juliet's smile might have seemed warm to anyone who didn't know her. 'Certain details have come to light that we wanted to discuss with you. Have you ever met a young man named Tyler Jenkins?'

We'd been unable to uncover a link between Zara and the petty criminal. The blank look on Chase's faced suggested he wasn't about to provide one either.

'No. Should I have?'

I flipped open the file on the sofa beside me and passed Chase a picture of Tyler. His smile was wide, his eyebrow piercings glinting. 'Do you recognise him?'

Chase examined the picture, then handed it back. 'Never seen him before.'

That didn't mean Zara and Tyler were strangers too. Chase had been in the dark about the direction of her latest hike. Perhaps she'd been meeting Tyler secretly as well.

Turning to the file, I pulled out a copy of the messages between Zara and Paloma. Chase's jaw tightened as he scanned them.

'These are private communications between Zara and Paloma in the weeks before she left your home on the third of August.' Juliet's smile was still in place, but her eyes were sharp. 'They show Zara's clear intention to hike through the New Forest, not head east of the city. Do you have any idea why Zara wouldn't have told you about her changed route?'

'I have no idea, okay?' Chase thrust the printed messages at me. 'For some reason, which we're never going to figure out, my girlfriend lied to everyone except Paloma bloody Robins about where she was hiking. You saw the board. Zara had been talking about the route east for weeks. I honestly don't know why she would have changed her mind or why she didn't tell me.'

The papers rustled as I shifted them into a neat pile and slotted them back into the file. I didn't know if Juliet noted the distinct lack of grief in Chase's outburst. He didn't wish his girlfriend had told him the truth so that he could have kept her safe, or wonder if he could have persuaded her to stick to her original plan if she'd been honest with him.

That didn't mean he was guilty. Chase wasn't a particularly verbose man. He could just be closed off, unwilling to share any layers of his grief with us.

'Paloma has refuted your claim that she was jealous about your and Zara's relationship.' Juliet gave no indication whether her mind was travelling down the same routes as mine. 'She said your relationship was strained, even if Zara wouldn't have admitted it.'

Chase rocked his head back, showcasing the patchy beard continuing under his chin. 'I don't know why you're listening to a thing Paloma says.' He straightened and spread his hands. 'I swear I'm not one of those men who thinks every girl must be into him. Paloma was gagging for it before I started dating Zara. She was gutted when we got together, no matter what she claims.'

A classic case of he said, she said. I was inclined to believe Paloma.

'I don't know why she's going on about me and Zara,' Chase continued. 'Zara was happy before she died. We both were.' Despite the perfect bliss he claimed, he didn't overtly mourn the drastic change to his life that his girlfriend's death had brought about. His hands flopped to his sides. 'The only reason I can think of for Zara changing her plans without telling me is that she wanted to surprise me. She was like that. Always doing things on the spur of the moment to make me smile.'

He wasn't smiling now. Apart from when he'd thought we were customers, we hadn't seen a positive emotion on his face. Perhaps that was the evidence of grief I'd been searching for. Chase may not have cried or been visibly shaken by his girlfriend's death, but he wasn't happy.

I needed to forcibly direct my thinking away from him. Whether Chase was unfeeling or tamping down his emotions, there were other suspects in the mix who could have killed Zara, who would strike again if I didn't get my act together.

I passed Chase another photo. 'Do you recognise this man?'

He squinted at the photo of Benedict Hogan that we'd mined from Instagram. Most of Benedict's pictures were of foreign beaches and complicated cocktails, but recently smiling selfies of him and Terence had crowded in.

'I think so,' Chase said slowly. 'He's a hiker?'

I handed him the group photo from Zara's Instagram. 'Does this help?'

Chase held a photo in each hand. 'Kind of? I remember he was part of a hike up round Tall Trees for Muscular Dystrophy. I can't tell you his name. I'm not sure I talked to him much.'

'His name is Benedict Hogan,' Juliet said.

Chase's face remained blank, which was beginning to infuriate me. I gripped my pencil, the wood digging into my hand. I had to keep a handle on my fizzing emotions. More than half of them had nothing to do with Chase.

Still, I wanted something other than vague puzzlement and annoyance from him. I wanted my suspicions either confirmed or denied so that I could stop wondering about him.

'Have you been in contact with Mr Hogan since this hike?' I asked, careful to keep my voice level and movements smooth as Chase returned the photos.

'No.'

I wanted to crumple the paper in my hands at his one-word reply. I placed the photos in the folder and tucked my fingers under my thighs. Chase wasn't trying to annoy me. I had to control myself and not let anything beyond this investigation cloud my judgement. Chase might be heartless or just not adept at showing his emotions. Not all men were as open as Ollie.

I swallowed down a pang of sadness. Worrying about my boyfriend was a distraction I didn't need right now. I'd have enough time after this case concluded to work through the mess I'd created when I invited Matt over last night.

'Do you remember meeting Mr Hogan prior to the hike?' Juliet asked.

Chase's bottom lip pressed outwards. 'Don't think so.'

'We believe he was a school friend of your brother's.' Juliet folded one leg over the other, her trouser legs smooth and uncreased. I needed to be more like her – cool and collected. Juliet never let her personal life impact her work. 'Did Neil ever mention him or bring Mr Hogan home?'

Chase's brows lowered. 'Neil never had time for me when we were kids. I didn't know his friends' names. I wasn't allowed to talk to them when they came over, wasn't even allowed to look at them in school.' He breathed deep, wrestling control over years-old resentment. 'I don't remember that guy from back then.'

'Neil hasn't mentioned Mr Hogan recently?' I asked.

A flash of anger crossed Chase's face, but was quickly smothered. I wondered if he disliked displaying emotion around us specifically or if he was this closed off with everyone.

'No. Neil visited a couple of weeks ago. He lives up in Yorkshire now with his girlfriend. Mum and Dad insisted we go out for Sunday lunch. All Neil talked about was their new house and his job.'

Asking more about that meal wouldn't help our investigation, but the temptation to prod at a subject that obviously caused Chase disquiet was strong. I wanted to break open his emotionless shell, see what was lurking underneath.

'Do you have any idea what Neil and his friends did for fun while at secondary school?' Juliet asked. Perhaps she wasn't interested in Chase's lack of emotion. If Juliet was ever questioned about the death of a loved one, she wouldn't be anything other than a blank slate.

Perhaps I needed to allow Chase the same benefit of the doubt I'd give her. Not everyone wore their emotions on their sleeves. That didn't make them guilty.

'I don't know,' Chase said. 'Neil didn't spend a lot of time at home. Probably out drinking and stuff.'

'Did he ever mention playing with fire?' I asked.

Chase's eyebrows quirked. 'Why would he mention that?'

'We have reason to believe Mr Hogan and your brother set fires in a number of estate outbuildings while at secondary school,' I said. 'There have also been several fires across Southampton and the New Forest in the past two weeks.' Ever since his brother's visit.

Chase's eyes flicked to the photos of Benedict at the top of the open file beside me. 'I don't think that can be true. Neil didn't have friends like him.'

He didn't comment on the timeline of his brother's visit and the fires. It didn't feel like evasion, more that the events weren't inextricably linked in his head.

'Like him, how?' Juliet asked.

'My brother's changed his act now, but at school he was a proper lad.' Chase's mouth pinched. 'He wouldn't have been mates with anyone he thought was better than him. I don't remember much about Hogan, but his posho voice would have put Neil off.'

Chase's brother hadn't answered his phone before this interview. There was a chance Neil had nothing to do with the fires Benedict set in his youth. It could be a strange turn of fate that Chase's sibling was at school at the same time as Benedict, a man who engaged in arson in his youth, and years later Chase's girlfriend died in a fire.

Juliet glanced at me, then grabbed the Dictaphone. She stood from the unevenly stuffed sofa. 'That's all our questions for now.'

Chase and I followed her lead. I stepped across to hold the door open for him. 'Please rest assured we're doing everything we can to find out what happened to Zara.'

Despite my reservations, I didn't want Chase to worry he was being unfairly targeted or that we were so preoccupied with him we weren't considering anyone else. That was a fear my family had lived with for too long; detectives zeroed in on my dad again and again while the bad man walked free.

Whether my meagre promise meant anything to Chase was hard to tell. His face remained stubbornly blank as he walked out of the room.

Ollie the Hottie. Sent 15:28.

> Hi Alice. I've arrived home and found Gabe's phone here. I know you don't want to be the one to tell her I'm back but can you encourage her to come home as soon as she can? I want to make sure she's okay. Thanks x

Detective Sergeant Nicole Stewart: Witness statement recorded with the permission of the interviewee on Thursday 7th August at 3:31 p.m. This interview is being conducted by myself, Detective Sergeant Nicole Stewart. The interviewee is Meridith Coates and this interview is taking place at her home in Oak Hill Holiday Park. This interview is concerning a possible sighting of a gentleman of interest in the investigation into the murders of Max Powrie and Barnabas Martin, among others. Ms Coates, thank you for making time to speak to me today.

Meridith Coates: No trouble at all, love. And please call me Merry.

DS Nicole Stewart: Thank you, Merry. You already explained this on the phone to my colleague, but can you please tell me why you believe the man who stayed in the caravan next to yours is the man we're interested in?

Meridith Coates: Because he's the exact spit of him. As soon as I saw the paper, I knew.

DS Nicole Stewart: Did you speak to the man?

Meridith Coates: Nothing beyond the normal hellos and goodbyes when we were coming and going. There are two groups of people here. For some of us, the caravans are our homes. For others, they're here for a few weeks and then they clear off. There's not much point chatting to anyone until they've been around for a while.

DS Nicole Stewart: Do you remember any details about the gentleman that would help us identify him?

Meridith Coates: Can't Sharon give you his details?

DS Nicole Stewart: Unfortunately, the gentleman paid in cash and the copy of his ID has gone missing.

Meridith Coates: That's damn bad luck. I don't remember much apart from that he had a white van. Never saw him with a kid or a barrel or anything.

DS Nicole Stewart: Can you remember the van's number plate? Or if there was anything distinctive about the vehicle?

Meridith Coates: Not a chance I'd remember the number plate. I have enough trouble with my own. The van was a bit older. Maybe. There was a scratch along one side. Looked like someone had tried to paint over it but they'd done a bad job.

DS Nicole Stewart: Okay. That's good to know. Did you ever see the gentleman speaking to anyone else on the site?

Meridith Coates: No. Not that I'd notice, mind. I didn't keep tabs on him or nothing. Shame I'm not a nosy parker, really. I could have been more helpful.

DS Nicole Stewart: You've already been incredibly helpful. I can't say for certain that the gentleman who stayed next door is the man we're looking for, but he is someone we would like to speak to and the information you've given gets us a step closer.

Meridith Coates: You're not certain, but I bloody am. I was living next to a kiddie killer and had no idea.

Gabe

I vaguely remembered the interior of Benedict's spacious terraced house from my frantic search after Artie was taken months ago. I'd believed Terence was involved, when really his strange behaviour was due to hiding his growing depression.

Juliet and I followed Benedict into a bright kitchen. We took a seat at a dining nook overlooking a square garden while he made drinks. It seemed to be a calling card of the well-off – a dining room for when they were feeling fancy and another table they used for meals the rest of the time.

His hands fluttering, Benedict set a cream kettle on a flaming gas ring then arranged a bowl of sugar cubes and a jug of milk on the table. His dark green shirt flattered his slim frame, his black hair pushed back from his smooth forehead. He explained, as he readied a pot of tea neither Juliet nor I had asked for, that Leo was at work and Terence was out on one of his long walks.

Benedict didn't seem to have absorbed the information that we were here to speak to him, not Terence or his younger brother. It wasn't the same posh insistence shared by Terence and his father that the police showing interest in them was preposterous. Benedict seemed genuinely confused that we would want to speak to him a second time. I wasn't aware enough to figure out if it was an act to appear innocent.

'I really have shared everything that could possibly be helpful,' Benedict repeated as he carried the teapot over to the table and sat on the cushioned bench opposite me and Juliet. 'Please ask whatever questions you need to, but I'm not sure I'll have anything new to say.'

I opened the thin file I'd set on the table. 'I don't know if you've been keeping up-to-date with the case, but we've identified the woman killed in the fire.' I slid a photo around the teapot. 'Her name was Zara Everett.'

The skin around Benedict's eyes creased with sadness. 'How terrible.'

'Do you recognise her?' Juliet glared at the teapot. She'd once described tea as warmed pond water. I suspected she would take the opportunity to throw any Benedict gave her out of the open window beside her.

'I can't say I do.' Benedict placed a strainer over my cup and poured a rich brown stream from the pot.

I slid a second picture next to the first. 'How about now?'

He set down the pot. Juliet's shoulders lowered as he picked up the photo from the group hike.

'Gosh. I must have met her then.' Benedict's dark eyes danced between the sweaty faces. 'I feel awful that I don't remember her. I do recall feeling terribly unfit. I signed up because my father has Muscular Dystrophy. I thought the hike would be an easy way to raise funds, but I could barely finish. My legs ached for days afterwards.'

'Did you speak to anyone during the hike?' I asked.

Benedict put down the picture and resumed pouring tea. Juliet's eyes narrowed as her cup filled.

'We all chatted as a group to begin with, but then it became clear some of us were vastly unsuited to a full day of walking. We fell behind.' Benedict picked up a sugar cube with a tiny pair of tongs. 'One of the organisers hung back with us so that we wouldn't get lost. That man.'

Benedict pointed the tongs at Chase.

'Do you remember if he spoke to you about anything in particular?' Juliet settled her hands around her steaming cup, giving the impression its presence in her vicinity wasn't wholly unwelcome.

'Honestly? All I really remember was what a miserable day I had.' Benedict poured milk, then angled the handle of the jug between me and Juliet. 'We look jolly in this picture, but I just wanted to go home and have the longest bath.'

Ollie would approve. I added a cube of sugar and milk to my tea, then sipped. The liquid wasn't nearly as warming as my boyfriend's arms would have been around me. I didn't know if that would be an option once I told him what I'd tried to do.

'Did you have contact with Zara or this gentleman after the hike?' Juliet asked.

Benedict shook his head. 'They called afterwards, I believe to organise another outing, but I'm afraid to say I ignored them. I wasn't putting myself through that again, no matter what the cause.'

I replaced Zara's picture with one from Neil Nolan's LinkedIn account. 'Do you know this man?'

Benedict regarded the photo over the rim of his cup. 'He looks familiar.'

Juliet and I waited. I sipped my tea. Juliet tapped one long finger on her cup. Birds sang outside, flitting between feeders.

'Is he one of the boys I told you about?' Benedict asked.

'He is,' Juliet confirmed. 'His name is Neil Nolan.'

The surname didn't cause a reaction. I moved the group photo from the hike closer to Neil's professional portrait.

'This is Chase Nolan.' I pointed at the man Benedict said had stayed with the struggling hikers. 'Neil's younger brother.'

Benedict's eyes widened and he set down his cup. 'Oh.'

'Did you know Neil and Chase were brothers?' I asked.

'No.' He swallowed. 'Neither of them mentioned the other.'

'Can you see why we would be interested in whether you've had further contact with Chase or Zara?' Juliet prompted.

'I can,' Benedict said slowly. 'But I can honestly say I haven't. And I haven't spoken to Neil since the police caught me. We went to the same school for another year, but he and his friends wanted nothing more to do with me.'

'Neil visited Southampton a couple of weeks ago.' I picked up the pictures and placed them back in the file. 'You didn't meet up with him?'

A lock of hair fell over Benedict's brow as he shook his head. 'I didn't. I had no idea he was here, haven't spoken to him in years. I wouldn't know how to get in touch with him if I wanted to.'

Benedict volunteering the information about his youthful arson suggested it was unlikely he was involved in the recent fires, and other things stacked in his favour too. He'd committed a crime as a miserable and impressionable teen but, as a grown man, he had a perfect life he wouldn't risk for a strange thrill. I didn't think Benedict would hurt Terence by destroying anything even nominally his or his mother's.

But once someone committed arson, they were far more liable to do it again. And there was that flicker of anger at Dunlow every time he was mentioned.

'Have you heard from Terence's father since the fire?' I asked.

Benedict's brows lowered, his jaw tightening. 'No. He doesn't seem to care how this has affected his sons.'

There it was: the reason we couldn't discount him. Benedict had experience of starting fires and his alibi was corroborated by a man known to lie to the police. With a motive of strong dislike towards Dunlow, Benedict had to stay in the running despite his mild manners and the artless care he displayed for others.

I slid a final photo across the table. 'Do you know this man?'

Benedict frowned at the picture from Tyler's birthday party. 'I don't. I'm sorry.'

Juliet flinched, then pulled her phone from her pocket. 'We need to go.'

I gathered the photos into the file, then trailed behind her to the front door.

'Thank you for your time,' I said, as Juliet strode down the neat path.

Benedict held onto the door handle. 'I'm sorry I couldn't be more helpful.'

I nodded, then hurried after Juliet. 'What's going on?'

She smirked as she climbed into her car. 'Nothing. I just didn't want to drink the tea.'

A huff of laughter surprised me. I couldn't remember the last time I'd smiled in the past few days.

My heart fluttered and I shook my head. Panic was a stupid reaction to laughing. It didn't matter if I let my guard down. The things I feared had ended long ago.

'Do you believe Benedict?' I pulled on my seatbelt, ignoring my thrumming chest.

Juliet rested her hands on the steering wheel. 'I'm not convinced he's as clueless as he wants us to believe.'

'Why would he have told us about the historic arson if he had anything to do with the recent ones?' I breathed deep through my nose to banish the last vestiges of nerves.

'He could have been getting out ahead of it?' Juliet turned the key in the ignition. 'Better to play dumb and innocent right from the start than be caught unawares.'

'Especially if he'd planned to lash out at Dunlow. He would also have had time to practise his confession,' I mused as Juliet checked her mirrors. 'The connection between the Nolan brothers and Benedict is strange too.'

'Strange, or a clue we shouldn't ignore.'

From: Paul Willis **paul.willis@mit.gov.uk**
To: James Knowles **james.knowles@police.gov.uk**
CC: Nicole Stewart **nicole.stewart@mit.gov.uk**, Leonard Dunlow **leonard.dunlow@police.gov.uk**
Date: **7 August, 16:29**
Subject: **Operation Mercury – forensic match**

James,

Have you had any joy with the CCTV footage from around the entrance to Oak Hill? We've just had the forensics back from the caravan and there are several matches for DNA material and fingerprints left on the barrel containing Max Powrie and the warehouse where Gabe was found.

I probably don't have to tell you this is the closest we've ever gotten to catching him. Scour every clip for a white van. We need the number plate and an idea of where he headed after he left.

I'll send someone to the chippy soon. It's going to be a late one.

Paul

Regulation of Investigatory Powers Act 2000 – section 32

REQUEST FOR INTRUSIVE SURVEILLANCE

REQUESTING OFFICERS: Detective Inspector Juliet Stern and Detective Sergeant Gabriella Martin

CASE NUMBER: 17293074

CASE DESCRIPTION: Homicide of Zara Everett and arson of an outbuilding on the Dunlow Estate in the New Forest on the 4th August

INDIVIDUALS FOR SURVEILLANCE: Benedict Hogan and Tyler Jenkins – their home and work addresses are attached

REASON FOR SURVEILLANCE: Zara Everett died in a fire deemed non-accidental on Monday the 4th August, though it is not yet clear whether the arsonist knew Zara was in the building or not.

Benedict Hogan has admitted to setting fires on similar estates as a teenager. Although he claims no knowledge of the fire that killed Zara, he has links to Zara and her boyfriend, Charles Nolan, whose brother, Neil Nolan, was one of a group of young men Benedict committed arson with in his youth. Benedict is also linked to the estate via his partner, Terence Dunlow. We're requesting the use of intrusive surveillance to monitor and record Benedict's movements. The use of such surveillance will allow us to determine Benedict's involvement in this arson and homicide, and the possibility of his continued relationship with Charles and Neil Nolan.

Tyler Jenkins's fingerprints were found on the front door of the torched building and several items inside. His DNA was also found throughout the cottage and on Zara's backpack and face. We have not been able to make contact with him either at home or at his place of work. We would like his home and workplace to be monitored so that we can make contact with him as soon as possible. Items belonging to Zara were found in Tyler's bedroom, which would have been on her person when she entered the Dunlow Estate. Whether Tyler was involved with the fire or not, it is likely he was one of the last people to see Zara alive. It is of the utmost importance we speak with him.

Gabe

I sat back in my chair. 'Are you sure we shouldn't ask for surveillance for Chase as well?'

Juliet frowned at her computer screen. 'A vague sense someone is acting strangely isn't a valid reason to have their every move watched.'

I couldn't seem to articulate anything beyond that. I swivelled to look at the evidence wall. Chase's picture was pinned beside Tyler, Paloma, and Benedict's. Where the others were surrounded by interconnected threads and notes, Chase's had blue lines of twine between Zara's final hiking board and his brother.

'He doesn't have an alibi for the time of the fire,' I offered.

'Not enough,' Juliet muttered.

I turned back to my computer. Juliet and I had debated our next steps when we got back to the station. We agreed we needed to speak to Tyler as soon as possible and watching his home and the chip shop was the best way to achieve that.

Tyler's possible motivations were a mystery. He had to have known Zara was in the cottage, since his DNA was found on her face and he'd taken her valuables. We had to assume she was a stranger to him. It sent chills up my spine that Tyler could have left the building and set it alight, knowing a young woman was sleeping inside.

Juliet was more suspicious of Benedict than me, believing his polite poshness made his anger at Dunlow seem less extreme. There were enough connections between him and the fire to justify surveillance of his movements. We'd floated the idea that Benedict could have been motivated by revenge against his boyfriend's father alongside scratching a pyrotechnic itch, but unless we found concrete evidence to link him to the fire I couldn't see him deviating from his innocent act.

Despite their closeness to Zara, Paloma and Chase had missed out on surveillance. There was no real link between them and fire starting. Paloma was totally annexed from it, while Chase claimed his brother wouldn't have involved him. We were waiting on Neil to confirm he'd ostracised Chase when they were teens. Unless Neil said he'd placed fire starting materials into his younger brother's hands, Angela wouldn't permit surveillance of Chase. She'd have no patience for my theories about him tipping into a murderous rage when Zara defied him by continuing her solo hikes. Angela would note that Chase claimed he didn't know where his girlfriend was and had evidence to back that up, then she'd allocate her finite funds to the case being run out of this station that had to be a priority. Even though it was doomed to fail.

We'd received a report about our four suspects' mobile phones while chatting to Benedict. Apparently all of them had been at home at the time of the fire. The absence of my mobile in my pocket today proved how fallible phone tracking was for confirming movements.

'Fuck's sake,' Juliet hissed.

My head snapped up. I didn't think I'd pissed her off too badly with my insistence that Chase should be watched. Part of the character needed for a detective was the tenacious inability to let go of threads less curious people might. Maybe I needed to learn when my inklings were based on detective instinct or a random attachment formed by my scattered brain.

Juliet wasn't looking across our desks. She glared at her phone, her thumbs jabbing the cracked screen, then stood up.

'I have to go home,' she announced.

'I can finish up here.' I turned my chair to follow her movements as she threw on her jacket and strode to the door. 'There's not much to do. Just admin.'

She paused in the doorway, blocking the view of empty desks. She opened her mouth, then closed it. Her knuckles whitened around her phone.

'Are you alright?' I tried. Juliet rarely tolerated personal questions, even ones that could be easily batted away. I wouldn't stop asking though.

'I'm fine.' Juliet's neat eyebrows lowered. 'Just look after yourself, okay?' Before I could respond to her uncharacteristic concern, she marched out of sight.

A mumble of indistinct voices drifted across the floor. One of them might be male. Hopefully Paul hadn't caught Juliet when she was already in a mood.

I frowned at my clunky desk phone. Actually, I hoped Paul did wander straight into Juliet's war path. That was the least he deserved for upsetting my parents at a time when my family was struggling to hold ourselves together.

'Can I second that motion?' Alice appeared in the doorway, dispelling my dreams of Juliet laying into her fellow detective inspector.

'What motion?' I snapped, then caught myself. It wasn't Alice's fault I felt frayed and bruised. 'Sorry, Al. It's been a long and frustrating day.'

'The motion you look after yourself.' She sauntered into the room, ignoring my waspishness. 'One way of doing that is leaving the station at a thoroughly decent time.'

I held in a cringe. Nothing waited for me at home. I couldn't rest there. It was a place to hide, to spend hours falling into myself to avoid the howling memories I could barely keep at bay.

But I had no good reason to stay here. Tyler was determined not to be found, Benedict was innocent until he proved himself guilty, and my theories around Paloma and Chase were a dead-end. I could shuffle paperwork and answer the emails clogging my inbox, but I'd have to head home in the end. At least if I left now, I'd be a little less exhausted when I came into work tomorrow. Even if I did spend the whole time at home curled up on the floor.

'Fine.' I pushed my chair back and grabbed my keys.

'Good girl.' Alice patted my shoulder.

'You're the worst,' I said as we walked out of the office together. I tried to ignore the blank screens on our way to the lift. My ribs felt too tight as I pictured the frantic activity one floor below.

'I am the definition of the best.' Alice's puffed chest was made more impressive by her stab-proof vest. She jabbed the button for the ground floor. 'You doing alright, Gabe?'

An impossible question to answer. Not without lying or weeping.

For a second, while we waited for the lift, I leant to the side and pressed into Alice's shoulder.

'Thank you for asking,' I murmured as the metal doors slid open.

That was the most I could offer. Alice was loyal and tried to be kind, but I didn't know how to lay out my mess with any but the gentlest hands to catch me.

My heartrate climbed when we stepped into the lift. My stomach swooped as it descended, then promptly jumped up my throat when the doors opened on the sixth floor.

Fear and annoyance collided. It wasn't enough that Paul had harassed my parents. I couldn't even leave work in peace.

But it wasn't Paul who shuffled into the lift. Nicole's eyes were bloodshot, the brown skin around them puffy. She angled herself away from me when the doors closed but the mirrored walls didn't allow for hiding as we glided to the ground floor. Her hands shook as she brushed moisture from her cheeks.

'Nicole?'

'Shit, Gabe.' Her shoulders hunched.

Alice shot me a wide-eyed look as the lift doors opened at reception. She stepped into the space and spread her feet wide, blocking anyone from entering.

I placed a hand on Nicole's arm and coaxed her around. 'What's happened?'

Cold panic slashed through my concern as more tears stole down her face. Anything could have upset her, but the likelihood was that it had something to do with the bad man.

She sniffed. 'You're the last person I should burden with this.'

I swallowed, then hardened the paper-thin walls around my heart. I could summon strength for this. Nicole had never leant on me before. 'You don't need to worry about me.'

Her arm jumped under my hand, her chest heaving with a sob. 'It's just. It was days ago, but I can't stop thinking about Max's autopsy.'

Thick blankness swamped me. I wasn't there for the examination of Barnabas's body, but that didn't stop me from conjuring images. I'd been to enough to imagine what it would have been like. My brother would have looked so small on the metal table.

I couldn't think of that. Couldn't let myself crumble. I gripped Nicole's arm.

'It must have been horrible.'

She nodded, her breathing uneven. I circled my arms around her and she rested her forehead on my shoulder.

My annoyance at Paul and his team dissipated. Working as a detective was a fucking thankless task. Even when we caught guilty parties, we had to live with the intimate knowledge of what they'd done. Paul had been doing his job when he called my dad. When a crime was committed, especially those like the bad man's, the painful ripples extended out to hurt everyone connected to it. Paul was doing the best he could in a shitty situation. Neither he nor his team enjoyed pushing my family to the limit. The evidence of that sobbed in my arms.

'I'll be fine.' In Nicole's words, I heard the lies I told myself. 'Lang and Mei better be ready for the longest cuddle when I get home. There's no way I'm letting go of them until I have to come back here.'

I think I smiled at her as Alice stepped aside and we exited the lift. I think I waved goodbye to them both at the station's side door. I think I held my head high as I walked to my car.

Cold enveloped me despite the lingering warmth of the sun peeking over the tops of the surrounding buildings.

Nicole was headed home to her husband and child, while I would be alone.

A childish part of me stomped and screamed, but I shut it down. It didn't matter how desperately I wanted to recall Ollie from his parents'; it wasn't possible. I'd already been a piss-poor girlfriend by almost sleeping with someone else. I couldn't drag him home after what I'd done.

I climbed into my car and rested my head back. I had to deal with this on my own. If that meant crawling into my hiding place as soon as I got home, so be it. I couldn't let the memories overtake me. I had to work tomorrow and prove I could be useful.

This dark time would pass. Paul would fail to find the bad man, just like all the detectives before him.

Life would return to normal. It had to.

Paloma Robins @WiseGirlHiker. Sent 17:29.

> Chase. Why the fuck have you blocked me on your account?

Zara Everett @SoloHikingGirl. Sent 17:30.

> Leave me alone.

Paloma Robins @WiseGirlHiker. Sent 17:31.

> I'd love to, but I need to know you're not going to spout shit about me to the police again. Back the fuck off before your lies get you in deep shit.

Zara Everett @SoloHikingGirl. Sent 17:31.

> I told them the truth.

Paloma Robins @WiseGirlHiker. Sent 17:32.

> You said I'm obsessed with you. PLEASE.

Zara Everett @SoloHikingGirl. Sent 17:32.

> You're the one who hunted me down after I tried to get away from you.

Paloma Robins @WiseGirlHiker. Sent 17:33.

> Boy, you are delusional. This is the last message you'll get from me. EVER. Stop saying shit to the police about me and we can live our happily separate lives.

Zara Everett @SoloHikingGirl. Sent 17:34.

> You tell yourself that. I don't look forward to chatting to you again when you create some new excuse to talk to me.

Call connected at 17:43.

'Tyler, what the fuck's going on?'

'What the fuck have you been saying about me?'

'What have I said? What are you on about?'

'Mum said the police went to my house. They saw a picture of you and got all excited, and that's when they found my stash.'

'Your stash?'

'Yeah, my—'

'No. Don't fucking tell me. I don't want to know.'

'How did the police know to look under my desk? What did you tell them?'

'Mate. Fuck. Can you hear yourself right now? What the fuck could I have told them? I don't know anything about your fucking stash. Or your desk and whatever. You know the deal. I don't want to know about the shit you get up to because then I don't have to lie for you. I couldn't have told the police nothing because I don't fucking know anything.'

'You haven't blabbed to anyone else about me?'

'I talk to you and Red at the chippy, and Mum at home. You know that. I don't have anyone else to chat to.'

'Alright. Fuck.'

'Don't tell me the details, but you're in trouble, yeah?'

'Fuck tonnes.'

'The police asked me about a woman who died in a fire.'

'Shit. Mate, you have to fucking believe me; I didn't have nothing to do with that. I swear.'

'I believe you. I don't know what shit you get up to, but I know it isn't killing no one.'

'This is fucked up. All I did was—'

'Ty. No. Don't tell me. But I'm going to give you some advice and you can take it or leave it; if you really had nothing to do with that woman's death, talk to the police.'

'What the fuck? Have they told you to get me to turn myself in?'

'What? Fuck no. I've been in this situation before, haven't I? Talking to the police is shit, but hiding makes you look more sus. Tell them what happened and your chances of walking away are much higher. You didn't kill her but someone did. If the police are wasting their time looking for you, then they're not out there finding the fucker who actually did it.'

'Calm down, J.'

'You know why this gets to me.'

'I know, I know. I've got to go.'

'Think about it, Ty. You've got to help find whoever killed her.'

Gabe

I simultaneously did and didn't want to get out of my car. I was desperate to shut the front door of my house and curl into the nook under the stairs. Hemmed in by the soft pressure of Ollie's coats, I wouldn't have to think, wouldn't have to feel, would barely exist. I could spend blissful hours hiding in nothingness.

But such a fugue state had consequences. I couldn't keep sleeping tucked into a corner on a hard floor if I wanted to succeed at work. To function properly as a detective, I needed to rest and eat and find harmony with the haunting memories.

I unbuckled my seatbelt, but didn't make further moves to leave my car. My indecision around what I'd do once I stepped through my front door was maddening. While a primitive part of me longed for the safety that another night of hiding would bring, I didn't know if I could keep allowing myself that escape. Scarily, I didn't know if once I stepped through the door all semblance of choice would be snatched away.

The bad man made me weak. Small. I couldn't fight the impulse to run, even though the need to evade him was long gone.

I took a deep breath, my chest aching, then grabbed my keys from the ignition. I climbed out of the car, my hands shaking as I slammed the door. The evenings stretched at this time of year. Streetlamps barely blinked to life as I walked along the road to mine and Ollie's house, the air thick with salty heat.

My key scratched the metal plate before slotting into the lock. My arms weak, I tugged the handle and pushed.

Into light. Paws scrabbling on wooden floors. Fresh bread and garlic.

My throat constricted as Artie barrelled into my legs. I knelt and pressed my hands into his thick russet fur. His back pulsed with pants as he licked my arms, his pointy ears brushing my face.

I wasn't alone.

'Gabe?'

Ollie's voice unlocked a vault I'd ruthlessly slammed shut the moment Angela said the bad man had struck again. Fortunately, I was already on my knees. They might have buckled if I'd been standing. Grief and pain and lashing anger had been leaking out around the edges of a poorly constructed cage for days. Now, they erupted free.

I bent to press my forehead into Artie's side, my chest heaving with sobs. Heavy footfalls heralded Ollie's approach. He nudged our over-excited Alsatian out of the way and gathered me into his arms. I gripped the back of his T-shirt, my face pressing into the soft fabric.

The familiar smell of his earthy bodywash was a balm, yet it ripped open even more of the broken places inside of me. I wanted to hide in his embrace forever, never emerge to face the brutalities of the world again.

Ollie rubbed my back, his bowed to make up for the height difference between us even when kneeling. I clung to him, my fingers digging into the toned muscles of his sides. He hadn't unlocked just grief over the bad man. Another compelling reason to stay cradled in his arms forever was because then I wouldn't have to tell him what I'd done.

Maybe it was better to confess here, one step inside our home. If Ollie decided he didn't want me around, I wouldn't have far to crawl. I didn't know where I'd go, but I wouldn't force my presence on him.

I made myself push away and wipe my face. Ollie didn't let me go too far. His hands wrapped around my upper arms, his grip sure. I wished I could trace the straight line of his nose, the winding patterns of tattoos across his arms, but I couldn't touch him again until he knew.

'I need to tell you something.' I didn't look him in the eye. I couldn't stand to watch the warm brown darken, concern swamped by rage. 'I invited someone here while you were gone. To sleep with them.'

Ollie stilled, his fingers tightening. 'What?'

Tears spilled down my cheeks. 'Ollie, I'm so sorry.'

'What the fuck, Gabe?' He pushed away from me on his knees, pressing my arms into my chest as he let go. 'I leave for a few days to look after my sick dad and you take that as a chance to cheat on me? What's wrong with you?'

The space between us yawned. I choked out a half-sob and curled into myself, my head lowering until it met cool wood. I braced my arms around my torso. Warm at my side, Artie whined.

'I don't know,' I whispered around gasping breaths. 'I didn't sleep with him. I swear. I couldn't. Everything felt wrong when he kissed me. I couldn't do it.' My chest hurt, but I tightened my arms. 'I just had to make it stop. All the noise. I needed it to stop. I thought I could make it go away. But I couldn't. I'm sorry. I'm so fucking sorry.'

'Gabe.' Warm hands gripped my shoulders, gently forced me upright. 'Shit, I'm sorry. I shouldn't have freaked out.'

I shook my head, crouching into myself as much as possible with Ollie holding me up. 'You should be mad. I didn't do it, but I wanted to. I wanted to forget. I wanted it to stop.' I pressed my fingernails deep into my palms. 'It never fucking stops. But I shouldn't have done that. Shouldn't have tried to. I'm sorry.'

'Gabe, that's enough.' Ollie shuffled closer and unwound my arms from around my chest. He tucked his thumbs into my clenched fists, pressed my hands flat on his thighs. His touch steady, he wiped tears from my cheeks and threaded his fingers through my hair. 'It's okay.'

'It's not okay,' I mumbled, refusing to meet his gaze. 'I tried to cheat on you.'

'But you didn't.' Ollie sighed. 'You said you didn't want to. That you couldn't.'

Fresh tears cascaded over my eyelashes. 'I just needed it to stop.'

Ollie kissed my forehead. The touch felt like forgiveness, pure and cleansing. I reached up and clung to his T-shirt, drawing him into another hug. Artie's tail thumped against the floor.

'We can talk about this in more detail if you need to. Later. When you're not so upset.' Ollie's arms wrapped around me and the blind panic consuming me abated. He didn't want me to leave. I could rest here, at least for a while. 'I'm not cross at you, Gabe. I didn't mean to flip when you told me. It's been a stressful few days.' He held me closer. 'Next time, you need to call me. No matter what else is going on, you need to let me be the person who helps you through the hardest days.'

I swallowed. 'Your dad was unwell. I couldn't call, couldn't make you come home.'

'You could and, next time, you should.' Ollie's voice was firm, his arms strong. 'You are my priority, Gabe. Even if there's other stuff going on, I don't want you facing horrible things alone.'

I sagged into his chest, the final fight abandoning me. I'd thought I'd done the right thing by dealing with the bad man on my own, but I didn't want to. I'd wanted Ollie here, and now he was. My two options for tonight weren't hiding away or fighting my demons alone.

I sniffed. 'How's your dad?' I needed to check. I might have been absent from too much of my life recently, but I still knew Ollie loved his family deeply.

'He's alright.' Ollie huffed. 'According to him, he barely had a stroke. He was outraged a hospital stay was deemed necessary by medical professionals.'

'And you're okay?' I wormed a hand free and pressed into Artie's soft fur at my side.

Ollie pressed his lips to the crown of my head. 'I'm tired, but I'm happy to be home. I missed you. I'm gutted you've been dealing with so much on your own.'

My nostrils blocked, I sucked in a breath through my mouth. 'The bad man is back,' I whispered.

Ollie's arms tightened around me to the point of pain but I welcomed the suffocating squeeze. I was safe in his embrace. No one could steal me away.

'I know, love,' he murmured into my hair. 'I'm so sorry.'

Call connected at 19:54.

'Paul?'

'Ma'am. Sorry to call in the evening, but I need immediate authorisation of surveillance and an on-call armed response team.'

'You've found him?'

'We believe so, ma'am.'

'Talk me through it.'

'I've been looking through CCTV footage with Nicole and Police Constables James Knowles and Leo Dunlow. Leo tracked a white van away from Oak Hill Holiday Park but none of the images captured a clear shot of the driver or number plate. James made contact with local businesses along the route and found a privately owned camera, which gave us the number plate. The car is registered to a man named Owen Westover. He's sixty-one years old, a lorry driver, originally from Northumberland but he's lived all over. He's currently renting a property in the north of the New Forest.'

'You're sure it's him?'

'I can't be certain until we've checked his fingerprints and DNA, but he's currently our strongest suspect. He's the right age to have been active for the last thirty-five years and has moved around in a similar pattern to the killer.'

'Alright. Get the forms over to me and I'll sign off on the teams.'

'Thank you, ma'am.'

'Just tread carefully, Paul. There are a lot of eyes on us. We can't afford another misstep.'

Day 5

Friday, 8 August

INCREASED POLICE ACTIVITY – A GREAT NUMBER OF POLICE OFFICERS AND VEHICLES WERE SEEN LEAVING SOUTHAMPTON STATION THROUGH THE NIGHT…

Scroll.

PUBLIC LEFT GUESSING – AFTER A CALL FOR HELP TO FIND THE BARREL MAN, PLEAS FOR FURTHER INFORMATION ARE LEFT UNANSWERED…

Scroll.

POLICE INCOMPETENCE LANDS MAN IN HOSPITAL – A WRONGFUL ARREST HAS SEEN SOUTHAMPTON PENSIONER PHYSICALLY HARASSED…

Scroll.

You have one new voicemail. Voicemail left today at 8:02 a.m.

'Hey, Leo. It's Teddy. It was a shame we didn't see you before we headed to bed last night. I hope you're not working too hard. Remember, you've got nothing to prove. Anyway, I was wondering if you chatted to Benny before you left this morning? I can't get hold of him and I can't remember if he said he was doing something today. Send me a text if you know where he is, and look after yourself.'

Call connected at 8:30.

'Hello, this is Detective Inspector Paul Willis.'

'Morning, sir. Mahira here. Just calling with an update from the surveillance team in Bramshaw.'

'Any joy?'

'None yet, sir. No one has arrived at the property.'

'Sit tight. He's got to come home some time.'

'We'll have a team changeover and debrief at 9 a.m. We'll call with another update at 9.30 a.m.'

'Thanks, Mahira. Fingers crossed it will be with good news.'

Gabe

I gripped my steering wheel as I pulled into a layby. Juliet and I peered at the tractor driver as they passed, though presumably Juliet had as little idea what Nicolas June looked like as I did.

I'd picked Juliet up from a side road near the station, her jacket thrown over one arm. The sun wasn't yet high in the sky but the day already promised to be scorching. Juliet's cheeks were red as she climbed into my car, which I thought was more likely due to heat rather than any interactions she'd had with journalists lingering outside the station.

I waited for the huge back wheels of the tractor to trundle by, then edged out onto the narrow road. We were on our way through the New Forest to question the farmer who'd called in the fire on the Dunlow Estate. I needed to focus, but my mind kept straying from our case. Not quite in the same way it had for the last few days, though.

Last night, I told Ollie everything about the bad man. All the arguments against sharing the entirety of my past with him were insubstantial compared to the overwhelming relief that, with my boyfriend home, I didn't have to fight the memories alone. Intimate knowledge of the worst experiences of my life hadn't seemed to make me weak in Ollie's eyes. He'd cried with me when I told him how the bad man stole me and my brother away, and cried again when I explained how Barnabas saved me.

We'd slept in our bed and Ollie held me when I woke from grasping nightmares. Part of me had hoped baring my past to my boyfriend would chase them away. An unrealistic dream.

The bad man was too close, had struck too recently, for my nights to pass untroubled by horrifying phantoms.

My heart felt lighter as I drove along another lane, past grazing wild horses. Since Max's body was found, every one of my actions had been performed through heavy sludge. That pressure was gone, my focus back, but my limbs ached as though I'd run for hours the night before.

Juliet hadn't commented on any change in me. She'd been glued to her phone for the whole drive, her hair in a severe ponytail at the nape of her neck. She wore a spotless white blouse paired with dark purple trousers. Her eyes had flicked over my rumpled blue shirt and grey chinos as she'd climbed into my car, but she either didn't care about my appearance or didn't find it too objectionable.

She didn't scrutinise my face for signs of sleepless nights or ask how the investigation to find the bad man was affecting me. I rolled my shoulders as I drove along the lane, checking the sides of the roads for more untethered creatures. Just as openness with Ollie soothed me, so did Juliet's complete lack of interest. She trusted that if I was here, I was ready to do my job. Her faith in me was bolstering.

I slowed when I neared an oncoming cyclist. Their navy tracksuit hood was pulled up, but bright blue curls snuck out from under the fabric. Their bike was black, some kind of mountaineering brand. The packed wicker basket on the front was incongruous.

I squinted at them. Their face was downturned, but one of the piercings on their eyebrow caught the sunlight as they passed.

'Shit.' I slammed on the brakes, then began the laborious process of turning my car around on the narrow lane.

Juliet looked up from her phone, frowning when she realised we were no longer travelling towards Nicolas's farm. 'What's going on?'

'I think Tyler Jenkins just rode past us.' I hauled the wheel to one side as I reversed, then spun it in the opposite direction.

Juliet twisted in her seat to get a better look at the cyclist disappearing down the winding lane. On a different day, when my body wasn't already spent to its limit, I would have jumped out of the car as soon as I recognised Tyler and depended on the element of surprise to catch him before he rode off.

I didn't put on the sirens as I zoomed back along the road. Tyler was the embodiment of a flight risk. To apprehend him, we had to get close enough for Juliet to chase him down.

It would have to be over a short distance. Even unhindered by high heels, Juliet wasn't a runner. Both of us just about passed our yearly fitness checks.

'There's a clearing to the left after the next turning.' Juliet tapped at her phone. 'Could be a car park.'

I wrenched the wheel to the side. The road stretched ahead. Empty.

'Surely we'd be able to see him if he was still on the lane.' I scanned the left side of the road. 'He couldn't have gotten away so quickly.'

'He wasn't that fast.' Juliet glared down the lane, the next twist distant enough that Tyler had to be close by. She pointed to the left, bashing her finger against the window. 'There.'

A single-track lane led into the forest. It didn't look like anyone had driven down it in months. Long strands of grass hissed against the underside of the car as I sped along the narrow trail.

This was our best bet at finding Tyler but, as I drove on and all we passed were tall trees and perplexed horses, doubt crept in. I'd caught a glimpse of the cyclist. It could have been someone else with blue hair. If Tyler was so determined to evade us, returning to the scene of the crime didn't fit.

I was about to suggest I reverse back to the road and we continue on to the farm when the trees opened onto a small clearing. At the far end, a young man with blue hair carried items from the bike's basket to an empty slot in a car boot where a spare tyre would usually reside. It was the modified Ford that Juliet had parked behind outside Tyler's house.

Accelerating, I drove over to the car then turned to block as much of the clearing as possible. The young man straightened as we climbed out of the car, clutching a bulging backpack. He slammed the boot closed.

Recognition flared stronger than in his bedroom. Tyler was definitely one of the youths who had jostled around Jordan at Melanie Pirt's memorial.

Multiple piercings lined up along the outer edge of one defined eyebrow. His eyes were narrowed, his shoulders hunched. His light brown skin contrasted with the blue curls toppling over his forehead.

Despite their differences, I suspected Tyler and Jordan were the same in essentials: both boys acting as men. Both incapable of keeping their toes firmly inside the line of the law.

'Who sent you?' Tyler took a step towards his bike.

'No one sent us,' I said, as Juliet came to stand beside me. We left what I hoped seemed a safe distance to Tyler but that Juliet could traverse in a few seconds to grab him if needed.

Tyler's eyes flicked to Juliet then met mine before landing on the lanyard around my neck. 'Fuck.'

'Tyler.' I edged forward as he stumbled back, reaching for his bike's handlebars. 'My name is Gabe and this is Juliet. We just want to talk to you. Please don't run.'

I couldn't discern his expression. Something like fear, but with a healthy dose of defiance.

'You want me to come in.' Tyler's voice was far deeper than Jordan's, rough and grating. 'That's what Mum said. And I talked to J. Jordan. He said that if I tell you the truth, you'll treat me fairly.'

Fairness was often discussed between Paul, Joanie, and their sons whenever Ollie and I joined them for dinner. Young children were preoccupied with the notion that everyone should be treated equally, especially when they felt they were being short changed. Most people, as they aged, realised fairness could be hoped for but not counted on. The world was random and difficult, human beings prone to self-favouritism at the expense of others.

This naivety compounded Tyler's youth. He might be able to drink and vote and drive, but he thought in the ways of a child.

'We always strive to be fair.' I attempted to exude calm, keeping my arms loose at my sides. I sensed extracting my notepad would cause Tyler to flee. 'Could you tell us how you were involved with the fire at the Dunlow Estate?'

Blush flooded Tyler's face and his knuckles tightened around the bike's handlebar. 'I had nothing to do with it.'

Juliet stepped forward to stand at my shoulder. 'Zara Everett would have had her mobile and purse on her person when she entered the cottage on the Dunlow Estate. We found them in your bedroom. How did these items come to be in your possession if you had nothing to do with the fire that killed her?'

'You've already fucking decided, haven't you?' Tyler snapped, flecks of spittle landing on the long grass between us. 'Here's a lad who grew up in a council house and was shit at school. He must be a criminal, right?'

It was difficult to believe Zara's purse and phone, along with the jewellery belonging to Timothy Dunlow's late wife, could have ended up in Tyler's bedroom without some wrongdoing on his part. It wouldn't be helpful to point that out.

'We want to hear your side of the story.' I hoped Juliet would allow me to form a rapport with Tyler before diving in and raising his hackles again. She might be confident she could catch him, but I'd rather not chance it. If we could convince him to come with us voluntarily, then he would be more cooperative during further questioning at the station. 'Can you please explain how Zara's things came to be in your room?'

Tyler's jaw clenched, but the high colour receded from his cheeks. 'I took them.'

I wondered whether in Tyler's mind *took* was synonymous with *stole*.

'Where did you take them from?' Juliet asked.

If Tyler were a dog, he would have curled his lip at her. 'You know where I took them from.'

'It's helpful for you to give us a complete account of your actions.' I spread my hands. 'If you fill in the gaps of our understanding, we can be as fair as possible.'

I thought mentioning Tyler's favourite concept would soften him. He shifted his weight, then dumped his bag in his bike's basket so he could push his hair back from his forehead. His nails were painted a chipped turquoise.

'I've got this scheme over here. People camp and they think no one will come along and take stuff from their tents. Sometimes, they leave caravans unlocked.' He pressed his thumbs together. 'I park my car somewhere nearby, then cycle to the sites. Wait until they go off and take anything that looks valuable.'

'Targeting tourists is a little different to stealing from a cottage on a gated estate,' Juliet said.

'Not really,' Tyler sneered. 'I was cycling to a campsite and saw an old man moving a load of boxes into the cottage. I tried the door the next time I went past. It was unlocked. Practically begging someone to go through his stuff.'

I'd heard similar justifications before. If someone didn't want to be burgled, they would implement better security. It was their fault their things were taken.

'I was looking through the boxes when I spotted a girl in the back room,' Tyler went on. 'I thought I was busted, but then she snored. She was totally out of it. Didn't notice when I went in and took the stuff from her bag.' He huffed out a laugh. 'I even poked her face and she still didn't wake up. I left right after that, though. Didn't actually want her to catch me.'

'Did you recognise the woman?' Juliet asked.

Tyler shook his head. 'I assumed she was a lost tourist or homeless.'

If Zara had belonged to either category, then the theft of her purse and phone would have been difficult to overcome had she survived the fire. I resisted the urge to ask Tyler whether it was fair that he'd stolen from a woman he assumed was in such a vulnerable position.

'Did you know Zara Everett before her death?' Juliet clarified.

'No. I looked her up, when I got home and went through her stuff. She was way too posh to spend time with me.' Tyler frowned, his lips pursing. 'I wasn't happy she died, though. She might not have been my kind of girl, but no one deserves what happened to her.'

His remorse around the death of the woman he'd stolen from seemed genuine. Jordan had been similar about Melanie. He'd hurt his girlfriend when she was alive but had been devastated by her death. There was no connection in their minds between their mistreatment and their grief.

'You left after you took Zara's purse and phone?' I checked. 'Did you see anyone or anything as you left that indicated what would happen to Zara and the cottage afterwards?'

'I didn't see anyone in the forest.' Tyler scrunched his nose. 'As I was riding to where I'd left my car, a van sped past. They came so close I almost stacked it into a tree.'

'Can you remember anything about the van?' I asked.

'It wasn't white,' Tyler said. 'I would have been able to tell if it was, even in the dark.'

'Did the van driver turn into the Dunlow Estate?' Juliet asked.

'Couldn't tell you. I was well away by then.' Tyler squinted. 'I guess they were headed in the right direction.'

I glanced at Juliet. If Tyler was telling the truth, this confession ruled him out as a suspect for the fire and Zara's death. My partner gave no indication whether she was convinced of Tyler's relative innocence, but I was inclined to believe him. We'd struggled to establish a motive for why Tyler would have killed Zara. It seemed plausible he'd simply committed another crime in the cottage before it was set ablaze later that night.

'One more question,' Juliet said. 'Have you ever set any other fires?'

Tyler was friends with Jordan, a young man linked to a previous blaze on the Dunlow land. If Tyler had set fires of his own, his lack of a relationship with Zara wouldn't matter. A history of arson would keep him firmly in our ring of suspects.

Although, nothing had been taken from the other estates. Their outbuildings had been burned seemingly for the sake of it, not for material gain. If Tyler was to be believed, items being purloined was his calling card.

'No,' Tyler stated, his piercings glinting as his brows lowered. 'I'm not interested in starting fires and shit.'

Tyler's operation worked far more effectively if he could come and go undetected. He'd even left his car at a distance so that no one could identify him via his altered Ford. Despite his intention to flee and the crimes he'd admitted to, I tentatively trusted he'd told us the truth about Zara and the fire.

'We'll need you to come into the station to repeat all of this on record,' Juliet said before I could think of some way to convince him to come with us voluntarily. She walked towards him. 'Tyler Jenkins, you are under arrest—'

'Like fuck I am.'

He swung his leg over his bike and pushed off.

Juliet broke into a run as Tyler slammed his feet onto the pedals. She reached for his hood but he whipped away down a winding path through the trees.

'I hope you never fucking find who started that fire,' Tyler called over his shoulder, before disappearing behind thick trunks. There wasn't much point calling for help to find him. He'd be long gone before anyone else arrived, lost in the tangled forest.

Bright spots of red decorated Juliet's cheeks as she stormed back to my side. 'What a charming young man,' she growled. 'Do you believe he wasn't involved in Zara's death?'

'I think so.' I fell into step beside her. I tapped my keys, allowing her into the air-conditioned interior of my car. 'I'm not sure Tyler has it in him to be convincingly duplicitous.'

'I agree.' Juliet's mouth twitched. 'Let's go talk to this farmer. If we're lucky, we'll crush all of Tyler's hopes for today.'

Call connected at 9:42.

'Hello, this is Detective Sergeant Gabe Martin.'

'Hi, Gabe. It's Matt here. How are you?'

'Oh, yeah. I'm fine. Thanks for asking, but is there something I can help you with?'

'I'm at the Dunlow Estate and I think you need to come over.'

'What's happened?'

'Timothy Dunlow asked me to accompany him into the cottage so that he could take another look through the boxes and retrieve those items that hadn't been too badly damaged. When we arrived, someone else was already in the cottage.'

'Who?'

'Man called Benedict Hogan. He's not hostile and has agreed to stick around until you get here.'

'Right. Juliet and I are nearby. We'll be with you soon.'

From: James Knowles **james.knowles@police.gov.uk**
To: Paul Willis **paul.willis@mit.gov.uk**
CC: Nicole Stewart **nicole.stewart@mit.gov.uk**
Date: **8 August, 9:53**
Subject: **Further details – Owen Westover**

Paul and Nicole,

Several documents attached to this email support the emerging hypothesis that Owen Westover is responsible for the deaths of Max Powrie and many other children.

The first is a map of places Owen Westover is known to have rented properties. There are gaps, but the movements we have been able to track correlate strongly with the abductions and deaths of children. He arrives in these areas up to a month before the children go missing and leaves around six months afterwards.

Mr Westover's employer – J&L Delivery Services – handed over a full record of his time working with them. They are based across the UK and Europe. They have accommodated Mr Westover's frequent moves as he is a dedicated worker. Uri Smith – Mr Westover's line manager – expressed shock and disbelief when we explained the reasons behind our interest in Mr Westover. His statement is attached as well.

Also attached is Mr Westover's record of annual leave, which correlates with the disappearances of children. His absences from work last for a week before the children are taken and until a week after they are found. Mr Westover is currently on annual leave.

Several of Mr Westover's present neighbours expressed shock that he could have been involved in the deaths of children. They described him as quiet and considerate. None of them has ever seen him in the presence of a child or a barrel. His neighbours have not seen him since yesterday afternoon.

Mr Westover paid for his most recent barrel purchase in cash. If he has bought other barrels in the past, there is no record of card payments at garden centres or similar shops at pertinent times.

I hope this is helpful,

James

Gabe

The three men waiting beside the burned cottage formed an interesting tableau.

Timothy Dunlow stood closest to the wreck, a frown tracing well-worn lines across his face. A missing tie was his concession towards not spending the day in an air-conditioned office but rather picking over the ruined possessions of his deceased wife in an uncomfortably warm forest.

Benedict Hogan was furthest from the cottage. His shirtsleeves were rolled up to his elbows, his clasped hands discoloured with ash. He and Dunlow didn't look at Juliet and me as we approached. Benedict didn't lift his eyes from the ground.

I wondered if Dunlow had met his son's partner before, whether he knew Benedict's name. Dunlow could be blissfully unaware that the man he'd found on his property was more closely connected to him than an opportunistic stranger.

Matt Lam stood between them, his grin wide. The corners of my mouth twitched in response. He didn't seem to hold it against me that sex had been unexpectedly withdrawn and replaced with a sad consolation the other night.

'Morning,' he said, as Juliet and I stopped before them.

'Hello,' Benedict mumbled to the ground.

Dunlow redirected his furrowed brow from charred boxes to us.

'Hello, all.' I pulled my notepad from my pocket. 'Mr Dunlow, Forensic Fire Brigade Officer Lam told us you came over this morning to take another look at the contents of the cottage. Is that correct?'

Checking why Dunlow was here wasn't strictly necessary, but forcing the older gentleman to speak when he would clearly rather glower in haughty silence was strangely satisfying.

'Yes. I'd looked through the boxes with the forensic team, but wasn't allowed to take anything away because they were still working.' The curl of Dunlow's upper lip conveyed exactly what he thought of being told to wait. 'Once I was given permission to remove my items, I asked to be escorted into the cottage again. This morning was the earliest Mr Lam was available.'

'I'm a busy man.' Matt shrugged his broad shoulders. The hint of a smile suggested he'd perhaps prioritised a plethora of other tasks over spending time in Dunlow's company.

I glanced at the cottage and my sympathy for Matt stuttered. Dunlow was difficult but he was his most human when speaking of his dead wife. There had been no rainfall since the fire but all Dunlow had to remember his partner by was currently bared to the elements. It was understandable that he would be anxious to see her things made safe.

'One more question, then we'll let you two get on while we chat to Benedict.' I ignored a sharp look from Juliet. She either didn't think it was necessary to speak to Terence's boyfriend alone or couldn't understand why I'd hasten Dunlow's search of the cottage. Perhaps a heaping of both. 'What happened when you arrived on the estate?'

'I saw someone in the cottage.' Dunlow's light blue eyes finally darted to Benedict. Red crept over the younger man's neck and cheeks, a steady stain so different to the uneven blush shared by his boyfriend's family. 'I asked him to remove himself from my property and he complied.'

I didn't imagine Dunlow had been quite so calm when he demanded Benedict exit the cottage. But then, I couldn't claim I would be unaffected if I found a stranger in my brother's bedroom.

'Thank you,' I said to Dunlow. Matt winked before following the older man into the ruined cottage.

'Benedict.' Juliet's voice was an icy contrast to the stifling heat surrounding us despite the tree cover. 'Why are you here?'

His eyes remained on the leaf-strewn ground. 'It's nothing nefarious.'

Speaking to Tyler then Benedict gave me conversational whiplash. The two men couldn't be more different, yet both were suspects for the same crimes.

'Can you explain what brought you here?' I infused my words with the warmth Juliet's lacked. I no more wanted to wait while Benedict bumbled towards another confession than she did, but there were other ways to encourage transparency than by slashing straight to the truth.

Benedict looked up, his deep brown eyes imploring. 'I wanted to help Teddy.'

I could practically hear Juliet's eyes roll even as she stayed perfectly still. She would never sympathise with foolish actions performed in the name of love.

'How would your coming here help Terence?' she asked.

'He was distraught when he learnt his mother's things were in there.' He nudged his head towards the cottage, hair flopping over his brow in an annoyingly handsome wave. 'Since he and his father have been on bad terms, Teddy has been working up the courage to ask for some of her belongings.'

'Why didn't Terence ask his father if he could take a look at the cottage himself after he discovered what happened?' Juliet asked.

'I don't pretend to understand what it must be like to have a parent who refuses to accept you for who you are.' Something other than perfect diction punctuated Benedict's words. He pressed his blackened hands together and angled his face away from the cottage. 'Teddy didn't feel he could ask his father, so I didn't push.'

There was that hint of barely concealed anger again, but would Benedict have returned here if he was the arsonist? He couldn't have known Matt and Dunlow would show up, so might have thought he would be able to pick over the remains of the cottage without arousing suspicion.

Benedict said he'd come here for Terence. Was that admirable, or an indication that he hadn't known what was stored in the cottage when he set it ablaze and was now riddled with guilt?

'Instead, you decided a better course of action was to trespass and commit theft?'

Benedict gaped at Juliet. Apparently, he hadn't viewed his quest to comfort his boyfriend as anything other than noble.

'Did you take anything before Mr Dunlow arrived?' I asked gently.

'Only this.' Benedict pulled a crumpled photograph from the pocket of his perfectly pressed trousers.

A woman with the same olive toned skin and thick auburn hair as her sons sat on a rolling lawn edged with trees. A toddler perched on one knee, his eyes obscured by round glasses. A young boy in a rumpled school uniform rested on the other.

Her face was alight with laughter, her teeth shining as she beamed at whoever held the camera.

'Strictly speaking, you should ask Mr Dunlow if he's happy with you taking that.' I wrinkled my nose. I'd witnessed firsthand Dunlow's casual cruelty and pettiness. If anyone would withhold a scrap of comfort to regain a semblance of control, it was the man picking through the boxes in the ruined cottage.

'I don't think that's necessary,' Juliet said.

I stared at her, but she gave nothing away. I couldn't tell if pity for Terence moved her to let this tiny indiscretion slide or if the idea of slipping something past Dunlow motivated her. She'd been suspicious of Benedict before. I didn't think she would be as affected as I was by finding him here.

'Thank you.' Benedict slid the photo back into his pocket. He bit his lip then blurted, 'Are you any closer to figuring out who started the fire?'

Juliet's eyes narrowed. 'Why are you so interested in the investigation?'

If Benedict was anything like his boyfriend, he would prefer us to work out of sight and out of mind. His curiosity could be a sign of a guilty conscience.

His brows gathered together. 'Who wouldn't be interested? A poor woman died. Of course I want to know her killer will face justice.'

Terence might be striving to be a better person now he'd removed himself from his father's influence, but I suspected there would always be a gulf between the man he hoped to be and the genuine consideration displayed by his boyfriend.

'Let us escort you off the estate,' I said.

Benedict shot one look towards the cottage before falling into step between Juliet and me on the wide gravel driveway. Dunlow's head was bent, his back turned. I waved a hand in Matt's direction. He grinned in return.

'He knows who I am,' Benedict murmured as we passed through the gates. 'He didn't ask a single question about Teddy or Leo.'

While Benedict and I paused, Juliet walked over to my car. I squeezed the key fob to let her inside, struggling to generate a reply beyond *Dunlow's an arsehole*.

Like Benedict, I didn't know what it was like for a parent to turn on me because of my sexuality. Mum and Dad were kindly bemused at best and confused at worst. I didn't doubt they assumed I'd been cured of my bisexuality now I was in a serious relationship with a man, but they didn't think that way to hurt me.

What drove a wedge between me and my parents was my refusal, growing stronger each year since Barnabas died, to submit to their desperate need to keep me safe.

'I hope the photo brings Terence and Leo some comfort.'

Benedict raised a watery smile. 'It will. They both loved their mum so much.'

I examined him as he dabbed delicately at his eyes with a monogrammed handkerchief. I didn't think he was acting, but a guilty conscience could look remarkably similar to sadness.

Perhaps Benedict didn't know what was in the cottage when he set it alight, but I didn't think that was the case. I suspected he was just a nice, if overly privileged, man caught up in a horrible mess.

However, I couldn't discount him yet. If more links arose, then I wouldn't be able to keep blaming his fully developed conscience for his reactions.

Benedict swallowed, shaking his head. 'Why is it that the best people are stolen away too soon, while the worst go on hurting those around them?'

He didn't wait for me to respond. He sighed and strode towards a silver BMW.

I pressed my fingernails into my palms, took a deep breath, and walked to my car. Benedict couldn't know how his parting comment would hit home.

Call connected at 10:31.

'Boss, I've got news.'

'Go ahead.'

'A man was seen entering the property five minutes ago.'

'And it's taken you that long to call? Is it him?'

'That's why I've not called sooner; we're not sure. He parked close to the property and entered quickly. He was wearing a hat pulled low over his face. None of us got a good look at him and the images we've got are unclear.'

'Did it seem likely he knew he was being watched?'

'Judging from his body language, I'd say no. He didn't look around or seem nervous. Just in a rush.'

'Shit. Deciding our next step would have been much simpler if we knew it was Owen Westover.'

'I think we need to enter the property soon anyway.'

'Why?'

'He collected something from the backseat of the car before he went inside. A big sack.'

'Oh God. Has he taken another one?'

'We can't be sure, but the size and heft would be about right for a child.'

'Okay, Nicole. Stay exactly where you are. I'm going to head over with the armed lot. If it looks like the man is leaving or if you have concerns for the immediate welfare of the possible child, then you have full permission to arrest him.'

Keith. Sent 10:33.

> I've been thinking about what you said last night, and I agree that you need to spend more time with the girls. We need more time together as a family. You, me, and the girls. We're all that matters. So I've booked a holiday – a week on the Isle of Wight over Christmas. Book the 23rd to 30th of December off. I'll show you the details when you get home. It shouldn't be a problem, since I can't remember the last time you had a break from work to spend time with your family x

Call connected at 10:42.

'Hey, Alice.'

'Hi, Gabe. We can chat later about how you're eternally grateful I corralled your boyfriend home for you. I'm calling on official police business.'

'Right. What is it?'

'We've had a complaint from Chase Nolan about Paloma Robins. He said she's been sending him threatening messages on Instagram. He claimed to be worried about his personal safety.'

'Okay. Leave this with me and Juliet. We're chatting to a witness in a minute, but then we'll swing over to Paloma's to get her side of the story.'

'I'll let Chase know it's all in hand.'

'Thanks.'

'Gabe?'

'Yeah?'

'I really did think it was the right thing to do: telling Ollie what was going on.'

'I know, Al.'

Gabe

Juliet hadn't spoken during the short drive to Black Hill Farm, her eyes glued to her phone even as her thumbs remained stationary. She hadn't commented on my conversation with Alice after it was shared through my car's speakers, my cheeks burning as I turned from a lane onto a single-track path through swaying green fields. Her jaw clenched when Nicolas June's wife explained on the doorstep of their picturesque farmhouse that after waiting ten minutes, he'd headed out to do watering. I'd thanked her and hurried my partner away before she exploded.

Juliet tugged at long strands of grass as we skirted the edges of fields, heading for a blue tractor trundling through yellowing stalks of wheat.

'Has anything cropped up from the surveillance on Benedict?' I asked. The silence needed to be broken before we met Nicolas. Despite his reluctance to chat, the farmer didn't deserve to take the brunt of whatever bad mood Juliet had plunged into.

I'd appreciated the quiet as I'd muddled through my mixed feelings towards Alice after her call. I was grateful to have Ollie home but it made me uncomfortable that Alice could see how badly I was struggling, that she felt the need to take matters into her own hands. I hadn't acted normally over the last few days, but my evident transparency made my skin itch.

Juliet threw grass seed into a hedgerow, startling a cluster of sparrows into the blue sky. 'Nothing. I suppose you want to discount him now?'

I frowned at the back of her head and told myself she couldn't possibly be cranky at me. 'I was never sure about Benedict. He came to the cottage to get a memento to make his boyfriend happy. He wouldn't have burned down the cottage if avoiding Terence's sadness was his goal.'

'Unless he didn't know what was in there,' Juliet countered. 'He's angry about Dunlow's dismissal of Terence. What if Benedict thought a fire on the estate would bring Dunlow down a peg? It was a method of equalising he'd used before.'

'Why would Benedict have come to the station to confess his teenage fires if he was guilty?' I watched Juliet's bound hair sway from side to side like a cat's tail. 'I know you think he was trying to control the narrative, but I'm not sure he's that calculated.'

Juliet tugged a strand of grass so hard that the whole plant parted with the ground, roots and all. She flung it into a patch of brambles and grabbed another. 'You're far too inclined to think the best of people. Benedict has a shaky alibi and has started fires previously. He has a strong motive to hurt Dunlow and he knew Zara. What if she had also pissed him off, then he followed her to the estate? He could have killed two birds with one stone.'

My plan to chat with Juliet before we met the farmer and ease her out of her funk wasn't working. She didn't usually indulge in such wild speculation or jab at our differences as though they were deficiencies. Something had happened between the Dunlow Estate and Nicolas's farm that had rattled her.

Steeling myself, I asked, 'Are you alright, Juliet?'

She dropped a handful of grass seed and spun around. 'Why wouldn't I be okay?'

I stopped a decent distance from her. She wouldn't lash out physically, but space between us gave her words less of a whip-like sting.

'Since we left the Dunlow Estate, you've either been silent or snappish,' I forged on to ground I usually left well alone. But usually I wasn't allocating the bulk of my mental energy to keep from wondering about what Paul and his team might be doing, how close they might be to giving up. I didn't have it in me to juggle Juliet's moods as well. 'If something's wrong, you can tell me.'

Miniscule movements ticked over Juliet's face, swinging between hints of outrage and annoyance to sadness and a cracked open vulnerability that made me want to pull her in for a hug. But she would never allow that. As I watched, she shut down everything flitting across her face. She turned and resumed walking along the edge of the field.

I pressed my lips together and followed. I didn't know why I'd expected Juliet to open up just because I was too tired to dance around her caged emotions. Asking how she was, pointing out her moodiness, was a mistake. For the rest of this investigation, I'd not only have to manage my own weariness, but work with a partner icing me out for daring to care.

'I got an unexpected message from my husband.'

I stumbled over a stone, but righted myself and hurried to catch up. 'Oh?'

'I apologise if I took my surprise out on you.' Juliet's voice had returned to its normal measured tone, her hands still at her sides as she strode on.

'It's fine.' I fumbled for the right thing to say. I'd longed for Juliet to confide in me. She'd chosen a moment when my brain resembled mush. 'I hope it wasn't a nasty shock?'

It was as impossible to tell what Juliet was thinking from the back of her head as it was from the front. Her shoulders might have edged up by half an inch.

'Most people wouldn't say so.'

While I puzzled that out, Juliet opened a gate and we stepped into a field of wheat. In the distance, a tractor turned. Huge metal arms sticking out on either side swung around with it. Water, no doubt laced with assorted chemicals, rained down on the parched crop as the tractor rumbled towards us.

Time was dwindling to respond to Juliet's strange pronouncement. Mentally exhausted or not, I couldn't let this chance pass by.

'Even if other people would say something is good, that doesn't mean you have to think the same.' I raised my voice as the tractor neared. 'You don't have to like something if it makes you uncomfortable.'

Juliet turned from the approaching tractor. Her grey eyes flicked between mine. Her mouth opened, but snapped shut when the whirring growl of the engine cut off.

I tried not to glare at Nicolas June as he climbed down from the cabin. He hurried over and held out a work-roughened hand.

'Thank you for coming out here. When you were late, I couldn't hang around any longer. Days like this can't be wasted on a farm. Now, what do you ladies need from me?'

Juliet looked down at him as they briefly shook hands. Nicolas was a similar height to me but much broader. His checked shirt sat across muscled shoulders, his green trousers encasing trunk-like thighs. His brown hair was greying, the tan skin of his face weathered by many years spent in the fields under the glare of the sun and lash of the wind.

'We're concerned that you've not made time to speak to us before today,' Juliet said, she and Nicolas apparently happy to forgo protracted introductions. If the farmer hadn't made arranging this interview so difficult and hadn't forced us to tramp across fields to meet him, Juliet would have appreciated his willingness to leap straight to the point.

'Like I said, a sunny day in August can't be wasted. Crops need watering, animals need moving. There's a thousand jobs to do on the farm in summer and the weather is never a help.' Nicolas grinned at us, unmoved by Juliet's stern stare. 'I would have made sure to talk to you if I had anything useful to say, but I saw the fire and called it in. Don't know anything more than that.'

I pulled my notepad from my pocket. 'What were you doing when you saw the fire?'

'Tending the pigs.' Nicolas jabbed over his shoulder with one grass-stained thumb. 'We tried getting all the sows pregnant so they'd give birth in the spring, but a couple didn't take so we had to make do with summer. I was out with one of the mothers, since she'd been making a fuss during the day. I don't like leaving them on their own when they're in distress.'

'When did you spot the fire?' Juliet asked.

Nicolas lifted his head and sniffed. 'Smelt it first, which is saying something when ankle deep in pig shit. Panicked for a second, thought something had gone wrong with the Aga at home, but then I saw flames in the trees across the way.'

'Did you notice anything strange before the fire?' I asked. 'Anyone coming or going from the Dunlow Estate?'

'Can't say I notice much over that way anymore.' Nicolas shrugged. 'It's been quiet since the chap and his sons left.'

'Did you see anything after you spotted the fire?' Juliet asked.

'Not a lot,' Nicolas said. 'The sow started birthing while I was on the phone. If everything's as it should be, the piglets shoot out like bullets. I had my hands full, making sure they were breathing and getting them to a teat. Hardly had time to look up.'

'But you said you didn't notice a lot?' I checked.

Nicolas wrinkled his sunburned nose. 'I saw a van haring along the lanes. Didn't think much of it. Lads are always coming up here, using the roads as a race course. Although, that's happened less since the Dunlows moved away.'

I gripped my pencil. Tyler mentioned a van as well. It could be chance they'd driven around these lanes at the time of the fire, but for now it was a lead.

'Did you note any details about the vehicle?' I asked.

'Too far away and too dark to see much.' Nicolas's eyes swerved to the cloudless sky. 'I think it was blue.'

I wrote that down. 'Any idea of the size or make?'

Nicolas shook his head. 'I just saw a quick flash of colour as it passed by the lights at the entrance to the farm, lass. Nothing more. I wouldn't be surprised if it was some joyride that had nothing to do with the fire.'

'Thank you for your time,' Juliet cut across before Nicolas could commence a rant about the misuse of the lanes by bored youths. For a man who claimed he didn't have time to waste, his detailed answers had kept us in this sunbaked field longer than was necessary. 'We won't keep you.'

With a cheery wave, Nicolas hopped back into the tractor. It roared to life as Juliet and I walked through the gate.

'I'll ask Maddy to check if Benedict has a van registered to his name or if he rented one on the night of the fire.' Juliet tapped at her phone. 'We can ask Paloma about it when we see her.'

'Get Maddy to check Chase too.'

Juliet wasn't determined to discount Zara's boyfriend, but was much more inclined than me to dismiss his involvement. She considered discrepancies between his and Paloma's stories domestic rather than criminal.

If my brain was fully functional, perhaps I would have been willing to overlook Chase too.

Ollie. Sent 11:49.

> Hey, I just chatted to Mum – Dad is doing fine. He's being released from hospital later today and Jessica has finally returned to help out at the farm. Look after yourself. I'll be home when you get here. Love you xxx

Recording started: 11:55.

Police Constable James Knowles: Everything's ready, sir.

Detective Inspector Paul Willis: Good work. Ruby, over to you.

Strategic Firearms Officer Ruby Douglas: Thank you, sir. Working with information gathered by the surveillance team, we have reason to believe Owen Westover returned to Birch Cottage approximately thirty minutes ago and has been inside the property ever since. Mr Westover was seen carrying a large sack, which may contain a child. Extreme caution will be taken as we enter the building to ensure the safety of any children inside. AFOs are stationed at the back door should Mr Westover try to flee. It is unknown whether the suspect is armed and he is believed dangerous. Bravo, you have the go-ahead to approach.

Authorised Firearms Officer Dev Afzal: Armed police! Stand away from the door!

[Smashing wood.]

AFO Dev Afzal: No sign of him in the living room. Advancing to the kitchen.

SFO Ruby Douglas: Hallway and living room clear.

AFO Dev Afzal: Kitchen cl—

SFO Ruby Douglas: Armed police! Down on the ground!

[Muffled voice.]

SFO Ruby Douglas: Down on the ground now, or I will have to subdue you with force.

DI Paul Willis: What the hell's going on?

AFO Dev Afzal: Suspect is cooperative, but it took a second.

DI Paul Willis: Is it him?

SFO Ruby Douglas: Sir, once Dev has searched the remaining rooms, I need you in here. Suspect is confused and seems to be losing consciousness.

DI Paul Willis: Ruby, is it him?

AFO Dev Afzal: Bathroom, clear.

SFO Ruby Douglas: I'm not sure, sir. Mr Westover? Owen? Can you hear me?

DI Paul Willis: Shit.

AFO Dev Afzal: Bedroom, clear. The sack's here. It's open. Full of laundry.

SFO Ruby Douglas: That's the whole building clear, sir. Suspect is unconscious. We need medical assistance in here.

DI Paul Willis: I'm coming in. James, get a paramedic in there.

PC James Knowles: Already on their way, sir.

Gabe

Juliet and I paused on the threshold of Paloma's flat. The monochromatic space had been transformed. Piles of colour-coordinated clothes formed bright lumps across the white sofa. The glass-topped coffee table was covered in patterned papers and photos. Scattered across the floor were boots in various states of muddiness and items I assumed related to hiking but could have been used as unconventional torture devices.

Paloma stood in the middle of the room, hands braced on her yellow Lycra covered hips. She didn't let grief dictate her fashion choices. Her brown arms, legs, and toned navel were exposed by a tight two-piece.

'I'm glad you've turned up. Now I don't have to lug all this down to the station.' She waved one hand briskly. 'Come in, then.'

Juliet raised an eyebrow as we joined Paloma at the epicentre of the colourful jumble. 'What is this?'

Paloma threw her pink and blonde braids over her shoulder. 'I want to show you everything between me and Zara.'

Without further preamble or overt curiosity around why we'd come to her flat, Paloma launched into a guided tour of the ordered mess. She explained that the clothes had been sent to Zara originally by different brands.

'She said they didn't fit right, but you've seen pictures of Zar.' Paloma gestured at the photos on the coffee table with a hand holding an expensive sports bra. 'I never pushed too hard, but it was pretty fucking clear these things didn't fit her in a way Chase liked.'

The clothes Zara had given Paloma were revealing. In her frequently updated Instagram posts, Zara had always been dressed in long leggings and tops showing nothing more exciting than her elbows.

'I've worn these on loads of hikes. They're my favourites.' Paloma bounced over to a pair of purple boots, their soles caked in mud. 'You can test them against earth from the New Forest or whatever. You'll see I've not been around there in ages.'

A sinking feeling dragged at me. Paloma didn't know why we'd appeared at her door or what Chase had accused her of, but she'd assumed she needed to defend herself. I wasn't sure she was motivated by guilt around her friend's death. As methodical as Paloma's display was, I could recognise her fear.

She grabbed the nearest pile of papers from the coffee table. 'These are more of our DMs, plus ones between me and other people. I was always nice about Zar, even when she couldn't see.' She brandished the printouts at us. 'Even when someone else slagged her off, I stood up for her.'

'Stop.' Juliet halted the frantic pile on of information. 'Why are you showing us this?'

Paloma looked to me. Something in my face must have confirmed I wasn't as clueless as my partner about why she felt the need to pre-emptively defend herself.

She picked up a pile of handwritten notes and held them out to Juliet. 'I know Chase has been stirring shit about me. He's probably one tiny nudge away from claiming I'm harassing him.' Her eyes widened as Juliet took the papers. 'Unless that's why you're here? The fucker.'

'Chase has expressed concerns over your interactions with him.' Juliet didn't look down at the notes in her hand. 'But why would that prompt all this?'

Paloma's eyes darted to me again, then narrowed when they landed on Juliet. 'Because I'm a Black woman suspected of the murder of a White woman. You think I don't know whose side you'll take if shit turns ugly? You've got a White dude claiming

I'm a crazy psycho, and then you've got me. You'll see exactly what all these brands saw.' She gestured at the piles of clothing across her sofa. 'You think any of them sent stuff directly to me? No. They saw a pretty White girl who preached that the world is a wonderful place and they dismissed the Black girl telling the truth. Because I seem paranoid. Too loud. Angry.' She huffed humourlessly. 'I've seen this story play out too many times before. I don't know if this will make a difference but if I can help you see the truth before you storm my home and wrongfully arrest me, then I'll do it.'

Shamed blush rose to my cheeks. I liked to think I was better than those who judged others according to the colour of their skin, but I hadn't considered how being involved in this investigation would affect Paloma differently to our other suspects. I should have realised she needed reassurance that her side of the story was respected, that she would be listened to and treated well. She should have felt safe enough that she wouldn't consider extreme action to prove herself innocent. I didn't know whether Chase was playing the system by saying Paloma was harassing him, but in this moment it seemed far more likely that the woman laying out all she could before us was innocent than a man I found it impossible to get a read on.

Unable to look Paloma in the eye, I glanced at the notes in Juliet's hand. Spidery handwriting wandered in increasingly wonky lines across each patterned page.

Juliet flinched when my fingers brushed hers, but she relinquished the letters. I flicked through them. Kind thank-yous for each time Paloma helped Zara with a hike, sweet notes marking birthdays, apologies for missed meals and promises to do better.

'These are from Zara?' I checked, shame melting away as my heart rate sped up.

Paloma nodded, her chin jutting. 'There's no hint of any kind of issue between us.'

True, but that wasn't what bothered me. 'Who wrote these for her?'

We'd seen Zara's handwriting on the intricate collages detailing each of her solo hikes. She'd dedicated Instagram posts to her preferred calligraphy pens. Chase had given us the board she'd started before setting off six days ago, covered in her looping handwriting. It proved she'd planned to go in a different direction, that she'd allowed her boyfriend to believe she was heading east instead of west from the city.

Paloma's face scrunched. 'Why the fuck would someone else have written them?'

Juliet took the topmost note. 'This handwriting doesn't match our sample of Zara's.'

Paloma's mouth widened into a smirk. 'You mean that pretty shit she posted on her socials?'

I nodded. The artful words on Zara's boards were nothing like this spiky scrawl. My eyes widened as recognition pinged in my tired brain. I'd seen this writing before; on the page Chase ripped from his and Zara's address book. I'd assumed he'd written Paloma's address.

'That arty stuff isn't Zar's handwriting. It wasn't, I mean.' Paloma's lips downturned. 'She got Chase to do the wording on those boards for her.'

I struggled to remember if we'd asked Chase if the writing on the collage he'd given us was Zara's. He'd certainly wanted us to believe that. He said she made the boards, so it made sense we'd assume she'd written all the looping words across them.

Chase had used the half-completed board to prove his innocence. He couldn't have known where Zara was headed because she'd pointed him in the wrong direction.

But if it wasn't Zara's handwriting, the collage could have been made at any time.

'Can we take these?' I pulled an evidence bag from my pocket.

Paloma's eyes danced between the crumpled notes and the clear plastic. 'Have you caught the bastard out?'

'These letters could be helpful,' I hedged.

The handwriting confusion Chase had prompted wasn't proof of guilt. Grief could have caused an oversight; he simply didn't think to tell us it was his handwriting and that he and Zara had started work on the board together before the hike.

Or it could have been a calculated move, designed to make us look elsewhere.

'Does Chase own a van?' Juliet asked.

Paloma tutted. 'Yeah. Huge, diesel-guzzling beast. I told Zara a thousand times he needed to get rid of it. It was no good for her brand.'

Juliet frowned, but passed over Paloma's concerns. 'What colour is it?'

'Blue.'

Keeping any hint of excitement off my face, I tucked the bag of notes into my pocket. 'We need to go.'

Paloma's eyes widened, but she didn't stop us from charging out of her flat. I scurried alongside Juliet's much longer strides as we raced to the ground floor.

'Hopefully Chase will be in the shop,' Juliet said. We pushed through the building's polished front doors and hurried to my car.

My heart thundered as I flung myself into the driver's seat and turned the key in the ignition. We might not have found Zara's killer, but this felt like a step in the right direction. Finally.

I flinched when my phone vibrated in my pocket. I pulled it out, then froze.

Call connected at 12:36.

'Hel—'

'What do you want, Paul?'

'Juliet? I thought I called Gabe.'

'You did. We're in the car. You're on speaker.'

'Right. Gabe, you there?'

'Hey. I'm here.'

'I need your help.'

[Pause.]

'What do you need?'

'We've made an arrest. It could be him, but we're not sure. I'd like you to see if you can identify him as the man who took you and your brother.'

[Pause.]

'Why?'

'Juliet, isn't that bloody obvious? Gabe's the only person who can ID him.'

'Were you able to extract DNA from the barrel Max Powrie was found in?'

'We were, and fingerprints. They match those taken previously.'

'Then you don't need Gabe to ID him. Once you've got the results, you'll have enough to make a conviction.'

'It would be helpful if Gabe would ID him.'

'No. You just want my partner to hurry along your investigation. You've got enough evidence but you need a little more patience to wait for the DNA and fingerprint results. What would actually be helpful is if you left us to get on with our investigation. We've got a significant lead to follow up and every minute spent talking to you is a minute wasted.'

'Gabe?'

'Juliet's right. We need to get on.'

'Fine. I'll let you two go then.'

Paloma Robins @WiseGirlHiker. Sent 12:43.

> The detectives suddenly got excited when I showed them some letters from Zara and they asked questions about your disgusting van. Turns out, you can't lie your arse off to the police and get away with it. If only Zara had been a little more savvy, maybe she would have been alive now rather than murdered because she wouldn't be your kept pet. You fucking sicken me. I hope you rot in prison.

Dad. Sent 12:45.

> Terence, I hope you are well. I met your partner at the estate today. I've retrieved your mother's things now. Should you wish to have anything but the photo Benedict's taken, then give me a call.

Dad. Sent 12:55.

> Benedict seemed like a nice man. It was kind of him to want something for you to remember your mother.

Dad. Sent 12:59.

> We should talk. I've let this go on for long enough. I never wanted you or Leo to leave. I'd like to see you.

Dad. Sent 13:02.

> I apologise for how I've hurt you.

Gabe

'The number plate for Chase's van is CN10 SUP.' Juliet looked around the car park as though a blue van might materialise. 'It's a Volkswagen Transporter.'

I nodded and pulled on the handbrake, leaving my car's engine running for a few more precious minutes of air conditioning before we stepped into the stifling heat outside.

Juliet had been absorbed by her phone on the drive to Chase's combined business and home. I'd used the journey to carefully construct a wall around Paul's request.

Clawing hands from the past had clutched at me, but I felt I couldn't say no. As the bad man's sole surviving victim, the solitary link between the horrors he inflicted and the rest of the world, I had to take even the smallest chance to stop him from ripping apart another family.

I'd felt myself sinking as I'd readied myself to say yes, the pathetic shield I'd built up during a night in Ollie's arms collapsing, when Juliet stepped in. She'd tapped her fingers on her folded arms, her glare burning into the centre console where Paul's name scrolled. He couldn't deny that what she'd said was true. Witness IDs were notoriously unreliable, especially those made at a distance of two and a half decades.

I could have argued, could have said I was happy to help and our investigation would have to wait.

But I didn't. I wanted Juliet to whisk me far away. I wanted to be unreachable until this man Paul had arrested was set free.

I didn't dare consider whether the investigation might end with a conviction, that they could have found the right man.

Hope was corrosive. If I believed no one would ever find the bad man, then I wasn't disappointed each time an investigation was pushed onto the back burner.

As much as I feared facing the bad man, I couldn't quite fathom that whoever Paul had taken into custody could be him. The bad man had always gotten away before. Even though they'd had a photo to work with, something no other investigation had, I couldn't see why this time would be different.

'Thank you for earlier. With Paul,' I blurted out.

Juliet looked up from her phone. She couldn't know how Paul's request had affected me, but she had saved me.

'We have a job to do.' She tucked a stray strand of hair behind her ear. 'Paul shouldn't have asked that of you.'

It would be too easy to draw more than she'd meant from her words. Paul shouldn't have asked me to ID the bad man because it would destroy me, but Juliet more likely thought he shouldn't have asked because we had an investigation to conduct. If Paul had asked during a lull, maybe she would have been happy to see me go.

I took a deep breath. I needed to put everything to do with the bad man to one side. If I wanted to be helpful as we questioned Chase, I needed my whole focus to be on him. Hopefully, he wouldn't try to run like Tyler had if we attempted to arrest him. I frowned. I couldn't remember if there was a door in the SUP shop's back storeroom. We would have to assume that the front wasn't his only escape route.

'The sign,' I gasped.

Juliet frowned at her phone. 'What?'

'There was a sign outside the SUP shop.' I rubbed at my face, consoled that I'd missed it by the fact that Juliet obviously had too. 'It had the same loopy handwriting on it as the collages. The offers on it changed between the two times we visited Chase's shop.'

Juliet shook her head. 'The handwriting isn't as damning as the van seen leaving the site of the fire, but it is interesting that Chase didn't correct our assumption.'

'It worked in his favour for us to look elsewhere, whether or not he's guilty.' At worst, Chase misled us purposefully because he'd killed his girlfriend. At best, he'd not thought to tell us it was his handwriting or he'd let us believe it was Zara's so that we would leave him alone while he grieved.

I took one last breath of cool air, hoping it would calm my fluttering heart, then switched off the engine. Even before I opened the car door, the heat outside pressed in. Unclipping my seatbelt, I tapped my pockets to check my notepad and phone hadn't escaped.

'Shit.' Juliet straightened, squinting against the sun's glare on the windscreen. She pointed at the far end of the one-way road winding around the circumference of the car park. 'Is that Chase's van?'

I peered across shining metal roofs. A blue van cruised behind an old-fashioned yellow Beetle. 'Could be?'

The road would force the van to pass nearby our parking space. It was so close to the Beetle that we couldn't read the number plate, even as they both turned a corner and headed directly towards us. I pulled my seatbelt over my chest and clicked it into place.

The sun was high in the sky, reflecting off the van's windscreen.

I placed my hand on the key, still resting in the ignition. 'Can you see the driver?'

Juliet shook her head, leaning close to the centre console but maintaining enough distance so that she wouldn't accidentally touch my arm. 'I don't think there's a passenger.'

The Beetle driver, obviously fed up with being tailed so aggressively, pulled over to the near side of the narrow road and put on their hazards. The blue van swerved around them.

The new angle gave us a perfect view of the van's number plate and driver. One second Chase held up his middle finger at the Beetle driver, the next his eyes widened when he spotted me and Juliet. He jerked into the middle of the road and sped past the row where we were parked.

I twisted the key in the ignition and reversed out of the space. Juliet slapped the button in the middle of the dashboard to switch on the discreet lights and siren.

'Where's your radio?' she shouted.

I weaved over to the exit of the car park. 'Glove box.'

A woman with three small children jumped back as I ignored the one-way sign and sped down the narrow road. I raised a hand in thanks as I passed. The blue van was visible at the end of the road.

Juliet scrabbled through the clutter in my glove box and grabbed the radio. As I raced down the road, she unwound the cable to plug it in and twisted the receiver. I stamped on the brake at the junction. My seatbelt dug into my chest as I jerked the wheel to the side.

'We've established he's not complying with our request to stop,' she said over the sirens before pushing the button on the side of the radio. Chase's intention to flee was made apparent as soon as he saw us. 'This is Detectives Juliet Stern and Gabe Martin. We are currently in pursuit of a blue Volkswagen Transporter van, registration Charlie November One Zero Sierra Uniform Papa, heading east along Swift Road. We have reason to suspect the driver of the vehicle, Charles Nolan, was involved in the fire and homicide on the Dunlow Estate on the fourth of August. He has not complied with our request to stop. Urgent back-up required. Over.' Juliet lifted her thumb. 'How much do you want to bet that Paloma tipped him off?'

'Shit.' I assessed the road I'd turned onto. Two men with overturned bikes stood on the pavement, gesticulating at the blue van. I gave them a wide berth as I sped past. 'Why would she do that?'

One possibility I'd not considered was that Paloma and Chase could have been working together. They might both have wanted Zara gone. It would have been a risk to flout their supposed animosity towards each other, but good cover.

'My guess is she said something indiscreet.' Juliet tapped the radio on her knee. 'Paloma spends too much of her life online to keep thoughts inside her brain.'

The radio cut in before I could decide whether Juliet's evaluation was harsh or fair. I thought Paloma blabbing accidentally was more likely than her aiding Chase to kill Zara. It would have been hard for Paloma to fake such sadness at Zara's death and consistent ire towards her boyfriend.

'This is Police Constable Alice To. I am on Archery Road and closing in on your location, ma'am. Over.'

'This is Police Constables Leo Dunlow and James Knowles, ma'am. We are coming over the Itchen Bridge and headed east. Over.'

Juliet detached my satnav from my window and pressed the button on the side of the radio. 'The van is currently on Church Road heading north-east. Once you're closer, we can make a plan to slow him down. Over.'

The van swung to the left at the end of the road. Seconds later, I did the same. We rattled along a residential road, Chase swerving to avoid parked cars. My heart thumped along to the wail of the sirens.

'On Swift Road.' Alice chirped through the radio. 'Thirty seconds out from you, ma'am. Over.'

Juliet swiped at the satnav. 'Perfect.' She pressed the button on the side of the radio. 'Alice, I need you to park across the southern end of Glen Road. James, get to the junction between Western Grove and Victoria Road. Over.' She stared down at the satnav. 'Unless we get unlucky and he turns right, we've got him.'

Juliet's knuckles whitened as Chase swerved right towards roads we had no chance of covering with only three vehicles.

'Fuck.' She activated the radio. 'He's going—'

A bus stopped across the road on the right. Chase dodged back into the steady stream of traffic on the left.

'Didn't catch that, ma'am. Over.' Leo's perfect diction was tinny on the radio.

'Ignore it,' Juliet commanded, the radio raised to her chin. 'Are you in position? Over.'

'Almost there, ma'am. Over.'

'I'm parked across the end of Glen Road, ma'am,' Alice said. 'I'm going to vacate the vehicle and clear pedestrians. Over.'

Juliet leant forward. 'Straight on and he's headed towards James, left and it's Alice.'

My hands were clammy on the steering wheel, the blasting aircon powerless against the sweat on my palms and under my tensed arms. I closed the distance between us and the van, other cars darting towards the pavement to create space. I raced around them, engine revving and sirens howling.

Chase turned left. I did the same.

We'd turned onto a winding residential road. By the time Chase saw the marked police car blocking the end, we'd trapped him. There were no side streets or alleys to escape down, not even a long driveway.

Juliet gripped the radio. 'He's headed towards you, Alice. Over.'

The van slowed. Chase had to realise buying time wasn't going to help. I'd gotten close enough to read the stickers decorating the edge of the rear windscreen. Various beachy brands mingled with turtles and exultations to stop polluting Britain's waterways.

'Chase running has to mean he's guilty, right?' I eased onto the brake.

'It has to mean something.' Juliet glared at the van's flickering brake lights. 'We don't know why Chase fled. If Paloma did contact him, she could have spooked him.'

'What if she didn't tip him off?' I countered. 'He could have seen us and panicked.'

'That's possible, but Chase hasn't given previous indications of anxiety. Something caused him to panic and Paloma knew about our most recent findings.' Juliet leant forward. 'Admit defeat.'

I glanced over. Her last comment wasn't aimed at me. Her eyes were glued on the van ahead.

It veered to the left side of the road. The brake lights darkened and space opened up between us.

'What's he doing?' I let the distance grow. I didn't want to smash into the back of the van when Chase realised he wouldn't be able to get past Alice's car.

'There's a bigger gap between the car and a lamppost on this side.' Juliet leant towards her window. 'Not big enough for a bloody great van to get through, though.'

Chase must have been desperate enough to escape that he would attempt to ram Alice's car out of the way.

'Alice, he's coming at the back of your car,' Juliet shouted into the radio over our blaring sirens. 'Get everyone clear now. Over.'

The instruction was issued too late. We had to hope Alice had already gotten herself and anyone else out of the way.

The van sped to the end of the road. The brake lights flashed, like Chase reconsidered at the last moment, but there was no stopping. The van slammed into Alice's blue and fluorescent yellow Vauxhall.

It hit with enough force to turn her car to the side. The van's tyres left thick black tracks along the road before it shuddered to a halt.

I slammed on the brakes and tore off my seatbelt. I left Juliet requesting medical assistance and threw myself out of the car. I ran the short distance to the van. The sticky hot air outside compounded the sweat coating my skin. Beyond the battered police car, Alice's arms were stretched wide. She shouted at people with raised phones to keep their distance.

I stopped at the driver's side door. The van's bumper had crumpled on impact, the bonnet popped open. The engine let out hissing trails of steam.

I yanked the door wide. The airbags had deployed, coating the inside of the van with white powder. The empty sacks sagged over the steering wheel and across the glove compartment.

Chase slumped in the driver's seat. His face was bloodied, the tracks of red from his nose and mouth stark through the dusty residue covering his skin. One of his shoulders rested at an unnatural angle.

'Chase?'

I watched his chest. No rise and fall.

The impact of the crash could have killed him. I pressed two fingers into the side of his neck, gritting my teeth. He was warm, but no pulse thrummed. He didn't move at all.

'Fuck,' I breathed, pulling my hand back.

Chase's chest heaved, and I flinched. Sweet relief flooded me as he coughed, red-tinged spit shining on his pale lips.

Heavy footfalls sounded behind me. 'Can I get past, ma'am?'

I stepped aside so that James could peer into the cabin. Leo carried a first aid kit. He opened it on the ground and passed over bandages, which James pressed under Chase's nose.

His eyes blinked open. He groaned as his jittering pupils alighted on the steam pouring from the ruined bonnet of his van.

'My baby,' he slurred. 'Lola.'

James frowned at the empty passenger seat. 'Is there someone else in the vehicle?'

Chase coughed feebly. 'No. Lola's the van.'

Juliet came to stand beside me. Both Chase and the van were in a bad state. The side door at the back had popped open with the force of the impact. The large square interior was stuffed. I couldn't tell if that was evidence Chase had planned to run and had packed up all his worldly goods, or if he used the back of his beloved van as a haphazard storage space.

The edge of a mattress stretched across the floor. Stacked on top were bulging plastic tubs, several deflated stand-up paddleboards, and an assortment of paddles.

'Juliet.' I stepped closer to the van and pointed at a piece of cardboard half-buried under a tangle of sandy wetsuits. 'Look at this.'

She bent to read the looping handwriting at the top of the collage.

My solo trip across the New Forest.

Call connected at 14:01.

'Hi, who's this?'

'Hello, it's Detective Gabe Martin.'

'Right. What do you want?'

'Paloma, did you contact Chase after we left your flat?'

'Why do you want to know?'

'There have been further developments in the case and it would be helpful to know if you told Chase anything.'

'What's he said about me?'

'Sorry, Paloma. I should have been clearer. It's not you we're interested in, but more the effect anything you said had on Chase.'

'Oh. Did he freak out or something?'

'Or something.'

'Well, yeah. I sent him a message. Told him you were interested in his van and stuff, that he was a piece of shit.'

'Thank you, Paloma. That's good to know. Could you possibly send a screenshot of that message to this number?'

'If it will help you put that arsehole away for a long time, then abso-fucking-lutely.'

ACCIDENT AND EMERGENCY TRIAGE FORM

DATE: 8 August
TIME: 14:15
NAME: Charles Nolan
AGE: 29

PRESENTING COMPLAINT: Car collision – head and neck pain, broken nose, chest contusions, dislocated shoulder

HISTORY OF PRESENTING COMPLAINT: Police officers report that Mr Nolan attempted to flee in his Volkswagen van at around 13:00. He drove his vehicle into a police blockade on Glen Road. On impact, the airbags deployed. As the van was travelling at speeds of over 40MPH, Mr Nolan's injuries are not considered severe for this kind of impact. Mr Nolan regained consciousness quickly and was treated at the scene. After applying a neck brace, paramedics placed his right arm in a sling. There did not seem to be significant head trauma beyond the damage to his nose. His right shoulder was dislocated and his chest has suffered deep contusions.

ON EXAMINATION: The patient is suffering mild whiplash. The patient can stand unaided. He is being monitored for signs of concussion due to his loss of consciousness and headache, but has reported no dizziness or nausea. There is blood on his T-shirt from his broken nose. There are no significant lacerations. The patient is alert and has many contusions across his shoulders and chest. Please note: Mr Nolan is under arrest and is being restrained via handcuffs attached to his bed.

PAST MEDICAL HISTORY: Mr Nolan's right shoulder was dislocated two years ago in a stand-up paddleboard accident on the Isle of Wight.

MEDICATION: Mr Nolan has been given paracetamol and ibuprofen.

SOCIAL AND FAMILY HISTORY: None.

REPORT COMPLIED BY: Senior Staff Nurse Consuelo Day

Call connected at 14:47.

'This is Detective Inspector Juliet Stern.'

'Hello, Detective Stern. This is Neil Nolan. I'm sorry I couldn't return your call sooner; I've been in back-to-back meetings all day.'

'Not to worry. Your timing is perfect.'

'I'm glad to hear it. I have five minutes, so what can I help you with?'

'Do you recall the details of your friendship with Benedict Hogan?'

'I'm sorry, but I don't know anyone by that name. When would we have been friends?'

'Mr Hogan claims to have become friends with you after transferring to Grove Academy.'

'I'm not friends with many people from secondary school anymore. I went to York for university and I've not lived at home since.'

'You don't remember Benedict Hogan?'

'His name isn't ringing a bell.'

'Did you ever commit arson as a teen?'

'Did I— What? Of course not.'

'Mr Hogan says he was encouraged by yourself and some other young men to start fires on landed estates.'

'I don't know who the bloody hell this Hogan is, but he's talking out of his arse. I didn't do anything like that when I was younger. I never would.'

'I see. Did you visit anyone from secondary school during your recent trip to Southampton?'

'No, I didn't. I was in the area for two days. I spent the bulk of that time with my parents and brother.'

'You haven't returned to the area since that visit?'

'No. I've been here, in York.'

'You didn't meet up with Mr Hogan during your visit?'

'How could I? I don't know the man.'

'You didn't speak to your brother about starting fires?'

'No. God. Does this have anything to do with Zara?'

'Do you know anything about her death?'

'I didn't know she'd died until Mum called to tell me. I don't know any details apart from what she's passed on.'

'You haven't spoken to Chase about it?'

'God. Has he got you calling him that too? Charlie and I haven't spoken since my visit.'

'Has Chase ever expressed an interest in starting fires?'

'Oh, is this where this is going? You've decided my brother is to blame for Zara's death?'

'Could you answer the question?'

'I can: no. Charlie has never expressed an interest in starting fires. I don't know where you've gotten that notion from, probably because he's the boyfriend and he's easy to blame, but Charlie isn't like that. He won't have told you this because it doesn't fit with his image now, but he was a loser at school. A nerd. He didn't have many friends, was desperate to hang around with mine. It was embarrassing, really. But what I'm saying is he hasn't changed, even if he pretends to be a cool guy nowadays. Charlie's still that wimpy kid inside. He wouldn't have the guts to start a fire.'

'What was your impression of Chase and Zara's relationship?'

'It was a bit pathetic, if I'm honest. Charlie worshipped her. I could never see why. If you're thinking he killed her, then you're barking up the wrong tree. He loved that girl for some reason. He wouldn't have ever wanted to hurt her and, if he had, he was too weak to do anything about it. Look, is there anything else you need? I have to get back to my meeting.'

'That's more than enough, Mr Nolan. Thank you for your time.'

Gabe

James and Leo guarded Chase's hospital room. As Juliet and I approached, James dropped his hand from the younger man's shoulder. Leo's eyes swam behind his black-framed glasses.

I had to remind myself that witnessing a car crash wasn't normal. Leo had been in uniform for a couple of months. I wasn't yet as hardened as Juliet to the stark realities of police work, but more events that would once have been shocking had become almost mundane.

I was more concerned with my aching back than lingering shock. After the adrenaline of the chase and finding the board in the back of Chase's van had faltered, soreness had made itself known across my arms and down my thighs. Days of neglecting my basic needs followed by the tension of the chase ground through me.

'Ma'ams.' Sweat patches matching my own bloomed on James's white shirt, his receding grey hair damp in the oppressive heat.

Leo straightened, his uniform pulling across newly formed muscles. He was still lanky but had bulked out since the investigation to find Melanie Pirt's killer.

Juliet's eyes fixed on the door to Chase's room. 'Has he said anything?'

'Not a peep, ma'am.' James gripped the shoulder straps of his stab-proof vest. 'Nothing since he was carted away in the ambulance.'

Before that, Chase had repeatedly bemoaned the fate of his van. Though his words were slurred by the gauze packed around his nose, he certainly had more to say about the damage to his vehicle than he ever had about the demise of his girlfriend.

I offered James and Leo a smile before following Juliet into the single room. I shifted a file in my hands and closed the door behind me.

Chase reclined on a hospital bed. His T-shirt had been cut off and he'd apparently refused a hospital gown to replace it. A blanket was tucked under his armpits, covering most of his chest but leaving the topmost purpling bruises visible. His right arm rested in a sling. His left hand stretched towards the mattress, where he'd been handcuffed to the bed's railing.

The blood had been cleared from his face, although his nostrils retained a ring of crusty residue below the brace on his nose. His black eyes were particularly impressive either side of the white padding.

'Whatever that bitch has said about me is a lie,' Chase growled.

'Hold on one moment.' Juliet pulled a Dictaphone from her pocket and rattled off the relevant information for an interview of a suspect under arrest. She placed it on the wheeled bedside table. 'Please continue.'

Chase attempted a frown, then blinked away the tears the expression provoked as it tugged at the tender areas of his face. 'I don't know what Paloma's been saying about me, but it's a load of shit.'

'Interesting.' Juliet pursed her lips. 'If you knew Paloma told us lies, why did you panic when she messaged you?'

Paloma had been wary when I'd called to ask if she'd tipped off Chase but her reserve switched to glee after I explained we were interested in how her message implicated Chase, not the other way around. My phone had buzzed for minutes on end as she furnished us with screenshots of their conversations.

Juliet and I had printed them in Boots while sharing a meal deal, rather than going to the station. I didn't think her reluctance to return to our workplace matched mine, unless she was concerned Paul would drag me away to witness an identity parade as soon as we scanned our ID.

I propped the file on the rail at the end of the bed and placed the screenshot of Paloma's most recent message on top of Chase's blanket-covered knees.

He didn't look at it. His eyes slashed between me and Juliet. 'I didn't read it. Not properly.'

'If you didn't read Paloma's message, then what prompted you to flee?' Juliet asked.

'I wasn't fleeing.' Chase emphasised the *e*, like the word Juliet had chosen was foolish. 'I actually didn't notice you behind me and then I was trying to get out of the way. Why would I assume a police car wanted me to pull over?'

Juliet turned to me, her eyes wide. We'd theorised before we walked into this room that Chase had lied to us by omission. Now he'd smoothly transitioned to bare-faced falsehoods.

'Can we go back to the beginning?' I interjected. I placed a picture of the collage detailing Zara's supposed plan to hike east of the city on his leg. 'Who made this?'

Chase's derisive sneer was ruined by the brace over his nose. 'I told you this already. Zara made it.' He rolled his eyes. Even that looked painful. 'And no, she didn't tell me she'd changed her mind about where she was hiking. No, I had no idea she was in the New Forest that night. Anything else you want to ask again?'

The crash had shaken something loose in Chase. This was the most animated he'd been in our presence. I didn't know if it was another act, thrown together in an attempt to cover up his guilt, or if the combined pain and medication his body was processing had cracked apart his apathetic mask.

I waited a beat. 'Did you help Zara make this collage?'

Chase's eyes darted down to the picture. 'No.'

'Not at all?' Juliet checked, her head cocked to the side.

Chase tried to glare at her. 'I didn't have much to do with Zara's hiking. It was her thing.'

'How did you feel about it?' I asked.

Chase glowered at me. 'What do you mean?'

'How did you feel about Zara having something separate from you, something she didn't involve you in?'

'Obviously, it was fine.' Chase smoothed the blanket over his thighs as far as the cuff around his wrist allowed. 'Maybe I should have tried to get more involved though. If she hadn't insisted on going off alone, she wouldn't be dead.'

Chase stated Zara's fate with an absolute lack of emotion. It almost seemed her death was an inconvenience, something he would rather have avoided but was working around.

'Did you and Zara argue about her preference for hiking alone?'

Juliet's question elicited another pained eyeroll. 'Did that bitch tell you that? Paloma was always looking for problems between Zara and me. I might have once or twice questioned whether hiking alone was the wisest thing, but Zara was a big girl. She made her own decisions.'

I opened the file and laid a letter beside the picture of the collage. 'Zara sent this to Paloma after one of their hikes.'

Chase barely looked at the note. 'And?'

'Do you notice the difference between the handwriting on the board and in the letter?' Juliet coaxed.

'Zara used fancy pens and shit for the collages. She didn't write like that normally.'

That could be true, but I was no longer inclined to trust anything Chase said. Not after he'd lied about the car chase. He saw us and he ran. Plus, someone put the board about the New Forest in his van. I suspected he had. The mystery was why he'd held onto it rather than destroying incriminating evidence.

'We aren't sure that's true.' I gripped the end rail of the bed. 'We have reason to believe you helped Zara make the boards and that the handwriting on them is yours.'

'That would mean you could have made the collage about the hike east of the city at any time,' Juliet said. 'You could have made it after Zara died, then used it to make us think you couldn't possibly have known where she was headed.'

Much of Chase's face was obscured by the metal brace and cotton padding on his nose. That left exposed was mottled by black and purple bruising. There was enough skin clear to showcase the blood rising to the surface.

He clenched his hand, the cuff around his wrist rattling against the bed's side rail. 'I didn't make that board. I didn't know where Zara was that night. Paloma is the only one who did. You should be questioning her, not me.'

I ignored his jab at Paloma. Like we should have done all along. 'We found another collage in your van.' I pulled a picture from the file and placed it beside the others. The cardboard was creased but Zara's plan to walk across the New Forest was unmistakable.

'I didn't put it there,' Chase snapped. 'You saw the back of Lola when you were poking around for no good reason. There's loads of stuff in there. Half of it's Zara's. I had no idea she'd put that board in there. Had no idea it existed.'

'Do you go in the back of your van often?' I asked, refusing to react to the nickname. 'Have you looked in there since Zara died?'

'Yeah.'

'You didn't notice this board?'

'I shoved stuff in there a couple of times.' Chase might have crossed his arms over his bare chest like a pouting child if one wasn't caught in a sling and the other restrained by cuffs. 'I wasn't looking for another board, so I didn't see it in there.'

I picked up the pictures spread over Chase's legs and slotted them into the file. 'We spoke to the man who called in the fire. He saw a blue van racing away from the Dunlow Estate.'

Chase swallowed, the unmarred skin of his cheeks burning a deep red.

'Can you see why we would have doubts around your account of that night?' Juliet pressed. 'You have no alibi. We have reason to believe you made a decoy board after Zara died and hid the true one in your van, so you would have known exactly where she was. A van very much like your own was seen heading away from the fire.'

'And you've lied to us,' I added, more than willing to hammer in the final nail. 'We were watching as you passed the car park. You saw us, you panicked, and you ran.'

The exposed sections of Chase's face turned an ugly puce, like the outrage building inside him needed some kind of outlet as he stuttered incoherently.

A flicker of doubt ignited at Chase's clear intention to continue protesting his innocence. I'd been confused by him from the start, but perhaps Chase and Zara's issues were domestic. Juliet had talked to his brother, who believed Chase too spineless to commit major crimes and clueless about fire starting.

Juliet had been excited by the collage we'd found in the back of Chase's van, but she hadn't jumped to any conclusions. Perhaps I'd missed something crucial and the true killer was already planning their next blaze.

'Chase, if you started the fire it will be better for you to tell us now.' I hoped the note of desperation in my voice wasn't clear. 'You're not going to be able to keep the truth from us for much longer.'

I wasn't sure if that was factual, but I had to do all I could to urge Chase to confess. I needed Zara's killer found, needed to know someone else wasn't going to lose their life in a terrifying haze of heat and choking smoke.

Crimson spread down Chase's neck, before he crumpled like an unsteady house of cards. His jaw wobbled. His balled fist loosened, his arm shaking.

He pulled his knees up, his back hunched. 'I didn't mean to hurt her.' His breathing shuddered. 'I swear I didn't mean to.'

Tears streamed down his face and his chest convulsed. Juliet and I waited in silence until he calmed, leaning awkwardly to one side to wipe his face on the blanket wrapped around his chest. The thrill of cracking the case was dampened by pity. My sympathy for Chase was severely limited because, no matter his intentions, he had killed his girlfriend. But it was difficult as someone cried not to feel a stirring of something.

'Shall we go back to the beginning?' I suggested. 'Did you know Zara was planning to hike across the New Forest?'

Chase nodded, then grimaced at the pain the movement must have awakened. 'You saw the board. She'd been talking about it for weeks.'

'You did hide the collage in your van then?' I checked.

'Yeah. I got that message from Paloma and panicked. I didn't know if you would do a more thorough search, ask if I stored things anywhere else, so I was going to get rid of it. I was shocked when I saw you in the car park. I was hoping I could get away and dump the board, then pretend I hadn't seen you.'

'Did you make the collage about the hike east from the city after Zara died?' Juliet asked.

Chase bit his lip. He flinched when his teeth dug into a bloody split. 'I was frantic the morning after the fire. I knew I had to do something to make it look like I couldn't have done it. I was in bed, surrounded by the other boards, when the idea came to me. I hid the collage about the New Forest in Lola and made a new one about a hike east.'

'It's your handwriting on the boards?' I clarified.

'Yeah.' Chase sighed. 'I hated doing it, told Zara I didn't want to help again after each one. We argued the whole time we made them.'

How strange that Zara had decorated her and Chase's home with reminders of their disagreements, but perhaps she didn't see the collages in that way. They were also mementos of her hikes. And Paloma said Zara was adept at ignoring the parts of her relationship that didn't fit with her rosy view of life.

'What did you argue about?' I asked.

'I hated that she went hiking alone.' Chase licked his lips, his tongue skirting around the cut in the bottom one. 'She insisted she was safe and took the right precautions, and she wouldn't accept that I was right. Not even after I showed her.'

'How did you show her?' Juliet folded her arms. I wasn't sure Chase's tears had any effect on her. I imagined that, in her eyes, Chase was guilty and now she was focused on gathering a full confession.

I didn't know if it was better to recognise criminals as real people or take Juliet's detached approach. I'd tormented myself for too many nights wondering where my brother's killer was at that moment, what he was doing. The thought of the bad man buying pasta or sitting in a doctor's waiting room horrified me; that a monster could walk amongst men and not be recognised.

Chase squirmed as much as he could. 'On hikes, Zara would often take shelter at night in random buildings, rather than camping. She said it was safer.'

My eyes widened, thoughts of my over-developed compassion and the bad man momentarily banished. 'Did you set the fires on the other estates?'

Despite Chase's confession that he'd killed his girlfriend, I hadn't made the link. I scrunched my toes inside my boots. We'd caught Zara's murderer but I needed to stay sharp. We wouldn't be able to pursue conviction if we didn't have all the facts.

'My brother taught me how when we were kids,' Chase said. 'Neil was bored one day when his friends couldn't come over. He was showing off, telling me how much more dangerous he was than me. His visit a couple of weeks ago put the idea into my head. If buildings like the ones Zara slept in during her hikes were set on fire, then she would think twice about going.'

Juliet frowned. 'Your brother was adamant that he didn't start fires as a teen.'

'That's because you've heard "History According To Neil."' Chase raised his hand as far as the cuff would allow to make an air-quote. 'Sometimes when he talks about what he got up to when he was younger, I genuinely wonder if he's got a screw loose. The way he tells it, him and his mates were loveable miscreants. Not horrible bullies.' Chase pressed his sore lips together. 'Neil started fires. He was a sick fuck. I wouldn't be surprised if he did loads of other shit for a laugh.'

The irony that Chase thought his brother sick because of his criminal leanings seemed lost on him.

'There have been a couple of fires in the city recently too.' I stretched my weary mind to recall the map on the wall of our shared office. 'Did you set them as well?'

Chase nodded, likely would have shrugged if able to without a great deal of pain. 'Practice.'

'You thought starting fires on the other estates would discourage Zara from hiking alone?' Juliet asked, unperturbed by Chase's blasé attitude to torching buildings.

'I hoped they would at least make her wary, but nothing would stop her.' Chase swallowed. 'I thought maybe she had to learn the lesson firsthand.'

He closed his eyes. Tears crept from behind his lashes. They soaked into the padding around his nose and traced over his quivering lips.

'What did you do?' Juliet prompted, her face blank as she stared down at Chase.

'I followed Zara to the New Forest.' He didn't open his eyes. 'I knew where she was planning to stop for the night. I parked Lola along the lane so that Zara wouldn't hear the engine, then trekked to the estate. My plan was to sneak up on her, scare her a bit. I needed her to see sense.'

'Why didn't you do that? Why set a fire instead?' The answers wouldn't bring Zara back, but I needed to understand how Chase's desire to keep his girlfriend safe had become so badly twisted.

'When I arrived, someone was in the shack with her.' Chase opened his eyes and more tears spilled free. He made no attempt to staunch them. 'I waited just outside because I was sure some stranger going in would scare Zara and then I'd be right there when she needed me, but she didn't make a peep. I went around the back of the place and looked through the window. It was dark, but I could see her. She wasn't looking for her phone to call me; she was asleep.'

'How do you know Zara didn't try to call you at any point?' I asked. 'You left your phone at home.'

Chase's damp eyes wouldn't meet mine. 'Accidentally.'

I searched his face but couldn't determine if that was a lie to support his claim that he hadn't planned to hurt Zara.

'That's why I had to get close to the window to see if Zara was okay,' Chase continued. 'It wouldn't have mattered if I did have my phone though; she didn't call. I don't think she noticed someone else was in there with her.' His jaw tightened. 'That's when I decided that if I wanted her to take my concerns seriously, I needed to do something she couldn't ignore.'

The simple fact was that at no point in the groundskeeper's cottage was Zara as safe as she would have been if she'd stayed tucked up at home, but Tyler hadn't hurt her. It was the man who claimed to love her and wished to keep her from harm who'd killed her.

Chase didn't seem to spot the flaw in his logic. In impressing the need for safety on his girlfriend, he'd become the biggest danger of all. She would be alive and well today if he hadn't been so determined to prove to her how unsafe hiking alone was.

'I had everything I needed to start a fire in Lola,' Chase said.

That he'd taken his arson supplies and not his phone when he hunted down Zara made a good case for premeditation, no matter how much he claimed he'd decided to torch the cottage on impulse after seeing his girlfriend sleep through Tyler's intrusion.

We'd found no materials used to start fires during a cursory search of his van. Chase had either removed them or he'd used the last of them when he'd killed his girlfriend. The forensics team would uncover traces to back up Chase's confession.

'I'd planned to start a fire somewhere further ahead on Zara's route across the New Forest, I thought that would make her see I was right about her hiking on her own, but what I saw changed my mind.' Chase sniffed, then winced. 'I was so cross she would put herself in such a dangerous situation, that someone could literally stroll in to where she was sleeping and she wouldn't notice. It was a matter of time before she got seriously hurt.'

Juliet turned to me with one eyebrow raised. Apparently, she found Chase's disconnect between his desire to see his girlfriend safe and killing her as strange as I did.

'The front door was already open, so I chucked the stuff in through there.'

I gripped the file, searching for words that wouldn't antagonise Chase before we'd extracted a full confession. 'Did it occur to you that instead of teaching Zara a lesson, the fire could end her life?'

I'd walked the fine line well. Chase's eyes filled with fresh tears. 'You don't understand how quickly the place went up. One minute there was this tiny trickle of smoke coming out the door. The next, flames were everywhere and the ceiling caved in.'

'Did you attempt to save Zara?' Juliet's question was sharp. She had to be thinking the same thing as me; no matter how quickly the fire had spread, if Zara's safety truly was Chase's paramount concern then he would have rushed into the cottage when he realised his lesson had gone horribly wrong.

Chase swallowed, his eyes glossy. 'There honestly wasn't time. I swear.'

'You didn't even try?' My chest constricted. Zara had trusted Chase, had bent so many aspects of her life to please him, and he'd wielded the one thing she refused to give up as a weapon against her.

'What do you not get?' Defiance edged Chase's words. 'There wasn't a chance to save her. I didn't expect the fire to spread so quickly and once it got going there was no way I could get inside to help her.'

If he really cared for Zara, he would have tried. True love was selfless.

I shuddered, my brother's final battle cry echoing loud in my mind.

'When did you leave?' Juliet's voice jogged me from distant memories.

'When I knew Zara wouldn't be coming out.'

The lack of grief when Chase talked about his girlfriend was gone, but the strange disconnect remained when he talked about her death. He was certainly sad about what had happened, but there was no yawning pit of guilt. Something had gone wrong and Zara had died. Chase didn't fully take responsibility for her death because it was a mistake.

He had started the fire, but carefully trod around shouldering the blame for Zara's death.

'When did you know she wouldn't come out?' Juliet pressed.

Chase slumped against the raised bed. 'When the roof caved in.'

I wanted to shake him. He should have been weeping and begging for understanding, not baldly stating how he'd left his girlfriend for dead.

'Did you leave then?' My voice was devoid of tone. I had to contain my roiling emotions. It wouldn't help to vent at Chase, to force him to understand what he'd done; that he'd ended Zara's life in a wholly avoidable and unnecessary way.

'Yeah.' Chase plucked at the blanket with his cuffed hand. 'Someone would notice the fire. I had to get away.'

I took a deep breath. The motivations behind killings didn't usually bother me this much. A combination of Chase's lack of comprehension and the bad man's attack had worn me down.

'That's everything we need.' Juliet picked up the Dictaphone and tapped the button on the side. 'We'll process this at the station. There was a chance this could have been classed as manslaughter but after hearing your fucked-up account of why you started the fire and your utter lack of attempt to save Zara, we should be able to charge you with murder.'

Juliet turned on her heel and pulled open the door, leaving a shellshocked Chase in her wake. He looked to me as she disappeared, his mouth hanging open.

I could have unpacked it for him, could have explained that he was the reason Zara had died. Her demise had nothing to do with the speed of the fire spreading or her desire for independence. I could have watched as he finally comprehended that if he hadn't lashed out, Zara would be alive today. If he hadn't been so determined to show her she was in danger, then she wouldn't have come to harm.

But my body ached with tiredness. I didn't want to spend a moment longer in this room than was necessary, didn't want Chase's cracked thinking to infect any more of my time.

'Goodbye, Chase.' I walked to the door.

'I really didn't mean to do it,' he called out.

I didn't turn around. Didn't reply. I left the room and shut the door behind me.

From: David Rees **david.rees@forensics.gov.uk**
To: Paul Willis **paul.willis@mit.gov.uk**
CC: Nicole Stewart **nicole.stewart@mit.gov.uk**
Date: **8 August, 16:02**
Subject: **Operation Mercury – forensic match**

Willis,

A full report is attached. The DNA samples taken from OWEN WESTOVER while he was being treated for dehydration at Southampton General are a match for DNA samples found on the BARREL containing the body of MAX POWRIE. They are also a match for the forensic materials found in the WAREHOUSE where GABRIELLA MARTIN was discovered after her abduction.

OWEN WESTOVER's fingerprints are a match for prints found in the TAR on the BARREL containing the body of MAX POWRIE and the BARRELS containing OLGA BERT and PRINCE BAILEY.

You got him, sir.

Rees

Gabe

I pulled up in the station car park, then twisted to grab the file from the back seat. Lethargy clung to me as Juliet and I climbed out of my car, heat rising through the soles of my boots and pulsing into my skin.

The victory of finding Zara's killer was weighed down by what could be waiting inside the station. During the drive from the hospital, Paul's request had harried me.

I couldn't identify the bad man. I couldn't face the monster who killed my brother.

I didn't know exactly what being in the bad man's presence would do, but every part of me screamed with the desperate need to run.

Level with the end of my bonnet, I stopped walking. 'Juliet?'

She'd stalked off, assuming I'd be close behind. She looked up from her phone, then spun around.

Juliet frowned across the distance between us. 'What?'

'I don't want to come in.'

She blinked, her phone clutched in her hand. She'd not been on holiday the whole time I'd been working at Southampton. Only since she'd moved in with her husband and daughters had she stopped coming into the station at the weekend. The idea that I didn't want to work had to be alien.

'I can't do what Paul wants me to,' I went on, my voice small. I didn't know he would ask again, but there was a chance. A risk I couldn't take. 'I'm sorry, but I can't do it.'

I wasn't apologising to the right person. When the bad man struck again, I'd have his next victim's family to answer to.

Paul couldn't have found my brother's killer. That was too good to be true. I wouldn't identify the man he'd arrested just in case, but I couldn't comprehend that it would be anyone other than a confused stranger.

I rubbed my forehead while Juliet stared. 'I need to go home.'

She marched towards me. 'Can I have it?'

Perhaps it was fortunate that I couldn't face going into the station since I was unable to comprehend a simple question. 'What?'

'The file.'

'Oh.' I'd forgotten I was holding it.

Juliet tucked it close to her chest after I passed it over, folding her arms across the red card. 'If Paul asks, I'll tell him you're unavailable for the rest of the day.'

Double waves of relief flooded me. Juliet wasn't fighting for me to come inside and she'd keep Paul away.

'Thank you.' Hot tears prickled the corners of my eyes. 'I appreciate it.'

'It's fine.' Juliet's gaze flicked up and down. 'Don't come in over the weekend. I'll deal with anything that comes up.'

I didn't care how awful I must look for Juliet to suggest I stay away from the station. Our case was almost wrapped up and the idea of not being around until everything to do with the bad man had quietened down was too appealing.

'Okay.'

'I'll talk to Angela.'

I sighed. 'That would be really kind.'

Juliet's eyes darted between mine. I didn't have the mental fortitude to unpick what she might be thinking. It was enough that she was helping now that the strange energy that had seen me through the days since the discovery of Max's body was deserting me.

'See you on Monday.' Juliet turned and walked towards the station.

I climbed into my car and hurriedly left. If Paul was hoping to ambush me, I wanted to be far away when he learnt I'd escaped.

Forcibly concentrating on driving, I weaved through traffic in the direction of home. The direction of Ollie and Artie and a safe place to release the howling sadness rising inside of me.

Paloma Robins @WiseGirlHiker
Shirley, Southampton

As many of you already know, I lost my best friend on the 4th August. The days since then have been a total nightmare – not only did Zara die but in the very worst circumstances.

We preached different ways of staying safe when hiking but all we ever wanted was to enjoy the world together. One thing we both did was make sure to check in during hikes with trusted friends and I'm devastated one of the people Zara trusted completely fucked her over. Make sure your hiking buddies actually have your back.

I can't believe my beautiful girlie won't be stomping alongside me ever again. The pictures show our most recent hikes (and the carb loading beforehand). All we have now of Zara are memories, and let's keep ourselves safe out there to honour her xx

Detective Inspector Paul Willis: Formal interview commencing at 5 p.m. on Friday the 8th August. This interview is being conducted by myself, Detective Inspector Paul Willis. The interviewee is Owen Westover, who has been given time to consult with a solicitor provided by the force. He has declined to have them sit in on this interview. This interview is concerning the recent abduction and murder of Max Powrie, along with several other children who were abducted and killed in a similar fashion over the last thirty-five years.

[Short pause. Paper shuffling.]

DI Paul Willis: Mr Westover, before I ask any questions I wanted to show you some evidence. On the table are documents JK009 to JK017. They account for your movements, showing a clear correlation between where the murders of children occurred and the properties you rented for short periods of time. DNA you provided earlier today has been tested against material found in the barrel used to transport Max Powrie's body. It was a match, along with material found in the warehouse where Gabriella and Barnabas Martin were held. We have also had positive matches between your fingerprints and prints found on the barrel containing Max's body and those containing the bodies of Olga Bert and Prince Bailey. Due to this evidence, we have strong reason to believe you have been abducting and murdering children for thirty-five years, after which you placed their bodies into barrels and left them in various waterways.

[Long pause.]

Owen Westover: Do you have any questions for me?

[Cough.]

DI Paul Willis: Did you murder Max Powrie and the other children?

Owen Westover: I suppose if you want to talk about it that way, then yes. I murdered them.

DI Paul Willis: How would you talk about it?

Owen Westover: Well, that's an interesting story. Have you got the time to listen?

DI Paul Willis: Yes.

Owen Westover: You understand my checking. A lot of people don't have patience for an old timer like me. Barely even seem to see me, most days. You're the first person who's ever asked about this.

DI Paul Willis: Please, go on.

Owen Westover: Thank you. I first felt the pull when I was in my twenties. I'd just left the army and was feeling aimless.

DI Paul Willis: You were honourably discharged following an injury?

Owen Westover: That's right. The car I was driving was attacked. No one else made it out alive. A bullet caught me on my temple, you can see the scar. It bled enough that I was left for dead.

DI Paul Willis: Would you say that incident changed you?

Owen Westover: Have you ever served?

DI Paul Willis: I haven't.

Owen Westover: Silly question. Only someone who hasn't been part of the machine would ask if it changed me. My injury was the final straw. I couldn't live under such a strict regime anymore.

DI Paul Willis: You said it was after you left the army that you felt a pull? What pull was that?

Owen Westover: I can't think how else to describe it. I've heard people talk about creative inspiration before. They feel compelled to make what is in their mind come true. My pull is the same.

DI Paul Willis: What did you see in your mind?

Owen Westover: That I had to take those children. They had to die.

DI Paul Willis: Why?

Owen Westover: Haven't you ever had a feeling that if you don't do something, then terrible things will happen? I felt the pull and knew that if I didn't follow, there would be dire consequences. I started with the young lass in Durham.

DI Paul Willis: This was Lisa Blunt?

Owen Westover: That's right.

[Paper shuffling.]

DI Paul Willis: Before you are a number of photographs. A full listing will be attached to this recording. We believe these are your victims.

Owen Westover: Isn't that beautiful? I've never seen so many of them together before.

[Short pause.]

DI Paul Willis: I wonder if you can talk me through how you chose your victims?

Owen Westover: It was the pull. I followed where it led. I'd get this itch in the back of my mind and I'd know it was time to move on. I'd up sticks and once I got to the right place, the pull would get stronger. Every day, I'd be on the lookout. Then I'd find them.

DI Paul Willis: There was no prior planning to how you picked the children?

Owen Westover: None at all. Luck and chance, that's all it was. I'd look up from reading the paper, see a child, and I'd just know. They were the one. I'd feel peaceful, after the deed was done. I'd often spend nights where I left them, staring at the water.

DI Paul Willis: Is that what you were doing last night?

Owen Westover: Yes. I sat on the bank where I said goodbye to little Max. Slept under the stars.

[Long pause.]

DI Paul Willis: I wonder if I can ask about one child in particular: Barnabas Martin.

[Laughter.]

Owen Westover: I remember him. Plucky lad.

DI Paul Willis: His murder doesn't fit the same pattern as all the others. You abducted him and his sister.

Owen Westover: As I said, usually I see a child and I know. But I looked at those two and I couldn't be sure. Not right away, at least.

DI Paul Willis: How did you decide which one of them to kill?

Owen Westover: No decision making to it. I took them both, hid them away. As I sat in the warehouse, I could feel the pull saying it would work out. It would become clear. I thought it was going to be the girl. Gabriella.

[Coughing.]

Owen Westover: Are you alright, detective?

DI Paul Willis: I'm fine. Please go on.

Owen Westover: Like I said, I thought it would be the girl. Gabriella came out to find me. But then Barnabas raced in. I couldn't ignore that. He wanted to be the one.

[Long pause.]

DI Paul Willis: Thank you, Mr Westover. This has been a good start. We'll take a break, then we can discuss the rest of your victims in detail.

Owen Westover: Even the ones who aren't here?

DI Paul Willis: This isn't all of them?

Owen Westover: Oh no, lad. Dozens of them were never found.

Unknown number. Sent 17:38.

> I seriously don't know how much longer I can do this.

Unknown number. Sent 17:59.

> Stick to the plan.

Gabe

I thought I would fall apart as soon as I got home, but I walked through my front door and all I felt was bone deep tiredness. Ollie hugged me and Artie pressed his furry bulk into my legs. I wanted to lie down and never get up.

At Ollie's command, I took a cool shower and changed into a loose T-shirt and a pair of leggings. I ate homemade pizza while sat on the sofa and didn't feel much of anything. The immense wave of emotion I'd braced for during the drive home didn't break. It was like everything was happening on a screen. I watched, removed from it all.

I jolted at a knock on the front door. Artie's claws scrabbled along the hardwood floor as he ran across the room. Ollie patted me on the leg, the gentle concern that had been wrinkling his brow since I'd told him I had no opinion on what we had for dinner melting into a smile.

'I'll get it.'

I sank further into the sofa cushions. I wouldn't have protested if they'd opened up and dragged me inside their downy padding. If I had my way, I'd not see anyone other than Ollie until I returned to work on Monday. My brain was soggy with the words and deeds of other people. I needed them to stop, just for a while. My eyes drifted closed as the front door swished open.

'Hi, Paul.'

I snapped upright. The dragging numbness that had fallen over me since my return home whipped away.

'Gabe in?'

'Yeah. She's here.'

For a panicked moment I wondered if I could hurl myself out of the wide-open window, but then Paul appeared. His stick thumped as he walked into the living room, the shadows around him darker and longer than in the rest of the house. His shirt sleeves were rolled to his elbows, the creased cotton evidence of long nights spent working. The ever-present bags under his eyes had deepened from lilac to maroon.

He had no papers with him, so wasn't about to force me to look at anything I wanted to run from, but his face was grim. My tired heart clenched. This moment inevitably came with each investigation to hunt the bad man. They couldn't find him and so the detectives arrived for one last meeting. Paul hadn't come here to ask for anything other than my forgiveness.

Ignoring the space on the sofa and the chair beside it, Paul sat on the coffee table in front of me. His long legs branched out on either side of mine. I didn't mean to make myself small, but I couldn't seem to unhunch. My shoulders curled in and my knees pressed together.

'It's okay,' I whispered. I'd heard the news he'd come to deliver many times before. Better to get it over and done with. 'You and your team did everything you could.'

Ollie sat down on the sofa beside me. His hand spread across my back. The circles painted with his fingers highlighted how bunched my muscles were. 'I hope you're up for sharing.'

I didn't understand what he meant, but then I looked away from Paul's lined face.

All the air left the room.

Paul held a Twix.

That meant one thing: he'd successfully closed a case. He always bought a Twix to share with whoever had been most helpful to the investigation.

I wasn't sure I was wholly inside my body anymore but had enough control to ask, 'You did it?'

Paul nodded. The action sent the tears trembling on his eyelashes tumbling down his stubbled cheeks. 'We caught him, Gabe. It's over.'

A cross between a whimper and a sob broke through me, and I was lost.

I'd never allowed myself to believe the bad man could be stopped. I hadn't let myself hope, hadn't dreamed of a life uninterrupted by his crimes. Even when it seemed Paul was close, I hadn't entertained the possibility that the bad man could be within range.

He'd evaded everyone before. Investigation after investigation.

Desperate parents on the front page of newspapers. Sketch artists always wanting more. The interviews where I relived the harrowing days in the warehouse again and again, each detective determined to extract a crucial detail others must have missed.

Only remembering the worst times with Barnabas, because that was all anyone ever asked about.

Dad's face each time a detective called.

The nightmares. Terrors in the dark.

It was all over.

A core of pure darkness had been lodged inside me for too long; the sure and faithful knowledge that the bad man would kill and kill and go on killing until the end of his days. I'd been certain he would stop when he couldn't do it anymore, not when he was found.

The darkness cracked open. Lay broken and exposed.

Paul had caught the bad man.

No more deaths. No more destroyed families. No more investigations dragging me and my parents through the same horrors we'd endured since I was eight years old.

Slowly, I became aware of the room again.

Ollie curled into my side, his arm firm around my back. Artie had jumped onto the sofa. His head rested across my lap, his soft whines vibrating through my thighs. Paul clasped my knee with one hand. The other mopped salty wetness from his face.

He still held the Twix.

I swallowed, curling my fingers into the soft fur behind Artie's ears. 'I'm not sure I deserve that.'

Paul chuffed out a laugh and squeezed my knee. 'Gabe, we wouldn't even have known the other man who bought a barrel from the garden centre was important if it wasn't for you. We would have continued running around like headless chickens with nothing to work on.'

The CCTV image would haunt me, but the horror of recognising my brother's murderer had to lessen now he'd been caught. The fear that I might encounter the bad man at any time had been torn away.

I didn't know how to live with this weightlessness, to be so free.

I laid a hand over Paul's. 'Thank you.'

He seemed to understand that a thousand words clustered behind those short two. I'd lived under an oppressive storm for so long. Paul enabled me to step away, to walk into the light.

BOBBIE'S BETS – the best way to bet responsibly

Dear Mr Andrew Haines,

Bobbie's Bets is inviting a select group of their most faithful members on an exclusive Christmas-time holiday on the Isle of Wight. You are one of the lucky few!

This loyalty reward includes an all-inclusive stay at one of Bobbie's favourite island hotels, plus daily adventures across the Isle of Wight. Take this once-in-a-lifetime chance to enjoy the island's beaches and beautiful countryside for free. There will of course also be ample opportunity to participate in special Bobbie's Bets sweepstakes.

This holiday is from the 27th December to 30th December and is for selected members only. Since this is an exclusive deal, we ask you do not share details with other Bobbie's Bets users until a special social media splash at the end of the holiday. To confirm your attendance, please return the attached form using the pre-paid envelope.

We look forward to seeing you on the beautiful Isle of Wight!

The Bobbie's Bets team

Call connected at 18:51.

'Gabriella?'

'Hey. Hi, Mum.'

'Darling, what's wrong?'

'Nothing's wrong. Can you please get Dad and put me on speaker?'

'He's here. Let me sort this out.'

'It's the button there.'

'I know how to do it, El. Gabriella, can you hear us?'

'Yes. Mum, Dad; they caught him. The bad man.'

'Oh my gosh. Ellis, oh my gosh.'

'Bloody hell. I can't believe it. After all these years.'

'I know. I can't take it in. But Paul told me it's him. He wouldn't say that unless he was certain.'

'Romilly, it's okay. Here's a tissue.'

'Dad?'

'Yes, pet?'

'Can we please not go back to not talking? I don't know what life looks like without this hanging over us, but I don't want it to be like it has been. I know you don't like my job and don't like me living down here, but please don't shut me out anymore.'

'Gabriella, I wasn't shutting you out. At least, that wasn't what I meant to do. I just found it too hard to talk to you when I didn't know if you were safe.'

'I'm safe now. We all are.'

Four Months Later

Teddy. Sent 13:04.

You sure you're okay? x

Benny. Sent 13:05.

I promise. Has your dad been anything but kind since we arrived on the island? x

Teddy. Sent 13:06.

No. But this still seems too good to be true. A year ago, he wouldn't speak to me. Now he's taking us all on holiday and voluntarily spending time with my boyfriend x

Benny. Sent 13:07.

We have to keep hoping he's permanently turned over a new leaf. We're just pulling up at The Albion. I'll message you as soon as we've finished lunch to let you know how it went, but try to have fun with Leo x

Teddy. Sent 13:07.

> He wants to look for dinosaur footprints on some random beach, so I'm not sure much fun will be had. I hope Dad is good to you. Love you x

Benny. Sent 13:08.

> I'm sure he will be. Love you too x

Gabe

The soft leather sofa had probably been chosen to set clients at ease. Watercolours of woodlands and lakes framed on the cream walls certainly had. The floor of the small room was polished wood, the late afternoon sunlight dulled further by net curtains hung across the window to create a greater sense of privacy.

In theory, I could spill all my darkest secrets in this room without incurring judgement. I couldn't see that happening, couldn't see how talking would help, but I had to try. I couldn't keep going on as I had been since the bad man was found.

The counsellor seemed harmless. Elsa was as short as me but twice as wide, dressed in an oversized grey tunic and black leggings. A yellow necklace rested on top of her rounded chest, the different-sized beads clicking each time she moved. Her faintly pink skin was dotted with freckles, her grey hair parted into a bob that curled around her face.

She'd used the first few minutes of the session to explain how our time together would work. I'd tried to listen as she explained being person-centred and her different qualifications, but my mind had inevitably wandered. A bookshelf sagged behind her, thick tomes with wordy titles weighing on the cheap wooden shelves.

'Gabe?' Elsa's almost white eyebrows drew together when I visibly jolted. 'Do you often find yourself having moments of detachment?'

I'd been zoning out more and more over the last few weeks. Juliet hadn't commented on it and Ollie said he didn't mind, but hot licks of shame burned through me every time. It was embarrassing for it to happen here. I'd paid to sit in this pokey room and fix my brain. I should be concentrating, not lapsing into nothing again.

'Sometimes,' I hedged, sure a counsellor would read too much into it if I revealed I hadn't retained focus on a conversation for longer than thirty seconds in weeks. Not without exhausting myself. 'It's not a big deal.'

Elsa nodded slowly. She was incredibly different to Juliet, primarily because she was interested in my thoughts and feelings, but in one way they were the same. It was impossible to tell what whirred behind the counsellor's blue eyes and wrinkled forehead.

'What has brought you here today, Gabe?'

'My boyfriend suggested it.' I wasn't about to tell this stranger everything, but that was an easy enough question to answer. I wouldn't confess I'd been resisting this for months, had come now because Ollie was visiting his parents and I wanted him far away when I tried counselling and found it as ineffective as everything else. 'He's been concerned about me, thought it would help to talk to someone.'

Elsa nodded, like people who had been convinced by their partners that they needed additional help walked through her door every day. Like it wasn't a sign of weakness that I couldn't deal with my problems on my own.

'What would you like to talk about?'

Nothing.

If I could never speak of all that had happened, never think of it again, then I would be perfectly happy. But something had gone wrong in my brain since the bad man was caught. I wasn't reacting how I should be now that the threat that hung over me for much of my life had been eliminated.

I tucked my hands under my legs and braced myself. I wasn't as sure as Ollie that counselling would help but I was willing to try if it meant we could move on. I wasn't the only one affected by my mind's current malfunction.

'When I was a child, my brother and I were abducted. I returned home, but Barnabas was killed.' An abridged version of events, but all I was willing to divulge. 'The man who took us was a serial killer, who struck many times since. I always found those times difficult.' I pressed my lips together. 'Four months ago, Barnabas's killer was caught. I thought that once he was stopped, I would get better, but I've gotten worse.'

Elsa's plump fingers threaded together on her knee. She didn't react the way others did when I laid out the bare facts of my past. Her face remained attentive and open, unmarred by overbearing pity.

'Can you explain how things have gotten worse?'

I cringed, but at least she hadn't asked for the details of our abduction. 'I always thought that if the man was stopped, then a lot of my problems would stop too.'

I couldn't say his name, flinched when anyone else said it.

Elsa nodded, like my assumption was reasonable. 'Can you tell me what these problems are?'

This wasn't a room where I could hide behind vague answers. If counselling was going to work, I had to tell Elsa what I was dealing with.

'I've always had nightmares and moments when I've been more fearful than other people.' My fingers tightened around the undersides of my thighs. 'I felt guilty every time the man struck again because I knew another family would be damaged like mine. I wished I could do more to stop him.'

'You said these feelings grew more intense after the man was caught?' Elsa nudged.

I bit on my lip, wrestling with the internal whisper promising that I didn't need to be fully present. It was louder in moments when the past continued to intrude on my present. A present that should have been full of freedom.

'In the months since the bad man was arrested, I haven't slept a full night without horrible dreams.' I hated that I'd accidentally told her his secret name, but that slip up seemed to open the flood gates. 'I'm a detective and I feel useless at work. You saw how I space out. My partner has to drag me behind her.'

Despite her lack of enthusiasm every time Maddy asked about her plans, I imagined Juliet had been glad to say goodbye and head off on holiday to the Isle of Wight. I'd been nothing but a dead weight for weeks. I'd seen Alice's concerned looks on nights out, despite my attempts to act normally. I bet she and Maddy compared notes on the slack they'd had to pick up for me since the bad man was stopped.

'I'm exhausted at the end of each work day,' I rattled on. 'I cry all the time. My boyfriend says it's okay, but I've never felt this sad before. There's this aching pit inside of me and I don't know how to close it up. I jump at strange noises, even jump sometimes when my dog barks.' I shook my head, blinking against the warmth rising in my eyes. It had taken me days to convince Ollie it was alright for him to visit his parents, that I wouldn't fall apart when alone. His concern highlighted how weak I'd become. 'The bad man being caught was meant to solve my problems, but somehow it's made them all worse.'

Elsa regarded me calmly, like I hadn't unloaded a whole mess onto her. At least that was what she was here for. Maybe if I could leave some of my chaos in this room, I wouldn't need to lean on Ollie so much. He claimed he still loved me, but I couldn't see how that would be true for much longer if I continued as I was. I bet a few nights spent in his childhood bedroom was a respite after all the broken sleep I'd caused him.

'I wonder if I could talk to you about your brain for a moment?' Elsa asked. 'It's trying to help and protect you, and sometimes it's easier to be compassionate with ourselves once we understand what's happening inside our minds.'

I blinked as she pulled a sheet of paper from a stack on the table beside her. I didn't know what I'd expected after such an outpouring, but a science lesson wasn't top of the list.

Elsa held up a cross section of a brain and I really did try to listen. My detachment from her explanation of the lizard part and how logic shuts down at times of extreme stress was of a different ilk to the drifting off into blankness I'd experienced before. All I could think as she pointed at different sections of the brain was that it didn't matter how clever the defence mechanisms were or that I was employing protective strategies ingrained since cave people ran from tigers.

What mattered was that my brain shouldn't have been doing any of this. The bad man had been caught. I should be happy. All my fears should be gone.

It was wrong in a way I couldn't seem to make anyone else understand that instead of lessening, the terror living in me since Barnabas and I climbed into the bad man's van had grown huge and unignorable. I'd been able to function normally before, had pushed away my past and gotten on with my life.

I stared at the illustration of a brain, Elsa's words a meaningless drone. I wanted my mind to work as it should. I needed to relegate the bad man to memory so that I could finally live a life free from him.

Barnabas hadn't died so that I could live like this – cowed and scared and distant.

I straightened, easing my fingers out from under my thighs. 'Sorry, Elsa. Could you please go over that again?'

If my brain was malfunctioning, I needed to understand how. Then I could fix it. I'd gather all the knowledge I could and vanquish this thing.

I wouldn't let the bad man steal any more of my life than he already had.

Call connected at 15:27.

'999, which service do you require?'

'Police. I don't reckon an ambulance would be any good.'

'I'll put you through.'

PLEASE HOLD. PLEASE HOLD.

'Isle of Wight Police Service. What's your emergency?'

'It's not an emergency, but I think you'll want to get down here sharpish.'

'What's happened?'

'A body's washed up.'

'Right. Where are you?'

'I don't actually know the name of it. Have always called it Cow Drop Bay. It's down from the bay, at Freshwater. It's the beach just along. You can only get here by swimming. That's what I did.'

'I know where you mean, and we can use your phone to find you. When did you discover the body?'

'Couple of minutes ago. Wasn't sure what it was at first. Scared the living daylights out of me when I climbed onto the beach for a rest.'

'There's no chance they're alive?'

'None at all. You'll see, or whoever you've sent this way will when they get here. They've been dead for a while. Can't even tell if it's a bloke or a lady.'

Acknowledgements

Left in the Ashes was a difficult book to write because of how much I drew on my own experiences to make sure that Gabe's mental-health struggles felt authentic. It is a privilege to be able to write about and hopefully bring more understanding of trauma and PTSD, but while it was cathartic at times it was also draining. The only reason I was able to write about this without finding it too distressing was because of the techniques I've learnt to quiet my fear when it grows louder. Counselling sessions have not only been a space to be brutally honest, but have been a place to learn about the ways in which my brain is trying to protect me. My first thanks for *Left in the Ashes* must be given to my brilliant counsellor, Gabi. She has helped me piece myself back together and find strength and understanding in the moments I have felt most lost.

For anyone who has felt any recognition when reading Gabe's struggles, I highly recommend seeking counselling. As a first step, you could read *The Choice* by Edith Eger. I felt so seen by her, and her story of healing and acceptance is wonderful. PTSD UK (and other organisations worldwide) also provide information and support for those struggling with traumatic experiences.

Writing the acknowledgements for the third book in the series is a funny business because although there are people to thank for their work on this story, there are also a whole lot of people to thank for the work they've done since *Close to the Edge* published. Please indulge me while I attempt to thank them ALL.

Thank you to my readers. As I said, this was a difficult book to write but I hope the story that has landed on the page is entertaining as well as emotional. I hope you've enjoyed diving into another instalment of Gabe and Juliet's story. It still feels incredibly surreal that there are so many people around the world who want to read the books I sit with my dog and write – thank you for making my dream come true!

Thank you to all the libraries who have championed the Martin and Stern series and welcomed me in to natter about my stories – Thornbury Library in South Glos, Camberley Library in Surrey, Lord Louis Library on the Isle of Wight, Salisbury Library in Wiltshire, and Lee Hub in Lee-on-the-Solent. I will always have a special place in my heart for libraries – they provided me with so much joy as a child and I loved working in them as an adult.

The biggest of thank yous to the readers, bloggers, and other bookish chums who have read the Martin and Stern series and SHOUTED about it. There are literally too many of you to attempt to name you all, and isn't that incredible?! It always brings me so much joy to read your reviews and see your love for my stories. And thank you to the lovely authors who have read my books and said incredibly kind things about them!

Many bookshops have welcomed me in to sign copies of *Shot in the Dark* and *Close to the Edge* or asked for signed book plates – thank you for helping me to feel like a real-life author. My biggest thanks to Berts Books, Tea Leaves and Reads, The Imaginarium, and Fourbears Books. Medina Bookshop, Babushka Books, and Isle of Wight Waterstones have all been particularly supportive – thank you for being my local bookshops and for being kind when I mumbled that I had a book coming out and would you mind getting in a few copies. Thank you in particular to Jonathan and the team at Isle of Wight Waterstones for hosting another launch. I hope my parents didn't bully you too much.

I didn't think it could be done, but of course I've fallen more in love with my brilliant agent since *Close to the Edge* went out into the world. Saskia Leach is an excellent agent and human being. Thank you for holding my clammy hand during all the weird twists and turns of publishing and for being so kind during some difficult moments this past year. I feel so grateful to have found an agent who is unfailingly in my corner, even when I'm being cranky or get confused. I am excited to write lots more books with you! Thank you also to the wider Kate Nash Literary Agency team who support me and Saskia – there's a lot you do that I don't see and I'm so thankful for you all.

Another reason that writing *Left in the Ashes* was tough was because I changed editor. Thank you Siân Heap for initially choosing the Martin and Stern series. Without your wise guidance, it wouldn't have kicked off so well and I found your feedback so helpful. And thank you to Louise Cullen and Alicia Pountney for making the transition to a new editor so stress free! Despite the change, I've felt like the feedback and advice I've been given has helped *Left in the Ashes* follow on closely from the first two in the series. It has been a joy working with you both, and thank you so much to the wider team at Canelo for all the time and effort you put into getting Martin and Stern into as many readers' hands as possible.

Some lovely chums read *Left in the Ashes* prior to publication to reassure me that it made a vague amount of sense. Nat Jones – thank you for being so encouraging and finding the right parts creepy. Chris Reddecliff – I'm sorry I didn't wedge your name into this one but your thoughts continue to be brilliant. Ben Britton – thank you for being one of my first readers and reassuring me that I'd gotten the balance between emotion and plot right. Mum – you read so many versions of each of my books before they come out and never fail to cheerlead for me from start to finish. Thank you.

A whole bunch of people with far more useful jobs and lives than me helped make *Left in the Ashes* as accurate as it could be. Thank you for allowing me to mine your experiences and wisdom to get as close to factual as a made-up story can be.

The biggest thanks as always to my Uncle Mark, who worked for many years as a police officer and reads an early version of every one of my novels. He gives me copious notes to make sure that the police procedure elements are right. Thank you to Emma Maher, who is a nurse and checked the medical details for me. Thank you to Shari Barrett for making sure Paloma's scenes authentically reflected a Black woman's experience of the police. Thank you, Richard White, for helping me with the wording for greeting a firefighter. And thank you to Ben, for figuring out the car chase with me.

Thank you always to my family of writers – Marisa Noelle, Sally Doherty, and Emma Bradley. I love you all very much not just because you're all incredibly hot, but also because you're always up for SHOUTING about books/publishing with me. You help me not feel so alone as I write books and help keep me (vaguely) sane. I love celebrating all the highs and getting stabby about all the lows of life with you three. Thank you also to Chloe Ford, who writes very different books to me but is always ready with a listening ear and great advice when I need it.

I continue to be terrible at naming characters, but I only needed help with one in *Left in the Ashes*. Thank you to Michelle Underwood and Debi Simmonds for giving me the name of Zara's foster carer.

I've had a weird old time of it on social media over the last year – Twitter used to be a really positive community for me but the amount of spam (of the sexy lady variety since I'm clearly irresistible) made it unusable. I've taken all my nonsense to Instagram (and occasionally BlueSky), where things feel a bit friendlier and there are many videos of dogs. Thank you to everyone who has continued to connect with me despite all the changes to online spaces – I really love chatting about my books (and cinnamon rolls. And *Traitors*) with all of you. I am especially grateful to everyone who voted in my address book poll.

I'm so thankful for all the new chums I've made through my books being published. I want to give a shout-out to my DM pen pal Daniel Aubrey, who has been such a source of support and laughter as our books jetted out into the world.

Wild and uncontainable thanks go to my friends who read the first two books in the Martin and Stern series and who I am now reasonably certain will pick up the third, too. Your support makes me so hecking happy and I love chatting to you about my books. Thank you for distracting me when my brain gets too full of murderous plots and for being better secret-keepers than me when I show you my covers as soon as I'm sent them. I'm not naming names because there are too many of you, but you're all wonderful and thank you for encouraging me to keep fighting for my dreams.

My family is, if possible, even more supportive than my friends. My mum reads all of my books multiple times and mine are the only books my dad has read since I was born. Thank you to Rhiannon for taking my stories on nightshifts and my nan for telling all her carers about my stories. Thank you to my family-in-law (is that a thing?) for reading all my murderous little books.

The hugest of thanks to my lovely husband, Ben. Writing *Left in the Ashes* was difficult at times, but you were always there with a cuddle and a reminder that the people I was writing about weren't actually real. Your determination that I follow my dream of writing is so lovely, and I love hearing your feedback on my stories. You've continued to ferry me about to events and signings, which I think is only partially because of the McDonald's and cinnamon buns I insist on afterwards. I'm so excited for new adventures with you. Thank you for always being proud of me and for being a constant rock when my brain is pesky.

And last but very much not least, thank you to Odie. You're still perplexed as to why I insist on staring at a weird square and making tapping sounds instead of giving you head pats for hours each day, but you keep me company all the same. Walks with you are the highlight of my day and I feel greatly blessed when you allow me to touch your ears. You are a brilliant dog.

CANELO CRIME

Do you love crime fiction and are always on the lookout for brilliant authors?

Canelo Crime is home to some of the most exciting novels around. Thousands of readers are already enjoying our compulsive stories. Are you ready to find your new favourite writer?

Find out more and sign up to our newsletter at canelocrime.com